AFTERLIFE

Also by Paul Monette

Novels

Taking Care of Mrs. Carroll
The Gold Diggers
The Long Shot
Lightfall

Poems

The Carpenter at the Asylum
No Witnesses
Love Alone: 18 Elegies for Rog

Nonfiction

Borrowed Time: An AIDS Memoir

Novelizations

Nosferatu
Scarface
Predator
Midnight Run

AFTERLIFE

by

Paul Monette

Crown Publishers, Inc., New York

Published by Crown Publishers, Inc., 201 East 50th Street,
New York, New York 10022

CROWN is a trademark of Crown Publishers, Inc.

Book design by Jennifer Harper

Manufactured in the United States of America

Library of Congress Cataloging-in-Publication Data

Monette, Paul.
Afterlife / by Paul Monette
I. Title.
PS3563.0523A69   1990
813'.54—dc20   89-48754
CIP

ISBN 0-517-57339-3

10   9   8   7   6   5   4   3   2

For Stephen Kolzak
my partner in time

From far, from eve and morning
And yon twelve-winded sky,
The stuff of life to knit me
Blew hither: here am I.

Now—for a breath I tarry
Nor yet disperse apart—
Take my hand quick and tell me,
What have you in your heart.

Speak now, and I will answer;
How shall I help you, say;
Ere to the wind's twelve quarters
I take my endless way.

—A. E. Housman

AFTERLIFE

1

If everyone hadn't died at the same time, none of this would have happened. Steven Shaw hung up the phone at the first break in Dell's harangue, then padded naked into the kitchen to stick the lasagna in the oven. He wondered if Dell would remember to stop for beer, which was why Steven had called him in the first place. Don't hold your breath. Steven opened the cupboard above the sink and lifted four Chips Ahoy from their plastic cradle, popping them into his mouth as he transferred the casserole from counter to oven. Margaret had dropped the lasagna off on her way to meeting a planeload of Valley dentists back from Zihuatanejo. "Put it in to warm at seven," she told Steven, who realized now he hadn't a clue what warm was. He set the oven at 400. On his way out he opened the freezer and took a Mud Pie, wrestling furiously with the cellophane as he headed back to the bedroom. The cellophane reminded him of unwrapping hypodermics.

Steven watched himself eat the pie in the bathroom mirror. For a man who'd ballooned in a year from 160 to 185, he'd exhibited remarkable concentration in confining the pounds to his gut. His armor against desire. He had no tan to speak of, a mockery of all the beaches he'd dragged his ass to over the years. Pale just now like his Scottish grandfather, despite the swath of hair that covered his chest and ran down his belly, courtesy of the bleak Slavs on his mother's side. His eyes were the color of cool tea, all cried out. Steven had no beer; he had no salad; no milk for the coffee; no peanuts; no bread. And seven people were coming in half an hour.

"Vic," said Steven to himself in the mirror, "what am I going to do?" The question was rhetorical. The man he addressed had been dead a year and six days, dragged under at the end by a mix of horrors that racked his skeletal frame and produced a continuous low groan which still seemed to rattle the house in the hills like a tremor. In or out of the mirror, Steven was in the habit of addressing Victor rather than himself. "Honey, I'm such a wreck," he sighed, meaning how could he possibly entertain.

He tossed the last quarter of the sweet into the toilet and flushed it away. Then turned to wash his hands, only to find the Dial in the dish had dwindled to a sliver. He bent to the cupboard under the sink: no soap. Annoyed, he yanked open a drawer. Among the low-dose medicaments were several small plastic cases embossed with hotel logos. He pried open one from the Nile Hilton and plopped out the little soap. As he crouched and lathered his hands, an aching perfume hit him like a bolt of African spring—patchouli and myrrh and sweet grass. Victor in the Valley of the Kings, cavorting in angular poses, mimicking the Pharaohs on the walls.

Fumbling now in a panic, Steven stuffed the offending soap back in its Hilton case and flung it into the wastebasket. Vigorously he rinsed his hands, trying to expunge the heady scent. Then had a pang of sudden fear that he would throw away everything that murmured Victor's name and be left with nothing.

"I can't—" he said to the mirror softly. "It's like I can't..." But he couldn't think what he couldn't do, there was so much. His shoulders began to heave as his face squinched up, for of course it was all a lie that he couldn't cry anymore. He just couldn't bring up much in the way of tears. Though his mouth was all contorted, bleating like a small animal in pain, he was bone dry.

* * *

A female evangelist with a rabid platinum grin, interviewed on "News at 6," allowed as how Jesus would never have cured a man with AIDS, despite his record on leprosy. "After all, there's limits," said Mother Evangeline. "These homosexuals eat each other's feces. Do you think people like that deserve a miracle?"

Dell Espinoza spent the next ten minutes calling KLAX, screaming obscenities, two out of three in Spanish, till they hung up on him and he'd dial again. His balcony doors were open, but the wind was strong in the shaggy palm outside, and its clatter muted his bellowing voice. The balcony looked down on a horseshoe courtyard, ringed by six bungalow units which rented from $390 to $550. But Dell could not have told you what kind of profit he was clearing. Though his dining room table was two inches thick with paperwork, he hardly managed to keep the bills current. It was his sister Linda who kept the books, while Dell took the summer off to relive the one before.

Which meant he spent a lot of time at night at Marcus's desk, where the papers were deep as a snowdrift. Dell did not expect to understand the scholarly side of it all, but reading his slow way through things, he'd started to sort the exuberant chaos of Marcus's work. The chairman of Marcus's department had told Dell the college library would like the historian's papers, at least the ones on the Mayans. So Dell was methodically separating the Mexico research from the gay stuff—the latter a blizzard of caucuses and panels, letters to Sacramento, testimony at countless hearings.

Just now Dell was angry at Steven, who would not share his fury over Mother Evangeline. But then, he couldn't persuade anyone to get as regularly angry as he did, erupting in uncontrollable rage if he had to wait too long in any line. Though Dell wasn't sophisticated about the mechanics of displacement, at least he knew he had reached the stage of yelling instead of crying.

He was due at Steven's in half an hour, having promised to get there first to help. In his green fatigues with the frayed cuffs and his mottled camouflage shirt, he looked vaguely like a mercenary cooling his heels between insurrections. In any case he didn't feel like changing clothes and acting as if it were Saturday night for real. Linda had left three messages for him that afternoon, but Dell had been up at the scattering site, sitting on his haunches like a glazed coyote. He picked up the phone to call her now, though he could just as easily have gone out onto the balcony and hollered across the courtyard.

At the second ring a recorded voice answered: "Howdy. Welcome to 976-LOAD, the hottest call-in service in Southern California."

It was a natural mistake. Calling the jerkoff line was as automatic to him as calling the hospital used to be. At twenty cents a minute, some months it cost him more than all his utilities combined, immersing him in the vast pool of random longing that coursed just under the skin of the city. A burr of static sounded in Dell's ear like the sea in a shell. Then a voice broke in: "Hi, this is Kevin. What's goin' on?"

"Not a whole hell of a lot," Dell replied, dryly charming. The kid at the other end was very nervous and very horny. Already Dell could tell that Kevin would never volunteer his number. Casually Dell drew a spiral notebook from the shelf under the phone, then turned through pages crowded with vital statistics to a clean sheet. He grabbed a well-chewed pencil. "So what do you look like?"

The response was immediate, precise as a military drill. "Five-ten, one forty-five, kinda dirty blond. Medium hairy. Twenty-four years old. Good abs, nice legs." The kid laughed, perhaps at the absurdity of speaking in the shorthand of the classifieds. The laugh pulled it all together for Dell. He could see the kid sharp as a Kodachrome. "Your turn," prompted Kevin.

"Lorenzo," said Dell, his own real name, which nobody in the States ever called him. "Thirty-three. Latino. We're about the same size." Dell looked across at the left-hand page of the notebook, where a man named Vito was represented by an extensive list of abbreviations and one descriptive notation at the bottom: *stepfather fucked him*. Dell had no memory of Vito whatsoever.

"Sounds like fate. I got a thing for Latin men."

"Yeah? Is it a big thing?" Dell retorted. The smutty grin in his voice set the invisible man to laughing again. The sound of it was so young it fairly took Dell's breath away. He glanced at the clock and tried to think how many beers he had in the fridge, so at least he wouldn't have to stop on the way. "Why don't you take my number?" said Dell, and recited it very carefully, as if it were the combination to a safe.

Sonny Cevathas sailed along Sunset, top down on the gray Mercedes. His curly gold hair was still wet from the gym, and he loved the feel of it whipping dry in the night wind, defiantly unstyled. There was altogether too much mousse in West Hollywood anyway. Yet somebody snapping Sonny's picture from the curb would have carried away a totem souvenir of the place. Twenty-eight and in a 380 convertible, fresh from a Bruce Weber locker room, Sonny was as richly surfaced as the run of billboards looming above the Strip on either flank. On the tape deck Linda Ronstadt was wailing "Desperado."

It was all an illusion, of course, like the funk glam of the crowd that waited on line for the early show at the Roxy. In truth the gray 380 was all Sonny had in the way of real property. His apartment was a room in someone else's, a mattress on the floor and a bureau full of Italian sweaters that belonged to Ellsworth. Sonny hadn't legally inherited anything. Twelve months to the day, he'd come home from Ellsworth's memorial service to find the locks changed at the Bel-Air house. Ellsworth's father stood in the upstairs bay window staring down at him, utterly expressionless. Sonny understood immediately that he had already lost the only person who could have protected him.

At the instant of being shut out, Sonny didn't even stop to wonder if he was giving in too easily. The Greek in him—a clan of manic depressives in Fresno, none of whom spoke to the others—could have exploded through the front door like Bruce Lee. Instead he'd turned on his heel and sprinted across the terrace to the garage, where he still had a key that worked, along with the fat key to the Mercedes convertible. The only other place he had access to was the cedar closet off the garage, so he ran in and grabbed a double armload of cashmere. Nobody tried to stop him as he drove away.

Now he swung onto Sunset Plaza Drive and zigzagged up the hill. His shoulders tensed at the thought of seeing Dell and Steven. Their Saturday widowers' gatherings had lately grown contentious and redundant, at least to Sonny. He would have stopped coming months ago, except he felt a certain duty. After all, when he came unhinged in the awful final vigil at Cedars-Sinai, staring Death in the face, it was Dell and Steven who kept him from going out the window.

None of the three had ever met before the waiting room on the ninth floor, where each had come to watch the world end. Victor was in 904, Marcus in 916, Ellsworth in 921. The death-watch lovers quickly became a kind of combat unit, reeling in and out of their separate chambers of horrors, outdoing one another with unspeakable details. By the time it was all over—Marcus on Tuesday, Victor Thursday, Ellsworth midnight Friday—the widowers knew one another better than anyone. Or at least how they cried and took their coffee.

Sonny reached up and fingered the amethyst crystal that hung from the rearview mirror. *No more thoughts.* He had put all that behind him now, every night but Saturday, and could feel the life-force urging him to move on. The only thing that got him here tonight was Steven's decision to make a proper dinner—with real people and real food, not just the three of them pissing and moaning over Chinese takeout. Once the widowers' spell was broken, they would all be free to negotiate their own Saturday nights.

He forked onto a narrow lane and wound around a ridge that was tinder-dry, raw with the smell of sage and aching for the first inferno of autumn. Steven's house stood on a point of land, a bungalow faced with rosy stucco and a red-tile roof. Sonny swung into the steep driveway and parked in front of the garage. He flipped the mirror to check himself out, and the amethyst swung like a hypnotist's medallion.

He got out of the car and loped up the steps to Steven's landing, the unspoken agenda of the evening in his outlaw swagger. There might be somebody new in there, ready for the spin of fate, a man whose heart was tuned like Sonny's to the higher planes, who loved himself so purely that no bad energy would ever gain a foothold. A man he would know from an ancient place, unafraid and wonderfully evolved. A Pisces would be perfect. No question about it, Sonny was in the market again.

*   *   *

From the kitchen Steven could hear his guests and knew it was going badly, even as he gaped at the salad bowl and the groaning array of produce waiting to be chopped. Margaret Kirkham, his co-pilot at the agency, was telling the others a merry tale about a tour bus lost in Costa Rica, and the trading of forty Mastercards for safe passage through a guerrilla skirmish. Margaret had brought along the over-divorced Lynn Heller, who laughed with aching abandon at everybody's stories. Also Ray Lee, the sleek Korean who ran the computer at Shaw Travel, up to his neck tonight in black Armani.

It sounded at first like any other dinner west of Laurel Canyon. What Steven was really listening to was the silence from Dell and Sonny, who were doubtless staring at Margaret with unconcealed contempt. Dell was still gnashing his teeth over the lady preacher on KLAX. How was Margaret to know that everyone straight had better duck? Sonny had clearly mistaken Ray for the half-blind date Steven reluctantly promised to invite. The real thing hadn't arrived yet, but meanwhile Sonny was outraged at the vast inappropriateness of the willowy Asian with rings on four fingers.

Steven wasn't going to worry about it. He had lately begun to notice—irritably—that meetings of the widowers' league always took place at his house. It was Steven who ordered the pizzas and Chinese takeout, Steven who always paid. He was sick of being the oldest, exceedingly put out just now because Dell had arrived with three cans of Coors, Sonny with nothing at all, and the two of them dressed like bums besides. The ripped knees of Sonny's jeans were not Steven's idea of a fashion statement.

He hefted a red cabbage, poised it on the cutting board, and whacked it in half with a cleaver. Neatly nicking the tip of his thumb in the process. It was scarcely a wound at all, and it didn't even hurt, but the blood bloomed and ran down his thumb, ghastly as Macbeth. He clutched his fingers around the thumb, made a seething sound, and suddenly felt queasy at the slipperiness of the blood in his hand.

"Don't ever get on a bus during a revolution," Margaret observed from the next room. "They're too easy to commandeer. So, Dell, I understand you've seen a lot of Mexico."

"You mean because I'm a spick?"

"Uh, no. But I thought . . . didn't your friend . . . ?"

"Marcus," Dell replied, softening a bit, as Steven ransacked a drawer for a Band-Aid. Damn them all for not getting along. The thumb was bleeding too much for the little strip of flesh-colored plastic. What he really needed was gauze and tape, but he didn't dare go to the medicine chest in the bathroom, for fear of confronting the ranks of Victor's prescriptions. Powerless to throw them away, he figured to use them once he got sick himself.

Now he wet a length of paper towels and wadded it around the clotting thumb. There was a burst of laughter from the living room as Ray Lee vamped, Joan Collins in high dudgeon. Fuck the salad, Steven thought, moving to sweep the vegetables into the sink. The doorbell rang.

Though Margaret would have answered, Steven bolted from the kitchen to get there first. Passing through the living room, he saw the five of them grouped about the fireplace. Margaret billowed in harlequin silk, while Lynn was tailored in white cotton, absurdly spotless. Ray refilled their wineglasses with effortless worldliness, more Blake than Alexis now. Side by side on the sofa, Dell and Sonny sat stiffly, as if they were waiting to see the dentist. Sonny should perk up in a moment, thought Steven, as soon as he saw Ted Kneeland.

Steven opened the door in the vestibule and grinned at Ted, unnervingly handsome as ever, tan as a Polynesian prince. "Long time," said Steven vapidly as Ted threw a bear hug around him.

The next second was very "Twilight Zone." Steven looked over Ted's shoulder and saw another figure standing under the porch light, a dark-haired man about Steven's age, with a hunted look in his eye. Of course he knew it was Mark Inman, but the name arrived a beat behind the face, since he hadn't seen Mark in two years. Steven flashed to the time before the nightmare, when he'd expended considerable energy avoiding the likes of Mark at parties. What was Mark doing up here? Had his car broken down in the street?

"Oh," said Ted, unclenching from Steven and glancing in at the group around the fireplace, "I thought this was a party."

"Mark, how are you?" Steven reached to grip Mark Inman's hand, then stopped because of the halfwit bandage on his thumb. Instead they locked eyes. Steven thought: Why is *he* in so much pain? He hasn't lost anyone.

"Look, Steve, I'm sorry. Ted said there'd be a lot of people—"

"All my fault," purred Ted apologetically. "We'll just stay for a drink."

"Don't be ridiculous," retorted Steven. "There's tons of food. Really." With his good hand he coaxed Mark over the threshold and watched as the two men exchanged a tentative look, feeling each other out. Suddenly Steven realized they were an item. He felt a curl of rage in his gut.

"Well, if I knew *you* were going to be here," said Margaret, sweeping into the vestibule, "I would have brought your tickets." She nuzzled the air beside Mark's cheek, then turned and held out a hand to Ted. "I book all Mark's reservations. He can't make a move without me."

As she introduced herself to Ted, Steven realized he didn't even know Mark was a client of the agency. That wouldn't have happened a year ago. "Where are you going?" he asked Mark.

"London. Just for four days." He grimaced, as if to reassure Steven he wouldn't be having any fun. Then Margaret put an arm around his shoulder and led the two new arrivals into the fray. As Steven lumbered back to the kitchen, he saw the laser look in Sonny's eyes, picking up on the unavailability of Ted. Steven let the swing door shut behind him and leaned his forehead against the refrigerator. He didn't want to hear about anyone going anywhere, which was why he stayed out of the office. Shaw Travel mocked him now with all its promise of freedom, the paradise beaches and Gold Card souvenirs. For Steven travel was over. He'd become a walking bad advertisement, like a misspelled sandwich board.

He was lousy at getting surprised too. Ted Kneeland had been a friend of Victor from the prehistoric time before Steven. Victor's furious loyalty had always kept a place for Ted, long after they hadn't a thing in common, save having been twenty-two. Ted cried the loudest at the funeral, practically writhing on the floor, offending Steven mightily. He'd been invited tonight only because Steven needed a man as ripe and simple as Sonny. Mark Inman was something else entirely—Steven's polar opposite, tough, superior, predatory. From the very first meeting years ago, the two of them had bristled and backed off for good.

The door swung open, and Dell slipped into the kitchen, vacant-eyed with boredom. Steven opened the fridge and tried to look focused on dinner. Dell laid a mild hand on his host's arm. "So who's the beauty?" he asked, squeezing Steven's biceps. Dell was the resident masseur, patting his friends like Labradors.

"Friend of Vic's. Used to be a model."

Dell nodded. "Creep. And the big shot?"

"Mark's in television. Major heartthrob. Eats gorgeous men for breakfast."

"Another creep. How come he's still alive?"

"Dell, don't wish it on people."

The other man shrugged in his mottled shirt, a smile playing in his hawk's eyes. He ran a hand through the stiff brush of his black hair and sauntered across to the sink. He didn't seem bored at all anymore. As he reached for the phone, he said, "Gee, Steven, you'll have to give me this recipe." Steven turned to see him staring at the mess of raw vegetables in the sink, blotched here and there with the crimson of Steven's blood. "HIV salad. Looks scrumptious."

Dell punched in a number. Steven had a sudden vision of the women walking in, all their hard-won reasonableness collapsing in the face of a viral bloodbath. He walked over and turned on the tap, using the spray attachment to rinse the blood from the greens. Beside him Dell spoke into the phone in a surly voice: "Yeah, is Mother Evangeline there? Well, tell her there's a bomb in her church." Steven stared at Dell. "It's set to go off in the morning. During the sermon."

Steven reached over and slammed the cradle. "What the fuck are you doing?" he growled.

"I can't help it, I'm a phone addict. When do we eat?"

"It's not funny. Go be a sociopath in your own house. I'm not going down the drain with you."

Dell was bored again. He bent to the oven and pulled open the door, peering into the raft of lasagna. Steven shoved the flat of his hand against Dell's shoulder, not even managing to rock him off-balance. Then he cuffed the younger man on the side of the head, so that Dell turned with a grin and hunkered into a crouch. They faced each other like stupid warriors, Steven having the weight advantage by thirty pounds. The oven was still open, pouring waves of Italian heat into the room.

"That's it, Steven," taunted Dell. "Let's have a little rage."

He started to bob in place, darting a hand for a quick slap to Steven's cheek. Then ducked and landed a soft punch to his belly, which set Steven to roaring like a grizzly. He caught Dell's head under his arm and wheeled them both in a circle, crashing against the counter. A crock of wooden spoons spilled over onto the floor. Dell yelped playfully, goading Steven on. They swung like a single beast, Dell grappling to yank Steven's hair. When Margaret glided in, Steven was trying to butt Dell's head against the refrigerator. Steven blinked at Margaret, panting now with exhaustion, and Dell slipped out of the armlock and stood up. He kissed Steven on the cheek and grinned at Margaret: "This is what we call safe sex."

"I guess Victor did all the cooking," she observed distractedly, pushing up her harlequin sleeves and making for the stove to rescue her casserole. "Why don't you both go out and . . . beat someone else up. I'll take care of this."

"Steven says I should be nice to you," declared Dell cheerfully. "Everyone's not the enemy, right?"

"Oh, so you've decided to woo me now." She laughed with wonderful carelessness. "Really, it's not necessary. I actually sort of like you the other way. Now go play."

She made a shooing gesture with one hand as she reached for a pot holder with the other. Dell beamed at her, blew another kiss at Steven, and headed back into the living room. The swing door swung like a saloon's, but Steven didn't follow. He stared at Margaret's back as she lifted the lasagna to the counter. He tried to block the thought of Victor, easy as a gymnast, charging around the kitchen cooking three things at once for a Monday-night supper, and tried not to hate Margaret for bringing it up.

He looked down at the floor and saw drops of red splashing like a bad Catholic joke. He held up the bleeding thumb and choked Margaret's name. She turned with a frown between her eyes to see her boss cocking his thumb in the air, forlorn as a hitchhiker. "Help," gasped Steven, for the thousandth time. And she moved swiftly to cradle him in her arms, he who was so lost and far from home, unanchored and alone, who would never again want a ticket anywhere.

Mark Inman, former boy and TV star, thought they were all assholes, but he wasn't proud of the thought. Though he had enough perks to choke a horse—car phone, half-acre granite desk, personal trainer—he'd just had a whole day of being abandoned and unloved. This despite two dozen calls from people who fawned and kissed the hem of his garment, even despite the fact that the glittering Ted Kneeland was crazy in love with him.

Mark himself was good-looking in an offbeat way, with nothing studied about him unless *that* was the studied part. Ted Kneeland called him a Jewish jock by way of body type, but at thirty-eight Mark had lost a certain edge, so you couldn't tell anymore what sport it was he'd played. Not out-of-shape exactly, he had a sort of arrogant indifference to the Renaissance bronze his body used to be. He had been a boy so long—decades—that when he grew up at last it was with a vengeance. In any case Mark did not require himself to be beautiful at all, as long as he got his share from men like Ted.

Mark didn't simply work in television. He was much higher up than that: chief executive officer of a company whose sole product and brand name was one Lou Ciotta. Lou was the crown jewel of the NBC Wednesday lineup—34 share—and no magazine went to bed without an update on him. He couldn't even divide his coke into lines without the input of manager, lawyer, publicist, but all of these were so many phone calls stacked in the airspace over Bungalow 19 on the Burbank lot. The bungalow was Mark Inman's starship. Input was one thing; the decisions were Mark's.

On Saturday the ninth of September, Mark was invited to a screening at the Academy, two black-tie affairs in Beverly Hills, and a power dinner at the crenelated house of a great white shark. He had canceled all of them at four o'clock, so he was batting 0 for 20 on the week's invitations. Ted, of course, had not expected to attend a single one, since Mark was not permitted to be so openly gay. No couples in double tuxes. Ted was accustomed to seeing Mark only late at night, when love was all the business left to attend to. Yet Mark had canceled none of it tonight to be with Ted. On the contrary, Ted would have been on his way out even if this awful week had never happened. Regrettably Ted didn't understand the finer points: he still thought they were made for each other.

Over a beer Mark listened sullenly to the china doll swathed in Armani. "The mall people have discovered Rodeo Drive," observed Ray Lee ominously, bravely filling the gap with Margaret and Steven away in the kitchen. Understandably Ray overcompensated, since the four other men in the room stuck to monosyllables, stalking one another with their eyes, and somebody had to talk to poor Lynn Heller. On opposite sides of the fireplace, Ted Kneeland and Sonny jostled like thoroughbreds pawing their stalls. Dell Espinoza, sunk in an easy chair, continued to look as if his pockets were full of explosives. The social fabric was stretched very thin by the time they got the call to come to dinner.

They all moved intently toward the dining room, breaking off conversation. Margaret had whipped together a bloodless salad and garlic bread in minutes, so the questionable lasagna was buffered on all sides. Everyone laughed when Steven swore he would never entertain again, even Margaret who believed him. They grazed around the table, a shred of manners surfacing at last as they helped one another to bread and olives. With their plates for ballast they moved outside to the brick terrace, which floated along the brow of the hill above the white-flecked tide of the city.

Somehow they fell into little groups that worked. Dell and Lynn straddled the chaise longues under the sycamore, its dry leaves rattling softly. Nearby Sonny sat cross-legged on the bricks beside a wooden bench on which Ray Lee perched primly, plate between his knees. Sonny rambled animatedly about his splintered youth, the nuclear exchange with his father that put him on the road at seventeen. Charmed though Ray was by the story, it was told for Ted Kneeland's sake, who slouched against one arm of the bench and talked to Margaret about poor Steven and how he was getting on. Margaret lied and swore there had been a noticeable turnaround.

Which left Mark Inman standing half in, half out of the dining room, poised on the brink with his pasta rapidly cooling. He seemed to survey the others, making sure they were all engaged but not committing himself. As if he were trying to choose the "A" conversation, or as if he had one ear cocked for a phone call that would draw him away from the place entirely.

Steven hardly noticed that Mark was waiting, as he put together a mechanical plate of food he didn't want. He was actually thinking about the two remaining Mud Pies in the freezer, but that would have to wait till later. He poured himself a glass of Finnish seltzer and turned toward the terrace doors, only to have Mark pivot neatly and smile at him. "Why don't we eat in here?" he asked conspiratorially. "I like to see what I'm putting in my mouth."

"Oh, sure." Steven gestured vaguely for Mark to take a chair, but instinctively he looked outside, as if longing for reinforcements. Steven sat down lightly on a chair opposite Mark. He poked at his pasta and took a guarded bite. For a moment he thought they were going to be lucky and not have to speak at all. Steven relied on other people's bouts of uncomfortable shyness in his presence.

But then Mark rolled his shoulders and stared at Steven's thumb. "I'm sorry I never wrote you about Victor."

"Mm," replied Steven mildly, on automatic pilot. "After all, it's not like we were friends."

"No, it was chickenshit of me. He was a really sweet man. I should've—" Mark stopped mid-sentence, shaking his head, as if he couldn't bear his own inadequacy.

Suddenly Steven felt weary and annoyed. "Don't worry about it, Mark. We had all kinds of people around. Besides, you hardly even *knew* him."

Mark glanced up bewildered. "But we—" And he stopped again, but this time Steven got it. He stared blankly in Mark's gray eyes till Mark looked away, visibly squirming. "It was ten years ago. I thought you knew."

Before Steven. As if Ted Kneeland weren't bad enough, his deeply tanned presence teasing Steven with all the summers of Victor's twenties. Why was it he'd never been jealous of Victor's past during all their eight years together, and now he was? He couldn't even remember asking Victor anybody's name from the deep past. Ten years ago Steven still lived in Boston, being tormented by a man who was half Portuguese and half crazed. Nino: faceless now, a character in a book Steven never quite finished. Who cared about ten years ago?

But Mark was clearly mortified. There was something almost endearing about the deep flush that washed across his face. He was not someone who ever had to back down in a business deal, and his temper was legion in the close quarters of Bungalow 19. It was other people who did the wincing and the flinching. Yet even as Mark struggled to frame an apology, Steven stood up, set his plate down, and walked away through the front hall.

Mark blinked after him, feeling stunned and ridiculous. He glanced outside to the group on the terrace, to see if anyone had noticed his appalling gaffe. But everyone was happily engaged in dinner chitchat, and Mark's gaze focused instead on Ted Kneeland, who happened to be laughing, his head thrown back, the sculpted swell of his chest taut against his shirt. A queer chill of contempt went through him. Ted wasn't just not beautiful to him anymore; there was something almost repellent about the Perry Ellis perfection. How long had they known each other? They'd slept together for five weeks, having circled each other for some months prior. They didn't know each other at all.

Sonny stood up and moved toward the house to get more food, and Mark hastily bolted from the room. Once in the vestibule he decided impulsively to leave. There was no way to apologize to Steven without making more of a fool of himself. Let Ted hitch a ride with the Greek kid. Mark's hand was on the doorknob when he heard Steven beckon from the room beyond: "Here, look at this."

Startled at the conspiratorial echo in Steven's voice, Mark walked into the study. Steven was standing at the desk with a big book open in front of him. Behind his head was a poster of an Italian hill town, a blue-streaked painted cart in a meadow beside a crumbling wall. Steven smiled as if there had been no awkwardness whatever. He pointed to a picture in the album, and Mark approached and dutifully bent to look. It was a Polaroid of Victor and another man, both shirtless, leaning shoulder to shoulder and laughing.

"Summer of 'seventy-seven, right?" asked Steven, precise as a scholar.

Mark's gaze widened to take in the pictures on both pages. Victor Diamond in his mid-twenties, scrappy and muscular and in constant motion, racing in and out of the camera's frame, as if he could be caught only by accident. Mark sighed. "He looks about eighteen."

"Vic always looked eighteen. I mean not at the end. . . ."

Mark could feel the sudden shiver of tension in the man beside him, like one who had looked too long from a high place. Scrambling for something to say, Mark touched a finger to the print of the two laughing boys. "Who's this?"

"Why, Ted of course," retorted Steven, recovering his balance.

"Oh, right." Mark recognized now the tilt of the chin, cocky and self-satisfied. More than ever he felt as if he'd never met this man. It was a case of mistaken identity, five weeks at the wrong address, like everyone else Mark ended up with. Abruptly he said, "Guy I knew just died."

Steven felt the empathy like a hot rush. They were standing side by side, and he reached out and touched the back of Mark's hand where it rested on the desk. Steven retracted all his censorious thoughts, now that the pain in the hunted eyes was real. Neither man spoke for a moment, Steven's fingertips resting on the vein that coursed from the wrist to the knuckles. He might have been taking Mark's pulse. Finally Mark, whom no one touched except in bed, began to talk in a cautious voice.

"Thursday night, out in Riverside. Nobody else was there but me, but it didn't matter. He was in a coma."

Still Steven waited, staring down at the pictures of Victor a decade ago. He only had a fear that one of the others would walk in before the story was done.

"I went out with him last winter," continued Mark, then hastened to qualify that. "Couple of months, no big deal. Then I had to go away on location, and when I got back he'd split. I just thought he was gone." The last word came out with a certain torque of bitter irony, as if "gone" were a whole other story. "Then last week his father called, because Brad left me a note. I don't think I was supposed to get it till after he died."

Silence again, and this time Mark's hand stirred under Steven's fingers, restless and unsure. Steven recalled the lame and useless remarks he'd heard by the thousand in the last year, how angry every attempt at comfort made him. All except Margaret, who never even tried but only asked the plainest questions, solid and dull as her lasagna. Steven said, "How old was he?"

"Twenty-eight."

Eight years less than Victor, five less than Marcus, three less than Ellsworth. Steven always asked how old. He read the obituaries only of men under fifty. He tried not to feel a spurt of triumph that Vic had lived longer than Mark's friend. But then, Steven spent so much time trying not to feel that he sometimes couldn't recall what was still allowable.

"I'm sorry, Steve, I wasn't even going to tell you that. You've had enough."

"I don't mind," Steven replied mildly. Since the night he last walked out of Victor's hospital room, nothing surprised him anymore. Nothing was too horrible or too much a reminder. He knew they were lying in comas all over the city.

"Nobody knows I even knew him. 'Mark,' he wrote, 'thanks for a wonderful time. At least I got a taste.'"

In one dispassionate room of his mind Steven waited for Mark to cry. It amazed him how much of the story Mark had managed without a break, and wondered now if he'd heard him right that it happened just two days ago.

"I can't cry," Mark announced with a certain psychic precision, as if they were playing chess by mail. At that he withdrew his hand from Steven's touch, restoring the equal distance, man to man. Nobody seemed to have anything safe or comfortable to say. Steven closed the album and turned to slip it back on a shelf, where Mark could see half a dozen more, leatherbound in a row. These, he supposed, were the sum of Victor's life, organized year by year, all of it compact enough to fit in a baby's coffin.

Steven turned back and shrugged at Mark. "It doesn't really matter," he said, "but nobody calls me Steve."

They locked eyes again, for the first time since Mark had entered the house, but now there was something antic in the look they exchanged. At last they had stumbled on a minor issue. "Steven," said Mark, trying it out in a diplomatic sort of way. Then they laughed, like two kids in a half-naked Polaroid.

Suddenly they were comrades, merry and sly. Mark Inman dug his hands in his jacket pockets, his car keys clinking dully. The ex-actor in him flashed a quarter smile. He wasn't half so tan as his boyfriend Ted, and besides, the squint lines around his eyes were deeper than the sun. Without moving a millimeter, Steven puffed his chest and pulled in his belly and started to think inanely about what diet he ought to begin tomorrow.

They could have happily gone outside and joined the others now, drawing the group together at last, a one-night family. They'd gotten through all the sad part. But plainly Mark had something more to say, for his face clouded again. Steven realized he hadn't looked in anybody's eyes in over a year, not since the light began to go for Victor. Not even in his own eyes, not even in the mirror.

"I'm positive," Mark declared with ashen calm. "I've known for a long time, but it's like I didn't believe it. Not till I was driving back from the desert the other morning. You know what I mean? Here I am—I'm going to die."

Steven nodded, unable somehow to lie in the face of so much naked truth. "Me too," he replied flatly.

Then Margaret billowed into the room, beaming with proprietary feeling. "Where the hell are the coffee filters?" When they looked at her blankly, too many fences down, she glanced from one to the other, her radar on red alert. Before Steven could think which cupboard, she said, "I'll find them," and backed out.

When they turned to each other again the two men looked askance, but only slightly, a bare degree from locking eye to eye. It wouldn't have much mattered what they said. *Where are you staying in London? You're lucky to have her in the office.* But now there interposed a small insistent beep. Steven slipped a hand in his pants pocket and drew out a small white plastic container with digital readout: his pill timer. He slid back the little drawer and scooped out two white capsules banded in blue. Mark's eyes were fixed on him the whole time, as if he was trying to memorize a code. "Welcome to the valley of the dolls," Steven said wryly.

He punched in the 4 A.M. call on the timer and slipped it back in his pocket. Now he needed a very tall glass of water to try to outwit the nausea. Thus they moved to leave without another word, back to the missed connections of a widower's Saturday night. They sauntered into the living room, not quite shoulder to shoulder, but effortless and casual. They were two grown men, as old as each other, and each, if nothing else, knew how to segue.

No one would have supposed they'd connected at all, from the vast indifference they maintained in the short half-hour that ended things. Sonny and Ted, the two beauties, were much more notable for the texture of their approach/avoidance. Brittle and clumsy, they talked without any of the fluid grace that marked their Olympian passage through the gym. Ray Lee was cruelly disappointed that no one had skimmed the latest *Star*. Indeed, as a group they seemed unable to dish with any flair, even at the most basic level of Liz and Liza. Ray wanted out of this cultural wasteland, as did Lynn Heller, whose own stomping ground was Beverly Hills and Malibu, where she was booked for the rest of her life.

Still, it was Dell who made the first move to go, murmuring to Steven that he had a phone date at midnight. All it took was one of them, and the general move began, gathering their jackets, making the vaguest promises to see one another again. Mark and Steven didn't even say good night. When Ted and Mark paired up to go, it was Ted who took care of the flashier good-byes, hugging Steven close and whispering in his ear. Between Mark and Steven there only passed the briefest nod, like moguls bidding at an auction.

Margaret remained behind and stood at Steven's side on the landing, waving with him as the others went to their cars. But though she stayed till well after midnight, till every plate was back on the shelf, nothing further was said about the private talk in the study. Margaret castigated Steven for the grim dryness of the lasagna, swearing next time she would bring it over hot from her own oven. When everything was clean she had a last cup of decaf, while Steven packed away the two Mud Pies. He declared an end to the widowers' Saturday club.

"Our weeds have officially changed from black to dark purple," he announced, walking his friend to the door with her Pyrex under her arm.

"Just to be safe," retorted Margaret, "I'm taking you out next Saturday night myself. They'll get the idea." This was above and beyond the call of duty, since Margaret had a b.f. of her own— Richard—whose unrepentant straightness required that he be kept separate from the bent world of Steven Shaw. But the drying up of Steven's grief was Margaret's primary mission. Hands-on action was required.

Poor Dell, thought Steven, *poor Sonny.* He watched Margaret fold herself into her white Toyota. The headlights flashed on, flooding the patch of chapparal west of the house. A coyote froze by the trash cans, then slunk away into the dry sage. Steven felt no fear or annoyance at the scavenger. Nothing surprised him anymore, even that he would pull back from his fellow mourners, who'd seemed for the entire last year more real to him than brothers.

He wasn't being entirely truthful, but couldn't say that to himself. He closed the door and reentered the emptiness of the house. "You little devil," he said out loud to Victor, "what did you ever see in *him?*" He cocked his head, seeming to wait for an answer, but not for long. Then he glanced down at his two bare hands, one with the clotted blood on the thumb, the other that had taken Mark Inman's pulse.

"I can't take care of them anymore," he said, meaning Dell and Sonny. There was no sign of protest. "I need..." he continued tentatively. "I need to..." But he quickly fizzled out, stumped for a verb, as if he couldn't translate fast enough from another tongue. He stared into the living room, where the gas fire still rippled in the fireplace. His party had vanished like a parlor trick. There was no more mud in the freezer. He couldn't even imagine what he needed.

2

Victor Diamond had worked for Pacific Bell on a four-day week—
in the business office, that is, not up a pole in a stud leather
belt heavy with tools. Nobody loved a weekend more than Victor.
He and Steven day-tripped with murderous abandon, malls and mu-
seums and endless capuccinos. But each free Wednesday was his
soft spot, his time for self-improvement and various errands so arcane
they seemed invisible. Also the occasional midday drop-by at the
baths, what Victor would later call his window of vulnerability.

He was diagnosed with a single lesion on his ankle in October, a
month before his thirty-fourth birthday. The next one, above the left
nipple, didn't appear till fourteen months later. In the meantime
Victor shook the fear and dread and convinced himself he was once
again a special case. He was still the only gay man in the western
world from northern Montana. Besides, he swore he never felt better
than he did in the fourteen months. He nicknamed his lesion Spot
and patted it every night when he took off his socks: "Good dog."

Steven longed so much to believe him, and there were so many
places left to see, that they defied it together from Bora Bora to
Moscow to Rome. Steven practically traveled free, there were so
many outlets hungry to seduce his client list. Victor took all the

vacation and medical leave they owed him at the phone company, without ever having to use the "A" word. So every two months they fled to a different poster, sharp as the blue-flaked cart beside the Tuscan wall.

When the second lesion appeared it wasn't given a name, but still he felt terrific, his energy inexhaustible. They flew to New York for Valentine's Day, then on to the Bahamas for a freebie at a mob resort. Steven didn't want him getting too much sun, but Victor wouldn't listen. "Stop acting like I'm fragile, it's bad luck," said Victor, collapsing under a banana palm, blond hair stiff with salt.

Right after that they started appearing in clusters, two or three every week, but Steven never dared to blame it on the sun. Still they traveled: to Sonoma for the opening of a winery, to Provincetown for a rainy Memorial Day. Victor was getting docked for missing so many Mondays at Pacific Bell, but he rather liked the three-day week, and still hadn't told his supervisor anything about AIDS.

He lost weight in the summer but not very much, and the proof of how stable he was were the men who had started to fall all around them, battered from weeks of pneumonia, curling into a ball. Their neighbor up the street was on a respirator for seventy-seven days, some kind of world's record. Victor was very early for L.A.; New York was already half gone. By autumn he was tired, but still they went away again, to Tuscany for real.

It was close to the unspoken second anniversary of Spot. Though now that mark was indistinguishable from a hundred others, none were above the neck, and Victor looked quite spiffy in his long-sleeved Brooks Brothers shirts. Steven had the pictures to prove it, on the last page of the last album in the study. Victor at a rusty table on a terrace west of Siena, with a view out over a tawny, smoky meadow dotted with cypresses. Victor's arms were open in a giant laughing embrace. He was singing a garbled aria, making it up as he went along. A cone of roasted chestnuts sprawled on the table.

That night or the next, Steven woke from a nap in the hotel room. The balcony doors were open to the chill November evening. The hotel was an old nunnery, with a cloister just below their windows. They were planning to eat a baronial dinner in the cove-ceilinged dining room, and had starved themselves all day to get ready.

Steven jumped up and ran to the light in the bathroom, thinking to scoop Victor out of the tub and kiss him all over, lesions or no. And found him sitting on the edge of the tub, naked except for his purple welts, staring into the mirror. He pointed to a spot along his chinline, below his ear. Steven bent forward with hammering heart. It wasn't even purple yet, barely a quarter-inch across. Victor said, "It's time to go home." And they never went anywhere again.

Sonny was the youngest of three Cevathas boys. The older two had worked construction for their father every summer through high school. Thus they were always ready, come September, to lumber into the backfield for Orange High, kicking butt through the brutal heat of the Central Valley fall. Sonny, youngest by half a dozen years, considerably leaner and golden-haired from the sun, followed suit in the summer of his fifteenth year and picked up a shovel for Athens Construction.

By the middle of June he had seduced the foreman, also a Greek and extremely married, who could not bear the guilty wages of desire and fired Sonny before he killed him. Stathis Cevathas, the rhyming patriarch of the family and the Greekest man in Fresno, never quite understood what had transpired. But with a sixth sense for the horrors of fate, he kept his third son clear of the business ever afterward.

It didn't deliver Sonny from the dreams of married men. At sixteen he was a bag boy at Safeway, working "12 Items or Less" from five to seven, when business types would stop off on the way home with the sudden lists of their wives. Sonny would stare them down in their three-piece suits, and every couple of weeks a white card would flash and exchange hands as Sonny gave over the paper sack. "Why don't you give me a call?" they'd say.

He did it in high-rise offices, as high as they rose in Fresno anyway. In BMWs and Jeep Comanches, in weekend cabins in the high Sierra. Once in a barn in a rusty sleigh, with a man who owned two mountains. Sonny never really felt gay; he had nobody gay to talk to. He never felt anything. Years later, a therapist at a walk-in clinic suggested that Sonny had spent his adolescence being sexually abused, but he never went back to find out why.

When he was seventeen he was meant to go to college, despite functional illiteracy. Stathis Cevathas had decided his questionable son would be a professional man. The Cal/State branch in the next county was willing to overlook the C's and D's on Sonny's record, being as Athens Construction had built the entire campus from the ground up. Sonny had no opinion in the matter.

He was required to make up a failing grade in Spanish with summer work, and his father hired as tutor the non-Greek loser husband of his sister Urania. The husband of Urania was a professor of Romance Languages at NYU, not a loser at all. He loathed the Cevathas clan of Fresno, but nevertheless spent summers there for his wife's sake. The Spanish lesson was from five to seven, necessitating a rearrangement of Sonny's hours as bag boy. It was only a matter of time between irregular verbs and fate.

One searing day in July, an ocean of heat surging across the valley floor, Stathis came home with terrible heartburn. He lumbered into the bathroom for Gelusil and drank it from the bottle, staring at a picture of his wife and three boys. His eyes welled with the fullness of life. Carol the wife was out doing good works of an Orthodox nature, and the backfield brothers were pouring concrete at a shopping center. The ache of love in Stathis's heart was so intense, he moved blindly to the room of his third son, feeling he would burst if he didn't hug someone.

He threw open the door and stepped inside, the king come to visit the prince. At first he couldn't even see what he saw. He averted his eyes to the desk where Sonny should have been sitting, with the Spanish grammar and the dictionary. Instead the boy was naked and leaning against the dresser, being fucked from behind by the husband of Urania. The rutting pair were strangely silent, no moans or gasps, and hadn't even heard the door open. It was Stathis who gave the first groan as his heart broke.

The husband of Urania, his pants around his ankles, turned and looked in horror. Instantly he pulled out of the boy. His big shiny penis swayed before him, foolish and ungainly. Sonny was more languid as he glanced over his shoulder at his father. His bare butt was still thrust out coyly, the look on his face more fascinated than surprised.

Rock-hard from a life of shoveling, Stathis lunged at the husband of Urania and threw him against the closet door. All of the screaming went on in Greek, but the motif word was *incest*. Though Stathis was three times stronger, the professor abominated his brother-in-law, so they were equally matched in passion. They grappled and gouged and crashed to the floor, spitting like Medea.

Sonny darted across to the pool of his clothes beside the desk. He slipped into his jeans and a work shirt, then sat on the desk chair to pull on his socks and sneakers. Even as his father and uncle rolled in fury, heaving up against the furniture, Sonny's mind was icy-clear. He swept the room with his eyes, abandoning all the paraphernalia of his childhood. He didn't really need a thing.

By now Stathis had started to scream—*cunt, whore*—and gladly would've turned his rage on the son who had blackened his name. But the husband of Urania had gotten the upper hand, pinning the patriarch to the floor and banging his head like a gavel. Sonny opened the center drawer and lifted out an envelope full of his bag boy savings. He took a last look at the clutter on his desk, almost wishing there was something worthy of a souvenir, but nothing sentimental caught his eye.

Sonny skirted by the two men on the floor and out the door. He flew down the stairs, the walls swirling with red and gold flocked paper. As he ran outside he had a wondering moment: *Could he really leave without any plan at all?*

A midnight-blue LTD was just pulling into the driveway. His mother was at the wheel, his Aunt Urania in the passenger's seat. Sonny grinned and waved, sprinting away down the sidewalk as if he'd been sent to buy milk and the evening paper. He never looked back and never wrote, thus escaping the wrath of Stathis Cevathas. Yet even as he took to the open road, to wander the next ten years, Sonny never lost the feeling of being a hairsbreadth away from getting torn apart.

When Lorenzo Delgado Espinoza arrived in Los Angeles, on the third of June in 1978, he had been on the road four months, overland fifteen hundred miles. The village he left behind, on the shore of a marshy lake south of Morelia, with a view to the humid slopes of Taucitaro, mountain of the lost gold, was not equipped with a telephone or even a post office. In order to send money to his mother and three sisters, Lorenzo Delgado had to ricochet every dollar through a cousin in Mexico City. The cousin creamed twenty-five cents off the top, as did the traveling lawyer who wound his circuitous way to the marshy lake three times a year. Even so, the Espinoza girls were the best dressed in the district school. On her sixteenth birthday Linda Espinoza was able to buy in the market at Morelia a pair of Calvin Klein jeans. This was what it meant that her brother had gone to the end of the earth to be a gardener's helper, armed with a leaf blower and not a submachine gun, but a revolutionary all the same.

By the time Linda was nineteen, her brother had reached the stature of myth. He'd been living in California for five years, moving from leaf blower to a truck of his own and a couple of assistants. The money orders increased proportionally, such that the cousin in Mexico City was able to reupholster his living room. For her part, Linda's mother vacated the mud house on the marsh and moved into town with her three daughters, to a house of concrete blocks sturdy as an air-raid shelter.

Beatriz Espinoza lit candles daily to her wonderful son. Within a year the prosperous older daughters had taken husbands. Linda began to write letters to Lorenzo Delgado, for at last they were on a postal route and could get their money direct. Linda gave sharp and ironic descriptions of her brothers-in-law, and of the doctor's office in Morelia where she worked as a receptionist. She always ended by asking, "When are you coming to visit?"

He never exactly answered her, but took to scrawling a note with the money order, sending his love to all. Linda wasn't remotely hurt. Her brother was so superior to the bewildered young men of Morelia, even to those who took off for the States themselves. Lorenzo Delgado, ten years older than Linda, had seemed heroically handsome when he left the weed-choked lake at twenty-three. He hadn't been saddled with wife or even girlfriend, his dreamy smile fixed instead on the life he would make for himself alone. Even at thirteen, with her black pigtail and her somber eyes, Linda understood there was more to life than settling down.

She expected nothing remarkable for herself. It was enough to think of her brother roaming the north, making his mark, and becoming something different. Linda stayed the same—going to Mass in the morning with her mother, smiling all day at the fretful sick in Dr. Sandina's waiting room, visiting her sisters in the evening, an old maid before she was twenty.

Then, just after Easter, when the bludgeoning heat of the dry season had settled down in earnest, a letter arrived from California, the Spanish formal as high school: "I am coming to Mexico City with a friend. I will travel to Morelia to see you on Saturday the 8th of May." Linda wasn't visibly more excited than the others, who buzzed word of the visitation far and wide in the family. Beatriz Espinoza prevailed on the vinous local priest to say a Mass of special providence for the safe journey of her son. Black beans and guava jelly simmered on the stove all week.

Even when he walked in the house, with his black brush mustache, she held back till the others had embraced him, sisters and aunts and neighbors. Then he picked out Linda with his eyes, standing beside the table where she sat and wrote her letters. They grinned in startled delight. She was brisk as a pony, her long black hair shivering. Her sisters were already wide as their mother, but Linda was spare and taut like him, with the same dreaming gaze. They were both too shy to embrace. Yet his grin was all the reassurance Linda needed.

He spoke to everyone else all evening, the waves of cousins who came from everywhere to greet him. Linda oversaw the food and passed out the Carta Blanca. It was only very late that they were alone with the fireflies, having sent all the others rollicking home. They sat out on the terrace on chairs made of branches, the air swooning with night jasmine. He thanked her for all her letters and laughed with her about the dull-witted brothers-in-law. He'd already answered everything about himself three times over—his apartment, his truck, the border, the dollar. The only thing he could think to add was his gringo name. "Dell," he told her, "with two L's."

Linda leaned toward him in the dark, chin in one hand. "And who's your friend?"

He blinked once. "Marcus," he said. "A professor. He comes to Merida to study the stones." He waved a hand vaguely to the east, toward Yucatán.

"He's nice?"

"Oh yes. Very nice." He smiled broadly, the mirror of her own, then reached across and took her hand. "Look, you don't want to live here. Why don't you come to California?"

She laughed deliciously then, as if he had guessed her deepest secret. "Why not," she replied without a moment's thought. Proving to herself at last that much was destined to happen to those who had no expectations.

On Monday morning Steven hauled the Hefty bag out the kitchen door and down the driveway, grumbling under his breath, hating all the dailiness of things. He kicked the rolled newspaper out of his way as he headed for the two battered trash barrels, tilted against each other in the curbside grass. The barrels were supposed to be up behind the kitchen steps, brought to the curb Wednesday night for Thursday pickup, but ever since Victor had gotten sick, Steven had abandoned the protocols of trash.

He reached for the rusty lid on the right-hand barrel, when suddenly a grizzled shape rose up, its lip curled and snarling. Steven yelped in terror, stumbling backward. The coyote bent to the ground again, where it had torn open a paper sack full of fast-food garbage. Steven sagged against his trash bag, gulping to get his breath back. The coyote, five feet away, seemed utterly indifferent as it shook a Styro burger box in its teeth.

What disoriented Steven most was the animal's lack of fear, no skulking away up the canyon as it had the night before. And what was it doing out in broad daylight anyway? Slowly Steven rose to his feet and began to back away. If the predators had lost all fear, the millennium was even closer than he thought. Then the animal came up off its haunches, ignoring Steven completely, perking up its ears as it listened to the wind. The ears did it: suddenly Steven saw it was a dog. Mangy and gaunt and yellow-gray as its wilder brother, but the ears were a lab's. His matted coat and his bony rib cage showed how long he had lived outside.

With a simian roar, Steven reached for a stick at the edge of the driveway. "Get the fuck out of here!" he bawled, smashing the lid of the barrel like a warped gong. His shouting grew wordless as he jumped up and down, banging the lid again and again. The dog looked over, head low, growling contemptuously.

Steven hit the lid so hard his stick broke in two. He shrieked even louder: "Get out! Get out!" Across the street, where an A-frame perched on the side of the hill, the garage door began to rise, as if Steven's screaming had tripped a sonic alarm. Then a moment later an old mint-green Caddy lumbered up the narrow street and turned neatly into the driveway. At last Steven stopped shouting. He was practically faint from exhaustion as he panted for breath. The dog hadn't moved an inch.

Out of the Cadillac stepped a wiry old lady in a tailored suit, a hat with a veil perched in her blue-white hair. "Morning, Mr. Shaw," she called with a little wave. "Is that your dog?"

"No," said Steven emphatically, stepping away from the barrels to put some distance between him and the offending carnivore. "I never even saw him before."

"Oh, I've seen him around," said Mrs. Tulare, bending to peer in her mailbox. "I tried to feed him, but he won't take food from me. Maybe you'll have better luck."

"But I don't *want* him," Steven insisted as Mrs. Tulare disappeared into the A-frame.

Now that Steven had stopped commanding, the dog loped away along the hill to look for heartier fare. Furiously Steven gathered the fast-food smithereens and shoved them into the barrel, dumping the Hefty in after them. He trotted up to the garage and got into the silver Volvo, dented at all four corners. It wasn't till Steven was halfway down the hill, a pearly September smog brooding across the city, that he caught a whiff of rotten cole slaw on his hands.

He felt a flutter of revulsion in his belly, and fought a memory of the smell of blood in the lab at Cedars. As he pulled into traffic on the Strip, heading east to Hollywood, he knew he couldn't show up at the doctor's stinking like a deli. Thus he decided, for the first time in months, to stop at the office on the way.

Shaw Travel was at the corner of Sunset and Laurel, upstairs from a tux rental place and across from Greenblatt's. The streetside windows, full of blue-velvet formal wear, looked like a Reno wedding chapel. Steven pulled around to the back of the building, where the parking space he hadn't used in months was empty and waiting. In the dumpster beside the back door someone had tossed out a pair of mannequins, nude and headless and cut off at the waist.

Steven trotted up the back stairs and used his key to let himself in. Instantly he could hear the buzz of activity, phones and terminals, though a dim-lit hallway separated him from the main office. He ducked through a door off the hall to his private office, about the size of a cabin on a freighter. The desk foamed with third-class mail that Margaret hadn't bothered to cart to Steven's house. On the wall above the desk was a big blowup of a silversword cactus on the black crater floor of Haleakala, eight thousand feet up on Maui.

Steven slipped into the broom-closet bathroom to wash his hands, noting fussily that the last person to use the sink hadn't wiped it for the next passenger. He tidied up assiduously and made a mental note that they had to change from bar soap to liquid: less germs.

He would have slipped out the back door like a phantom, leaving no one at Shaw Travel any the wiser. But as he moved into the hallway, he came face to face with a young woman who gasped and jumped back. She stared at him as if he were a cat burglar. "Hello, I'm Steven Shaw," he said mildly, offering one of his squeaky clean palms.

"Oh," she replied, the light dawning. "I've talked to you on the phone. I'm Heather."

They shook hands warmly, and then Steven had no choice. He turned and headed into the main office. The room was unpartitioned, with army-green metal furniture, a small bureaucracy in a country on the brink of war. Margaret looked up from her desk by the front windows, phone at her ear. Her eyes widened impishly at the sight of the ghost who hadn't crossed the threshold in six months. At another desk Ray Lee crouched before his computer screen with savage punk-cut hair, spouting numbers at a fleshy middle-aged couple sitting opposite. Heather quickly returned to her own desk, apparently having thought better of taking her break just now.

Steven nodded absently at his staff of three and moved automatically to the free desk in the corner. The computer was on and waiting. He pressed a sequence of keys, and the system booted up the client file. He had done this hundreds of times, but never quite so thoughtlessly. He would've sworn he wasn't going to punch in Mark Inman's name until he saw the green letters appear on the screen. The system thought for a moment, then went for the name: *Mark Inman, 2200 Skyway, LA 90046.*

"We thought you'd never get here," Margaret purred beside him, patting his belly.

"I'm not here," Steven corrected her. "I just came to use the facilities."

"You want to see his file?"

"Whose file?" he asked with a certain stubbornness, even as she pointed to Mark's name. "No thanks. I'm on my way to the doctor."

"For what?" No tension in her voice, no smothering worry.

"Numbers," he said, turning to go. Heather was huddled over her corporate rates. Ray Lee, darting past to grab some folders, murmured to Margaret and Steven: "They're taking a second mortgage to go on the QE2." Margaret followed Steven down the hall and out the back door. They stood together a moment on the landing, looking down at the pair of mannequin torsos tumbled in one another's arms.

"Lynn says Dell's the most stimulating man she's met in months," declared Margaret.

"She probably needs a new gardener."

"Listen, he really fired her up. Now she wants to get involved." Margaret drew out the last word dryly and gave a languid shrug, which was her way of punctuating. She didn't pretend to understand such things, she just reported them.

"I hope she's good with explosives."

"Oh, Lynn's very game," she countered. "Her whole life she's been looking to meet a stranger on a train. If someone will just bump off her father, she stands to inherit Brentwood. Call as soon as you leave his office, okay?"

Steven nodded dutifully, then trotted down the stairs. He glanced up at Margaret as he got in the car, smiling at her puckishly, feeling he'd been too abrupt. She leaned on the railing with folded arms, her hair glinting copper in the bright noon sun. She didn't look worried at all, about Steven or anything else. If it was an act, Steven would have known by now. They had worked together for twelve years, since the days when Shaw Travel was a two-button phone in Steven's apartment.

Which made Margaret Kirkham thirty-five, though in Steven's mind she remained as young as the day he met her, in much the same way that Victor stayed eighteen. Of the three it was only Steven who ever got older—exponentially so in the last two years, to him anyway. After driving up Hollywood Boulevard to Dr. Buckey's office, he parked in an aimless gray garage, then sat for forty-five minutes in a packed waiting room, reading *National Geographic,* twice reaching into his pocket at the sound of other men's beepers. The exhausted boy across from him was peppered with lesions all over his face. He wore a *Cats* T-shirt and Walkman earphones. Steven squirmed at his own girth, how it mocked the thin and ancient boy with the sleepy eyes, swaying to the silent music.

Dr. Buckey, admitting Steven to the inner sanctum, did not specifically ask how he was feeling, the question being faintly out of place in a nuclear war. Beefy as a tenor himself, with fingers that never stopped flexing, Buckey opened Steven's folder and drew out a sheet of blood work. He scanned it closely as Steven, sitting on the tissue-covered table, made a last futile stab at nonchalance.

"Your T-4 is 289, Mr. Shaw," Buckey observed pleasantly. "White blood count, 4400. You're doing very nicely."

Steven flushed with accomplishment, the good student as ever. He didn't even hear the next part. Wilted with relief, he pulled off his shirt and let Buckey poke at his lymph nodes and peer in his mouth for patches. The hard part was over. Somehow Steven had squeaked in under the wire again. No plummet and no red flags: he was stable.

The T-cell test was a sort of latter-day College Board score, with the top of the class assured a slot in some immunological Ivy League. For a year and a half Steven's numbers had bounced around from the mid two hundreds to high threes. When they were up, Dr. Buckey said he was doing fine; when they were down, he said the numbers didn't mean very much. Other men had abandoned Leonard Buckey because he made it all seem like helpless guesswork. When Steven would ask about the latest drug-of-the-month, Dr. Buckey would say, "Well, there are people who say they do better on that." And then he would flex his fingers.

Actually, Steven liked Dr. Buckey *because* he had no bedside manner. It was a curious relief after Victor's doctor, who had been so sure the answer was around the corner, if only Victor would just hold on. Steven preferred a helpless fatalist, even as he answered Buckey's catechism: no night sweats, no fevers, no diarrhea.

"If you don't lose some weight, Mr. Shaw, you'll be dead of a coronary before you ever get AIDS."

He patted Steven's belly in the same way Margaret had. Steven was beginning to feel like Buddha. He didn't retort that Buckey was just as overblown as he, because he knew this place wasn't a democracy. As Buckey filled out the bill, Steven looked over at the shelf above the blood-pressure gauge, where a cluster of Plexiglas frames were full of pictures of Buckey's wife and children. The dividing line between the two men could not have been more sharply drawn. And the prospect of a coronary suddenly seemed as lush as an oasis, like dying in your sleep at ninety.

The bill was sixty-five dollars. As Steven handed his VISA to the receptionist, Buckey instructed him to come in again in three months. They shook hands philosophically, a certain understanding between them that nothing of a medical nature had just transpired. In December they would try to have the same non-meeting again, everything blissfully stable. Buckey called in the next patient, who happened to be the sleepy boy with the lesions. He came in bent like an old man, but what made Steven turn his face away was the yearning in the boy's eyes. This one wanted to be healed. He still trusted that Dr. Buckey would find him a magic bullet.

Steven passed guiltily through the waiting room, eyes straight ahead, not wanting to doom anyone else with his awful dose of reality. Tears welled up for Victor as he groped across the desert wastes of the parking garage. It wasn't till the Volvo lurched out onto the boulevard that he permitted himself a small throb of being alive. He didn't feel like murdering anybody in traffic. For the first time in weeks he felt he might make it home without a dozen glazed doughnuts from Winchell's.

To be sure, it was only the most provisional kind of alive. It wouldn't have done to ask him where he'd be two years from now, because the answer was still "Dead." But the stasis of his numbers gave the next three months a sort of burnish, like the light in Margaret Kirkham's hair. He wasn't going to be sick between now and Christmas. He never would have verbalized it so, especially to himself, not wanting to spoil his record as a fatalist. But for now, anyway, the white had gone out of his knuckles.

At Hollywood and Fairfax, traffic slowed to a crawl around a broken-down sanitation truck. Its tattooed crew, up since dawn, sat on the rear bumper dozing like cats as they waited for a tow. Steven inched forward, patient and serene, opening the glove compartment to fetch himself a diet mint, just nine calories. Instead he pulled out the Thomas street guide, the spiral-bound Bible of the Southland grid. Back and forth from the brake to the gas, he moved toward the light at Fairfax. One hand on the wheel, he leafed through to the index, trying to act random, stopping at S. About halfway down the third column he spied *Skyway Lane: 23, E-6*. Quickly he thumbed to Map 23, Hollywood and the hills. He traced the E longitude to Mulholland Drive, east of Laurel Canyon.

So he lived up there, thought Steven, dispassionate as a realtor. Then on the map he spied "Skyway," a squiggle off Mulholland on the spine of the mountains. The view would be out to the Valley, the opposite of Steven's. A car behind him pounded its horn, and he looked up startled. The road ahead was clear. Steven lurched forward and took the turn, nodding guiltily at the sanitation crew as he passed.

Four minutes later, heading uphill to his own aerie, he sucked the diet mint with innocent abandon. He swung onto his winding street and sailed the Volvo into the garage. Scrambling out, he paused at the top of the driveway, trying to think what to do first with the rest of his life. Down below, the 2 P.M. haze was pale as sherry, hunched across the city like a bad sleep. High up where Steven was, the sun beat unambiguously on the hills, scorching every vacant lot. Overhead a pair of hawks circled the canyon, their wings utterly still.

Steven lifted up onto his toes like a diver. *Wish small,* as Victor always used to caution whenever a cake was lit for anyone's birthday. With a lazy smile and nothing decided, Steven headed around to the front of the house. He went past the front steps and tramped through the ivy, ducking behind a white oleander. A couple of copper pipes with faucets stuck out from the house foundation.

He opened both taps full force. There was a surge of pressure from under the house, then a sputter as several sprinklers began to spray. Steven hadn't watered in months. The ivy and stunted shrubs that covered the hill below the house had done the best they could, brown and crumpled at every edge, holding out for the rainy season. Anything too possessed with being green was long gone in Steven's yard. More than once, Dell had offered to hook up an automatic system with a timer, but Steven never pursued it. Let the desert reclaim itself, he decided grandly, wistful for the millennium.

Now he surveyed his half-acre, the sprinklers playing on the dusty prow of the hill. A lunatic idea bloomed in Steven's brain: the hillside covered with ferns and orchids. He thrashed around to the side of the house, skirting a sprinkler's halo, making for the faucet on the northeast corner. All along this flank the lantana, thriving on thirst, had blanketed the slope in a twisted thicket. To reach the tap Steven had to crash his way through a maze of branches.

As he bent to turn the water on, he saw the dog, curled in a shady hollow in the underbrush about four feet away. Its nose was on its paws, its glowering eyes on Steven. The animal growled threateningly, just this side of bared fangs. "Fuck you," retorted Steven.

He turned the faucet on hard, and the sprinklers in the eastern quarter burst with spray. Since one of these was a bare stone's throw from where they crouched, it began to rain lightly through the bushes. The dog didn't move from his burrowed place, or even lift his head. Getting wet was the given of a rainy day. Ringed around him in the hollowed-out cave in the bushes were the stubs of bones he had scavenged on Wednesday nights. The two of them blinked at each other with studied indifference.

"Just don't get any ideas," Steven murmured disdainfully, rising out of the brambles.

He slogged to the front of the house again, the squish of mud around his shoes. Across the hill the sprinklers' mist was shot with minor rainbows. Irrelevantly Steven wondered: If he had Thanksgiving here, could he keep it to eight people, since eight was all the movable chairs he had? A startling thought for a man who, except for his funeral, never planned anything more than two months in advance.

He was trying to wish smaller than Christmas, apparently, thrown for a moment back to life Before, when he and Victor took in all their circle's refugees for a plate of turkey. Even as he smiled at the memory, he stopped in his tracks in the ivy, soaking wet from the knees down, squinting into the afternoon sun. Aside from Margaret Kirkham and now Mark Inman, he couldn't think who else to invite.

Ray Lee, perhaps, and maybe Heather, though it wouldn't do to make Thanksgiving a company picnic. Of course he had to include Dell and Sonny, being as it was a holiday. But he couldn't avoid the sinking feeling of having no one left for the eighth chair. Then he remembered Dell had a sister, even though he'd never met her. He felt better already, just having his table full, and rambled around to his front door, candying yams in his head. Drenched in the fullness of his reprieve.

When Mark got back from London, ready to kill, there were a hundred and nineteen calls on his call list. His plane touched down at two-thirty, and he told the driver to take him directly to the studio. He was still reeling with jet lag from flying the *other* way four days ago, but since he'd never had time for jet lag before—a wimp's condition—he wasn't buying it now. No, this was the start of dying. There wasn't a test for it exactly, any more than he could put his finger on a symptom. He just felt sapped. And even if no one could tell him how long, he knew it was only a matter of time before the shrunken shell of him went into its final spasm.

He sat dully in the back of the limo, hands hanging limply over his knees. His briefcase lay bewildered beside him. He could've returned ten calls between LAX and Burbank, but he didn't. At the

Dorchester he'd confined his telephoning to doctors, all over Europe, trying to get a straight answer about drugs. It was quickly obvious there was no sure deal on a magic bullet. *Maybe, maybe not,* they told him in Paris, Zurich, Stockholm. He thought he'd explode if he heard them say "promising" one more time.

The guard at the Barham Boulevard gate waved them in, with a fawning smile at the smoked-glass window in the back. The limo wound its stately way through the outskirts of the lot, past the post-nuclear silence of a dusty New York street. Behind the executive building a row of tall eucalyptus trees swayed lazily, trailing along the ridge of a dry wash where savages used to slaughter noble cavalry. At the end of the ridge stood a cluster of thirties bungalows.

Mark climbed out in his Bond Street grays, the driver promising to leave off his luggage at the house on Skyway Lane, also to lay in milk and juice. Mark stood on the bungalow stoop for a moment, as if he had suffered a brief amnesia. For two years he'd rocketed through this door at full throttle. Now there was something oddly timid about his hand on the screen door latch, dangerously quiet, like men who arrive at work one morning smiling, with a bullet for everyone.

Connie Hinton, Mark's dogged secretary, was up from her desk and firing the instant he stepped inside. "Lou's in Chicago, he wants to buy a horse," she said without preamble. "A million two, and he doesn't have his checkbook." She followed her boss as he headed silently into his inner office. Everything here was gray, and as subtly tailored as the Bond Street suit. The window blinds were tilted to banish the afternoon light. "Eric's been calling all morning," Connie continued as Mark went around his desk. "He tried to call your *plane.* Paramount's upped their offer, Sid says no, Angela wants him to do it."

Eric was Lou Ciotta's lawyer, Sid his bug-eyed manager, Angela his wife. None of them knew that Mark was gay, or at least they never said so, at least to Mark. Connie, who would've taken this job for half the pay, so mystical was the place to her, knew everything but didn't speak either. "Ted Kneeland just called," she added neutrally, about as far as she went into lifestyle matters.

Mark stood at his desk but didn't sit down. The full list of the hundred and nineteen calls was typed out on three neat pages, edge to edge on the blotter. He sent Connie out to gather all the principals of the Paramount deal, then glanced down the roster of players who wanted a piece of Lou. Still he did not sit down, the briefcase still in his hand.

The fifth season of "Hard Knocks" was scheduled to commence two weeks from Wednesday. By spring the show would be ready for sale to syndication, and then Lou would have enough cash to buy all the horses of Arabia. The Paramount deal was for a feature, a good cop/bad cop comedy, to be shot during Lou's hiatus. Angela, formerly Miss Arizona, who shopped with a murderous vengeance day after day, never lost sight of the golden goose in all of this. Eagerly she encouraged Lou's product spokesmanship throughout the western world: batteries, soft drinks, fitness parlors.

On the wall opposite, Lou Ciotta grinned from a shiny Cibachrome print, the prototype for a poster that had sold seven million units in the last two years. Lou's bedroom eyes were full of dirty linen, and he wore a baby-blue tank top that showed a lot of pumped and hairy cleavage. Mark's job was to graph the national turn-on that Lou evoked, working with total abstractedness, since Lou did nothing for him personally. He'd sat through countless meetings poolside at Lou's house in Malibu, himself in a tie and Lou in a tank suit, peaceable as a eunuch while Lou scratched his voluminous basket.

Connie buzzed: Sid Rawls on the line. Mark picked up and went into automatic overdrive, parsing the Paramount deal. Quickly they worked out a counteroffer, its tax loopholes intricate as crochet. Sid didn't ask how London was or tell a joke. The deal was all there was between them, until the end, when Sid tossed out, "So, who's the lucky girl you're bringing Sunday?"

Mark chuckled dryly. "Sorry, I haven't got that far yet," he replied, but promised he'd drop by Sid's house after the show. He hung up and glared at his week-at-a-glance, where Connie had written in red for Sunday: *EMMYS, 5 P.M.* His jaw tightened decisively. He tapped a number and flicked the phone to the speaker box, moving around to swing his door shut.

"Hello?" Ted Kneeland's voice was bright and inexhaustible, like the boy himself.

"Hi, it's me."

"Hey, welcome home. How's Fergie and Di?" Like a cheerleader with a megaphone. "I decided I'm cooking you dinner. Nothing drab and English, I promise."

"Listen, I'm busy tonight."

"Oh, I thought we said..." Mark could hear the younger man shift gears and swallow the protest. Ted was right, of course: there *was* a date. "No problem. I'll come by later." In just five weeks he was so well trained.

"Look, Ted, I want to be alone right now. I'll call you, okay?"

There was a moment's silence, during which Ted must have calculated the odds of pushing the point. Not worth it. "Right now" was forever, as far as they were concerned. Or maybe Ted was shrewder than that, stopping to wonder what he had left behind in Mark's house. A pair of jeans, a couple of CD's, nothing that couldn't be replaced. "Yeah, sure," he said evenly. "Take care, huh? I'll see you around."

That was how easily it was done, as economical as a telegram. Mark's pace seemed to quicken now as he swung the door open again, his private deal done with. He tossed the briefcase onto the sofa. Connie called out the executive's name at Paramount, and he flicked off the box and grabbed the receiver, flinging down the new offer like a gauntlet. Before Paramount could catch its breath, Mark was on with Lou's publicist, leaking the counteroffer. A call to the network, one to the agent, then touching base again with Sid. For the space of five minutes Mark seemed fully reconnected, but as soon as the circle of calls was done it all dissipated. Sitting down at last, he felt bloated and queasy, as if he'd just wolfed down a dozen doughnuts.

Nobody knew anything. Mark talked to his Studio City doctor like a bachelor, the way he talked to the excitable women he took to black-tie functions. They knew and they didn't know; they didn't want to know. Eighteen months before, he had taken the antibody test anonymously at a gay clinic, sitting for twenty minutes' counseling with a man who knew only his first name.

Ted's five weeks was short by the usual standard. Typically they lasted about three months. Even Ted would have lasted the full nine innings, except for the call from Brad's father in San Bernardino. Until that night, Mark had succeeded in plotting his course on the good side of the percentages. There were guys who were going to squeak through and survive this thing, and he meant to make the cut. Otherwise he kept his fluids to himself, or shot them harmlessly into the air, like a gun on New Year's Eve.

Connie lobbed him a bunch of sucker calls, the kind he could put away with his eyes closed. The main piece of business right now was trying to find Lou Ciotta himself, whose chestnut stallion stamped the ground impatiently, longing to be in his retinue. Every few minutes, like a tongue on a sore tooth, Mark would glance at his call list, dissatisfied and impatient, trying to find someone he felt like calling. Mostly it was the standard cast of those who lunched too much. Some were gay and wanted checks. Some were friends who never missed a screening, but even they didn't know he was dying.

It wasn't till his eye swept the third page for the fourth time that he registered his own name: *Rob Inman*. Sometimes Connie typed *Your Dad* instead, and among the list of agents' names it sounded as if an Indian mystic had called. The number beside the name, beginning with 305, was indelible as a tattoo.

The static on the line was heavy when Rob Inman picked up the phone in Fort Lauderdale. "Hello," they called to each other, sailors on a stormy deck. "I said I was in London," Mark repeated slowly. It was considered too much of a fuss by the elder Inman to call back and try for a better connection.

"The show last night was a dog," complained Rob Inman, ignoring London pointedly, unless it was a short in his hearing aid. "Where did you dig up that landlady? She don't know how to play off Lou, and she don't look Italian either. You need a *guy*."

"Thanks, Dad. I'll have the casting people call you. How you doing?"

"*I* should be a Nielsen home," announced the old man. "Roz Schwartz is a Nielsen home, and she don't watch nothin' but soaps and Oprah."

Mark laughed and asked how Roz was doing, but the question got drowned in the static. The bristle of one-upmanship between

Rob and Roz was the one safe topic, much to be preferred to what followed now, the recitation of the mortal ills of the father. Cholesterol 280, triglycerides up, suspicious swelling in the prostate. Mark never paid much attention, considering it a form of white noise, but lately there was anger too. Mark had blood counts of his own, as well as a chain of swollen lymph nodes in his neck.

Yet even the list of ills was to be preferred, compared to what came next. "It's her birthday next Wednesday," declared Rob gravely. Mark said he knew. "She'd be seventy-one," his father went on, the catch in his voice sharp enough to override the static.

Mark didn't think about his mother unless he had to. When she died eleven years ago, after three sudden months of cancer, people told him it was a blessing. Mark agreed with everyone who said it—agreed with everything anyone said, however vacuous. At the time he was still an actor; still straight. No end to the ways he could duck.

"What are you planning for Wednesday?" he interjected when the old man paused between memories of the house in Manhasset, sold so Rob could flee to the waiting room of Lauderdale.

"Nothing special. Roz and me'll go to the track, maybe get a bite. I try to keep busy."

He had never yet said he and Roz were an item, however an item worked in south Florida. They had separate condos across the pool. They each had children in California—once, Mark endured an appalling call at the office from Nelson, son of Roz, inviting him to a barbecue. Sometimes Mark thought his father wanted to say more about Roz, but he never seemed to give the right cue.

"So who's your date for the Emmys?"

Mark chuckled a bit louder this time. "I haven't got that far yet," he said.

"You mean you got Friday and Saturday first. Hell, you can go three for three."

Mark never picked up on the playboy talk, but that didn't stop it. A fantasy of the old man's, from a youth cut short by marriage. Yet it was only after Eileen died that Rob started thinking about what he'd missed. The blondes he saw at the Emmys mocked him. It was a most ambiguous consolation that one of these walked in on the arm of his only son.

"When you coming down to see us?"

"Oh, I'll get there," Mark replied, the answer as rote as the question, their way of saying good-bye. Thus it was uncharted territory— Wile E. Coyote running off a cliff—when Mark added haltingly, "We need to sit down and talk."

Even as it tumbled out, he loathed the banality of it. There was a startled silence at the other end. Mark saw the two of them sitting on the condo's narrow balcony, overlooking a Pitch 'n' Putt, but he wasn't sure which he wanted to say: gay or dying. Probably both, but he hadn't got that far either.

"Well, you come on down whenever you like," replied his father briskly. It wasn't clear why they couldn't do this talking on the phone. "Least we can help you blow your savings on the ponies. We'll be watchin' for you Sunday night. Good luck."

"Thanks, Dad, but I haven't even been nominated."

"You're a winner in our book, son." The sincerity in his voice was real, even if the clichés were slightly askew. All Rob Inman could do with his heart was wear it on his sleeve. Their actual good-byes were clumsy and glancing as ever, the work of two men who avoided embracing. They hung up at exactly the same moment so nobody had to do it first.

Connie buzzed in with lightning speed: "We found him. They're transferring now. On two."

Mark waited for the prince of the Wednesday lineup, his eyes moving without thinking to the graven image of same across the room. Lou Ciotta, the current national mascot, radiated health. Untold thousands of hopeful actors looked as good, the beautifully unemployed with their bad glossies and puffed résumés, but this one happened to have won the lottery. Happily he was also a moron, so he never lost sleep wondering if he deserved it.

Two flashed, and Mark picked up: "Hey, Tiger."

"Okay, what's the problem? If I want a fuckin' horse, it's *my* business."

"I don't know about the problem," Mark responded smoothly, poising pen over paper.

"Eric's doin' this trip on Angela—like we can't afford it. I don't want to hear that shit. It's all I ever heard growin' up."

"Eric's just being protective," said Mark. On the memo pad he wrote *horse*.

"Call the bank and get 'em to wire the money. Today." End of discussion. Mark wrote *1.2* under *horse*. "Now, about this picture. Angela says the other guy's got all the laughs. *I* want the laughs."

"Lou, you've got just as many laughs. It's a buddy picture. You're both hysterical."

"Yeah, well, either they change it or they can sit on it."

Underneath *1.2* Mark wrote *laughs*. "I think it's a little premature. Counteroffer's two and a half mill. They may tell *us* to sit on it."

"Whatever," Lou retorted dismissively, as if the deal-making procedure were beneath his notice. The full tantrum would wait till the deal was done. "Angela needs a new psychic. Make sure he does house calls."

"What's wrong with the one she has?"

"He don't do channeling." Under *laughs* Mark wrote *channeler*. "Listen, what am I gonna get her for her birthday? I was thinkin' a boat. What do you think?"

"Why don't you get her a feed bag?"

"What?"

Mark set down the pen beside the memo. "Well, it's like this, Lou. I don't really give a fuck."

There was an odd aphasic pause at the other end, longer than Ted Kneeland, longer than Rob Inman. Mark glanced across at the poster again, to savor the shit-eating grin that had vanished just now in Chicago. Lou said: "This is a joke, right?"

"I don't think so, Lou. *You* get all the laughs, remember?"

Mark could hear him breathing heavy, as if he'd just worked out, a photogenic film of sweat gleaming on his charmed torso. "Listen, if this is some kind of fag shit, I don't got the time. Talk straight to me, man. What's the deal?"

"No deal, Lou. I was just thinking, maybe Angela can get it on with the horse. That ought to channel her pretty good."

There was a noise like a bull elephant's trumpet as Mark replaced the receiver quietly in the cradle. He stood up. Nothing sentimental cluttered his desk—no picture frame, no monogram, no paperweight. He came around and made an automatic move toward the sofa for his briefcase, then stopped himself. He took a last look around, amazed to think there was no mark of himself here to erase. He gazed at the black Italian leather chair behind the desk. It only seemed to dawn on him now that he'd killed the man who sat there. Bloodlessly: the next keeper of Lou Ciotta's flame could move in tomorrow.

Mark turned and left the office. So silent was his crime that when he strolled out of the bungalow, Connie assumed he was going across the way for a meeting with an executive. They still had a hundred and nine calls to go, but she was convinced they could do it before the day was done.

Scot-free, Mark walked away down the eucalyptus alley, the trees creaking overhead in the furnace breeze of September. A tumbleweed skittered down the New York street. Ghosts of cavalry and Indians waited for "Taps" in the dry wash. The list of names on Mark Inman's desk would never be cleared, but for once he was unencumbered by all his previous lives. For a dying man, in fact, he moved with a marvelous stride.

3

D ell pulled his mustard-yellow truck into a Pioneer Chicken stand on Alvarado. The noon heat was rotten as the dumpster in the parking lot, drizzled with flies. He had two men working in trees in Hancock Park, and he'd promised to bring them lunch. Already late, he drove past the takeout window and nosed in between the dumpster and a bank of three pay phones.

A couple of Bloods were dealing crack, using one of the phones as an office. They fastened their glittering eyes on Dell as he stepped to the right-hand phone, but saw right off he was too normal, not on the edge at all. If it had been past midnight, they might have killed him on principle, but now he was just another greaseball, meek as a burro, his truck full of tooth-shy rakes and caked shovels.

Dell drew a square of paper from his work shirt pocket, though he'd already memorized the number. When they answered at the Department of Water and Power, he asked to speak to the commissioner. He didn't exactly disguise his voice, though he did try for a resolutely American twang, so as not to implicate his people. "Yeah," he said to the bimbo who answered the commissioner's phone, "you got a reservoir up by Castaic, right? Well, you got a problem."

"I think you want the engineering department, sir."

"Oh no, honey, I want you. See, I just dumped a gallon of blood in there."

"Let me transfer you to Violations."

"It's AIDS blood." Finally there was a pause, a break in her bimbo stride. "See what I mean? You got a problem."

He hung up. As he strolled over to the takeout window, the Bloods were selling a gram vial to a scrawny girl about sixteen, indifferently pregnant. The glazed boy who took Dell's order was serenely abstracted from the crimes of the Pioneer parking lot. There was a bucket of chicken for everyone, pimps and dealers and terrorists all. Dell went away with two bags brimful of junk, and not another thought about his threat to the public safety.

He checked on the men in Hancock Park, who had stripped four trees of their summer growth. He listened, straw hat in hand, while the matron of the house berated him for cutting her elm too close to the bone. Then he raced to the Westside to give bids on two big landscape jobs. Then he made his maintenance rounds, leaf-blowing and watering in the hills above Franklin. These were his oldest clients, who still paid him only fifty a month.

He knew every green thing in their yards and liked the quiet, for no one was ever home. The autumn blast of heat had killed off all the annuals, but under the trees the flowers would not quit—beds of impatiens, baskets heavy with fuchsia. His grief was at its lowest ebb in the old hill gardens, as he hummed and showered the ferns with spray. Expertly his thumb controlled the flow of water from the hose, as if using a nozzle would be cheating.

He didn't even listen to the radio in the truck as he made his rounds. A proper terrorist would've been glued to the news, waiting for a bulletin. He picked up his crew in Hancock Park and left them off at a corner on Olympic, where crowds of brown men waited every morning for day-work. He got home around five and dozed in front of the tube. He didn't seem to pay much heed to the local news, hardly rousing himself when Linda came in to cook up some rice and chicken.

But there was no report of the incident, though the news stayed on till seven, through four different segments on the National League playoffs. Every half-hour saw an update on a plastics fire in Reseda and a baby born in a hammock. Dell was silent as he ate his supper, Channel 2 droning irrelevantly, while Linda read him a long rambling letter from one of their sisters—a christening and a funeral, all in one week, the seamless web of celebration in the dusty squares of Morelia.

Abruptly Dell stood up when he finished eating, crossed to the television, and slammed the button to turn it off, the only sign that he was impatient. Still, Linda didn't take it personally, even when he disappeared into his room without another word. If anything, she thought he was doing better with the pain. Better than she by a long shot. She cleared the dishes and sponged the plastic tablecloth, tears for Marcus stinging her eyes. But she didn't require any special attention. She kept her sorrow secret. As long as Lorenzo Delgado looked all right and didn't cough, sad was happy enough.

Cross-legged on his bed, Dell pulled the scrap of paper from his work shirt and dialed another number. "Channel 4 Action News," said a man's clipped voice, reeling with self-importance.

"Yeah, how come you don't got a story about the blood in the reservoir?"

"What story would that be, sir?" Instantly alert, yearning for an anchor spot.

"I stole it from a lab. It's contaminated with AIDS. I sure hope they got a good filter up there in Castaic."

"Are you claiming responsibility? Are you a group?"

Dell laughed. "No, man, I'm just a nut. I don't belong to anyone."

He heard a beep and click on the line and hung up fast. He didn't really believe they could trace the call, but he didn't want to be recorded either. He ambled into the kitchen as Linda was finished washing up. She said she was going around to collect the rents. First of October already: at least they had left behind the anniversary month. She was wonderful with the tenants, mostly single mothers, who were never on time with money. More like a resident social worker than a landlady, Linda filled out their ADF forms and wrote their letters home to Costa Rica.

By ten it was on the news. A spokesman from the Water Department said there was no cause for concern. The reservoir in question wasn't in use and would be brought on line only in severe drought conditions. No evidence of the alleged vandalism had been uncovered by department workers, but the footage was vivid all the same: a crew of men combing the shores of a pristine mountain lake in white space suits, helmeted, with walkie-talkies bleating.

A nice counterpoint to the anchorman's insistence: "There is absolutely no way that AIDS could be transmitted in this manner." Even a gallon of blood was scarcely a part per billion of water. More plutonium fell on Castaic Lake on an average day.

Nevertheless, there were seven thousand calls to the Water Department between ten and eleven. Linda came back with partial payment on two of the four rents and found her brother prone on the sofa again, flicking the remote from station to station. The switchboards were clogged to the point of gridlock. A hastily briefed dork from the Mayor's staff reiterated that nothing had happened and nothing could. No Castaic water was flowing through the system. Every faucet in the L.A. basin was being served by pure Colorado River runoff. The reporters shoved their mikes in his face: "Can you say without any doubt that the water supply is completely safe?" The dork brayed with frustration, trying to talk reason, but the answer was clearly no.

"Stupid, crazy people," Linda hissed in contempt, switching her black ponytail. It wasn't certain whether she meant the vandals, the officials, or the hysterical callers; she may not have known herself. Dell chortled and scratched at his mustache. Linda was pleased to see he didn't let the ignorance and lunacy get under his skin. She didn't say how little of the rent she had collected, how many dollars from how many months were owed by the Cabrillos and the Rodriguezes.

She did say, though, with a casualness that was most unlike her that she would leave him his supper cold tomorrow night. Asked it more than said it. He frowned up at her, not knowing how to tell her she owed him nothing. He'd explained to her often enough that he didn't need to be cooked for, that the last thing he wanted was Linda in a dutiful role, tied like the women of Morelia. He didn't ask about her plans for tomorrow night. It was none of his business.

"This girl I ride the bus with," she said. "Emilia. She asked me to go to Disneyland." Her brother didn't say anything, just nodded as he watched the TV screen fill up with a map of California, all its reservoirs dotted in blue. Linda shrugged. "I've never been there. Everybody should see it once, right?"

At last he turned from the news, as if he finally heard the flinching in her voice. "Yeah, well, you make sure you go on Space Mountain," he said briskly, his onyx eyes shining with intensity. "And the Haunted Mansion. I don't care how big the line is."

He spoke with the same insistence, at once protective and daring, with which he had commanded her to leave the concrete blocks of Morelia—the dead-end spinster's life, shuttling between her mother's house and Dr. Sandina's office. Smiling now, she swore to follow Dell's itinerary to the letter. She wished him good dreams but didn't embrace him. Their closeness didn't allow them to touch; they were both too formal and too discreet. Only once had she ever held him, just after Marcus heaved his final breath, and she'd drawn away as soon as Dell released the first roar of pain.

"I'll get you a Mickey Mouse T-shirt," she said.

"They're all gay, you know." He was playful now and teasing, one eye on the news, but not quite wanting her to go yet. "Mickey, Goofy, the duck—every single one of 'em."

"Mickey's not gay. He's got Minnie."

"Minnie's a dyke."

She laughed. "Don't tell anyone in Morelia. That's like saying the saints are gay."

"They are."

"Now you sound like Marcus."

They both laughed now, remembering the caucuses in the living room on Lucile, Marcus shaking his head about some politician or bishop. The closeted ones did the most damage, sabotaging the gay rights planks, throwing a red scare around Marcus and his petitioners. Whenever Marcus heard a homophobe spewing hate, he'd cluck his tongue and roll his eyes, convinced it was all thwarted desire.

As Dell watched Linda move to leave, quick and lively now that she had his permission for the outing, she looked thirteen again, the girl he'd left behind when he first came north. The pang of love in his heart was a constant wish for her happiness. He tried not to feel too protective, even resisted imagining what this Emilia looked like.

49

He had never seen his sister naked, never thought of her fired with passion. Such things couldn't be spoken of. Minnie Mouse was the closest they'd ever come.

He couldn't seem to focus on the news anymore. The final editorial note was sounding, the anchorman reassuring the viewers that nothing more was at issue here than a crackpot prank. "We owe it to what is most decent in all of us not to panic," he intoned, "to rise above our basest fears and ignorance."

Very stirring, though by noon the next day the DWP would measure a twenty-two percent drop in water consumption throughout the L.A. basin. Looking on the bright side, it was the first real stride anyone had ever made toward water conservation, but nobody looked on the bright side. For days after, there would be footage of the run on bottled water—bottled *anything*, as long as one didn't have to drink disease from the kitchen tap.

Now that he'd set it in motion, Dell had no plans to escalate the matter. By the next night's news they would be calling it "bloodmail," and every AIDS organization would roundly condemn the irresponsibility of the terrorist act. By then Dell would be feeling so abstracted from his own deed that they might have been talking about somebody else entirely, even after Channel 4 produced a composite based on the tape of his call: *hispanic male, mid-thirties, probably gay.*

He stripped to his shorts, grabbed the spiral notebook from his bedside table, and sprawled in bed with the phone on his chest. The first few numbers he tried were busy, for these were the midnight callers, restless and wired. Then he left an identical dirty message on two machines—calling on a CB from an eighteen-wheeler, looking to find some action at a truck stop. Not his scene especially, but according to the spiral notebook that's what these two liked. They really ought to meet each other, thought Dell. What did they need a middleman for?

The first one who answered was Kevin, the kid in Manhattan Beach who still lived with his parents and said he was twenty-four, though he sounded about sixteen. Kevin liked nothing better than to suck an uncut dick. Never been fucked, he hastened to add, the assertion falling somewhere between anxiety and a dare. Mostly he liked Dell to do the dirty talking—which Dell obliged, bringing Kevin to a quick crescendo, so loud it seemed the parents couldn't help but hear, unless they were full of a midnight rage of their own. For his part, Dell didn't even bother to take the aforesaid member out of his shorts.

When Kevin was done gasping, Dell inquired how things were going with his father, a foreman at Hughes Aircraft who thought queers should be gelded. Kevin chafed about wanting a life and a place of his own, to be gay for real. Sternly Dell assured him there was time enough, then warned Kevin as he always did about playing safe, though he knew the young ones felt immortal. AIDS was a middle-aged death to them, like middle age itself.

"Hey, Lorenzo, I'm hard again."

"Yeah, well, put it back in your pants. You gotta get up for school."

Kevin gave a wild derisive laugh. He loved the pull between them, big brother/kid brother. Dell had been checking in with him now for almost a month. The spiral notebook page was covered with scribbled details—Kevin's last term's grades, his workout routine, the four dudes he hung out with, the girlfriend he pecked good night.

"So when am I gonna meet you, guy?" asked Kevin, stuck in his little world.

"Someday," Dell replied, already pulling back like a camera, till the scene was small and far away. Some night they would know they were ready, he seemed to say, but it didn't sound soon. In the country of 976, meeting was like commitment, a marriage doomed from the start. *Someday* meant no. Reality would only spoil it. Face to face they would see that one was still in high school, the other one old enough to be his father. Then what fantasy would they play?

Yet both of them knew they would speak again. Dell never said a word about himself, or anyway not the truth, especially that Marcus had died of AIDS. In a jerkoff scene it was very bad form to bring up one's lover, let alone the holocaust. Dell was content to be a kind of scoutmaster to his 976 crew. When he called around he changed like a chameleon—sometimes Italian, sometimes twenty-five, top with bottom urges, rapist, virgin—anything not to be one particular man, especially himself.

He lay there with the phone still perched on his chest, paging

51

through the notebook. Nobody seemed to fire him tonight. His hundred men with their vital stats were too familiar, too predictable, as hard to quicken as a sleepy wife. Of course he could go back into the pile, pay his twenty cents a minute to the LOAD line and start a new page. But he already had one of every kind.

Below in the courtyard he could hear Nola Cabrillo coming in drunk with her date. She was squabbling and hissing at the scarfaced brute Ramon, but she would let him in anyway. Her two kids, five and three, who babysat for each other, would pretend to be asleep on the sofa so no one would yell at them. And later on, after the wails of pleasure, Ramon would beat her up; and none of the tenants would call the cops because they wouldn't come. Nola Cabrillo was just a domestic incident.

Dell put the phone and the notebook back on the bedside table. He turned off the light and pounded his pillow, scrunching up and staying on his own side of the bed. Almost unconsciously, not moving his lips, he prayed his double prayer. First to God, if there was a God, that He should reunite Dell and Marcus Flynn in heaven. This heaven was like a library where Marcus would be sitting and reading, parsing his glyphs with wonderful concentration. He could always read even with Dell lying beside him flicking the remote control, watching three stations at once. The second prayer was to Marcus himself, that he should protect his widows.

Don't let me drag her down, he said to the dark inside him. *Don't let me get in trouble.*

Between God and Marcus he could only believe in one at a time, and Marcus always won. God was back in Morelia, the queer priest in his gold cloak seething for the altar boys, Beatriz and her useless novenas. God didn't have enough rage. No doubt the pederast Fathers of Morelia would have found it remarkable that Dell was praying at all. Let him keep it secret if he liked. The thin thread of his nightly prayers would one day lead him back to the confessional. There they would stuff him with sin, bringing him home to the prison where he'd lived before Marcus Flynn.

But Dell was much further gone than that. He believed the opposite of everything, now that the anger had gone underground. It was all mixed up in his head with the Mayan gods of fire and blood, the stories Marcus had told him about the altars high on the pyramids, where a prisoner's heart was torn from his chest still beating. That was the God Dell yearned for late at night, a force equal to his own fury. Not even revenge was enough of a reason to believe, for he couldn't pin the enemy down to any one man. Chaos was what mattered. Watching the world unstring itself, with just a snip of the thread here and there.

Not that he wished to hurt anyone, except maybe God Himself. He lay there curled on his side in bed, his empty arms resting on the spot where Marcus used to sleep. To go forward at all anymore, it wasn't a matter of faith but will. Because he was a gardener he would be up at 6 A.M., but everything else had changed. He didn't trust the red sun would burn off the morning fog, or that he would be strong enough to work. Every single night before he went to sleep, he had to be finished with the world, in case he woke up too sick to go on. All he knew was this: before he went he would do what he had to, whatever it was, to let them know his people wouldn't go quietly anymore.

Dell used to complain that Marcus would have been better off marrying Linda. From the day she arrived—with a suitcase full of her mother's crochet, enough doilies to last three lifetimes—she and the professor were captivated by each other. In her mind she had expected an older man, cerebral and laconic, probably stout, requiring silence in order to work. But he loved to talk and waste time in the kitchen, gulping pots of tea. He darted and feinted like a middleweight boxer, with his flattened nose and broad Midwestern vowels. There was nothing bookish about him: he was all ideas.

She had sworn it would only be a month's exploratory visit, not really believing she'd find a life of her own, content to watch her brother's for a while. Marcus swept her up, grilled her in English, swamped her with idioms. Her resident status was permanent to him from the very beginning. Dell was away all day, overseeing his teams of yardmen and tree crews. Marcus took her to K-Mart and Ralph's and Farmer's Market. Linda saw the furious mix of peoples—broods of children, old women with vinyl shopping bags. Nobody fit in any better than Linda. The poverty and chaos of East L.A. were at least a step up from Morelia.

Besides, she couldn't be more alone than she had been there. In the afternoons Marcus would work in his study, counting the jaguars on Mayan glyphs, and Linda would sit on the terrace writing long letters home to her mother and sisters. She mentioned Marcus only obliquely—never in the same breath with Lorenzo Delgado—but the subtext was that she had a protector. She said it for their sake, not her own. It helped her to dare to think they would let her stay, since clearly she'd had no luck finding a man in the shadow of Taucitaro.

She began by helping Rosa Diaz, who came to clean on Wednesdays for Dell and Marcus. Rosa was in her fifties, iron-gray, and disdained to speak any English. She took on Linda not as a favor to Dell, but because all her own daughters and nieces had better jobs—some even had maids of their own. Linda went with her to fussy apartments up and down Wilshire, cranky retired couples seething with smudges and cobwebs.

Linda did kitchens and bathrooms while Rosa attended to subtler matters, dusting and tidying, watching the soaps as she made up the beds. Linda felt like Rosa's maid, but she wasn't proud. Within a few months she had three clients of her own, friends of Dell and Marcus. Her English was good enough now that she could tell a joke. She pronounced herself ready to seek a place of her own to live.

Marcus wouldn't hear of it. By then they were a family of three, eating suppers around the table, and Marcus always making plans for Saturday outings to Magic Mountain and the Salton Sea, as if he was determined to be Linda Espinoza's tour guide to all of California. He insisted she couldn't move out till she'd found a proper roommate. In this he was more conservative than the brothers-in-law she left at home. But secretly she was glad because she loved being with the two men, seeing how much they loved each other, always jostling and teasing. Her small room at the back of the apartment on Lucile was all she needed. She lived there quietly so as not to be a burden, not even playing the radio Marcus gave her unless both men were out.

And though it took her awhile to be invisible, she was curious and fascinated by the gatherings that took place in the cluttered living room, where Marcus read four different daily papers. Large florid men in bracelets battled back and forth with buzz-cut types in leather vests, as they worked out the wording for a letter of protest. Sometimes the smoke was suffocating, the room sour with political sweat and coffee breath, as ten or a dozen men and women accused one another of betrayal.

Linda would stand in the doorway, listening. The arcana of gay and lesbian politics were difficult to sort out. Some rode their agendas like dead horses. Linda could never understand why they bothered to meet at all if they couldn't agree more. What she loved best were the times when Marcus would speak, patiently and softly. He would always focus the talk back on people—gay teens especially, lost and bashed in high school, no one to talk to but drug dealers. No wonder every group would choose him to lead the delegations to Sacramento.

"Is my sister a dyke?" Dell had asked suddenly one night, curling to sleep beside the professor. Marcus, a strict insomniac, was propped on pillows and slogging his way through a bad dissertation.

"I don't know. Would that be so awful?"

"No," Dell retorted defensively, "but you have to admit it's a little, uh, queer, brother and sister."

"Sounds like self-loathing to me." Marcus reached down and twisted Dell's ear, and the darker man growled and ducked beneath a pillow. "Wherever she's going she'll get there by herself. You're just worried about what the parish priest would say. Don't sweat it, dear, you're already damned in hell."

Dell peered out from under the pillow. "I just don't want some fat-ass dyke puttin' the moves on my little sister."

"Tsk, tsk—sexist stereotype."

"Yeah, well, if I'm such a pig, you should marry *her.*"

Which he did in the end, though Dell had only been fooling. It wasn't a white wedding, not in June, not happy at all. Just five or six friends in the garden below the apartment on Lucile, an aching clear Sunday in February, presided by a lady judge. Linda wore a navy dress with a crocheted shawl sent by her mother. Rosa Diaz bought a bouquet of nasturtiums wrapped in tinfoil. Everyone cried.

Marcus stood up from his wheelchair and leaned on Dell's shoulder, his other arm curled through Linda's.

"I now pronounce you," said Margo the judge, "husband and wife. May you thrive in joy."

And the three of them folded in, Dell and Linda and Marcus, and cried if not with joy, then a sense of completion. It wasn't a green-card marriage. Amnesty was on the way to becoming law, so Linda would've become a citizen soon enough. This union was to assure that the cousins of Marcus—rabid bird-dog Baptists sniffing the spray of death all the way from Missouri—would not swoop down and take everything when Marcus died.

In the end she took care of both men. Three meals a day and still kept up with every client, cleaning apartments where nothing was dirty, then home to dispense the medicines. She learned to give IV so he wouldn't have to be in the hospital. By the time he was bedridden most of the day, his beautiful mind beginning to wander, she dealt with all the doctors too.

"I am his wife," she said with furious dignity, her shivering mane swept atop her head.

It wasn't that Dell wasn't wonderful. He would sit by Marcus's bed all evening, holding the professor's hand and reading the papers out loud. When the fevers were high he would wipe Marcus down with cold cloths, humming softly. Then later during the sweats he toweled Marcus dry, tweaking his nipples to make him laugh. All night like a guard on duty Dell watched him sleep, no matter how much Linda pleaded with him to rest.

Late afternoon was the best time. It was Marcus's strongest hour, with the terrace doors wide open and the wind chimes dozing, the white sun bellying down on the western hills. Dell would be home from work and showered, wrapped in a towel and lying beside the professor. The IV drip would be going into a catheter in Marcus's chest. Linda would bring in a tray of melon and iced tea—they had to keep his fluids up—and they'd sit and laugh and tell stories.

Linda had no stories, not about herself, making do with the ba-roque affairs of the neighbors in Morelia. She much preferred coaxing details out of Marcus, hearing his limpid, eloquent voice as he re-counted his trips to Yucatán, his shyness of other men. It was only the year before he met Dell that he started dating the men he marched with. Till then, he would say, he was gay only in theory. Then Linda would make them repeat again their chance and sudden meeting, so perfectly California. Bumper-to-bumper traffic, southbound on the 405—Marcus in lane 2, Dell in lane 3, flirting like truckers all the way to Laguna. How else did professors and gardeners meet?

"At last," said Marcus, swatting a thin hand at Dell's bare chest, "I found myself a Mayan king in the flesh."

"He means a Mayan dick," retorted Dell, and they all erupted laughing.

Linda was sure that if they filled the room with life there would be no chink for the dark to enter. She panicked only when they had to bundle him into the car to go get a test. Then the three of them would seem very small, without a chance in the world. Her terror was that he'd have to go into the hospital. She never forgot the teeming wards of Dr. Sandina, the blue-gowned orderlies wheeling their useless machines and wiping down the walls of dying. As long as she and Dell had him safe in the apartment on Lucile, they could make their stand, night by watchful night.

"What are the two of you going to do?" he asked one day.

She turned startled from the terrace doors, thinking he was asleep. Dell wasn't home yet. Marcus's face was liver-gray, the skin stretched tight along his cheekbones. She smiled. "As soon as you're strong, we're going to take you to visit the family. See if my sisters can figure who's married to who."

He didn't seem to be listening. That was what he had lost this month: the hawk's intensity of his eyes as he leaned forward to listen. "Don't spend money on anything churchy," he said. "Keep it simple, and scatter the ashes up in the hills." He nodded vaguely toward the window.

"Stop it," she hissed.

She hurried over to check the drip, tapping the IV bag to see how much was left. He reached a hand—so thin you could almost see through it—and stroked her bare arm. "Bunky," he said gently, "don't be like that." Bunky was a girl in a book he'd read as a kid, who rode a stallion bareback on a beach. "I can't say it to Dell. You have to let me." Her eyes didn't move from the tubing. Milliliter by milliliter, the clear liquid seeped into his heart. "There's life insurance," he continued, his voice quickening now, savoring what was still concrete. "Maybe you can buy some units. But don't go back to Mexico, all right? And don't let *him.*"

"You're not going to die. I won't let you."

"It'll be very hard for a while, but you mustn't go back. This is where your life is now." His hand slapped the mattress beside him, though he meant the city outside. If he had been stronger, he would have stamped his foot. "Linda, promise me."

For a moment she pretended she didn't hear. The wind chimes mocked them, thoughtless and bored. At last she nodded. He tugged her hand. "Now come and cry," he said. And she sank to the bed and clung to her husband's neck—but carefully, for he was so bone-thin and frail. "I know, I know," he whispered, rocking softly, his cheek against her hair.

It was good she had it out then, before Dell got home, before the tea and the stories. An hour later they laughed as loud as ever, the terror and misery all but vanished. Of course she couldn't cry later, once he had slipped beneath the waves. Three weeks delirious, neither awake nor asleep, his mouth slack in a gape of disbelief. Linda and Dell sat on either side of the hospital bed, curtains drawn against the horrors of the ward.

And when Dell staggered away to use the bathroom, Linda leaned close to Marcus and spoke with tender force. "Marcus, you can let go," she said, "it's all right. We'll stay, and we'll buy a nice building. I'll take care of him." No sign that he heard. His useless breath whistled like wind down a canyon.

At the memorial service she and Dell stood side by side on the steps of the auditorium. The students and faculty shook Linda's hand and said they were sorry, then murmured and nodded to Dell as they turned away. The gay people went to Dell, clasped him tight and keened for all their losses. Linda remembered several from the meetings in the living room on Lucile.

She picked up the box of ashes herself from the mortuary, riding with them beside her in a shopping bag on the number-four bus. For weeks she kept the box on her windowsill, beneath a hummingbird feeder that hung from the eaves—a Christmas present from

Marcus her first year in L.A. She held her breath whenever a bird would hover close, dipping its slender beak in the feeder's honey cup. She wanted to believe it was Marcus, his spirit alive in the blur of wings, but wanting didn't make it so.

When two months had passed and the rainy season started, she told her brother the time had come for the scattering. He had moved about twenty feet since Marcus died, from wailing and beating the pillows to staring sullen at the TV set. Dell shrugged listlessly but didn't protest. He left all the forms to Linda.

They drove late at night in the pickup, weaving along Mulholland Drive, past dozens of cars nosed off the road and pointed at the view, rapt couples swimming in one another's arms. They pulled off onto the shoulder near Outpost, no houses in sight, and walked uphill through the wet sage in the moonlight. Linda cradled the box in her arms. Dell had never once held it. He wanted to bring a shovel from the truck, but Linda was very firm about Marcus's wishes. *Scatter,* he'd said.

By way of compromise, she counted fifty paces up the hill and stood on a cracked rock beneath a towering century cactus. Its great spear of a stem shot ten feet into the night, exploding at the top in a clot of white blossoms. "This will be our place," she declared, staking claim to a mourning ground.

Dell stood slightly away from her as she lifted the top from the box. She had no fear of remains. In the moonlight she saw the box was full of white knobs and broken shells—more gravel than ashes. She flung out an arm as if freeing a bird, and the gravel flashed in the sage like buckshot. She could feel Dell flinch beside her. She looked at the sky to keep the tears in. Over the brow of the ridge the Big Dipper was rising, but that wouldn't help her mark the place, for she had no idea which stars were fixed.

"You want to say something?" Linda asked quietly, widow to widow.

"Fuck it all," he declared, bitter and finished, and trudged off down the hill.

Prime Time at The Body Works was five to seven-thirty. The actor/ models had the place to themselves in the afternoons, but then they would have to hustle home for their white shirts and black bow ties. Copies of *Drama-Logue* and *Daily Variety* littered the floor by the treadmills. By five the working class would start arriving—tie clerks from Bullocks, paralegals, men who provided assistance. The men's aerobics hour from five to six was as rigid as a Ballanchine class, and to miss it was to miss the point entirely. Norm, who led the class, had single-handedly raised the tone from early-bird disco to Olympic trials.

Six to seven was weights. By now the professional class had started to filter in, the lawyers and dentists and realtors. Nightly the choice would have to be made: chest, shoulders, abs, or legs. In the age of triage a man couldn't work on everything; focus was all. Here was where the social cutting edge was honed, in the little groups that formed around the bench press and the lats machine.

These were the guys who had always been chosen last in the schoolyard, banished to the outermost outfield, and now they made up for lost time with murderous concentration, forming a sort of Little League of lost preadolescence. In the mindless banter and short-hand of the weight room, they recovered the willful merriment of boys. And given the fact that they pushed so hard, showing off their bodies muscle group by muscle group, it wasn't surprising that they traded numbers and paired off for weekend nights. The Body Works was a dating pool where one could be certain at the minimum of a proper ratio of fat to body weight.

If five to six was the dance of life, and six to seven boys' phys ed, seven to seven-thirty was the waters. Ripe and glistening, they would strip off their second skin, the bicycle shorts and tank tops, T-shirts from the *Nebraska* tour. White towels round their waists, they lumbered into the steam room or the sauna opposite. In the milky smoke they were languid and muzzy, a Rousseau dream of the tropics. They stared at each other dry-eyed in the crackling air of the sauna, their superheated skin prickling, as if they longed to dive in the snow. In the Jacuzzi they sat in churning water chest-high, a circle of missionaries being boiled by cannibals.

But in all of the waters, especially the showers, what they were doing mostly was appraising one another. Mirroring themselves, catching a glimpse of who they used to be or where they were going. They did not exactly represent the seven ages of man, for the first two and the last were banished utterly from The Body Works. But the arc from twenty to fifty was played out in top form, worked on and sculpted and purged of excess flesh. Were all of them gay? The question was moot. Straight ones did slip in every now and again, actors and other archetypes of fitness, but they kept their affections private. Mostly their sexual preference was themselves.

Sonny Cevathas was one of the gods of Prime Time. His own waitering schedule was clustered on the weekend, so that all he needed to pick up during the week was a couple of lunches. Not that he ever missed a day at the gym, sometimes going twice if he felt like a swim in the morning. It was only a block from Dirk Ainley's apartment, where Sonny occupied the cubbyhole second bedroom, hardly room for a mattress and an orange crate full of New Age texts. Even though Dirk was away more days than he was home, shuttling back and forth to Hawaii on American, Sonny never felt the place was really his. It was temporary quarters. The Body Works was Sonny's living room, his office, and his yard.

He was principal dancer of the 6 P.M. aerobics class. Norm the instructor, who had a terrible crush on him, would let Sonny choose the music from a box of tapes. There were a dozen regular Adonises in the class, but Sonny had the edge of being mascot. His regular place was first row far right, where he flung himself into a thousand hieroglyphs. It was Norm on the foot-high stage in front who issued the orders and counted off, a drill sergeant with a slight twinge of the ballerina, but it was Sonny the class watched.

More than an athlete or dancer, he capered like a figure on a Greek vase, erotic and in-the-body and far beyond it too. He sweated like a bandit, shaking it like rain from his hair. He wouldn't have dreamed of cruising here, or connecting up with anyone. This was the warm-up, all for him.

Upstairs in the weight room was where he made his connections. He had no regular workout partners, always keeping his options open as he moved from station to station. For a while he'd spot a buddy on the bench, somebody from his own league of aching youth.

The two of them would trade off and pump, watched by their elders longingly, as if the tableau might at any moment burst into a Matt Sterling saga.

Then Sonny would wander off and do curls in the mirror or sit-ups on a slant board, hundreds of them, till one or another of the older men would be transfixed. Sonny always knew who was watching him, and which of several different ones was ready to make a move on him. Usually thirty-five to forty, better than a hundred grand a year, and looking for something permanent. It didn't make Sonny a gold digger that he let them watch or even ask for an evening.

He'd go out with almost anybody once, if the guy was spellbound enough. Sonny's youth and beauty were a magic circle. He didn't think of himself as jaded or a cynic. He simply chose his own reality, as a warrior chooses his fights. He was the existential object.

He could see Sean Pfeiffer approaching for twenty minutes before he said a word. Eyeing Sonny through the baffle of mirrors that sheathed the place, never looking directly, staying busy with his own workout, but moving inexorably. Sonny was working out with the wooden pole behind his shoulders, swinging back and forth at the hips with abandon, where there already wasn't an ounce of fat.

"You gonna do chest?" Sean asked, sidling up and addressing him in the mirror, staying clear of the pendulum swing of the pole.

"Shoulders," Sonny replied.

It didn't bode to be a very scintillating encounter, but these things always began with body mechanics. Sean was forty-five or there-abouts, running to fat at the waist, his hair spiked like a razorback, trying to look younger than he was. His eyes were blank as binoculars from staring across the gym at men like Sonny. To fill up space he fretted about whether to trade in his XJ-S for a convertible, then about his imminent trip to Australia, where he'd be unable to work out for two weeks. Fearing to lose his hard-won pecs, he sighed: "I wish I could take a trainer with me."

At last Sonny stopped bouncing and put the pole aside. *Shoulders* was still the only word he'd spoken. Now he turned to Sean and grinned. "Great. When do we leave?"

Sean laughed at the sudden flirtation. He was some kind of banker, or perhaps it was even more raw than that and he was in money, pure and simple. He had a house at the top of Trousdale Estates and was on the road constantly, very nice situation for a boyfriend. Sure, said Sonny, they could have dinner tomorrow. An invitation that had been building for weeks, as Sonny let Sean come closer and closer. Did he find Sean hot? Put it this way: it was hot that Sean found *him* hot. As Sonny trundled downstairs to the locker room, he realized with a certain irony that Sean was only six years younger than his own father. There was something hot in that as well.

But then, hot was very imprecise, or at least in constant flux. And never to be trusted, since it evaporated as quick as it flared, usually by the end of the second weekend. Sonny shucked his tank top, shorts, and jock, letting them lie in a heap on the floor as he grabbed his towel from his locker. Twice in the last year his jock had been stolen while he was in the shower. It neither bothered him nor turned him on that there were guys out there with fetishes of him. The queer thing was—as he stepped under the shower, arching his nakedness into the driving spray—he wasn't all that wed to this body that stopped traffic.

It was the metaphysical side of him that was truly in competition form. Those myriad men who only knew him by the candlepower of his body were on the wrong track. Not that his body wasn't a temple—just now with the water coursing down its sinews like a cloudburst—but he didn't want heathens supplicating there. In the early years it used to be enough for a man to be a Pisces. Like Ellsworth, all they needed to do was hear Sonny out when he spun his tale. Now he wanted an old soul, a fellow prince. Wanted them to understand that this Sonny with the warrior's form and the gold hair was just one of a hundred incarnations.

Toweling dry in the white-tiled vestibule, he stroked his vivid limbs in full view of a dozen others who could see they were lesser gods than he. Yet Sonny always gave them the chance, men like Sean Pfeiffer, even as far as going to bed once. After all, it often required the full body to put them in touch with the not-body. This, he had come to see, was where Ellsworth had failed him, by keeping Sonny's body at the objectified level of pure desire. If only Ellsworth could have broken through metaphysically, he never would have gotten sick at all. In his own way Sonny had truly loved Ellsworth and tried not to judge him. He understood that different men had different karmas to enact. But the last of the grief he felt was indistinguishable from a sort of moral posture, that a man made a journey of his own devising.

No shadow of the sickness was on him as he padded back to his locker. It wasn't just him: the sickness did not penetrate the walls of The Body Works. If people got sick, they had the decency to stay home. There had to be a sanctuary somewhere where AIDS did not intrude, where people really meant it when they said they were feeling great.

Sonny slipped back into his jeans and a sweatshirt, reeling with well-being, drunk on endorphins. He knew he had made the right choice not to be tested for the virus. The real test was the vast aliveness he felt at the end of Prime Time, gathering up his workout clothes and stuffing them in his gym bag, feeling a throb in his groin from the smell of his own sweat. He sauntered through the locker room and out, waving and nodding to several men as he went, including Sean, who blinked at him, dazed at his own good fortune.

Sean Pfeiffer, thought Sonny, would definitely bear some further investigation. At least he had the proper urgency. Perhaps he could be led beyond the body. Sonny walked out into the lambent evening, the traffic streaming by on Santa Monica Boulevard like a river of light. He stood at the curb, perfect and untouchable, waiting for the WALK sign. His own heart was in no danger, that was the most important thing. After all, it could take forever to find an old soul. In the meantime, Sean Pfeiffer might be just the thing he needed for the next plateau.

Finally they had lunch.

Mark had been out of work ten days before he answered the phone, content to stare at the answering machine as Lou Ciotta and all his minions called in on the hour, slimy with apologies. Mark walked around the house on Skyway Lane in his boxer shorts, unshaven. It astonished him to realize that his maid, pool man, and gardener had had the house to themselves for years, while Mark was only in residence from eleven at night to seven in the morning. He felt vaguely guilty being in their way, but knew they would all vanish as soon as he got sick. Meanwhile, one day at a time, he could feel himself recovering from the telephone.

It was an accident that he took Steven's call. He was having a cliché nightmare, the lid of a coffin being lowered over his face. He bolted awake from his third nap of the day and grabbed the phone unthinkingly, like oxygen. When he heard Steven's voice, he thought at first it was about airline tickets. He was about to say his travel days were over when Steven suggested lunch—a Sunday drive up Topanga Canyon. Mark was too groggy to think of a reason not to.

Steven had no idea that Mark had severed relations with Bungalow 19, nor that heaps of lawyers and network men were frantic to woo him back. Driving out Sunset to the beach, they made an odd pair of retirees. Despite the Hawaiian shirt that covered his ample belly, Steven didn't look ready for golf or senior discounts. Mark, even with ten days' beard and nothing pending, tore at the wheel of his big boy's Jeep, negotiating traffic like a killer deal. They weren't out of work so much as off it. Vigorous still and in their prime, they looked fit enough to work construction.

By the time they wound their way up Topanga, the blasted gorse of the beaten hills parched to the brink of conflagration, they were having a gentlemen's disagreement as to how long they had left. "Two years max," insisted Mark, parsing it like a contract. "But that's if I stay above water. Soon as I get sick, I'm checking out."

"You don't know that," Steven replied with a certain superiority, as if he'd heard the suicide brag before. "You'll probably want to fight for a while, and besides, the drugs might keep us going. Five years, maybe ten."

"Ten," scoffed Mark with a growl of impatience, and Steven wasn't sure if ten years seemed to Mark impossibly optimistic or beneath contempt.

They stopped at a sprouts-and-granola inn at the top of the canyon, sitting on a porch above a dry creek bed, their Zen salads dive-bombed by wasps. They compromised on three good years of marginal stability, suicide not included. Cautiously they traded T-cell numbers—happily in the same neighborhood, or somebody might've been walking home. Mark was leery of the blue-and-white capsules, admitting as much when Steven beeped at one-fifteen and gobbled them with his iced tea. Mark was willing to risk a further dip in his numbers and wait for more data.

Steven didn't press him, not having much faith in the medicine himself. It was only that he'd spent so many months fighting to get Victor onto the drug, then pleading with Victor to take it. He kept waiting for the conversation to change. He was sick of talking immunology. Mark drove his knife and fork as furiously as he drove the Jeep, attacking his hippie salad with a vengeance. He barked at the shoulder-blond waiter, demanding rolls and dressing on the side, clearly annoyed by the waiter's easy straightness, by the fact that he didn't flirt with either of the ticking men from the city. When Mark had at last exhausted all the numbers and the odds, he started to ask about Victor. Nice uncomplicated questions about Montana and their travels.

It wasn't behaving like a date at all. Not that Steven would have known what to do with it if it had, but he felt quite mournful turning down dessert. If he was going to be alone, he might as well have the brown rice cheesecake. Yet Mark was trim and meant to stay that way, even if he was dying, so Steven stuck to coffee laced with three packets of Equal.

There was a sudden cry from the next table, where a burly man was cuddling with his girlfriend. A wasp bit him on the cheek, this after the waiter's assurance that they were harmless. The ensuing ruckus was oddly cheering to the two men from the leper kingdom. Suddenly the rim of the canyon was charged with violence. The white-gold grass beyond the dry wash bristled in the October heat, alive with snakes and spiders. As the man was led away wailing off the porch, threatening to sue, Mark flashed a dirty smile at Steven.

"Besides," insisted Mark, always doubling back, "my insurance is fucked. I'm only covered for eighteen months unless I get a new job. Then what? I gotta go into County?" County was downtown, a public hospital swamped by the indigent, a scream made into a building. Mark shook his head stubbornly. "Sorry, I'm not sticking around for that. And *what* new job? Who's gonna hire me? 'Please describe your general health.' Dead."

Steven looked into the restaurant, where a gaggle of laughing girls was trailing around the buffet table, loading up their plates. All of them untouched. Now this Sunday date was in danger of turning into a suicide pact. "Well," Steven replied carefully, "sometimes people stick around for other reasons. So they can stay with people they love."

His gaze remained on the breezy girls. He could feel the stillness across the table, but also sensed a certain coolness—not aloof, just very self-contained. Obviously Mark didn't have anyone to stay for. The girls spilled out onto the porch, bearing their bountiful plates. They took a free table and sat in a magic circle. None of the wasps would bother them. Mark stretched and waved for the check.

Did he want Mark's body? He couldn't have said. He studied the play of muscles in the other man's forearms as Mark signed the credit-card slip. He wasn't anything like Victor, whose motions were antic and fluid, his heart pouring out of him like laughter. Mark didn't laugh. As an actor he had been conventionally handsome, Ivy League WASP when it came to casting, despite being a lapsed Jew, and with every gesture predetermined. Not like Victor at all, careening with spontaneity, shrieking hello.

Steven walked out of the inn behind Mark and studied his walk—shoulders high, a cowboy's sway in the hips, very butch. But did Steven want all that? Did he want to see it naked? He had not, even unconsciously, checked out Mark's frontal equipment, not even glanced at the rise in his jeans. This was probably not a good sign. They hoisted themselves into the black Jeep on either side, and Mark headed down the hairpin canyon. The bright western arc of the sun caught them full in the face. The smell of sage in the empty hills was distinct, but it needed the first winter rain before it sharpened and broke your heart. No rain since April. Last year it rained in September, the day of Victor's funeral. Everything was late this year.

As to equipment, Steven had scarcely glanced at his own in months. Even at his randiest, in the dim days of his youth, it seemed a waste of spirit to jerk it off. Now he had left it alone so long it had seemingly forgotten all its tricks. Yet something quickened in Steven, sitting beside Mark Inman, especially now that they were quiet. The ocean appeared below in the final V of the canyon. Something he understood about Mark the moment he'd walked into Steven's house three Saturdays ago. Here was a man as isolated, as *dis*located as he. That was the turn-on.

"How's Ted?"

Mark's face wrinkled in a frown, as if he could hardly remember. "That's all over," he said tartly, shrugging it off. "He's a jerk." Traffic was smooth on the coast highway, just a beat too early for the beach folk to be heading home. Steven made a small murmur which could have been agreement or dissent. Mark started over. "No he's not, he's a kid. It doesn't have anything to do with him. It never does. Two, three months . . . that's like forever to me." He pouted his lips as if the taste was sour, then clucked his tongue. "I'm such a shallow queen."

"Is he negative?"

"I don't know. We played it safe, so nobody had to ask. Is anybody negative?"

"Yeah. Certain genetic freaks."

They laughed. As they sailed through Pacific Palisades—Republican ladies staggering down the sidewalks under the weight of boutique loot—they kept playing catch-up with a pickup truck full of retro surfers in the next lane. The skinhead driver was lobster-red, and his buddies in the back slouched on each other like puppies in a cardboard box. Mark fixed on the one in the orange shorts and rattled off something obscene that Steven didn't quite catch.

He had never been very good at on-site cruising, and especially at the cold appraisal of flesh in the passing parade. Victor had let no beauty go by unnoticed, scaling them one to ten, while Steven couldn't bear the thought of being noticed noticing. For politeness's sake he leered along with Mark, but couldn't imagine bedding down any of the boys in the pickup, and not just because of the numbness of his dick. They were all too straight. There was something faintly appalling about straight men these days, as if they had all been deferred from the draft, 4-F, ridiculously healthy.

The dozing surfer reminded Mark of an earlier dude—ten years ago, or was it fifteen? Nothing much to remember really, beyond the stupid good looks, except Mark had been just as young himself, so the memory was of two hot men. "I used to meet him every Monday at Unemployment," Mark recalled, more wistfully than Steven had ever heard him. "We'd get our checks and go back to his place and fuck."

The pickup turned north on Veteran, bearing its gods away, but Mark kept talking, filling in his ancient Mondays blow by blow. Steven was at a loss. He couldn't quite see how the past and the present meshed for Mark, who shuffled through his men like a deck of cards. For his part, Steven had no one to talk about but Victor. Somehow he couldn't go back beyond those eight years. The carnal game, the chase and capture—all of that took place in another life, as unreal now as porno. So he looked away and laughed thinly, while Mark laid the slovenly Mondays to rest.

By the time they drove uphill to Steven's house, it was less like a date than ever, or perhaps just like a blind one. Unconsciously Steven's hands balled into fists, for he couldn't think of another thing to say. He was nearly forty-one years old, and his tongue was tied like a high-school kid's. Would a hug be too much to say good-bye? Would a kiss be too effeminate? It suddenly seemed the height of folly, that two men who'd been in the game so long could ever connect at all. Somebody had to be young and undefended, or else forget it.

"He's probably dead by now," said Mark, drawing up in front of Steven's house. Steven had ceased to hear as they came around the hill, but assumed he was still talking about the guy from Unemployment. "We'll have to do it again," said Mark, clapping a hand on Steven's shoulder, man to man. Steven looked into his grinning eyes and was seized again by the curious rage he'd felt the night of the party. What right did this man have to be courting death, who hadn't lost anyone real? Steven remembered clearly now how it used to feel to dislike him—cocksure and riddled with power.

"Yeah, well, I'm free for the rest of my life," Steven replied wryly, and reached across and mussed Mark's hair. The gesture was casual, kiddish, more than anything meant to cover Steven's annoyance, the uselessness of two grown men.

But Mark, who took everything opposite, seemed startled and cornered by Steven's touch, as if he finally understood the ambiguous blurred attractions of the afternoon. Steven scrambled out of the Jeep. They shrugged good-bye with careful smiles. He watched Mark disappear down the hill, then went in the house and slumped in a chair, blank for an hour over Victor. Nothing new in that, except there was starting to be a place inside him that was worse than tears.

If they weren't going to be an item, perhaps they would try to be buddies. That was how Steven read the next call, ten days later, time enough to draw the line in the dirt between them. The message on Steven's machine asked if he wanted to go to a meeting at the gay center. A drop-in group for seropositives, what they called in the crisis trade a "rap/support." No reference whatsoever to their Sunday lunch.

Steven was surprised that Mark would even consider such a gathering, given its potential for whining and general bullshit. Dysfunctional himself when it came to groups of strangers, since Victor's death he had avoided all movies and malls and public events. The only groups Steven ever saw anymore were at funerals. But yes, he told Mark's machine, he'd be there Thursday night, and agreed it would be easier if they went in separate cars.

Gay and Lesbian Central was a former hooker motel on Highland, deep in the tatters of Hollywood, a warren of makeshift offices around a central court. Runaways sat on folded chairs waiting for someone to make it all better, dreading another night on the street. Meanwhile, underpaid staffers churned about with sign-up sheets, putting groups together: gay fathers, the semi-recovered, bulimics and overeaters twinned like Laurel and Hardy.

In Polo shirt and jeans, Steven walked over to the main counter, where a dyke in a hooded sweatshirt sat before the switchboard, fielding the night's calls. When she answered she was very brisk, her voice as clipped as her mackerel hair, making it clear that she didn't consider herself a hotline. Haltingly Steven started to ask where the seropositives were. She pointed upstairs before he even finished the "sero" word, making him wonder how sick he looked.

The battered meeting room was about the size of a second bedroom, with two tiers of carpeted benches built around the walls, and perhaps a dozen people sitting, mostly men and mostly younger. Mark sat across from the door and smiled as Steven came in. The meeting had already started, so Steven took a quick seat beside a boy with a platinum buzz-cut and a cluster of earrings along one lobe.

A middle-aged man—too thin, too gray—was railing at the group about his doctor. "Just the art in his office looks like a fuckin' museum! Why should he get rich off us? By the time I croak, he's gonna have a house in Malibu."

"So what?" asked a pumped-up man on the tier below. "It's not his fault you're sick. Stop displacing."

"I'm not *sick*," the thin man shrieked.

"It's no one's *fault*," clamored a voice beside him, a willowy girl in Esprit pastels.

She, it turned out, had been infected by a hemophiliac boyfriend, the only man she'd ever slept with. Dead now, proclaiming till the very end that he was "innocent." The girl, Marina, had nowhere else to go for support besides Gay Central. The same was true for the black woman next to Mark—Charlene, who got it from a man who shot speedballs.

In fact they were all bizarrely different from each other, random as a planeload of refugees. And as far as Steven could tell, nobody listened to anyone else. They were all too angry, too upset, and everything got lost in cross talk. Before ten minutes was up Steven was feeling extremely claustrophobic.

The hemophiliac's girl was especially hard on a tall sandy-haired kid who sat under the wheezing air conditioner. He declared he had no intention of getting sick, and all the people who did were full of bad attitude. He was maybe twenty-five. "There's too much negative shit in here," he concluded with a grimace. "Can't we lighten up?"

"Listen, Andy," Marina hissed at him, "my Jim had great attitude, and he died like a vegetable anyway. So don't tell me to look on the bright side. We're all going to die here."

"Easy, easy," said the buzz-cut boy by Steven, who turned out to be the facilitator. "Let's keep it to feelings, shall we? Let's not judge. Try to say 'I,' not 'we.'"

Marina apologized to Andy. Steven looked at his watch. He knew already he would never open his mouth in this group. He couldn't begin a single sentence with "I," and besides, he liked being judgmental. He'd already judged the whole room, in fact, with its rancid smell of old Reeboks, and found them all wanting. He was damned if he would be their token widow.

At least he wasn't the oldest. Following up the facilitator, a bearded type in a tweed jacket said he felt like the group's gay uncle. "I'm fifty-seven years old," he announced proudly, "and when I came out there were no parades. It doesn't surprise *me* that they're letting us die." *They* were the Feds, whose informed neglect was a leitmotif of the group's rage. "But I'm not gonna go quiet. They'll have to drag me outa here kicking and screaming. I've seen those camps where they locked up the Japanese." He folded his arms, proud and stubborn. For a moment the room was charged with defiance.

Who did these people love? thought Steven as an envelope was passed to him for the night's donation. Who loved them back? He slipped two dollars in, guilty as a parishioner. The uncle was taking care of his mother, eighty-three and bonkers, and only hoped he wouldn't die or be shipped to the camps before she went. Nobody in the group told him the idea of camps was paranoid. An initiative on the November ballot required all those infected with the virus to be on a master list in Sacramento. The state health commissioner— Dr. Mengele to his gay friends—would be given broad power to quarantine at will. "Yes on Proposition 81" was running sixty/forty in the polls.

"Don't matter where I die," said a red-faced man with a Southern accent, "long as I don't die alone."

Vic, thought Steven, his mind reaching out still, trying to pull Victor back from the edge for a year, then trying to help him go over. Steven had missed the actual moment by ten minutes, gulping Sanka in the hospital cafeteria. Died alone.

Then suddenly Mark was speaking, slow and uncertain, and Steven looked over. Mark held out the palms of his hands, as if backing the world off. "I used to be an actor," he said. "Closest I ever let anyone come was Row G." He laughed, but nobody else got the joke. "That's where the critics sit," he added lamely, unsure where he was going now. "I even had a series for a while. I was twenty-eight, but I played nineteen. I let the camera get *real* close." The irony in his voice was fierce, but the rest of them continued to look perplexed, as if Mark had come to the wrong room.

"Excuse me," asked Marina, "but what's that got to do with AIDS?"

"Nothing, really," Mark admitted with a shrug. "Except now I want to be close to people, and it's too late. I'm on my way out, and I *still* put up all these walls."

"It's never too late to fall in love," observed the Southern man. "I do it at least once a month, whether I need it or not."

They all laughed. The ball bounced back to the uncle and his mother—something Charlene could relate to, since her mother and grandmother both lived with her. A straw poll was taken around the room, and it turned out no one had told his family but the thin gray man, whose American Gothic mom and dad had advised him to go to church and disinvited him for Christmas, saying they were keeping it small this year.

Steven wasn't interested in anybody's family, especially his own, strewn across southern Ohio in sullen bungalows off interstates, never quite living in one town or another. He checked in with the parents once a month, usually Sunday mornings when his father was out hunting. His mother would give him an automatic chronicle of his sisters and cousins and all their brood, the union layoffs and small arrests. Never a word about Victor since he died, or the grief or Steven's precarious health. Steven's life didn't exist at all, which was fine with him. Or Victor's father would call sometimes from Montana, drunk and late at night. He'd cry and tell Steven how sorry he was, and when he was done he would say, "Good night, son," making Steven blush.

He wanted to veer the discussion back to relationships again, but he couldn't be the one to do it. Back and forth the group played with the family issue, Steven tuning out. Telling meant nothing to him. Ever since Victor left the phone company, since the day the first lesion bloomed on his face, everyone waited for Steven to be next.

Finally Andy piped in: "I'd like to go back to what Mark said." Steven perked up and smiled crookedly. "I'm twenty-six, and I feel like I'm never going to be with a man again. I don't know which is deader, me or my dick."

Murmurs of assent around the room. The Southern man—Emmett—drawled the tale of a boyfriend who walked out on him the day Emmett found out he was positive.

"Sounds like you're lucky to be rid of him," said Mark. "He sounds like an asshole."

"Yeah, I guess," sighed Emmett. "But I miss the body heat."

Marina objected again. She didn't come to the group to listen to the problems of gay dating. She'd apparently been a regular at the Thursday rap for months, and had evolved to a sort of den-mother status, in her own mind anyway. She was more than a little appalled by the constant refrain of the men, who still acted as if their major goal was finding a boyfriend. Survival was their main job, she told them, and for once the facilitator didn't stop her from saying "we."

So the boys backed off from their lonely hearts, as conversation shifted now to medication and research. Everyone seemed to be taking something different and was armed with newsletters and offprints, fierce as an eighth-grade science project. Not that the line wasn't utterly blurred between science and metaphysics, as several people shared their regimens of macro suet and imaging. Andy was especially eloquent here, with his peaks of self-hypnosis.

Steven didn't hear a word of it. He'd become aware that Emmett was cruising Mark from the moment of his freefall declaration of love. The Southern boy was chunky, with sloe-gin eyes and a constant antic smile, overripe and slightly bruised, like a fallen peach. He raised his eyes to the ceiling when Marina dampened the boyfriend talk, a look meant solely for Mark. And all through the rest of the meeting Emmett stretched his legs out, hitched at his crotch, plumped his hair, a veritable symphony of self-consciousness. Steven couldn't see how Mark was responding to the dumb show of courting, but figured Emmett wouldn't keep it going if he weren't getting teased back.

High school again. Steven was suddenly back in the bleachers beside his buddy Daryl, who squirmed and strutted in his seat as he locked eyes with Lisa Connor, the flame of his roaring pubescence. In the gloomy algebra of life, Daryl had been to Steven what Lisa was to Daryl, but all unrequited. Steven had sat stone still in the bleachers, swallowing his hard-on, his knee in a faint as it brushed Daryl's thigh.

The last thing he needed right now was a repeat of Daryl Sawyer. Yet he found himself staring across at Emmett with the same lip-curling contempt he used to feel for Lisa Connor. Hussy. Cow.

The meeting broke at eight-thirty, with Tim the facilitator coaxing them to return again. The group fell into twos and threes as they gathered their things. Steven watched Emmett stand up and stretch his back, rolling his hips forward in a lurid thrust. Steven, who couldn't somehow avoid the view from crotch level, noted the curve of the boy's Southern dick, heavy in the cradle of his sweatpants.

Emmett's eyes danced as he leaned past Steven toward the upper bench where Mark was sitting.

"You want to grab a bite?" asked Emmett.

Steven felt his stomach tilt, thinking of Mark's face buried in Emmett's groin, the queasy porno of jealousy. But it was the uncle who answered yes to Emmett's invitation. Steven turned bewildered to find he'd got it all wrong. Mark was crouched on the upper bench, scribbling his number on a scrap of paper, then handing it to Tim the facilitator. The look that passed between them was careful and correct, but there wasn't any question where they were going.

Steven felt doltish and slow, watching the uncle and Emmett saunter out together, wishing now he'd been nice to someone so he wouldn't have to leave alone. But he must leave now, that was clear. It would be more humiliating to wait for Mark, who stayed crouched while Tim borrowed his pen to write a number of his own. Steven prayed his face wasn't burning as he trampled past Andy and out of the room. It didn't even cross his mind then that anyone looked at him, that Andy might have been lingering there in the doorway hoping for an older man.

The dyke, still on the phone, was powdering her coffee with Coffeemate. She winked at Steven as he passed. The street kids on the folding chairs looked up like a litter of spaniels at the pound, and Steven shrank with guilt, wishing he could rain down dollars on them. He stepped outside, gasping with an overwhelming sadness, which for once had nothing to do with Victor. That was the saddest thing of all.

"We didn't hear much from you," said a sudden voice beside him. Statement of fact; no accusation.

He turned. It was Marina. "I don't think I'm the group type," he said, trying to be as direct as she.

"You sent me to Holland," she replied without any transition. He stared at her, confused. "I was on my way to Israel, and you convinced me to lay over in Amsterdam." Steven nodded vaguely, amazed that he'd ever been so forceful, even in the throes of Shaw Travel. "All those Rembrandts and Van Goghs," she declared with a wondering smile. "I always meant to call and thank you."

Steven made a scoffing sound, modest as Mother Teresa. Not that he could recall the encounter. He'd probably suggested the layover flight because he got a better cut from KLM.

"Now that I'm afraid to travel," she said, "those little side trips seem more special. I'm sorry about your friend."

Steven made another sound of dismissal, but this one sputtered. She laid her hand on his arm, and he froze as if someone were trying to put in an IV. She knew too much about him. He didn't want to be solicited anymore. But she seemed content to have him say nothing in reply, and he looked beyond her shoulder and waited for the touch to be over. Then the door opened behind them, and Mark and Tim walked out, close in conversation, too absorbed to notice Steven and Marina. The two men turned and headed down Highland shoulder to shoulder, and Steven felt like Barbara Stanwyck peering in the final window.

"I'm too hard on the boys," said Marina, withdrawing her hand at last, leaving a numbness on his arm. "I guess it's because I'm not ready myself. To love, I mean." Mark and his new boyfriend had reached the black Jeep, parked at the curb about halfway down the block. "Are you?"

They were figuring out whether to take one car or two. Whose place to go. Steven forced himself to look back at Marina's face, framed in a tumble of curls. "Am I what?"

"You know . . . open."

"I guess," he replied, deflated. Not till now did he think of her as a fellow widow. She'd only been engaged to the bleeder; only known him two years before he got sick. But Steven wasn't in the mood to act superior. "It's all a mess," he admitted. "I can't make it work anymore."

Marina nodded gravely. "I'm never going to have a child," she said. "That's the hardest part."

There was no self-pity, only a kind of amazement. She looked so spunky in her white silk blouse with the floppy bow, not wilted at all by her two hours in the locker room with the guys. Steven reached out and touched her arm in the hollow of the elbow, just where she had touched him. Out of the corner of his eye Steven saw Tim trot across the street to his car, jump in, and peel off in a U-turn to follow Mark.

"Main job," said Steven gently. "Survival, right?"

"Yeah, right," she sighed. "See you next Thursday, huh?"

And she strolled away before he could tell her no, he wasn't coming back. He couldn't stand the responsibility. Why else had he sat in his house for a year, avoiding the phone, avoiding daylight? They all took off into the night—Marina, Emmett and the uncle, Mark and Tim—and Steven was left on the sidewalk, stupid as a panhandler.

He knew the difference between jealousy and love. He spent the next few days de-escalating. Maybe they could be buddies, maybe even friends, but not yet. He didn't blame Mark for any of it. Steven had whipped these emotions up all on his own. There was a message on his machine the following day: "How did you sneak out of there last night? There was something I wanted to tell you." Well, it would wait.

He didn't have anything else to do, but that was nothing new. Margaret brought him supper one night, veal chops and twice-baked potatoes. She asked him only once about Mark, whom he dismissed with airy vagueness, as if they hadn't laid eyes on each other since the party three weeks ago. There was tension between Margaret and her boyfriend Richard, because he'd been pestering her to go away for a three-day weekend, and she was too busy running Shaw Travel. "He mopes when he thinks you get all the attention," Margaret declared. "He says I spoil you. But I spoil *everybody.*"

Steven was really quite recovered by Monday night. Saturday and Sunday he went to Forest Lawn to visit Victor but managed not to cry. The anniversary echoes seemed to have subsided. Mark was just a symptom of the residue of pain. At least, thought Steven, he'd held himself from blurting it out. No hopeless declarations to take back.

It was nine o'clock and he was standing on the back terrace, peering along the side of the hill. In the dark he couldn't see if the dog was in his burrow beneath the lantana. "Hey," Steven called gruffly, tossing one of the veal bones. As it thumped to the ground, he could hear the animal scramble for it, crashing out of the thicket. The barest shadow of him was visible beyond the light that poured from the house. "Now get out of here!" Steven barked as the phone began to ring. The dog growled horribly, hunkered over his bone. Steven padded back to the kitchen, slamming the door on sentiment.

It was Mark. "How come you didn't call me back?"

"Oh, hi." Steven opened the freezer door, determined to be casual. "I was out of town. In Santa Barbara. Sailing."

"Look, Steven, can you come over?"

"Why?" He reached for the Häagen-Dazs. He could hear the upheaval in the other man's voice. He couldn't stand how much it excited him.

"I'm freaked out. There's a spot on my leg. I think I've got a fever."

"You don't get a fever with KS."

"Will you please come look at it?" Vulnerable, but not whining.

"Sure. Ten minutes."

He hung up and went directly to the garage, not realizing he still had the carton of butter pecan in his hand till he got in the car. He hadn't asked for the address, because he knew it from the computer. Hadn't asked directions, because he'd driven there so often in his head. He took the back way, winding through the hills to Laurel Canyon.

They had no contract for this part, the call in the middle of the night. As he tore up the pass to Mulholland, Steven could have been seething about being taken advantage of. After all, he never would've called Mark with a spot, he would've called Margaret. Well, he would call Mark now. It went without saying that the spot would be nothing. Steven would not countenance another case of KS.

From Mulholland he saw flashes of the plain of lights below, but when he took the turn onto Skyway, the full candlepower of the Valley swept the night to the far horizon. He pulled into the brick driveway at 2200. The house was more woodsy than he would've expected, shaded by Chinese elms. As he came to the front door, he wondered how he looked, besides fat. He lifted a hand to the knocker, and the door swung open.

Mark stood there in baggy white boxer shorts, wincing as if he had a toothache. Nobody said hello. Steven strolled in, manfully keeping his eyes in the middle distance, looking at everything else but Mark. House very tailored, country pine. Terra-cotta floor scat-

tered with Indian rugs. Steven was on the brink of observing something banal about Santa Fe when Mark grabbed his bicep and led
him over to a pool of light. "Look at this," said Mark, propping his
foot on a table. "Tell me it's not."

As if from a very great distance, Steven leaned forward to study
the flank of Mark's inner thigh. Jewish jock indeed: leg muscles hard
as a diver's. The spot in question was about four inches below the
baggy cuff of the shorts. It was purple, all right. "But it's not raised,"
said Steven, reaching out a forefinger and rubbing it gently. "See, it
fades when I press it. It's just a bruise."

"You can't be sure," retorted Mark, his voice tight and accusatory.
Yet Steven could hear the relief behind it, the grasping at straws. A
palpable shudder rippled across Mark's bare torso as he ran his hands
through his hair. "Man, this is driving me crazy. I can't live like
this."

Mark reached out, his hands shaking—not reaching out *for* anything, but somehow it was the easiest thing in the world just then
to embrace him. Steven enfolded him in a bear hug—no nonsense,
nothing sexual, not even sentimental. Just two guys. Mark let it
happen, sagging against him, head on Steven's shoulder, first time
he ever noticed Steven was two inches taller. Steven stood there
mute as a redwood, cradling Mark's ribs in his open palms.

It couldn't have lasted five seconds. Nobody tipped his hand. "So
when did you first start working as a paramedic?" Mark asked playfully, leading the way to a wide-hipped leather sofa by the windows.
He flung himself down on the sofa—Finnish, about four grand—
with a slap like a wrestler hitting the mat. He punched the cushion
beside him to indicate Steven should sit down. Which Steven did,
curling in the opposite corner, one leg tucked under him.

"Look at all the shit he sends me," Mark declared with contempt.
"I feel like a fuckin' game show."

He waved across the room toward an improbable clutter of toys:
a stationary bicycle, a VCR, a stork-like Italian desk lamp, a video
camera, a telescope, all heaped by the window as if waiting for a
Christmas tree. This was the booty with which Lou Ciotta was trying
to woo Mark Inman back to work. A new gift arrived every third
day. For no one believed that Mark was seriously retired. It was just

a matter of soothing his ego, time for another absurd raise. They thought he was being coy and temperamental.

"How much of a raise?" asked Steven, blunt as a visiting nurse. When Victor was sick the nurses would ask the price of everything.

Mark shrugged. "Fifty, a hundred grand. Lou made sixteen mill last year. I figure I'm worth the moon and the stars to him." He was mocking himself and the system both, but there was an undertone of bad nerves, as if self-disgust alone were not enough to distance him from the folly of his former life. "Every day I don't take his calls, my price goes up. Lou's a very superstitious man. He thinks it'll all go away if he loses me."

"I don't watch television," Steven observed as politely as he could.

"I wish *he*'d get AIDS. I'd like to see that on the cover of *People.*"

"Don't wish it."

But Mark wasn't listening. He was hyper after the fear, tensed and ready to spring. His muscles twitched with crossed signals, as if he wanted to beat himself senseless. He glanced out the window and down the mountain, the Valley like a fallen galaxy. "How do you stop waiting for the other shoe to drop?"

"My therapist told me I had to live for today and cut out all the bullshit. So I fired him. I think he was a closet Scientologist."

"Do you believe anything?"

"No."

The moment of silence that followed was like the opposite of a prayer. Steven stared at Mark's heap of toys; Mark continued to gaze out the window. If it gave them any comfort to be godless together, they made no show of it. Mark turned from the window and lolled his head on the back cushion, fixing a look on the other man's face. His arm stretched out along the back of the sofa, but didn't quite reach Steven.

"So is that what you do?" asked Mark. "You live for now?"

"I guess. It's what—ten o'clock? By eleven-thirty I should be in bed with Ted Koppel and a package of Oreos." Steven smiled puckishly. "That's what I live for."

Casually, off-handedly, Mark let his hand fall from the cushion to Steven's knee. "Doesn't sound like you leave much room for the unexpected."

Steven stared at the sudden connection, trying to ascertain if the knee maneuver was a comrade thing. Then he looked up and made a last stab at irony. "Hey, I'm open," he said, California earnest. "I mean, we could have an earthquake between now and eleven. I could get pinned in the rubble." He shrugged. "Fuck Koppel."

Mark brought his other hand to rest in the crotch of his shorts—a gesture that may have been neutral but, coming right after the knee, narrowed the options considerably. Mark wasn't exactly playing with himself, but the nervous scowl of a sick man had vanished. His eyes were unnervingly still, his mouth a trifle surly. It was a dare now.

There wasn't time to wonder what was predetermined, whether it started three weeks ago or three seconds. Perhaps it depended on who was counting. One thing was certain: though Mark had made the offer, it was Steven who had to cross the distance. It felt like a kind of surrender to physics, inevitable as falling. He rolled forward across the field of butterscotch leather, closing the distance, grappling his way into Mark's embrace.

They didn't exactly fit. Their bodies groped and tangled, torso to torso and throwing heat, but there was an instant suspicion that nobody was in charge. Steven's mouth fell mutely against Mark's neck, in the vampire spot. The stubble of their beards rasped together. Once more Steven found himself cradling the armor of muscles that played across Mark's back—this time gripping him close, almost lifting him off the sofa. Why did it seem so tentative, then? They were locked as tight as wrestlers, yet somehow Mark wasn't touching him.

They meant well enough, but that was not the same as desire. Five seconds into it they had already flailed too long. Steven clamped his mouth to Mark's as if he needed oxygen, or maybe to keep them from saying the wrong thing. And knew right away: Mark didn't kiss. He let it happen, even put his tongue into play, but he didn't want it. Steven should have known from ancient times that the ones who don't cry don't kiss. It was the kind of thing Victor would have understood instinctively.

Worse, they didn't know each other well enough to stop and reconnoiter, but too well to cut and run. They were beached here now, no way to turn back. Like the last man in a long race, the best they could do was finish. Steven tried not to be sad, also not to think, but felt an awful weariness in his limbs. The kiss was plainly a small truce, stalling for time. It looked as if one was trying to save the other from drowning, but it wasn't clear who was the lifeguard.

Somebody had to say something, give it some kind of direction. Finally Mark gripped Steven's hair and pulled his mouth away. "Go down on me," he whispered, pushing him underwater.

At least it got them off the dime. Obediently Steven's tongue slicked down across Mark's belly, a snail's spoor on the skin. He tugged the waist of the shorts, yawning it wide enough for Mark's dick to spring free, something unambiguous at last. Steven bent and took the head of it in his mouth, tasting salt, as he tucked the waistband under the balls. Mark's hand never loosened its grip on his hair, guiding him but also holding on, not sure if he was the driver or the rider. As Steven crouched forward and swallowed him whole, Mark hissed a sharp intake of breath. Then for a moment no sound at all as the first wave carried them out.

Easier now that they didn't have to face each other. They got into a rhythm fast, Mark heaving deep into Steven's throat, groaning for both of them, a spill of wordless obscenity. In short, the generic blow job. Ten years ago it would have been over in two minutes. Even now there didn't seem to be any room for languor. It was all heading in one direction, the only thing still up in the air being the matter of fluids, whether to come in or out. Then suddenly Mark was swimming back to shore. He stopped pumping, put his hands on either side of Steven's head, and lifted him away. "Wait—just wait a sec, okay?"

Steven was embarrassed to look him in the face, as if he might find out he was doing it wrong.

Mark grinned at him playfully. "Get naked," he said.

Steven sat back on his haunches, breathing hard, and blinked at the man lying before him. Curiously he felt more shy than before they had tumbled into this. "That's all right," he replied in a husky voice, his throat still thick from the workout. "It doesn't matter."

Mark didn't quite get it. More than anything he wanted not to be selfish here, though that was precisely how it worked between him and the likes of Ted Kneeland: *You do me, maybe I'll do you in the morning.* As if to prove he could do better, give equal measure, he reached out a naked foot and tapped the front of Steven's jeans. "Come on," he demanded impatiently. "Now. Before the earthquake."

Steven was almost somber pulling the sweatshirt over his head, like a kid ordered to go to bed too early. It wasn't that he was tentative about his body. He looked rock-solid enough as he tossed the gray sweatshirt aside, snagging it on the Italian lamp. His big shoulders and hairy chest were as brute as a fullback's. Even his belly had a certain working-class demeanor, redolent of beer in a sawdust tavern. Yet he seemed almost professorial as he stood up from the sofa and tugged the front of his 501's, undoing the buttons.

A young man might have mistaken Steven's tense self-consciousness for carnal heat, but there was no way to tell what Mark was feeling beyond the tautness in his groin, which he stroked idly to keep it in gear. Steven kicked off his shoes, then bowed to remove his jeans. In his brick-red Jockey shorts he looked more like a kid than ever. He opened his mouth to speak, then seemed to think better of it. With a swift yank he whipped the briefs down and tossed them aside.

His dick was as respectable as the rest of him, but not engaged. It swung there, pendulous and bloodless, a slight flare at the head. Peacefully asleep. It was Mark's turn to look in the middle distance. A gentleman doesn't point and always assumes a gun is loaded. Up was understood. For decency's sake alone, it was Steven's move. To his credit as a warrior—that quixotic mix of bullet-biting and Zen calm—he hardly missed a beat. With nothing further to hide, he clambered back onto the sofa, moving to bury his head once more between Mark's legs.

Mark hitched up onto his elbows, watching with dismay. The nervous scowl was back. "What do you like?" he asked, affecting a smutty undertone. The question posed the whole world over, to try to get pleasure to work. What he couldn't say—it would've sounded too much like an accusation—was: *Isn't this what you wanted?*

"I want to eat your balls," retorted Steven coarsely, snuffling close to the objects in question. The subtext being: *You guys go on ahead, I'll catch up later.* The valiant lie of the wounded soldier.

The spoken lines they'd learned in other places, from other men who'd passed them on like a secret language. Somehow the old forms were better than nothing. If you're all dressed up and the band is playing, as Victor used to say, then you might as well dance.

They even enjoyed it a little. Steven was hungry enough as he tongued the scrotum, unleashing the funk of locker rooms all the way back to the seventh grade, beyond even Daryl Sawyer. Besides, he didn't have to be hard himself to feel a pang of intimacy, especially knowing Mark was groaning on his account. And the groans were real: Mark wasn't performing here like he did for the kiss. His dick didn't care about Row G.

Admittedly, the final engagement was automatic, two minutes at best. But if *now* was all they were after, they got it right enough. Steven's cheeks were fat as a squirrel's, tugging the ball sack till it ached with heat. Mark straddled him like a motorcycle, worked himself to the top pumping with both hands. When he got very close, he didn't cry out but swallowed it, deferring perhaps to Steven's sleeping tiger.

And there was a moment at the end—at crest of tide—when they would have done anything to stay like this forever. It didn't matter that they were out of phase, as long as they could be out of time. For an instant anyway, they felt more than they thought. Mark arched his hips, pulled by the moon, and the spurt of white spilled across his belly to his breastbone, a line of liquid pearl retracing the downward trail of Steven's tongue.

Immediately after, they probably wouldn't have minded being two men in the bushes again—if only to facilitate surfacing and escape. Steven released him and slumped to the side, his cheek against Mark's thigh, covering where the spot was. Mark rested a hand on his head, making no move to disentangle. It wouldn't do to let the silence go on too long. Always best, even after a minor tremor, to check for survivors.

"Thanks," said Mark. "I thought I'd forgotten how."

Steven chuckled amiably. "Hey, it's like riding a bicycle."

"What about you?"

"I think my bike got stolen."

"No, really. You want to get off?"

"Sometimes. In the morning when I'm half-awake, so I hardly notice." He shifted uncomfortably, but perhaps he was just trying to shrug. "Oreos are simpler."

Mark pulled him by the shoulder, thinking to bring them face to face again, but Steven veered away and reached to the floor for his shorts. Cleanup wasn't urgent here, since neither one was a fallen Roman. It wasn't as if Mark was acting sticky or squeamish. But there was something very tender in the gesture as Steven moved to contain the spill. In one neat swipe he cleaned Mark's belly, then briskly dried the head of his dick, even as it lapsed to half-mast. Steven balled the shorts and tossed them down again.

Then he scooted up so they were lying side by side. Curiously their bodies seemed to fit better now, with the hard part over. Steven settled his head against Mark's shoulder. "I don't think I could go through what you did," said Mark. Then, as if this might be misinterpreted to refer to the rigors just completed: "I mean last year."

"You just do it," said Steven.

"I don't even know what to say to you half the time. I feel stupid."

"Mark, you don't have to apologize. You're fine."

With the evidence all expunged, not including being naked, there was no way of telling they'd made love at all. Pillowed side by side, they were more like a pair of combat vets in a foxhole, between shellings. At least they weren't so afraid of silence. After a long moment of looking out at the inland sea of light, Mark wondered aloud: "Don't you think we'll make better friends than lovers?" Steven didn't answer right away, but that was fine. Undoubtedly he would have said yes after a decent interval, even if he was wrong, even if he was lying. But then the phone rang, making them jump a little. The second ring kicked in the answering device, informing the world at large that Mark was never home.

"I never answer the phone," said Steven.

"But I just called you. You picked right up."

"A mere fluke," he replied as the beep sounded.

"Hey, Tiger, it's me," purred Lou Ciotta, his bedroom voice echoing off the tape. "How come you don't wanna talk to me? How many times I gotta apologize? Angela'n me don't care who you sleep with. You're my goom-bah. What you want from me, huh? So I'm an asshole sometimes. Don't mean I don't love you. Why don't you come out to the beach, have a steak?"

"He's coked to the tits," said Mark dispassionately.

There was a clunking sound, as if Lou had dropped the phone. Then another voice came on, raw and charred like barbecued meat. "Yeah, Mahk," murmured Angela, half in a slur, "we're family, right? Lou and me, we got more money than brains. Widdout you, hey, we're in the toilet. I got your chart right here. You got long life, good health, success—*if you stay with the family.* This is not bullshit. You come here and I'll show you. Bring your boyfriend."

Imprecisely, blind and in the dark, she hung up the phone in Zuma Beach. Mark and Steven—containing the laugh throughout her spiel, fearful her radar might pick it up—now let spill. They rocked nicely against each other like a couple of co-conspirators. They didn't need to speak about any of it, they shared it so completely.

And the laughing gave them just the right transition. There was nothing clumsy or tentative in Steven's rolling away and off the sofa. He reached for his sweatshirt from the lamp, sending it teetering like a whooping crane. Mark seemed willing to let it end here, grateful that they'd managed to come through with such light casualties.

Steven squirmed his head through the neck of the shirt, relieved to tent his belly again. "So how's Tim?" he asked, and the irony had returned intact, as if after a bout of amnesia.

"Tim who?"

Steven sighed. "How quickly they forget. Tim the facilitator. Tim from Thursday night."

Mark looked no less bewildered now that he had placed the name. "What're you talking about?"

"Well, didn't you ... I mean the two of you ..." He petered out. Stalled in the intersection, he bent to retrieve the brick-red briefs.

"Steven, he's straight." Mark laughed effortlessly, still in the muzzy swoon of release. "He fuckin' *announced* it. I guess you weren't there yet. At the end he was pestering me for the name of an agent. He wants to be an actor." Steven's mouth made a motion of saying *Oh,* but without a sound. As he put a foot in the briefs, Mark protested. "Don't put those on—they're all messed up. Here, take these."

He leaped up from the sofa, pulled off the white shorts, and handed them over. Steven, grateful not to have to grin and bear the ick factor, accepted the loan gratefully. He tried not to romanticize the moment as he slipped into Mark's underpants. This was not a favor bestowed on a knight.

"You promise it's nothing, right?" asked Mark, pointing again to the spot on his thigh, as if there had been no interim.

"I promise," Steven replied, and did up the buttons of his 501's.

"Here, take something." Mark walked over to the corner full of treasure, hugging himself excitedly. "You need a camera? You want this lamp?" His ass was faintly luminous, given the bronze of the rest of him. Steven shook his head slowly, a fount of desirelessness, but Mark insisted. "Come on, take *something*. The stuff's just gonna keep coming. How about this?"

And he picked up the telescope—black matte finish, two feet long, too phallic for words. But strangely he hit the right nerve, a place where Steven yearned for something he'd never got for Christmas, when his father gave him a .22 instead. He didn't nod and didn't reach out, but Mark knew he'd won the point.

He stooped and laid the instrument in the velvet bed of its case, then snapped it shut. When he rose to present it to Steven, he was flushed with pride, a kid not notable in his green years for sharing his toys. Steven—who couldn't stand things, who hadn't acquired any tangible goods since Victor died, not a sock—hefted it by the handle, swinging it gladly as he followed his naked companion to the door.

"Thanks for making a house call, Doc," said Mark, pulling the door open a foot, not quite enough for Steven to leave. He seemed not the least disconcerted to be undressed. Steven was feeling more naked than he.

"Couple of aspirin, lots of liquids," Steven drawled. "You'll be fine by morning."

Mark drew the door open wider, standing slightly behind it in case a car went by. "I guess we'll uh . . . you going to the meeting Thursday?"

"Maybe. We'll see."

Still they hovered in the doorway, still no answer to Mark's co-nundrum. They were closer here than when they were kissing, more open-hearted and casual, free of whether they liked it or not. Finding it hard to let the moment go, perhaps, the gong they couldn't unring. Friends were not the same. They understood they'd never be so naked again. From now on they'd have to be dumb as boys, elaborate as straight men paying no attention to one another's winkies, snapping towels in the locker room. The male bond: everything but desire.

And no good-byes. As the door swung shut, each of them gave a small vague wave, hardly more than the twitch that passes between a pitcher and a catcher. Steven could smell night jasmine somewhere nearby and made a hasty step toward the Volvo, needing no floral reminders. He knew just what to say to himself as he drove away. If he'd wanted it, he'd have wanted it. There were other things besides passion, which only frizzed the nerves and left you vacant for days after. One grew too old for boyfriends anyway. Better to know it now than later. A bad case of missed connections, that's all it was.

Just two guys, resolved at last. Steven careened down Laurel Can-yon, glad they had brought the moment to its crisis so now they could move along to something real. He chose to think he was happy. The canyon pass was unbearably still, his the only car. If an earth-quake had struck just then along the Inglewood Fault, it would have brought the whole mountain down around his head—but none did. The ground remained the ground, and Steven was free to go home.

The ice cream beside him on the seat would go back in the freezer and be as good as new tomorrow, except for a few ice crystals. Otherwise nothing had altered. Though he now possessed the where-withal to seize the riddled dome of the star-shot sky, Steven would have protested that he was an ordinary man again, lucky to be alive. The nice thing about friends was being able to leave intact. Tender was better than carnal; intimate didn't require a hard-on. It was all turning out to be very postmodern, dating in the apocalypse.

$$5$$

No matter where he landed, Sonny was always lucky with room-mates. Something—an energy, a polar drift—guided him to people possessed with a gift. He could see it all as a pattern now. Every couple of years he needed to hole up and incubate the next transition. Just then, a safe place would present itself, an island in the river. *Oasis* was his hieroglyph, green his color, six his number. Of course he didn't know any of that at first. Life taught him the order and character of his life by repetition.

First was the girl with the green shock in her long blond hair. He met Romy in a greasy spoon near the Embarkadero, the very night he walked out on the lighting designer. He hadn't actually planned to walk out for good; he was mostly trying to escape a roomful of overly decorated men, lit like African violets. Sonny ordered eggs and sausages. Beside him, Romy scooped a handful of pearls and agates from her purse, laid them on the counter, and worked out for him his place in the XVIIth Dynasty: Pharaoh's cousin on his mother's side. Sonny was nineteen.

He slept in Romy's bed for seven months, a sword of chastity between them. Of course he still cruised and woke up in other places, having morning coffee with perfect strangers. That was just desire.

But Romy was further evolved than the men he met and discarded. She was the first philosopher he had ever known who could walk through the walls of her own metaphysics.

They lay around in their underwear, dropping tabs of acid like vitamins, and Romy would lullabye him with the scope of his ancient kingdom. Pharaoh's cousin, she said, commanded the land below the Second Cataract and personally oversaw the painting of Pharaoh's tomb. Synchronicity alone demanded that the two of them should drive down to L.A. for the Tutankhamen show, and they sailed down Route 5 on purple haze.

They stood in line for half a day at the County Museum, swooning with the fumes that wafted from the La Brea Tarpits to the east. "The bones of mastodons," she murmured, waving a scarf at the primal ooze. You could not just stand in line with Romy; there was always something shimmering at the edges.

The Tut exhibit was mobbed, and they went around it arm in arm, Romy gasping with recognition at every gilded shape. "This was my period, I know it," she whispered, her arms wrapped around him as they stood before a Plexi case in which an alabaster cat with emerald eyes sat on its haunches. "I used to worry that I was just a handmaiden, or even worse a slave. Now I can feel my lineage was royal."

Sonny wasn't listening. He was staring through the case at a square-jawed man in black-rimmed glasses—thirty-five, no wedding ring—who wasn't looking at the cat either. By the time they reached the hammered gold mask of the boy-king himself, Sonny and the guy were rubbing shoulders. Romy melted into the crowd, no prearranged signal required.

His name was Larry. From Houston: lizard boots and a Stetson in his room at the Beverly Hilton, discreetly shed for his sojourn in L.A. He had a smutty mouth and a fantasy that Sonny was his little brother. A speculator in real estate, beachfront on the Gulf. "The Second Cataract," murmured Romy when Sonny told her. He laughed; for him it was just a weekend lark. It was Romy who convinced him to go when Larry proposed to take him home to Texas.

"Life doesn't happen, you make it happen," she said, the shimmering green of her eyelids playing off the green in her hair. Their good-bye was in the Hilton lobby. She pressed a brass scarab into Sonny's palm, which she'd bought at the Tut souvenir pavilion. "Never forget, you are a prince of Thebes. Whenever you come to an oasis, think of Romy."

Houston lasted about five months, with endless humid commutes to the Gulf. Larry would oversee the demolition of rows of beach-board bungalows, then follow the progress of his poured motels and mini-malls. The memory trace of Athens Construction wasn't lost on Sonny, even to the burly foremen who stared at him with fam-ished eyes as he sat in Larry's pickup.

But Sonny wasn't giving it away anymore. He didn't ever love Larry, though he liked the little-brother part, especially in bed. Other than sex, Larry didn't expect much from Sonny, which seemed a fair bargain, like getting paid to eat sandwiches. Sonny worked out in a gym on Montrose for two or three hours a day. He took a few units in business at U of H, but ducked the exam. Otherwise he drifted in Larry's wake. The Texas men they bothered with, coarse and unreconstructed, were a bracing change of air after the lighting queens of San Francisco.

If Sonny missed anything, it was metaphysics. Romy had been for him like a book of changes, tapping the well of the deep past, un-leashing his uniqueness. He couldn't seem to do it on his own. All the Gemini data in all the astrology columns left him cold. He needed a medium tuned to him alone—needed to *be* a medium for someone else's gifts, as he had been for Romy. It wasn't the same as being desired. Whatever it was he yearned for, his love life was the opposite.

After Houston he landed in Provincetown, with a lyricist who wrote only eight lines in the year he was beached with Sonny. There followed a spate of sane and passionless roommates, the sort who divvied the phone bill to the penny, while Sonny tended bar in Boston. His boyfriend at the time was a dean at Somerset College. The dean, married with four, was able to transfer the incomplete from Houston. Sonny put in a semester of night school, the dean's car waiting afterward under the elms. The diploma was left on his bedside table.

Sonny felt nothing; he had no plans. He still had nobody gay to talk to. All that he had to say seemed to fit the space of a single

night. He was twenty-four, and he wanted to be a man now—
enough of being everybody else's kid fantasy. The gold in his curly
hair had tarnished. His bright, astonished eyes had narrowed, squinting like a scout. The summer after the dean he pulled in, flicking
the remote in his Comm Av apartment, watching reruns of "Lucy"
and "Beaver." At night he ventured out to tend bar at Foley's, a
watering hole that was blissfully straight and single.

He passed for straight himself that summer. His roommate at the
time was a film student who came home every night reeling from
the movie of his life. Aaron would shake his head and talk about
"Boston women" as if they were a breed apart, impossibly self-
possessed. Sonny grunted sympathetically, man to man, one eye on
"Bewitched." He set Aaron up with free drinks at Foley's. They were
summer buddies, all the carnality focused on the blondes Aaron
couldn't score with.

His student film was a docu-portrait of Signora Guardi, a psychic
from Somerville with a sign in her dining-room window: PAST AND
FUTURE READINGS. Aaron would come home and play back his Super
8's on the walls of the apartment, laughing delightedly at the cracked
ideas of his seeress. Sonny watched, casually tagging along for the
next shoot. They stepped into an apartment whose curtains were
drawn for good, the atmosphere redolent of sausages and marinara
sauce. She was garbed in a flowered housedress, the bags under her
eyes like black crepe. She didn't require a crystal or a trance. Aaron
asked her questions, and she chatted about the future, very matter-
of-fact, the triumphs and pitfalls that lay ahead for Michael Jackson
and Cher.

Modestly, even reluctantly, she would speak of things predicted
in the past. She had a near-perfect record on the Oscars and the
Triple Crown. Sonny hung back and tried not to lock eyes with her
son Carmine, who took time off work to oversee every interview,
to make sure the Signora was not ripped off. He stood by the sofa
in his blue delivery uniform and stared at Sonny. The Signora confined her predictions to *National Enquirer* matters—earthquakes, serial killers, cancer cures. A crackball, just as Aaron had said. The
movie was only a comedy after all.

When the film ran out, it was time to leave. Carmine walked Aaron to the car, wanting to ask in private about the foreign rights. Signora Guardi offered Sonny a sweet from a dusty bowl of hard candy by the door. He took a green one. She said: "So how come you never been in love?"

He sucked the lime for a moment. "No reason," he replied with careful indifference.

"Well, it's time." Sonny looked at her. She shrugged her lower lip in a very Sicilian way. "How long you supposed to wait? A thousand more years?"

She made a scoffing sound at the stubbornness of time and sent him on his way. He walked to Aaron's car without so much as a nod good-bye to Carmine; they hadn't even been introduced. Nevertheless, Sonny got the number off the panel truck in the driveway: GUARDI MOVING AND STORAGE. He met Carmine the following night at the Guardi warehouse in the South End. Married with twin girls. The next weekend Carmine drove a shipment of country furniture to New York, and Sonny sucked him off twice in the back of the truck on the way down.

He didn't even pack a change of clothes. They unloaded sturdy fat-legged tables and chests of drawers into the rear of a store on Amsterdam Avenue. The antique dealer, exhausted with connoisseurship, haggled halfheartedly with Carmine. It didn't much matter what it cost, since the markup was so precipitous. Jonathan Clare, the dealer—older than he looked, younger than he talked—paid over a check to Carmine for the truckload, then asked Sonny if he'd like to have dinner. Carmine eyed them briskly back and forth, shrugged and left. He wasn't a sentimental man.

Sonny barely registered this phase, except to notice that Jonathan's apartment was the mirror image of the lighting designer's on Sutter Street. It was all transition now, a sort of free-fall that had begun the moment the psychic opened the window. Sonny plummeted toward love. All through August Jonathan had a marvelous time, driving Sonny back and forth to the Hamptons to show him off to clients. Sonny stood in a green Speedo on innumerable bleached decks, staring out over the rippling dune grass.

He was unfailingly polite to all the summer millionaires, never locking eyes. Jonathan wasn't deluded and didn't pretend they were going anywhere. The sex was perfunctory, though here too they were courteous to a fault: quick spurts and hand towels. Jonathan was avoiding the real summer, having opted out of his share in the Pines for the first time in a decade. Too many housemates sick. In the Hamptons at least, his clients never discussed night sweats and purple bruises.

Nevertheless, Sonny woke up beside him in moonlit guest rooms, and Jonathan's pillow was drenched, the sweat streaming off him. It didn't mean anything to Sonny. Discreetly he moved to the other side of the bed, beyond the circle of damp. He had no idea what sort of man he was meant to fall in love with, but this excited rather than troubled him. He imagined a figure moving toward him, nudged perhaps by a seer of his own, heading for a crossroads. Sonny could feel the imminence. His past was about to slough like a snakeskin.

By September he had visited with Jonathan all of New York's summer camps, but no man touched him. Seized with bouts of colitis, Jonathan grew irascible and insisted Sonny stay in a separate room. When the ailanthus trees turned yellow in the alley behind the store, they went together to an auction in Tribeca. Jonathan sat with his bidding paddle, eyes keen for a bargain despite the wilted look on his face. One after another, ungainly blotched paintings were knocked down in the high fives. Sonny fidgeted.

Then a big painting with a ladder and a chair nailed to it crept toward two hundred thousand, and the room began to murmur. It wasn't the money that made Sonny turn, it was more like a surge of power. He saw the paddles waving as the action narrowed to two bidders. Two-eighty, then three hundred. Jonathan coughed dryly beside him. Sonny could see that one of the green paddles was numbered 66. He lifted slightly off his chair to look.

Number 66 was a man about thirty in a rumpled suit, matinee-idol good looks and the wary smile of a fallen aristocrat. His face was slightly puffy, as if he'd just woken up from a nap. Three-forty. Three-fifty. His eyes flicked away from the auctioneer and locked on Sonny. The planets shifted. Sonny, pounding with joy, lifted a tentative hand. He was either waving at 66 or telling him to wait. The gavel came down.

"Four hundred ten thousand, to you, sir," announced the house to general applause. For an awful moment Sonny thought he'd bought it. Two or three people around 66 beamed with exhilaration and hugged him, pulling his gaze from Sonny, who left his seat abruptly as the next lot went up. Jonathan glanced sideways to see him go, never sure if Sonny was leaving a room for good.

Sonny staggered into the vestibule, his heart throbbing. He hugged his arms, squeezing the useless strength of his biceps. Huddled in the hollow shell of his body, he tried to think who to be. An armed guard at the door could see he was deranged, but clearly no harm to anyone but himself. Sonny could not recall the family he always said he was from, or the country town or the college. In the space of ten seconds he went through an entire adolescence of uncertainty. Having tumbled easily into a hundred beds, armed with one night's story, suddenly he had forgotten how to dance.

"That was a very expensive look," said a voice behind him, sultry and ironic. "Lucky for you, I wanted the picture." Sonny turned, a mask of confusion on his face. 66 grinned. His eyes were the color of black jade. "Don't worry, it wasn't my money. It never is. I'm Ellsworth."

"Sonny." He looked away shyly and didn't shake hands, for fear he would tremble. "Congratulations," he said lamely, then laughed to think how earnest he sounded. "I don't think I get modern art."

"Neither does my father. Modern money is what he collects." The voice was smooth as bourbon. Stupidly Sonny stared at the open throat of Ellsworth's shirt. He didn't know where to rest his eyes, so skilled at looking at nothing when other men looked at him. "Are you bidding?" asked Ellsworth. "Or can we get out of here?"

"Could we just have coffee first?"

"He wants to know my intentions." Ellsworth folded his arms, brimming with amusement. "Dishonorable," he admitted with a small shrug. "But fate is fate, right?"

Indeed it was. Sonny grinned slyly, his sudden adolescence falling away like scales. The bond of destiny established, they walked out together into the rainy night, leaving the gang of art consultants to settle the details of Lot 31. They zigzagged through the city, stopping for coffee twice, buying a pair of umbrellas at an all-night Walgreen's.

Sonny could not recall ever laughing so much with anyone, as Ellsworth spilled the tale of his checkered dynasty.

The father was a Florida toy magnate, the mother addicted to plastic surgery. Ellsworth had been disowned three separate times for being an invert, but the old man always took him back, needing an invert's eye to build his art holdings. Ellsworth was pensioned off in L.A., a continent away from the Aryan supremacist barbecues of his parents. He came East only to buy immortal objects.

Sonny invented nothing, laying out his dim youth in the hot flats of Fresno. Then all the glancing men he could remember, though his first rule had always been that no man in his life should know another. It took them nearly three hours to reach the East Fifties, pants drenched to their knees, shoes ruined. By the time they got to River House—the Second Cataract at last—Sonny felt what he always knew he would feel. That the married men at the Safeway, and all their kindred who fell in love with him for a night, were part of somebody else's life, a man who wasn't a prince.

They cavorted among the baronial trappings like a couple of orphans loose in a castle. They ate peanut butter and banana sandwiches. They necked in the library and rollicked in the old man's bed as if the elder Downs were squinting through a peephole. Two nights they curled in each other's arms, never restless.

"You realize what I'm giving up for you?" asked Sonny in mock dismay, standing naked in a window arch, flinging out a hand at the hive of the city below.

"All your sons," said Ellsworth, "unto a hundred generations." In a tent-like Sulka robe of his father's, he backed Sonny onto the window seat, grappled into his arms, and bit his neck softly. "Are you lost yet?"

"Uh-uh," Sonny retorted, tickling him to break the clinch, then pinning him in turn beside the open casement. A summer breeze drowsed in off the river. They hadn't shaved in two days. Sonny whispered: "It's all happened before, you know."

And at last he repeated the ballad Romy used to croon to him in the old kingdom off the Embarkadero, waiting all these years for a bloodbrother. He told it now playfully, interspersed with kisses, the first time he'd ever met a man's hunger with an equal measure of his own. Always before he had let them want him. More than their wives and children, more than their land and chattels. He could make them give over everything for the hour they played with him.

"Who does that make me? Pharaoh?"

"I'm not sure yet." Sonny licked at the head of Ellsworth's dick and tasted pre-cum. "Clearly royal. Maybe not immortal."

"Just as long as you understand, darling, I don't believe any of that shit."

"You don't have to. I'm the channel."

He dove down and swallowed the other, his throat slack with passion. Ellsworth gripped the gold in his hair and heaved over and over, gritting his teeth with love. It hurt to come, and they cried out in protest, then collapsed in a heap on the window seat. As they groaned and laughed, Ellsworth spoke with a certain awe. "Egypt, I have to tell you," he drawled, "you were born to live in the Eighties."

He must have bruised a muscle because he could feel it throb in his armpit as he walked home Sunday night from the gym. But then, he'd been tense all week, ever since Sean took off for Sydney. The dinner they'd planned had been put off three different times, on account of some business crisis. Sean apologized ripely, swearing to make it up, but all they had time for was a quick drink the night before he left, no chance to turn up the heat. The full overnighter would have to wait till Sean's return—what Sonny considered his real audition. Meanwhile, he had discovered how very rich Sean was. It wasn't banking but cable franchise, and the money was all his own, no checks doled out by a patriarch. A situation, in other words, that was starting to look quite princely.

When he walked into the apartment, he wasn't really surprised to hear the television in Dirk's room, loud with the door half-shut. He was used to Dirk's abrupt arrivals and departures. They weren't exactly friends in any case, so Sonny didn't feel impelled to duck his head in. They had made it work as roommates by keeping on separate flight paths.

So he made himself a couple of bologna sandwiches and went in his own room. After he ate he fell asleep. When he woke at ten he was utterly refreshed, and decided to drop by Rage for a beer, since it wasn't a zoo on a weeknight. He pulled off the dun-gray sweatshirt and bent to his laundry basket, shaking out a black T-shirt with a zap sign across the front. As he slipped it over his head, tight and sleek along his torso, making his nipples hard, he heard the TV again from Dirk's room.

It had been playing all along, all through his nap, but only now did it strike him as queer. Still very loud, blaring a sitcom, as if the station hadn't been changed or the volume, ever since Sonny came in. He crossed the living room and pushed open the door. He saw Dirk's uniform laid out neatly on a chair, blue and heroic. Dirk was in bed with the covers pulled up to his chin, maybe asleep. It wouldn't have seemed weird at all if it hadn't been for the television, so loud in the room that it hurt Sonny's ears.

"Hey, Captain, you think we could break the sound barrier some other time?"

Dirk tossed his head on the pillow and grunted. Taking this for yes, Sonny moved to the set and hit the dial just as the canned audience erupted in laughter. On the screen was Lou Ciotta, bellowing at his brainy wife, the prizefighter and the professor. Suddenly mute.

"You want to go grab a beer?" asked Sonny, just to fill up the silence, since he knew there was something wrong.

"I can't get warm," said Dirk in an oddly muffled voice, peering now over the blankets. It was strange that someone so tan could be so pasty-faced. His eyes were hollow with exhaustion, and this in a man with the cushiest run in the business. Sonny walked over and laid a hand on his forehead. Like fire.

"You got a fever," he said, almost accusingly. "I'll get you an aspirin."

He walked into Dirk's bathroom and opened the cabinet above the sink, avoiding his own face in the mirror. The shelves were cluttered with the gray tubes and jars of Clinique, cheek by jowl with a box of Four-X rubbers. Sonny grabbed a bottle of Tylenol, filled a glass with water, and went back to Dirk. "Here," he said impatiently when Dirk made no immediate move to sit up.

With a weary moan, the co-pilot came up on one elbow, the coverlet falling away to his chest. It didn't make sense how thin and frail his torso seemed. Sonny had worked out any number of times with him, had seen the fine broad barrel of that chest hardly a week ago. Dirk took the two white pills and popped them in his mouth. As he tilted back his head to drink, Sonny could see a patch of white fur along the inner side of the lower lip. Sonny's chest began to pound.

"Did you call the doctor?" he demanded as Dirk sank back on the pillow, shaking his head no. "Well, don't you think you better call him?"

"It's just a bug," murmured Dirk.

Sonny practically lurched from the room, hurrying out of the apartment as if he was late. He trotted down to the garage and pulled the Mercedes out, though it was only a few blocks to the bar and parking was always a hassle. There was such a wall up between him and Ellsworth's illness that he didn't let the memories flood back in, refused to see again the white patches that foamed over Ellsworth's tongue, or hear the amulet phrase they had repeated over and over: "Just the flu."

Sonny didn't know Dirk very well, but they'd traded sufficient sexual banter, the high points and fine points of their respective voyages, for Sonny to know the bottom line—or perhaps it was the top line. Dirk Ainley didn't get fucked. This wasn't especially a matter of pride or superiority. Actually Dirk felt guilty about it, to find himself hung up on such an unliberated posture. Nonetheless his ass was never in the air, so there wasn't any way he could have picked up the virus. For all the shifting definitions of what constituted safe, one article of faith still held in the bombed-out world they moved in: if you'd never been a bottom, you were home free.

Sonny had put it out of his mind entirely by the time he parked on Hilldale. He walked quickly to the boulevard and ducked into Rage, nodding at the bouncer, who passed him through without the five-dollar cover. It was mildly crowded, maybe two deep around the bar. Sonny stepped up and waited to order, casting his eyes around. In the first sweep he picked up six men cruising him—pre-cruising actually, not at all sure they were worthy of him. At the end of the bar was an ordinary man, forty-five easy and clearly not a devotee of Prime Time. Mournfully smoking a cigarette, he looked at Sonny with a certain hunger in which there was no hope.

Sonny took his beer and walked around, passing four other men who were much more suitable and much more ready. "Howdy," he said, extending a neighborly hand to the smoking man, "I'm Sonny."

The guy was from Oklahoma City, for God's sake. He could barely keep from gaping, he was so flabbergasted that Sonny had approached him. He answered every question earnestly, as if he were being interviewed for a job. He was too overwhelmed to ask anything back, but Sonny was marvelously open, spinning his own Sinbad tale from Fresno to Rage, including his metaphysical detour as Pharaoh's cousin.

Within five minutes he made Charlie Bekins of Oklahoma City feel irresistible and witty. When Sonny leaned over to laugh, he grazed his knee against Charlie's, bumped his shoulder for emphasis. Even as he drained his first beer, Sonny declared with insolent good humor, "So why don't we go back to your place?"

Charlie nodded in a dumbstruck way, not even sure it wouldn't cost him. He had a literal closet back home full of Matt Sterling and his ilk, and no amount of autoerotic swooning had ever made him believe he would have one in the flesh. But yes, even if he had to sign away all the traveler's checks hidden in his boot, they would go back to his place.

Which turned out to be the Beverly Hills Hotel, Bungalow 14. Sonny had to laugh at the synchronicity of that, as he followed Charlie down Sunset in the 380. He was going to spend the night first-class, he who would have happily curled up on a couch somewhere so long as he didn't have to go home.

The immortal part was over very fast, a double jerkoff in which they barely nodded to each other, let alone touched. But they were very nice, even gentlemanly, and the Oklahoman was quickly sound asleep, leaving Sonny to order a midnight breakfast from room service. He shut the bedroom door and sat in the bungalow living room in the white terry robe with the BH logo. When the food was wheeled in twenty minutes later, the night waiter turned out to be a face from across The Body Works.

An actor/model/waiter named Bud, as beautiful as Sonny, who competed for the same rich forty-year-olds in the dating pool. They both knew the situation could just as easily have been reversed, with Sonny in the green bolero jacket and black pants. They laughed as if they were playing prince and pauper, Bud whisking the covers from the eggs Benedict and shrimp cocktail. Sonny signed the bill with a flourish and added a ten-dollar tip, then locked eyes with Bud.

"There's an awful lot of food here. Why don't you pull up a chair?"

"Can't, I got orders."

"What about later?" persisted Sonny, the white robe yawning open.

"Yeah, well," replied the other, rolling his shoulders in the monkey jacket, "I go on my break at one."

One was fine. It gave Sonny the chance to take a shower and wash his hair with a spate of complimentary BH products. He toweled dry in front of a full-length mirror for the second time that night, this time examining himself inch by inch to make sure there were no bruises, sticking his tongue out. Everything checked out fine, and even the aching muscle under his arm had started to mend. He was brimming with health.

By the time the waiter returned, Sonny was dozing on the hearth before a crackling fire. Bud woke him coming in, and Sonny stretched and groaned, shinnying out of the robe. Nothing required negotiation. Sonny watched the other strip out of his waiter's mufti, dispassionate as the locker room. They didn't even say hello. All the feeling was in their dicks as Bud came down on top of him, head to crotch. They fed on each other, enjoying it precisely the way they enjoyed a workout. It was Charlie Bekins who would have enjoyed it hugely, but he was sleeping serene as a deacon in the bedroom, missing the chance to see Jeff Stryker come to life. He surely would've gotten more out of it than they did.

Not that they weren't good at it: they came at the same time, their sixth sense for muscular contraction pulling their mouths away at the last possible moment so they shot free and clear, not a drop ingested. Thus on their deathbeds neither one would blame the other. They cleaned it up within ten seconds, using the pink BH napkin.

Three minutes later Bud was dressed and gone, leaving Sonny with the ancient pledge of their common faith: "See you at the gym."

Actually Sonny was horny again before the creak of the room service cart had faded down the pathway from Bungalow 14. But that would've been true even if he'd had another and then another encounter—the desk clerk or the car valet, whoever still might be available in the night's dead center. Sonny was being very disciplined, for him, to get himself dressed and out of there, without even a black swim in the pool of stars. And without a backward glance at Charlie, who wasn't so Oklahoma City as to dream they would wake in each other's arms. It was in the nature of a tumble with Sonny to wake up wondering if it happened at all.

He drove back into West Hollywood, knowing now how the next part would unfold. He hadn't decided any of it consciously. As usual, sex was the way he made the decision. Passing Rage, he felt a tug of raw intensity, watching the guys emerge in pairs as the 2 A.M. curfew fell. He left the Mercedes in the loading zone outside the apartment house, top down, trotted up the stairs, and soundlessly let himself in.

Dirk's light was off. He listened in the bedroom doorway, the co-pilot's breathing heavy as a winter tide. He actually thought of going and getting the Tylenol, since it was close to time for the next dose, but then they would have to talk. It was Dirk who had chosen to be here, wherever the journey was going. Sonny had nothing to do with it. If a man who couldn't possibly have the virus had it anyway, then he got what he wanted.

He was able to do it all in two trips. The laundry basket, the orange crate full of books, an armload of clothes on hangers, and one frayed suitcase. This was twice as much as he really needed, but his life was already edited down enough to fill only half the 380's trunk. He left the apartment keys on the board in the kitchen. No need to leave a forwarding address, since he never got any mail, and as for phone calls, the only one that mattered was Sean Pfeiffer's, and he wouldn't be back for ten days.

By quarter to three he was driving up into the hills above Sunset, turning in at a cul-de-sac, passing a line of ranch houses that hung out over the mountain on stilts. At the end was a vacant lot where a bungalow had been accordioned by a mudslide. Sonny had parked here on several occasions, at the lip of the view, to make out with certain men from The Body Works, certain men he didn't want to go home with.

He balled up a cashmere sweater of Ellsworth's to make a pillow, then eased the car seat backward till he was nearly prone. He stroked the amethyst crystal that swung from the rearview mirror, then looked up at the starlit night serenely, almost philosophically, as if he was camping out in the wilderness. As he unhitched the buttons of his jeans and drew them down over his flanks, the memory of passion aroused him—the man from Oklahoma chomping his nipples, Bud hunkered above him. Though no one could bring Sonny off like he could himself, he needed all his men to do it—dozens and dozens, trailing back into the deep past, each of them brief and glancing but in the mass like a force of nature.

He stroked and stroked. No man who had ever touched him was left out, for here all his lives were intact—the confederate soldier, the knight, the monk, the oracle, all his dreams in time. Every civilization had him, high on a mountain moaning in the night. He was the crux in which desire became pure spirit. He ran his other hand across the beautiful ripples of his belly, very nearly grasping what it all was for. He came with his eyes locked on the gibbous moon, viscous and thick and white.

Then he lay there free of encumbrance, smiling softly, the zap sign glowing on his chest, the sap cooling on his abdomen. Once more he had proven to himself that he wouldn't be sick. He was too much a moving target. No wonder he needed no permanent home and no baggage, even now, ten years after he'd run from Fresno. Saving himself for the big score, in the person of Sean Pfeiffer. All he needed was an interim arrangement, and it came to him now like everything else, in a burst of understanding.

The next oasis was Steven Shaw.

6

Steven was very good about bringing in the mail. He would hear the van at three or three-thirty and hurry on down to the box, sometimes even chatting giddily with the postperson, a black woman with hair as big as Oprah's. As he trotted back up the steps, he would rifle through the pile, sorting it into bills and letters and junk. Then he'd head straight for the alcove off the kitchen, which Victor had used as a kind of menu central *cum* potting shed, where he'd plan parties and arrange flowers. It had a big greenhouse window above a butcher-block counter, the window full of cymbidiums, the counter stacked with exotic cookbooks.

Briskly and efficiently, Steven would toss the bills into a cardboard carton, where they would wait till Margaret flustered in and paid them. This did not keep things from being turned off sometimes—the gas, the cable, the phone. But that was all right, since Steven didn't expect connections to be made anymore, and besides, it was an adventure to see what one could go without.

The junk mail went in the trash, of course, but not before Steven had rifled through it, bracing himself for the sight of Victor's name. For still the realty circulars and brokerage come-ons would arrive, the computer lists incapable of accepting death. Today a flier from a wine shop, promising a special gift for Mr. and Mrs. Victor Diamond, the Mrs. being Steven. Actually he liked this part, the persistence of Victor's name, even as he flung it into the barrel.

Two letters today, one from Montana and one from New York. The Billings address he couldn't place, a woman's hand, some cousin of Victor's or a high-school pal, two sides of a flower-bordered page full of stiff and formal sentiments. Not that Steven opened it to see. He tossed it into a shoebox where half a hundred other well-meaning thoughts lay sealed. The New York letter, Tiffany-crisp, was from an old friend of Steven's, an opera queen who'd had a crush on him fifteen years ago. Into the shoebox.

As he came around into the kitchen proper, he found Sonny Cevathas leaning into the fridge, in white sweatpants and nothing else. He turned around holding a carton of milk and poured it over a bowl of cereal. He grunted pleasantly to acknowledge Steven's presence, but no more than that, so skillful was he at not intruding. Steven watched him balance the bowl, a glass of milk, and two sweet rolls on his arm, his waiter's skills acute as he headed out the back door.

He'd been there four days now. The guest room beyond the garage had its own door, so they only met by chance, passing like ships. Steven had taken Sonny's plea at face value—"I need a place for a while"—and he didn't feel used. If people had asked him any number of things, he probably would have said yes. He was accustomed by Victor's illness to being overrun and invaded. In those last months the guest room had been filled with a stream of friends and family, coming to say good-bye. Compared to that, Sonny's being there hardly registered at all.

In addition to which, however charged his presence was to the men of The Body Works, Sonny didn't do anything for Steven. Steven watched him through the kitchen window, laying out his breakfast on the wooden bench under the bougainvillea, squinting up into the late-October sun to make sure he was getting its optimum light. No tanning rays available mid-autumn at four o'clock, but the burnish of the sun was perhaps its own reward. He scooped up a spoonful of Wheaties and thrust it in his mouth, eyes closed as he rhythmically stretched his neck.

The phone rang by Steven's shoulder, and he plucked the receiver, speaking without preamble. "This boy thinks he lives in a movie."

"I'm picking you up in forty-five minutes," Mark announced. They always began mid-sentence now. "Don't ask."

"He had a date last night. I heard them come in around one, and I watched the guy leave this morning. I feel like the housemother."

"Steven, it's your own damn fault. If he feels so fuckin' homeless, let him go stay at the Y."

"Where are we going?"

"If I tell you, you won't come. Just be ready."

"But how will I know what to wear?"

"Full leather."

As Mark hung up in his ear, he saw Sonny turn his head expectantly. The grisly dog came loping out of the bushes on the hill, his matted head slung low in that peculiar mix of cowering and threat. Steven felt a prickle of anticipation, waiting for Sonny to flinch and back away, breaking free of the self-possession. Instead he hunkered forward and held out his arms, and the mangy creature trotted up. Just to see its moth-eaten tail wagging—almost a spasm that twitched its hindquarters, as if the will to happiness was rusty—jarred Steven and made him feel curiously alone.

Sonny hugged the dog about the neck, pressing his own bare flesh to the racked fur. How did they have the time to become an item in just four days? Steven felt betrayed—worse, jealous. The last thing he needed right now was Huck Finn and Lassie in his backyard, friendship truer than true. By the time he flung open the kitchen door, the dog was already lapping the mush at the bottom of the cereal bowl, tenderly held in Sonny's hands. The bang of the door broke the spell. The dog skittered a few feet away and shot Steven a hooded look.

"That's not mine," Steven announced, pointing a finger at the mutt.

Sonny laughed, the sun crinkling his eyes. "Hey, he's not anybody's. He's just out there."

"Well, I don't want to encourage him."

Sonny nodded, studying the beast, who hadn't wavered his eyes from Steven. "Yeah, well, he don't look too encouraged. I was thinkin' I'd give him a flea bath."

"Look, you can have him if you want him. When you leave, I mean. I just don't want him domesticated *here.*"

"Got it," Sonny replied curtly, not mentioning the bag of veal bones he'd brought home from the restaurant last night, or watching Steven himself hurling dog biscuits and epithets from the terrace in equal measure.

Steven ducked back into the house to get ready, but wore no leather at all. He assumed they were going to something highly gay, some cheery fundraiser for the dying, where the young would be ruthlessly casual and the middle-aged overdressed. Steven, who was finally losing weight on a sort of popcorn and melon diet, stuck to a colorless, shapeless look. The worst that could be said of the way he dressed—Mark said this—was that he didn't look queer at all. Which was why Mark teased him about wearing leather chaps and harness, or a beaded gown for Halloween, just a week away. Steven was the only gay man in the Hollywood Hills without hair products, Mark would tell him disapprovingly.

In any event it didn't matter where they were going. Now that they were best buddies, they hung out together some part of every day. They would have played catch if they'd had the right gloves. Mostly they ate, lunches in diners and takeout suppers, Steven eschewing fats with Lenten rigor. Nobody loved too much. The incident of the mismatched blow job was almost two weeks behind them. They even laughed about it sometimes, but carefully. Meanwhile they cruised the world they wandered through together, exchanging indecencies about waiters and cops, confining themselves to what was fuckable in the abstract.

Steven heard the Jeep honk, jumped in his Reeboks, and hurried out. Mark had pulled up behind the Mercedes, which Sonny was washing, still in his white sweatpants. The two men were teasing back and forth as Steven slung himself into the Jeep. "Yeah, make me dirty and hose me down," called Mark to Sonny, who held the hose in one hand, his body slick from the backspray.

"Listen, dude," retorted Sonny, "you meet me up by the gas pumps later, I'll grease you up real good." They laughed; Steven smiled. As

Mark swung out and passed the Mercedes, Sonny touched his earlobe and nodded. "Very hot."

They swung away down the hill, and Steven looked over at Mark. *"What's* very hot?"

Mark didn't answer till they reached the red light on Sunset, by which time Steven had ceased to bristle. It was part of the theater of gay life to which he held no ticket: talking dirty. He could talk very sweet, sometimes even blunt and tough, but he couldn't get his tongue around these fantasies of dudedom. The common dream pool—locker rooms and barracks and heavy-metal shops—went right by him. He felt vaguely inadequate that his own erotic stomping ground was men in tuxes, very Cole Porter, or tumbling naked in the surf. No hosing required.

At the light Mark craned his head around to show Steven his left profile. "This," he said, a finger fluttering his earlobe, in which there was a single silver stud.

"When did you get that?"

"Yesterday. I ordered a diamond, but you have to wear this for a week. It's like a training bra."

"But what if it gets infected?"

"It won't."

"Did the person who did it wear gloves?"

"Steven Shaw, headmistress."

They turned right at the Beverly Hills Hotel and headed up Cold-water Canyon. The boxwood hedges on either side were as claustrophobic as the Brothers Grimm. Steven didn't know if he was annoyed at Mark for the post-punk affectation or pissed at himself for daring nothing of his own. His hair had hung exactly the same on his forehead forever. Weren't widows supposed to kick free and go blond overnight and plunge their necklines?

Well, not him. But even so, he wasn't sad or even really grumpy. There was a charge in him whenever he and Mark went out on a jaunt, as if they were teenage boys who would make something happen or else. About two miles up the long hill, Mark turned in at a blind driveway flanked by rows of cypresses shivering at the sky. About fifty feet down the cypress alley, they came to gates like at Blenheim, with a turreted Norman gate house looming to one side.

Steven looked questioningly at Mark, who announced himself into a brass trumpet device affixed to the gatepost.

"Mark Inman and guest, to see Lou."

The Norman tower stood mute for a moment, fixing invisible eyes. Startled as he was, Steven didn't move a muscle, knowing from Mark that Lou Ciotta was bodyguarded like a drug lord. Without a word of acknowledgment, the gates swept open, and they headed in. Around the next bend the cypresses stopped at a stretch of lawn so green it made Steven's teeth ache. The Norman mini chateau crested the hill with buttresses and vast expanses of diamond-paned windows.

"I thought they lived in Malibu."

"Just weekends. This is the winter palace."

The drive swept into an oval cobblestoned court. A couple of wolfhounds loped across the grass to greet them. Steven didn't ask why, after a month of avoiding all contact, Mark had decided to enter the lion's den. Lou Ciotta's name was never mentioned between them, though Steven had finally looked him up in *TV Guide* and watched an episode. A few times late at night he'd peered at the autumn sky through the telescope, but otherwise he thought of Mark's past as past for good, like his own. He couldn't imagine what Mark was thinking in bringing him here, but he felt a spurt of adolescent anarchy to think they were going in.

They parked beside three black cars—a Bentley, a Porsche, and a Ferrari, like three stallions grazing the edge of the wide electric lawn. Mark smiled at Steven once, to ask if he was ready. Yup. Together they walked up the wide stone stairs to a balustraded terrace. An oak door fierce as a moat yawned open, and a butler from Central Casting, tailcoat and gloves, looked down his nose and murmured, "Mr. Inman."

He led them across a domed foyer hung with tapestries and heraldic banners. They had left California far behind, but not Beverly Hills. The butler glided open a pair of paneled doors and stood aside to let them enter. Steven knew right away from the circle of faces that someone from the gate house had called ahead, though they were only a hair less stunned than total surprise.

Lou and Angela sat on a Louis XIV settee, in bilious matching sweatsuits. The manager and the lawyer, Sid Rawls and Eric Beemer, huddled on either side of them like donors, briefcases open on their laps.

"Marco," Lou said simply, shrugging his palms like a three-card monte dealer. "So. How's it goin'?"

He flashed his 34-share smile. The others all seemed to be waiting till the moment was complete between him and Mark. Steven's first thought on looking closely at the star was that he and Sonny were the same age and the same type, street-smart and slightly pugnacious, but painfully eager to be liked. Angela curled up beside Lou's shoulder in a kittenish way, her teeth bulging slightly behind her lips like a pit bull's, her red hair teased into a foaming frenzy.

Mark put an arm around Steven's shoulder. "Every Thursday at four o'clock," he said, "we meet up here to strategize. See, we like to get away from the studio. Feels more like a family. Right, Lou?"

"Yeah. And it ain't the same widdout you, pal." Lou Ciotta brimmed with sincerity, his heart going out to the prodigal CEO, but he also couldn't stop shifting his eyes to Steven. "So who's this? Your lawyer?"

Now it was Mark's turn to look bruised. "Lou, would I do that? This is Steven—my boyfriend." He squeezed Steven's shoulder, and Steven flashed a gelatinous smile.

"Well, hey, it's about time." Though the other two men looked as if they had swallowed turds, Lou Ciotta was bright and victorious. He stood and thrust a meaty hand at Steven. His eyes were slightly bulged, glazed as if he looked at the world through a film of Vaseline. Coked to the tits. "This one, he keeps his life in a box," said Lou, cocking his head at Mark. "Now that we got you here, you'll see how Lou Ciotta works. What's his is yours. Angela, meet Steve."

"Pleasure," she said, gathering herself from the sofa, shaking her hair like a tambourine.

"Lou," interjected Sid Rawls, "we gotta finish this deal."

"Fuck the deal," sneered the star, his bedroom eyes still riveted on Steven. "We got company."

He slipped an arm through Steven's and led him across the gleaming parquet, past gilded tables cluttered with Meissen shepherdesses. The former Miss Arizona followed with Mark, and the squirming courtiers, Sid and Eric, brought up the rear. Through French doors they passed out onto a terrace, where a table was laid for tea, the baroque sterling service heavy enough to ballast a ship. A starched maid poured, her Irish as thick as the butler's English. She pointed the way to the scones, plates pyramided with sandwiches, trifle, pies. It was all so BBC, one half-expected a voiceover from Alistair Cooke at any moment.

"I don't even know what we were fightin' about," sighed Lou as he and Steven took their cups and plates to wrought-iron chairs at the end of the terrace, looking down on a rose garden dotted with marble nymphs and satyrs. "Bury the past, right? So how long you two been together?"

"Uh, not long," said Steven mildly, swallowing a petit four. He wasn't sure what tack he was supposed to take. Since he was so unaccustomed to watching sitcoms, he was extremely unprepared to be appearing in one.

"Me and Angela, it's been four years, and I still get a bone whenever I see her. You know what I mean?"

"Yes, well, this is my second marriage," Steven replied demurely.

Then Angela appeared beside them, cozying next to Lou on his chair. She smiled at Steven. "Did he tell you this house belonged to Cary Grant?"

"Gary Cooper," Mark corrected, taking the chair beside Steven.

"Oh yeah," replied Angela, unfazed.

"This man is a genius," Lou declared, reaching forward to squeeze Mark's knee. "Lou Ciotta wouldn't even be here widdout this man's vision. He'll be runnin' the network someday. You better treat him right." This to Steven, accompanied by a playful slap to the shoulder, knocking a dollop of tea into Steven's saucer. "Or else you gotta answer to Lou."

"Oh, he treats me real good," Mark put in, turning a fatuous gaze on Steven. "He fucks me and everything."

Steven choked slightly on a bite of scone. Lou Ciotta nodded gravely. "We don't have no problem with that. Do we, Angela?"

"Uh-uh. Hey, live and let live, right?"

She grinned at Steven, who smiled peakedly, licking the Devonshire cream from his finger. Then everyone drank his tea for a moment, surveying the manicured acreage below. The sun had set behind the ridge, taking with it the Indian-summer glow that had suffused the roses all afternoon. An Asian gardener, reed-thin and stooped, moved among the rose beds, clipping blooms and laying them in a basket. From the terrace they could hear each clip of the shears, mournful but unsentimental.

The flow of servants in Lou Ciotta's house was as entrenched as the staff of a landed duke. Yet Lou and Angela themselves seemed strangely removed from it all, like a couple of orphan children. It looked to be as unreal to them as it was to Steven and Mark. They'd come into this life with the suddenness and speed of a lottery win, and deep down they probably believed they could lose it just as quick.

Sid and Eric had meanwhile disappeared, deciding it was simpler to take their tea in private. Presumably neither one would've been quite so forthcoming or openminded on the sodomy question. Indeed, there didn't appear to be much more to say, even among the foursome. Angela stroked the back of Lou's neck, where tufts of gorilla hair sprouted from the sweatshirt.

Steven wondered if he was meant to reach out and play with Mark, but his hands stayed gripped around his Wedgwood, not quite ready to fondle in public, even for the charade's sake. He'd never touched Victor in public, except surreptitiously, and tended to freeze when Victor, younger and easier, nuzzled against him. This was not the same as being in the closet, but there it was: a reservoir of uncertainty, a fear of being marked.

Lou Ciotta set his tea plate down on the glass-topped table before him, all his cakes untouched. "Me and Mark need to have a little talk," he observed mildly, and Angela dutifully rose to her feet. Leaning forward to Steven, with the full saccharine smile that had brought her to third runner-up in the Pageant, she intoned softly, "Why don't I show you the house?"

So they'd finally gotten down to it: the wives and the husbands. Purring with anticipation, Steven got up to follow her. He glanced over his shoulder for a parting dirty look at Mark—half dirty really, no hosing required. And was startled by the tenderness in Mark's face, thanking him but more than that, promising how they would laugh at this.

Yet she wasn't half as appalling as she'd seemed. As they drifted through the music room and the library, then through an awesome banquet hall chilly as a meat locker, she didn't act grand in the least. There was disbelief in every gesture, pointing out the musicians' gallery, the Regency silver, the phases of the moon on the grandfather clock. She seemed to have an instinct that Steven would like the details. She was generous and enthusiastic, leaving nothing out, sharing the secrets of her mansion girl to girl.

In the kitchen she opened the freezer and the ovens to show how much they could accommodate, then introduced him to the cook, a stout and white-bunned Scottish woman who gave him a half-curtsy, clearly disapproving of the help and the guests being chummy. It was the help, in fact, who were clearly most appalled by Angela Ciotta.

Then up a spiral stair to the second floor, where the hall was hung with a gallery of forbidding portraits, hard-bitten WASP ancestors of nobody who lived here. Angela pointed at one overly gowned and scowling gentlewoman and grimaced: "Has this one got a broom up her ass or what?" And she and Steven laughed like a couple of upstairs maids, reeling arm in arm into the master bedroom.

The ducal bed was hung with oceans of brocade. The dressers and fat armoire were country French, burled and honey-colored. In contrast, one entire wall was stacked with video equipment high-tech enough to launch a Trident missile. Balcony doors flowed to an upper terrace that commanded the twilight view all the way to the ocean. Every surface in the master suite was filled with baroque-framed pictures of Lou and Angela in a thousand lovebird poses. Steven cooed admiringly, as he had throughout the tour, but Angela could have cared less about the bedroom. Even as he lingered to stroke the mane of a carousel horse, she tugged his hand and led him into her true domain.

The bathroom. More green marble than a Biddle bank. A tub that would have happily bathed four at a time, in an alcove floor-to-ceiling with windows, blue with the gloaming sky beyond. Angela pulled him around excitedly, throwing open the mirrored doors to the sauna, the steam room, the massage table. Facing the tub were a sofa and chaise upholstered in white silk, perched on a white fur rug, the whole ensemble fit for a Hamburg brothel. Breathless in their sudden palship, the wives plopped down on the sofa. All they needed to make it perfect were peignoirs with maribou sleeves.

"This is where I chill out," declared Angela. "Nobody comes in here—not even Lou. The rest of this house, I'm like *on* all the time. I mean gimme a break. These servants are always *grading* me, like they worked for the fuckin' Queen Mother or somethin'. Please— I'm a beauty-school dropout."

She laughed with conspiratorial delight, and Steven couldn't help liking her, the bad girl thumbing her nose at all that arch propriety, Nero's rotten empire ceded to his horse. She told Steven he had ancient eyes and demanded to know his birthdate down to the minute so she could have him cast by Salou, her channeler. Then explained this one particular life she was working on rebirthing: the mistress of a medieval king, probably Italian, who gave up her jeweled palace to enter a nunnery. There was even some aura suggesting she may have become a saint.

"It all fits, 'cause like I was brought up Catholic and now I live in a castle." As she sailed through the parallels, she reached and opened the drawer of an inlaid table beside her. Out came an eighth of Peruvian flake and a small mirror. She flashed a bright smile at Steven, who shook his head no. Carefully she tapped out a couple of lines.

"You shouldn't do that, you know."

She had her straw poised above the first line. She shrugged. "Lou don't like to do it alone."

"That's not a reason."

"Yeah, it's stupid," she said, capitulating right away, this girl who wanted so hard to please and nobody was pleased. She laid the straw on the mirror and put it aside on the table. "I'm gonna stop soon anyway. Fuck, I'm so polluted I can't even have kids. Disgusting, right?"

Steven nodded, the moment not requiring any further remarks from the headmistress. He felt sorry for her, even a bit protective.

This was curious, for three months ago he would've been spitting with rage, to think these decadent hets could abuse themselves, squandering years, while men like Victor clung to their last days, sweet and clear and wasting no drop of time. *These* were the ones who deserved to die, he would've been thinking, seething like the very Baptists who crowed when the faggots died. For once he didn't want to take out Victor's death on someone. He didn't even care that they hadn't mentioned AIDS. On the contrary, he was relieved that Angela didn't know, that she wasn't hovering or flinching or covering her ass.

"Hey, Steve, c'mere." She winked at him and headed for a fourth mirrored door, clicking it open. As he followed her in, he was surrounded by a smell of cedar and sweet gum. She flipped on the overhead lights, a row of spots that tracked along the ceiling like in an art gallery. Except it was her closet, bigger than the master bedroom, with clothes racks wrapping the four walls. Angela spread her hands to show it all off, though there was something of an embarrassed shrug in the gesture as well. Blouses, skirts, little nothing silk dresses—dozens on dozens of everything. One corner was fitted with tiers for shoes, shining as if they'd never been worn, like a shoe museum.

"I've died and gone to Bonwit's," said Steven.

"I have a shopping problem," Angela shared with a rueful sigh. "I can't decide, so I buy stuff in every color. Besides, Lou don't like me to wear the same thing twice. Like his mother had one nice dress or something. What do they call that?"

"Overcompensating."

"But hey, I give it away like crazy. My sisters, my old girlfriends— they leave here with both arms full. I'm like Santa Claus." She reached out and touched her white-polished fingernails to his sleeve. "You see somethin' you like, don't be bashful." Steven swiveled his head and gaped at her. She laughed. "I don't mean for *you*. But maybe you got a sister—or even your mom."

He laughed back, but with her, not at her. He wanted more than anything just then to let her know he liked her, improbable though it was and despite her appalling money. He was sisterless, he explained, and his mother wore only housedresses, but because she

116

looked so crestfallen, he allowed as how maybe Margaret would like something from Angela's closet. He didn't know Margaret's size, of course, but that only meant a challenge to accessorize. Hats, scarves, belts—they finally settled on a linen shawl, hand-painted with birds. Angela was triumphant as she folded it up.

"Do you gift-wrap?" asked Steven dryly, and they were off again laughing.

Then she went to the Cinderella corner, where all the ball gowns were hung, rank on rank of gossamer. She pulled out a crepe sheath, green ink with a white appliqué in front that looked curiously like the zap sign on Sonny Cevathas's T-shirt. She demanded to know Steven's honest opinion as she wriggled out of her sweatshirt. She wore no bra, and her tits were firm and girlish, the nipples dark and Sicilian. Steven stood his ground, casual as could be, but he realized he'd never been two feet from a naked lady before. He suddenly felt quite racy, and was disappointed when the pants came off to see she was wearing panties. She shimmied into the sheath and turned so Steven could zip her.

"This is a very A event," she explained. "Streisand. The Spellings. I don't want to look like a hooker."

She swept the cascade of red hair off her shoulder and twisted it up on her head, spearing it with a bone comb. Steven knew exactly what she wanted, the sort of gay man with drop-dead taste who would know instinctively how she should look. Steven had never been this man, could scarcely remember to match his own shoes, and wore plaids that clashed. Victor was more what she was looking for, always running over to Margaret's to help her dress for a date.

"Is this too much?" She opened a drawer in an apothecary chest and drew out a velvet box from among a muffled clutter of jewel cases. She opened the lid and lifted out a tiara, glutted with emeralds and diamonds. She turned to the mirror so she could fit it into her hair. "This is not my Miss Arizona crown. It belonged to a Russian princess. We're not talking rhinestones." She studied the effect carefully, no longer dazzled herself by the jewels. She sighed. "Why does it look like rhinestones on me?"

He reassured her about everything, about the tiara, the dress, the satin pumps, kept telling her over and over how pretty she was. But here in her own mirror she actually looked miserable, doomed to pick out every flaw, night after night as she dressed for the A event. Steven didn't have the heart to tell her that the only thing wrong was how skinny she was from all the drugs.

She began to disrobe again, laying everything out on the chaise for later. A good Catholic girl, she turned the conversation back to Steven. "You're so good for Mark," she said with vivid good cheer. "I never seen him so relaxed."

"Really, it's not what you think. We're more like . . . brothers or something."

She faced him again, naked except for the black panties. "Don't tell me about love," she offered. "I'm Italian. It's the national sport."

"Oh, I love him all right. Whatever that means." Steven tried to sound breezy—tried too hard. "But gay men are very weird about sex. They can't do it with people they like."

She folded her arms and tilted her hips, in a very hookerish pose. Her lips pursed in a little bow of perplexity, her brow furrowed. "You tryin' to tell me you don't like to fuck someone you love?"

"Well, not me specifically. I sort of like to, actually, but—"

It was very problematic now, her not knowing anything about Victor and the nightmare. Not that she was trying to put him on the spot. She seemed genuinely interested, as if this were her hobby, more than clothes or chateau life. She turned away to duck back into her sweats, and once more Steven felt an odd thrill of melancholy, to lose the field of her nakedness.

"I'm not blaming Mark, you understand. He's a sweetheart. Besides, *I'm* the one who's dead from the waist down. It just isn't the right, uh, karma for us."

She almost seemed to wince at the California bullshit of the last remark, she who was the paradigm of the New Age consumer. Perhaps she understood that Steven was grasping at straws, not speaking out of any real faith in the wheels of the spirit. She pulled the comb from her hair and let it tumble down again. "Sounds to me like you're tryin' to talk yourself out of it."

"There's no it," Steven replied precisely.

She sidled up to him and took his arm. It was time to leave the inner sanctum. Whatever private truths were stated here stayed here.

"All you gotta do," she said, "is go slow and don't be jealous. Mark, he's like Lou, he's gotta fuck everything that moves. Oh, I know. Mark thinks his love life's such a big secret, but hey, people talk. He likes those humpy West Hollywood boys. But that's not a *man.* He's not gonna settle down with one of them."

Thus having given her final word, she led him back to the real world, keeping hold of his arm as they retraced their way through the upper hall and down the spiral stair. Steven didn't protest any further that he and Mark weren't an item. But he was feeling rather flush at Angela's inference that he was such a man. He hadn't thought of himself as a man, pure and simple, since before Victor got sick. An old man sometimes, a used-up one, but not the genuine article. Did he only believe it if a straight person said it?

Lou and Mark were framed in the front door waiting for them. Steven knew right away that Mark had told the boss about his antibody status. Lou looked strained and uncomfortable, not nearly so blasé anymore about who was fucking whom. He could hardly hide the fear and pity as Steven disengaged himself from Angela and stood by Mark, feeling ridiculous with the shawl over his arm.

But Angela was sunny and ebullient enough for all of them, eagerly praising Steven's eye for fashion. She invited them back for whenever they liked—dinner, the pool, a weekend out in Zuma Beach—pathetically eager, as if nobody ever visited either of them. She didn't seem to pick up that Lou Ciotta wasn't seconding what she said, that he didn't exactly shake hands with his guests, though here Mark made it easier for him by clasping Steven's hand.

"And if he don't come, *you* come," declared Angela to Steven, staking the ground of their special kinship.

The Ciottas came out to the terrace and stood at the balustrade, duke and duchess, as Mark and Steven crossed the cobblestones to the Jeep, hand in hand. "Don't worry about nothin'. I'll take care of it," Lou called out to Mark, a brief resurgence of his best Mafia don self-assurance.

"Don't be a stranger," Angela trilled beside him, one hand fluttering the air in a showgirl's wave to Steven.

Who found himself waving back in virtual pantomime, a gesture he wouldn't have been caught dead in before today. He and Mark broke the handhold and jumped in the car. They swept away down the drive, the wolfhounds gamboling after, saying nothing until they turned into the cypress alley. Then Mark reached over and fingered the fringe on the shawl in Steven's lap.

"This is darling," he said. "You can wear it over the harness and go as Laura Ashley."

Steven fixed him with a dead-bolt stare. "You think I could have a little warning next time?"

"You did great, babe."

Steven tried to remain in a wounded huff, but he couldn't sustain it. There was too much to dish. By the time they reached Sunset, they were talking on top of each other, roaring about the overdetermined tea and Cary Grant and the lugubrious retinue of servants. They swung down Melrose shrieking with glee, Steven spilling the details of the boudoir. *Why does it look like rhinestones on me?* would be their anthem from now on.

Boisterous and bumping shoulders, they rolled into Johnny Rocket's diner and took a booth, the oldest adolescents in the place. They ordered the burgers and fries they'd never quite got their fill of in high school. Steven fed quarters into the table juke so they could debrief each other to a rockabilly beat.

It had all been very calculated on Mark's part. He'd been out of work six weeks, and they were closing fast on the sixty-day AWOL clause that would let them break his contract. He didn't care about the job anymore, or if he ever worked again, but he was too much of a businessman not to hedge his bets. Because what if he didn't die so soon? He had enough put away for a couple of years, maybe three if he sold his house, but then what? He decided to come clean to Lou and try to trigger a disability settlement, an area so gray you could hardly read the print in the contract.

"I got him feeling so sorry for me, I figure he'll break his butt with the studio. Fuck, if I get disability, we can retire to Hawaii." He rolled his eyes at Steven and hitched up the sleeves of his leather jacket, cocky as if he'd just robbed a bank.

"But what did he *say?*"

"When I told him? Well, he pushed his chair back a couple of feet, and he stared at my teacup. You could tell he was trying to figure out what I'd touched in the house. Then he said, 'Did Steve give it to you?' "

"Thanks, Lou. Patient Zero over here."

"Then he asked me how long I had. I said two years." At Steven's sudden frown, he flashed defensive. "It *sounds* better. If I don't look like Camille, he won't get in there and fight."

"So what was *I* doing there?" asked Steven, waving his last french fry in the air.

"Ours is a tragic love, dear. We cling together in the whirlwind. It's practically a movie of the week. He loved that part."

Steven's beeper went off, and he washed his pills down with a chocolate malted, screw the popcorn and melon. Mark was stunned at his affectionate defense of Angela Ciotta, killer shopper and chatelaine of Coldwater Canyon. He accused Steven of being simply perverse, Steven who was usually such a misanthrope, especially about the overfed and unplagued straights of the Westside. Steven stood his ground and kept insisting that, despite being a moron, she was sweet and had a certain intuition.

They ogled the buns of the counterman. They rollicked across the street to the punk newsstand and scooped up an armload each of tawdry magazines. They headed back to the Jeep, pumped still with adrenaline from the adventure and wired on a fast-food high. They slapped each other five as they got in, and Steven leaned over and flicked Mark's ear.

"Very hot," he said with a certain smutty undertone. "I can't wait to see the rhinestone."

It was barely nine o'clock when Mark pulled up in front of Steven's, but both of them could feel the nimbus of exhaustion waiting on the down side of the day's excitement. They were so attuned to each other now that they didn't have to push it, didn't have to prove they could dance all night. Tomorrow was soon enough. They said good night without touching, being as they had no audience. Steven trotted up the steps as Mark gunned away, then turned as the Jeep roared back in reverse. Mark jumped out with the shawl, swept it   '
around his shoulders, and strutted up the steps like Carmen.

"You forgot your wrap, Miss Thing."

"So butch," said Steven dryly, tugging it gently off his friend.

"Genderfuck." Mark winked. "The last taboo."

Then the phone began to ring in the house, and Steven had to fumble fast to get the door open, letting Mark go a second time without a kiss good-bye. Steven ran through to the kitchen, not even turning on any lights, and grabbed it up on the third ring, an instant before the machine.

"Steven, it's Margaret."

''*Please*—I was just going to call you. I spent the day with a Russian princess, and I've got a major acquisition for you." He batted the wall switch with an elbow and flung open the shawl on the white-tiled counter. It looked even more costly and exotic outside the Aladdin's cave of Angela's closet.

"Steven, there's something I haven't told you—"

"The background's coral, it'll go just great with your china-doll skin. She's a redhead too."

"I just got home from the hospital. It's Ray."

A synapse seemed to malfunction in Steven's brain. His first thought was to protest: *No, no, that's over with.* Meaning Victor. He couldn't imagine who Ray was; the only Ray he knew was Ray Lee at the office. Which was exactly who it was, though Steven kept resisting, even as the details tumbled out.

"He's been having pains in his joints for months—some kind of arthritis. He's been on a cane for a couple of weeks. Then last night he had this stroke. His left arm's paralyzed, and he slurs when he talks. He's all upset, but you know how proud he is."

Steven continued to stare at the hand-painted birds on the linen, tracing a parrot's wing with a finger. "But he's too young to have arthritis," he said with a certain sullenness. Ray Lee was barely thirty.

"Steven, it's *AIDS.*" Only now could he hear the irritation and weariness in her voice.

"But he's not—" Steven stopped abruptly. Not what—not gay? Of course he was gay, the impish Korean who could do simultaneous impersonations of Linda Evans and Joan Collins, Ray who would *love* this shawl. What Steven meant was that Ray Lee wasn't sexual. He seemed somehow above all that, androgynous and rarefied. He had even been some kind of monk for a while, or at least he'd gone to monk school. Steven had always considered him rather lucky, to be so removed from mantalk and the purely carnal.

"We'll have to close the office for a couple of weeks," said Margaret, sad but firm. "I can't do the hospital *and* Shaw Travel. Unless you want to go in, but you don't." No accusation there, just a statement of fact.

"What about Heather?" asked Steven automatically, amazed to have remembered the name.

"Heather quit yesterday. She's been acting weird ever since Ray got the cane. She's scared. I can't deal with it."

Steven felt a vast protective urge, for Margaret more than Ray. She'd brought him into the office a year ago and trained him. She loved orphans, and Ray had no one, not even a wizened mother to write home to in Seoul. Margaret had even admitted he'd become a sort of replacement for Victor, at least for her. Now Steven offered all of himself, without any qualification, just as Margaret had done for him. He would spell her at County General; bring in meals when Ray got home. More than anything, he would be there as now, for the last phone call of the day. No problem about the office at all. Shaw Travel would take a collective vacation for the next two weeks, per order of Steven Shaw himself. Done.

"You won't be so glad at the end of the month," observed Margaret, ever the rueful manager. "We've already got no business. We're riding on the hubcaps as it is."

Steven wouldn't hear another word. All she was to think about was getting Ray Lee on his feet. He promised to join her at the hospital tomorrow afternoon for the conference with the neurologist. Skillfully he got her to finish up the thousand details of the hospitalization—Ray Lee's cat, his towed car, his unpaid rent, all of life that ground to a halt at the hospital door. Then he managed to turn the talk to Angela Ciotta, and before they were through Margaret was laughing, gasping really, demanding to know the worst.

For Margaret's sake he dished poor Angela mightily, even going so far as to trash the green-ink sheath. "She looked like a hooker," he lied, just for the laugh.

By the end of the story, Margaret was punchy, a laugh that could just as easily have been tears. But the feeling of being strung like piano wire had broken, and she was ready to go to sleep. With a promise to meet her at the coffee shop across from the emergency room, Steven purred a final good night and hung up feeling satisfied. Doubtless he would be feeling a good deal less plucky tomorrow, when he had to actually sit at the counter where he'd been eating pie while Victor died; but one day at a time.

He trailed back through the darkened living room to where the front door stood open. The moon was practically staring him in the face in the western sky, three-quarters full. He stepped outside on the landing to gaze at it, thinking idly that he ought to go in and grab the telescope. His eye fell to the street below, and there was the black Jeep, just beyond the driveway, across from Mrs. Tulare's house. Not exactly hidden, but Steven wouldn't have seen it if he'd stayed in the house.

Oh, how he wished he'd stayed in the house. He could actually feel a dull throbbing ache behind his breastbone, as if Novocaine had worn off. He slipped back in and shut the door, leaning his forehead against it a moment, trying not to think. Then he turned and floated through the dark of his own house, gliding open the glass door in the dining room and emerging onto the back terrace.

It was utterly still, the moon cold on the stripped white trunk of the eucalyptus. Steven turned left past the garage, trying now to stop himself, loathing every footfall. The guest room was pie-shaped, tucked into the fold of the hill beyond the garage, a kind of afterthought. The bathroom was in the wedge end of the pie, its small square window flinging light on the chaparral as Steven came around. He flattened against the wall, ridiculous as a spy, and peered one eye in.

Nobody there, the shower dripping. But just the sight of Sonny's gym clothes tangled on the floor, the jock in a sweaty ball as if he'd just peeled out of it, tilted Steven's stomach like a roller coaster. And Sonny did nothing for him.

He couldn't see into the bedroom, since the bathroom door was nearly shut. Nor hear any voices, though there was music playing. Still he had room to snap out of it. The point of no return was the corner. He groped through the sagebrush like an Indian scout. Then the point of no return was the side window, its banded light filtering through the blinds. Steven had a sudden panic, even as he held his breath and inched forward, that the blinds would be drawn enough to baffle his line of vision. He lost his last scruple as he hunkered down and came up to the sill like a periscope.

Mark and Sonny were at either end of the sofa watching the television, the backs of their heads about four feet away from Steven. Shockingly, they were simply sitting there, dressed and everything. They might have been watching a football game. Except on the screen were two men fucking.

The blond was on his elbows and knees in the bed, presenting his ass to a hairy overmuscled thug who stood by the bed dicking him— long, deep thrusts accompanied by a rhythmic slapping of the blond boy's cheeks. An indifferent disco beat thunked along in the background, not quite drowning out the slaps and moans, the grunted obscenities of the thug.

Otherwise there were no production values, and the set was like a motel room in hell. Not that the sleaze and bluntness weren't intentional, but leave it to Steven to feel the emptiness at the heart of it—the Pauline Kael of porno. Far from feeling left out, he was relieved not to be watching it with the guys. It might have engaged him if the scene had been two men kissing. But this—did people still go this far? It seemed like a loop from ancient history. And why was the thug not wearing a rubber?

Steven was far too literal for fantasies. Indeed, he might have tiptoed quietly away and left it at that. A little burned not to be invited to the party, but let it go. It was only a movie. Then suddenly Sonny stood up, and his ass was bare, his jeans around his knees.

He turned toward Mark, a surly pout on his face as he hawked spit in his hand. Then he reached to stroke his swollen dick, which was wrapped with a length of rawhide that also bound his balls, the ends of the string trailing between his legs. He was standing now so he blocked Steven's view of the video, but the moans and the guttural dirty talk still punctuated the disco beat.

"Yeah," grunted Sonny, cheering on the thug. He mauled at his knob, squeezing out pre-cum, seeming to present himself to Mark for inspection. "We should get us a kid," murmured Sonny, half to himself, "and work him over good. Get him real down and dirty. Right, dude?"

For a moment Mark didn't move, sitting on the sofa watching Sonny instead of the video. Steven had a weird and sudden thought, a hope almost, that Mark wasn't really involved in any of this, but just waiting for a break to excuse himself. Then Mark reached out and gripped Sonny's balls, pulling him toward the sofa, the pressure so intense that Sonny's head lolled back and he let out a fierce, abandoned groan, drowning out the video at last. Steven's chin was on the windowsill, his jaws clenched, wincing that Mark might be hurting the boy. He felt hopelessly naive and out of his depth, scared even, but worst of all he could feel the blip of arousal in his groin.

It all happened very fast now, as if there were a script at work. Mark rose up off the sofa—him with his pants down too. One hand still gripping the ball sack, he yanked up Sonny's T-shirt, baring his rippled abdomen and chest. Still Sonny's head lolled back, his big hands swaying at his sides, not touching his dick at all now, letting Mark set the carnal agenda. Mark leaned forward and took one of Sonny's nipples in his mouth, biting it softly, or maybe not so softly if the growl in Sonny's throat meant anything.

At last Steven could see Mark's face in profile, the single-minded hunger as he worked his mouth, the dull glint of the stud in his ear. Several steps behind, Steven wondered irrelevantly why they didn't take their clothes off. They both looked faintly ludicrous with their pants at half-mast, held back somehow from a full embrace. Then it occurred to him that this was how they wanted it, immediate and anonymous, the stolen moment and the dirty little secret.

Mark stood up straight, eye to eye with Sonny, and they traded a humorless smile of dazzling coarseness. Cocking his head, Mark motioned Sonny over to the bed. Sonny obliged, crawling onto the mattress and holding the pose, elbows and knees, of the blond on the video screen. Except in the interim the blond had vanished, and the thug was now being sucked off by a crewcut lad beside a pool. Mark paused on his way to the bed to watch for a moment, as if he didn't want to miss anything.

Even by inching all the way to the corner of the window, Steven found that the bed was mostly out of his range and in the dark to boot. He had to flatten a fish eye against the glass, but even so he could only half see Mark reach out and stroke Sonny's butt. Words were passing between them, slinky with innuendo, but Steven couldn't quite hear.

He had a second of being absolutely crazed, wanting to tear the casement window open. He couldn't bear the shadows and the whispers. They had no right to withdraw from him now. He felt entitled, as if his peeping had made it a threesome. And when he heard the grinding of his own teeth, felt his hands gripping the front of his shirt as if he would rend his garment, he finally recoiled in a kind of horror, pulling his head from the sill. Now he wanted out of there fast, as if the slightest further glimpse would take the last shred of his dignity.

He turned to the right and began to burrow through the lantana toward the driveway. His hands were getting cut up pretty bad as he pushed the web of branches out of the way, but then, he deserved it for being such a sneak. He was at pains to make no rustle or crack a branch, and gritted his teeth as a twig snapped back in his face, drawing a line of blood like a dueling scar along the cheekbone. He was almost out of the woods. He could see the pavement ahead, lit by the streetlight at the bottom of the drive. Then his foot came down on the serpent.

Hard to say who hollered the loudest. The dog let out a yelp as he sprang from his lair, and the shock made Steven scream. But the worst of it was being cornered, the two of them grappling and colliding as they scrambled to kick free of each other. The dog growled and bayed in panic. Steven wanted to strangle it, bellowing at the beast to shut up, unaware of the irony of his own roar. The dog got away first, barreling through the last of the thicket, clearing the path for Steven, who crawled out panting onto the driveway.

The guest-room door swung open, and Mark was there on the threshold, buttoning up his jeans. Tentatively he asked, "Are you all right?"

Steven was still on all fours, scuffed and rumpled and grimy. He peered up at Mark. "Yeah, sure," he replied, coolly enough given the situation. "This is part of my wilderness training."

Mark stooped beside him as he sat back on his haunches, brushing the shmutz from his clothes. "Steven," Mark said quietly, and though there was reproach in it, still more was there an indescribable tenderness. He knew exactly what had been going on, and Steven avoided looking at him, examining a tear in his sweater, trying to think of an exit line. Mark repeated his name, even more quietly, and reached and brushed the hair off Steven's forehead. "Come on, we'll go make some coffee."

Steven's eyes flashed at him now. "No. You're busy," he hissed, writhing at the thought of being patronized.

Mark shook his head plaintively, pointing a thumb over his shoulder in the vague direction of Sonny. "This doesn't mean anything," he said. "It's got nothing to do with you and me."

"Uh-huh. Will you just go back in there?"

"I don't want to make you crazy. I love you."

"Then do it in your own house."

At last he made Mark flinch, if that's what he wanted to do. An awkward silence fell, but neither moved to leave. Steven wondered if Sonny was still waiting spread-eagle on the bed. Probably this little crisis was just another kink to him, and Mark would come back even hotter. Steven, distanced from all of it, couldn't have said just then what turned him on. Given carte blanche—any man he fancied, whatever he wanted to do—he still would have been out the window looking in.

Yet most surprising was that he actually didn't feel so ridiculous right now, sprawled in his own driveway. If anyone had to see him like this, it might as well be Mark. At least it was who he was for real, no pretense left. He certainly didn't feel embarrassed. There was a certain giddy freedom that went with losing face, and a curious sense of release as well, almost as if he'd gotten off.

He turned his head with a crinkled grin. "Hey, go for it, buddy," he said to Mark, the adolescent balance all restored. "*Somebody* might as well get laid around here." Then he put a hand on Mark's knee to brace himself and stood up, groaning involuntarily at a sudden twinge in his hip. At the first grapple with the dog, he'd bashed the side of the house. He was going to be very sore tomorrow.

They were standing side by side now, looking off down the canyon as if they'd done no more than come out to watch the moon. "I don't think you realize," said Mark, "I'm as whacked out as you are." He was speaking rather carefully, formally even, not quite trusting the sudden breeziness in Steven's tone. "The man I used to be," he said—groping for it—"I mean, that's over. It's like that video." Again he gestured vaguely toward Sonny's room. Steven didn't ask if it was the thug or the blond Mark used to be. Even in his addled state he understood it was some of each. "Fuck, nobody's even touched it since . . . uh, that time with you."

Mark frowned. His declaration of solidarity hadn't come out quite as solid as he hoped. But Steven didn't bat an eyelash. "All the more reason," he retorted briskly. "Take it when it comes."

He nudged Mark's shoulder with his own, furthering their conspiracy but also clearly pushing him back to Sonny's arms, full permission granted. If there was anything shy or unresolved here, it was in Mark. He couldn't seem to match Steven's antic mood. He would go back in there, all right, knowing an easy way out when he saw one. But it felt as if he was doing it more for Steven's sake than his own. And Sonny didn't seem part of it at all, which was probably par for the course. Assuming they picked it up more or less where they left off, it would be over in ten minutes. Fifteen if Mark took a shower after.

He stepped to the threshold again, hand on the doorknob, and turned for a parting shot. "This is the kind I'm used to," he declared with a shrug, bleakly ironic, nothing if not self-critical. "I don't know how to do the other kind."

Steven smiled indulgently, not planning to say a thing. "I love you too," he replied.

Mark was half in and half out, so the playful smile could have been for Sonny as much as Steven. A second later the door clicked closed behind him. Steven limped across the driveway, making for the front door. The dog was lying low in the bushes below the steps, shrinking at Steven's approach but somehow standing his ground too. Steven stopped on the bottom step and peered at him over the rail, making a low sound in his throat, somewhere between a moan and a growl.

After a moment the dog responded in kind, a purring grumble from deep in its lupine past. Then Steven raised the pitch and volume, his lip curling back in a snarl. The beast followed suit and rumbled even louder, though still not raising its head from its paws. The tail Steven had stepped on looked as if it ached to wag, but it stuck to the rules and played dead. The standoff lasted about a minute.

Then Steven started to laugh and tottered up the steps. He wasn't thinking about Mark and Sonny. Who crossed his mind as he headed inside was Angela. He wondered how she was doing at the A event, and his mind flipped back and forth, imagining her in the tiara and the green-ink sheath, then naked except for the panties.

He went into the kitchen, past the counter where Margaret's shawl lay open, and into Victor's alcove. Angela would have a lot to say about the scene in the guest room, proof of her contention that Mark was at war with himself. Steven, she would have insisted, was still the only man in his life. Steven chuckled to think about it, what sort of man he looked like, peeping in the bushes and dumped in the driveway. He was going through drawers of madeleine pans and plant food, balls of elastic bands, Christmas ornament hangers, the ephemera of a life that used to work. He didn't know what he was looking for, only that he was looking.

The last time he said he loved somebody was to Victor, of course, but not like this. When Victor was dying the words were different— a kind of protest, a kind of clinging, the final declaration at the border. This was something else, more glancing and provisional, with a small L. He wasn't sure he believed it even so. There ought to be some other word for in between, less charged, easier on the backswing. He opened the second drawer from the bottom, string and twine and packing tape. There, snaking its way among the scissors and church keys, was a length of rawhide.

A-ha, he thought, drawing it out. It coiled and shivered around his hand. He turned and headed for his bedroom, limping a little still. After all this time he was finally going to come out and play. All by himself. But a new man had to start somewhere.

7

The ghoul on the corner of Santa Monica and Larrabee was so tame as to be almost invisible. It was still early, with a misty rain clouding the streetlights and slicking the empty street. The boulevard was closed to traffic through Boys' Town from six till two in the morning, but the revelers had only begun to straggle out. A tall man in a bridal gown waved at the door of Revolver. Three beefy white boys cavorted arm in arm in matching spangled pantsuits—The Supremes, 1966. One of them carried a portable cassette player, to which they were all lip-synching "The Happening."

The sixties had the right retro feel for a Halloween so deep into the plague years. There was Donna Reed and Mary Poppins. The trash/flash thrift marts had yielded up a queer sexless mix of tube dresses and white patent leather, the bruised-girl look, innocent and nasty. Somewhere along the interface between Edie Sedgwick and Twiggy.

The ghoul watched impassively. He wore a black nylon jumpsuit that zipped up the back, the front of it painted Day-Glo green with a skeleton's bones. He had a black fright wig, and his face gleamed with white greasepaint, the eyes hollowed with iridescent red. Not like a skull at all but a voodoo head, weirdly androgynous, a lady of the evening straight from hell. Every other dragster and costumed man seemed to be part of a group, or they met one another and shrieked with recognition. But not the ghoul: he was alone and meant to stay that way.

Perhaps it was a kind of shyness, the same that had kept him out of drag. He stood like a man in a bar who would never go up to anyone. The early girls were there for a reason, because they knew the camera crews from the local affiliates had to get their footage by eight in order to go on at eleven. When the carnival reached full throttle, with hundreds passing back and forth along the boulevard, the curbs would be three deep with hets who drove in from the Valley to see the queers at play. The ghoul was somehow not one thing or the other, neither reveler nor spectator. Even on Halloween, it seemed, a man could carry his closet around.

Only once did he seem to stir with a proper haunted passion. Out of the alley by Video West came a troupe of four men in jeans and leather jackets, hardly a costume at all. Each of them held aloft a placard on a stick. One bore a picture of the President grinning like an imbecile, AIDSGATE printed across his face. Another said STOP THE GENOCIDE. The ghoul stood aside to let them pass, and as they stepped out onto the boulevard, the four began to chant: "Help us, we're dying! Help us, we're dying!"

All of them under twenty-five, hair punked up and swaggering, they didn't look as if they were dying in the least. They seemed exultant and full of fire, more alive than anyone else on the street, which may have been why the ghoul looked after them so longingly. The revelers and drag queens cheered at the arrival of the little protest march. The bride and several others, King Kong and Glinda the Good, trailed along in the marchers' wake, swelling the ranks as they headed for the Channel 7 Minicam crew.

The ghoul had had enough. He turned away—regretful, somehow in exile—and headed up the side street. Above him someone leaned over an apartment balcony and hooted: "Hey, dead man!" The ghoul looked up to see a man in a glitter tuxedo holding a lighted pumpkin, waving as if he were on a float. The ghoul waved back vaguely and hurried along the darkened street, urgent now as a vampire trying to outrun the first pewter streaks of day.

He loped along and turned at the next corner, fishing in the jump-suit pocket for a jingle of keys. Then he suddenly froze in his tracks. Across the street a truncated three-wheeled vehicle was double-parked beside a pickup truck. A female cop stood with one foot on the bumper of her clownish cop car—PARKING ENFORCEMENT stenciled on the side—and laboriously filled in the blanks on a ticket. The pickup was parked in a red zone, underneath a streetlight. Very cut and dried: a twenty-eight-dollar fine, the envelope provided with the ticket. Yet the ghoul stood in a shiver of something like terror, his hands in his pockets kneading his thighs, as if he were about to be sentenced for murder.

The female cop finished her paperwork and tucked the ticket under the pickup's windshield. She glanced in the ghoul's direction as she folded herself back into her little three-wheeler, but the getup didn't appear to stir her fancy. She drove away and around the corner, making for the next hydrant.

The ghoul visibly relaxed, moving across the street and plucking the ticket off his windshield. The door of the truck was never locked, since anything worth stealing—the garden tools, the blower—were jumbled together in the open bed. Dell Espinoza climbed into the cab and reached across to the glove box. He flung the ticket in with fifty more, an avalanche of violations. From the visor he took a packet of Mexican cigarettes, drew one out, and lit it. He had stopped smoking two weeks after he met Marcus Flint, and started again four weeks ago, right after the first water scare.

He drove over to Fountain and headed east to Hollywood. Beside him on the seat was a potted gardenia, with three blooms fully articulated. The fragrance was absurdly intense, plangent with summer. Dell rolled the window down, and the wind ruffled his fright wig. He was thinking about the four young men with the placards. He figured they must've marched in Washington two weeks ago. Dell had seen the pictures in the gay rags—waves of marchers from every state, men and women being dragged off the Supreme Court steps. These were the same men and women who used to sit in the living room on Lucile, but younger and younger now, kids who were radicalized in college or even high school. Marcus would have been overwhelmed with joy to see it, aching for his own gay students to know themselves before they learned to love the prison of being safe.

Dell was stirred himself by the swaggering boys, but unlike Marcus he had no wish to join them arm in arm. He stayed at a certain remove, just outside the door the way he had on Lucile, letting the rhetoric filter in as he lay on his bed. He was never a man of words, never one for a group. Not that he didn't feel a yearning envy for the boys. They were bonded and fierce and rollicking, as if not being alone somehow gave them a way to laugh about it. Dell couldn't imagine laughing. No wonder he didn't quite believe they were dying.

He'd called the water department again four days after the first incident. By then the lunacy was at full pitch, with farmers in the Imperial Valley fearful of using tainted water on their vegetables, demanding Colorado runoff. This time Dell reported that he'd sabotaged the Hollywood Reservoir. But no mention was made of the threat on the news that night, or the next day either, even though Dell had called all three networks from the Pioneer Chicken phone booth.

Apparently the authorities had decided the threat was psychological, and they weren't going to give the AIDS terrorist any sort of forum, especially before an election. Dell watched the hysteria play out around his original call, the pleas for reason and the flood of information, and realized what was missing was demands. So he put in a call to the County Board of Supervisors, who were withholding funds for testing sites, and warned that if the money wasn't released, one of the supervisors would be abducted and injected with the virus. This had a nice Red Guard ring to it, and Dell used the same script when he called the Federal Building, demanding release of a drug that people were smuggling in from China.

A brief, vague reference surfaced on the evening news, but again they withheld the details. It was merely indicated that the Castaic terrorist was continuing to make crank calls. Voice analysis had convinced the police they were dealing with a gay hispanic man in his mid-thirties, probably dying of AIDS, probably in the last stages of dementia. This enraged gay activists, who demanded to know how you could ascertain a person's sexual orientation from his voice.

Confronted at a news briefing, head pig Sheriff Noonan raised a bushy Irish brow, held up a limp wrist, and said, "The lisp gives 'em away every time." At which there was an immediate outcry, but the sheriff didn't apologize. He knew his constituents.

In any case, the last thing the gay community needed was another criminal. Even Dell could see that. The psychos who picked up street kids and dismembered them, molesters running Cub Scout troops— there was more than enough material already for the tabloids. Dell suddenly realized Marcus would be ashamed of him if he hurt the larger cause of his people. The crank calls stopped; the bloodmail died. Still the composite of the suspect would resurface at the sheriff's weekly briefings, as he trailed through the laundry list of unsolved crimes. But Dell Espinoza had got away scot-free because his terrorist days were over, just like Patty Hearst's. The phone was reserved again for the normal sort of interchange—getting off with the 976 crowd.

He drove south to Third and headed through Koreatown, the lettering of its signs looking more like code than language. But if the Koreans owned the stores on Third, the polyglot mix of peoples here in East Hollywood ran the gamut: Vietnamese, Pakistanis, Latinos from every banana republic. Thirty years ago it was all white-bread. The old Congregational Church, at the corner of Emery Place, where Dell pulled into the parking lot, stood serene in its gray stone skirts. Only the purest Aryan need apply, its yearning steeple seemed to proclaim.

Dell nosed the pickup into an empty space by the parish house, one of a set of outbuildings that ringed the ragged park behind the church like a cloister. He glanced at his face in the rearview mirror, checking his makeup. He reached over and cradled the potted gardenia in his arm, lugging it after him out of the truck.

Even in the misty dark there were children laughing under the trees, clustered around the open double doors of the parish house. As Dell approached across the grass, he could see them dressed as pirates and witches and Saturday-morning heroes. They bore a certain tribal resemblance to the revelers of West Hollywood. Their parents stood by in raincoats, hovering over them with umbrellas. The kids turned and laughed when they saw the grown-up ghoul.

The parents smiled their careful polyglot smiles—Thai, Bengali, Mayan—and parted to let Dell through.

He stepped inside to the ruckus of a party breaking up. Dozens more children milled around Sunday-school tables, covered with the detritus of cider and cookies. Here too the melting pot was the operative principle. All the old Congregationalists were long gone, fled to the burbs. The immigrant parents moving among the tables were proud and happy, trading off cameras and helping the little witches fix their masks. Dell stood beaming benevolently. For a moment it seemed he had come to the opposite place of his isolation and darkness, that he shared in the triumph of the new Americans, gathered together in fellowship. He may have even wished it.

But that wasn't why he was here. His red eyes scanned the room and picked out the whitest woman, a honey blonde in her mid-forties, sleek in a beige wool suit. She was clearly more expensive than all the immigrant mothers. Standing beside her was a pale young man in a pinstripe suit and glasses, murmuring in her ear as he read from a sheaf of memos in his hand. The honey blonde nodded, taking it in, but the serene encompassing smile never left her lifted face. She began to speak, and at the first sound of her lush and lulling voice, the room fell into a reverent silence.

"My friends, my children," said Mother Evangeline, "the laughter we hear tonight is the joy of salvation. We are the true family of God." As her eyes scanned the faces of her sheep, she caught sight of the ghoul, bigger than all the costumed kids. Mother's gelatinous smile flickered, as if she didn't quite get the joke, but Dell was grinning at her so sweetly she went right on. "All our enemies are on the run," she declared, her bell-like tone gleaming with the language of the pulpit. "The heathen and the pornographer, the whore and the sodomite. They are the ones who bring hell to earth, and it's time we sent them back where they came from." Beside her the pale young man fretfully shuffled his memos. "Ours is the kingdom, don't ever forget it. And thank God for AIDS. Sometimes He is a God of wrath before He is a God of love. And we are His army. Remember that next Tuesday. Yes on 81!"

At this she flung out her arms like a politician, and her flock cheered, especially the children, waving their witches' wands and pirate swords. Automatically Mother Evangeline began to move to-ward the doors, as if she was late for her next appearance. The bespectacled man followed earnestly behind. As her parishioners stood aside, some of them seemed to want to reach and touch her garment. They were all ex-Catholics, and the old ways of idolatry died hard. They loved Mother Evangeline's evangelism, her Nieman's vestments and her enemies lists, but they also wanted a Blessed Virgin.

Mother played them skillfully, now intimate as a radio shrink, now aloof as a prophet. Just at the door she stooped to smile at a young Filipino boy dressed like a little policeman. His flustered father behind him whipped the hat from the boy's head, and Mother reached out and stroked the jet-black hair.

"Do you love Jesus?" she asked, almost a whisper. The boy nodded gravely. "You'll grow up to be one of his soldiers," she said, running an appreciative hand down the brass buttons on his blue jacket.

She rose to her feet. The father was tipsy with joy, looking as if he would gladly let the blood of his firstborn if the evangelist only asked. As Mother turned and waved a hand over the group in a final benediction, Dell stepped forward. "Mother," he said prayerfully, and she looked at him once again as if there must be a joke here, one of the adults in costume for a reason, perhaps to do magic tricks for the children. "I brought this for the altar," said Dell, shrugging the gardenia in his arm. "For All Saints. To pray for the soul of my own beautiful mother."

"Of course," she replied, smiling thinly, as if it was all a bit Roman for her taste. "Kenneth will let you in."

She continued out the doors to greet the overflow, and the young man nodded for Dell to follow. They passed Mother Evangeline gathering little soldiers into her arms. Walking beside Kenneth across the courtyard, Dell kept the gardenia hoisted up between them to discourage conversation. But Kenneth seemed to have other things on his mind, still shuffling his memos like a Tarot deck. They reached the oaken doors of the church, and Kenneth pulled back his jacket to unhook a ring of keys. He unlocked the door and let the ghoul precede him.

In the vestibule the only light was the EXIT sign above the doors, but Dell moved forcefully through the curtains and into the sanctuary, not wanting to seem unfamiliar with the geography. Two coronas of electric candles lit the altar at the north end, but otherwise the high stone space was dank and cursed with darkness. Again Dell moved forward, single-minded as a choirboy. He nodded at the Jesus cross that hung from the velvet backcloth.

Besides the candles, the altar was bare, no flowers or holy vessels. Dell set the gardenia down dead center, turning it so the blooms all faced him. He stepped back a foot to study the effect and became aware of Kenneth standing to the side, waiting not so patiently, fingering his memos like beads. Dell hadn't thought this through at all, didn't know how he would get the moment alone he needed. Perhaps it was the sanctity of the place that gave him the inspiration: he turned to Kenneth, a supplicating wince suffusing his red-rimmed eyes.

"I'd like to pray for her," he said meekly.

Kenneth's mouth twitched, and his shoulders squirmed in the pinstripe suit, as if he might be being asked to join in. This wasn't the meditative branch of theology. Dell waited quietly, letting the other man clutch for a way out.

"For sure," said Kenneth. "Why don't you just let yourself out when you're done. The door'll lock behind you."

He shuffled away a couple of feet, but almost as if he didn't dare turn his back on the ghoul. Dell wasn't sure how he knew, yet he understood in that moment that Kenneth was queer. A flutter in the hand that held the memos, a slight uncertainty in his gait—not so much the mark of being gay as being in the closet, as if he were suffocating in his own skin. Dell didn't know how to use the knowledge, except to stand in contemptuous silence while Kenneth skittered out of there. As if Dell's own openness—the savage pride he had learned from Marcus—shone through his black disguise, banishing the other man.

And suddenly Dell was alone in the church, carte blanche. He'd figured if he was lucky he'd get half a minute, just enough time to douse the altar, but now his mind raced with bigger plans. He stepped forward and retrieved the gardenia, then darted across and through the curtains into the vestibule. Ahead were the double exit doors, to the left a dark hallway. His heart pounding, Dell headed into the shadows, not even fearful of bumping into a wall. He was seized by a sort of radar now.

He hadn't expected to encounter Mother Evangeline herself. Last night when he heard her radio sermon—exhorting the faithful to "vote for God"—he only knew he had to desecrate her temple. The first door he tried on the right was the choir room. Its windows faced the grassy courtyard by the parking lot, where the families were gathering their goblin troops, getting ready to go home. In the dim reflected light from the lampposts, Dell could see racks of choir robes along one wall and an upright piano facing crooked rows of folding chairs. Nothing worth desecrating here.

Dell withdrew and closed the door, continuing down the hall, bearing the drunken perfume of gardenia wherever he moved. The next door to the left was a windowless storeroom. Dell hazarded flipping on the light. Here were the altar linens, the candle snuffs, a couple of dusty prie-dieus. But the most unwieldy object was a great bronze plaque that used to be fixed to the church facade, proclaiming with Gothic certainty: NEIGHBORHOOD CONGREGATIONAL CHURCH.

What had replaced it on the church porch was a ribbon of glowing neon—FAMILY CHURCH OF ETERNAL LIGHT—but everyone knew the place as Mother Evangeline's. Here in the storeroom lay the quaint trappings of the old religion, pointless and shorn of power. Mother required none of it, preferring instead the video booth installed at the back of the sanctuary, giving her cable access beyond the dreams of a neighborhood preacher.

As Dell flipped off the light and continued down the hall, he could feel a curious memory trace of his days as an altar boy, when he'd wait for Father Diego to finish his confessions. Even at eight years old Dell kept his sins to himself. Bearing the holy water into Mass behind Father Diego, he'd known he was damned eternally, twice damned for daring to touch the implements of transfiguration, and all because he diddled his cousin Alvaro. Now he felt that strange thrill of damnation again, moving deeper into the dark.

He still wasn't sure what he wanted. Right now it seemed enough to be penetrating the secrets of his enemy. It wasn't an act of terrorism happening here, nothing so direct. He didn't need this to be public, didn't care what statement it made. This was just between him and her.

He opened the next door down the hall and entered. Right off, the smell reminded him of Marcus, though he couldn't place it. Not enough of a smell to make him cry. Once again the light from the lampposts in the courtyard filtered through the Venetian blinds. It was some kind of central office, partitioned into several desk areas. Of course: Marcus's office at school. A queer amalgam of ink and Xerox paper and the must of files.

Idly Dell moved from desk to desk, not even taking care to stay away from the windows, so magic had his intrusion become. Luckily he was wearing black. The paperwork on the desks appeared to be financial, dull as any other business, money in and out. Dell stooped and set the gardenia down on one of the desks, as if it had finally become too heavy.

Unconsciously he sniffed at one of the blossoms as he dug his hands into the luscious earth. He groped for the root ball, lifting it gently away from the pot. It came out easily, spraying dirt on the desk surface. Gently he set it down among the papers. No matter what chaos exploded in the next five minutes, the gardenia would remain inviolate, ready to be transplanted.

He reached again into the clay pot, scraped some earth to the side, and hefted out the wide-mouthed gallon jar he had hidden under the bush. Carefully Dell screwed off the lid, releasing into the dry-ink office air a smell that was rank and horribly sweet at once. Trying not to splash it, he tilted the jar and poured the blackness onto one of the desks, messing the papers. As he moved to the next desk and poured some more, already the smell had taken over, awful as the drain at a slaughterhouse.

A turkey farm, actually, out in Riverside. Dell had seen the advertisement in the *Times*—"Come out and pick your own bird for Thanksgiving!" He'd driven out that morning in his pickup and asked to buy some blood. The disconcerted farmer and his wife had never been asked that before. They tried to keep the whole experience free of blood. Their customers picked a feathered friend in the barnyard, and then later came back and picked it up, plucked and trussed and squeaky clean. They didn't even want to think what a dark-skinned man might want with blood. But Dell got the farmer aside and gave him fifty, so he shrugged and emptied the blood drain in the barn, straining out the feathers.

Now Dell had left a spoor of turkey blood on every surface around the room, ruining any work Mother's staff planned to pick up tomorrow, plus three IBM Selectrics. Then he moved to the filing cabinets along the wall opposite the windows. He pulled out a drawer and poured the slick and clotting liquid over the neatly ordered files. He didn't know what the files contained, but assumed they were part of Mother Evangeline's master plan of hate.

Already two-thirds of the gallon was gone, and he'd only completed one of the cabinets top to bottom. Now for the first time he doubted. With five more banks of files, he'd only made the smallest dent in the bureaucracy of hate, a single trunk line bombed as the engines roared to Dachau from every capital. Perhaps he should have poured the whole of it on the altar after all, like a terrible bodiless sacrifice, a gout of blood streaming from the cross. He stepped to the window and peered through the blinds. Only a few kids remained, still trying to play as their parents coaxed them toward the cars. Dell was seized by hopelessness, thinking about the four young men with the placards against this army of intolerance, a children's crusade in a thousand churches.

Dispiritedly he turned back to the room, moving past the filing cabinets. The far wall was dominated by a huge blowup photo of Mother Evangeline, standing in a field with her arms open, a sea of children gathered at her feet. This was the picture that usually accompanied the mailings of Eternal Light. It also appeared on a billboard on Route 10 to the high desert, where the church ran a retreat—eight hundred dollars for three nights in a tent on bread and water, to simulate the forty days and forty nights of Jesus.

Dell approached the photo wall and climbed on a chair. Until now he'd been quite fastidious as he flung the blood around, making sure none spattered on his hands or his costume. He'd put a thirty-five-dollar deposit down at Western Costume, and he never threw money away. But now he had reached the stage of having nothing to lose, so he tipped the jar and poured blood in his cupped hand. He was standing eye to eye with Mother as he smeared the offal across her face, digging his fingernails into the paper, scoring her cheeks.

The blood dripped through his fingers and sopped the black cuff of his costume. Again he took a handful and drooled it down her body in the picture. With a wet finger he began to write in the sky beside her head. D–E—dipping his finger in the mouth of the jar again—A–T–H. He meant that she was Death, but it felt good just to write on a wall, making the mark of his gang of one.

Only then did he notice that the counter below the blowup picture was covered with computer equipment. Two terminals with screens, a laser printer—all alien territory to him. But even in the dim banded light he could see the vents on every piece, so he happily tipped his jar and funneled blood into the works. There was something peculiarly atavistic in the gesture, a deeper clash of alien magic than blood on any cross.

As he finished the last of the jar, the final drips on the printer, it gave him the deepest satisfaction, acting like a gorilla. He was finished now, or at least his ammunition was. He set the jar down and was turning to go when he caught sight of the plastic unit at the end of the counter, like a miniature file cabinet. He felt a pang of defeat to think he'd overlooked something. He reached to wipe a bloody hand on it, then registered the printed sign along the top: MAILING LIST.

He pulled open one of the drawers, full of computer disks. It was like an electric surge, not knowing where a thing would lead him till he got there. He turned and gripped the clay pot, poured out the last of the dirt, then began removing the disks in bunches. He worked with incredible swiftness. Finally the stakes were high enough that he feared getting caught in the act. There were four drawers, about twenty-five disks in each, and the clay pot was nearly full to the brim by the time he was finished. Though he knew next to nothing about the technology, he could feel the weight of the names he was stealing—ten thousand strong, a million.

He skulked to the door and retraced his steps along the dark passage, the hero returning from hell with the devil's own address book. He reached the double doors that led to the courtyard. One bloody hand on the knob, he pushed it open enough to peer out.

The coast was clear, all the budding Hitler youth scattered to their homes, gnawing their candy. Dell capered out into the mist-shrouded night, bearing his vessel of names. The pickup truck was the only remaining vehicle in the parking lot. He stowed the clay pot among the shovels in the bed, then got in and peeled away.

He was light-headed with merriment, perversely enjoying the caked feel of his bloodied hands. He knew he stunk like Death itself. As he ran yellow lights on Alvarado, he grinned to think what a cop would do if he got pulled over, a Frankenstein monster covered with blood who'd taken the holiday too literally. But the magic of the moment held. Having got away with the store, he was a full-fledged outlaw now, at least for tonight. It would take an entire posse to catch him, marshals and G-men and vigilantes.

Traffic slowed as he came into Silverlake, low-riders out for an evening's haunt. In the next lane was a BMW with a het couple inside. They had noticed the ghoul in the pickup, and they were waving at him with unconcealed delight. Dell rolled the window down, twisted his face in an exaggerated grimace, and waved back. His red-streaked hand was grisly. The woman in the BMW gave out with a mock shriek of horror. Dell blinked a red-rimmed eye and announced with lascivious glee, "It's real."

When he reached the apartment complex and pulled into the garage, he wondered for a moment if he should have tossed the evidence, disposed it like a body in a dumpster. But it felt too good to heft it in his hand, bearing the urn up the back stairs to the garden court. Besides, somebody might want it for further mischief.

He stowed the pot in the utility closet at the back of the kitchen. Then he stripped off mask, wig, and jumpsuit and stuffed them in the trash, fastidious as a hatchet murderer. Fuck the thirty-five dollars. He tramped to the bathroom and turned on the shower. As he dried off after, the only evidence of his ghoul status was a faint red rim in the hollows of his eyes, where the circles were already dark and tortured. He pulled on a robe from behind the door, a robe that used to belong to Marcus, and he was moving toward the phone beside the bed when the doorbell rang.

It was only nine o'clock, the witching hour barely begun, but he knew it was Linda. He was always too proud or diffident to go across to her, and sometimes when he was on the sex line he didn't answer, pretending not to be home, though of course she knew he was. But tonight he could think of nothing better than talking to his sister, even if he couldn't tell her what he'd done.

He shrugged into a pair of Jockey shorts under the robe and hurried out to the living room. As he opened the door, he was already talking. "I hope you saved me some supper," he growled playfully, teasing her like a patriarch.

She stood with a shy smile under the porch light, a blanket over her arm. Instinctively he reached out a hand, but just then she moved back a step. "Lorenzo, this is Emilia," she said, drawing the other woman into the light.

She was dressed like Linda in jeans and a Mickey Mouse shirt, but was shorter and rounder, with a brown moon face and spiky hair. "Hey," said Emilia cheerfully, no shyness at all, "she never stop talkin' about you."

He was flustered right from the start, ashamed to be so undressed. He bustled them in, sat them down on the sofa, insisted on getting a bottle of wine. As he fumbled with the cork in the kitchen, he could hear her talking to Linda, chattering really. He couldn't make out the words, but the playful tone was clear, the bursts of laughter, so unlike the sober quietness of Dell and Linda. He tried not to feel resentful. He poured the wine into three jelly glasses, then dumped a bag of taco chips in a bowl and placed it on a tray with the wine. He was determined to make Linda proud.

He strode into the living room and set the tray on the table, gallantly offering glasses to the women. Animatedly he told them about the carnival crowd in West Hollywood, the opulent drag and celebrity send-ups. Emilia roared. Linda reached for the bowl of chips and offered them to her friend, who grabbed a fistful.

"This guy I do his house, he's a big fat queen," she said, plumping her own full breasts with cheeky nonchalance. "Every year he model his costume for me. This year he have a beaded gown, fit him real tight." She made a slinky motion with her hips, then took a gulp of wine, making a smacking noise as she set the glass down. Dell winced at the broken cadence of her English. "He not a pretty girl," Emilia clucked wryly.

How was she good to Linda, that's all he should care about. They had been seeing each other for weeks. She made Linda laugh, that much was obvious. They probably laughed in bed. No men ever laughed in bed anymore, he thought.

Somehow he missed the transition, as Linda took the folded blanket from the arm of the sofa where she'd laid it. "We brought this to show you before we send it," she said, modest again and not quite meeting his eyes. Even Emilia looked subdued now. Dell was puzzled, but he could see how excited his sister was as she moved to the dining-room table. He and Emilia followed. If Linda was happy, then nothing else mattered. As she began to unfold the blanket on the table, Emilia was beside him. She put an easy arm about his waist. So, he thought, they would be a family, and Linda would have somebody when he got sick and died.

She undid the last fold and drew it out to its full width, holding the two corners where it flowed off the table. It was a flag, he thought at first, green on a yellow ground. Then he read the name sewn in red across the center—MARCUS FLINT—and below that the dates. The green figures were cutouts like Mayan glyphs, appliquéd around the name. Dell stared without any expression.

"It's for the big quilt," said Linda breathlessly. "The one that was in Washington. Emilia did one for her husband too."

He could feel Emilia squeeze his waist, and he stepped away, bending to study the panel closely because he didn't know who to look at or how he felt.

"I a widow two years," declared Emilia. "My husband, he get it from a needle."

There wasn't any superiority in the disclosure, just the matter of fact. But Dell Espinoza got angry at infinitely smaller things. He felt a spurt of white rage at the slovenly stranger beside him, bearing her official heterosexual grief, but because he was in pain he turned it on his sister. "Haven't you had enough yet?" he demanded in a seething whisper, watching Linda's eyes flinch. "When are you gonna start to live your life, huh?"

Emilia seemed to move back a couple of paces. In any case, she ceased to exist; now she was no longer family. "I'm sorry," said Linda, her voice quavering, fighting to endure the punishment stoically, without tears. "It's like a memorial, all of them together. We don't have to be so alone."

Dell made a slashing motion with his hand, cutting the sentiment off. "He wasn't your husband," he trumpeted with savage contempt. His hand thumped his bare chest, a gorilla again. "He was *my* husband."

A wave of tears was in her eyes, but she would not let them spill. She still held the corners of the quilt panel. Carefully she folded it again, closing the window on memory. In the tense silence that followed, she tucked it as carefully, as ceremoniously as a flag off a coffin. When she was done she hugged it to her chest and would not meet his eyes. He was furious at her shame, her cowering submissiveness. It wasn't what he meant at all.

"I won't send it," she said quietly.

He wanted to gather her into his arms. She didn't know she was the only thing keeping him from the edge, the last thing of life that mattered. But he was stuck in his foolish pride like any of his moron brothers-in-law, ridiculed by the love he had gotten wrong between the two women. It almost made him feel cuckolded. "Send it," he said, cold and blunt. "I don't want it around here."

She nodded and stepped by him, and he didn't reach out with an aching hand. Emilia, sober as a sentry by the door, fell into step with Linda as they headed outside. *"Buenos nochas,"* the plump woman said punctiliously, bowing to her host as she left.

And now it was as if it hadn't happened at all, his victory over the forces of darkness. The million names of his enemies frittered away in the closet. His mask was over, his brazen disguise evaporated like the wisp of an old nightmare. He stood dumbstruck in his borrowed robe, neither reveler nor spectator, and couldn't even make himself plod to the phone for a little relief. The darkness was over the world, and he and Linda would never escape it. Half alive, they would wander the world like ghouls, locked in a death embrace, afraid to love anything else except each other.

146

8

"Hey, wake up and smell the coffee, guys. I'm alive." The sandy-haired boy hunkered on the upper bench, elbows on his knees, his rangy frame like that of a cowboy sitting astride a fence. "This group is a fuckin' downer," said Andy, caustic with contempt. "Sometimes I think you guys wanna die."

"Excuse us, Mary Sunshine," said the thin gray man. "If your life's such a dream, then why don't you join a Tupperware group? We like a little reality here."

"I, not we," cautioned Tim with an upraised finger.

The planeload of refugees numbered about twelve tonight. Sometimes there were twenty-five or thirty, lined up body to body on the carpeted benches. But all the regulars were here. Charlene, philosophical and far too patient, knitting her cocoa hands quietly in her lap. Emmett from Tallahassee, who lost his heart twice in October, unrequited, and stood determined to be in love by Christmas. The bearded uncle, Fred, racked with certainty that his mom would be putting the star on the tree this year for the last time.

But please, they had Thanksgiving to get through first. November 11, and already the holidays yawned before them like a primal swamp, full of the bones of mastodons and the bodies of lost explorers. Nobody in the group had informed his blood family about his antibody status, except for the thin gray man, whose people had basically told him to make a reservation for one with a TV dinner. Several members of the group were planning to make the annual pilgrimage to home and hearth, and dread was thick. Not that they didn't feel it every year, but now the stakes were dizzily raised by what could not be said.

"It's bad enough they ask if I'm seeing someone," said Marina, looking lost tonight in her big Italian sweater. "They knew Jim died, but they don't know how. They keep waiting for me to get over it. My sisters'll flaunt their kids, and I'll want to die."

"Uh-uh—don't use the 'D' word," Mark piped in, and a ripple of black laughter went around the little room.

"Sorry," said Marina, wincing. "But how do I sit there smiling and passing the gravy, pretending I'm dating, when all I want to do is crawl in my mother's bed and cry?"

No answer. The gay men looked at the floor and the ceiling, unable to imagine such a wish. Tim the facilitator licked his lips delicately and offered: "So maybe you should tell them?"

"And ruin Thanksgiving?" retorted Marina, bitter and comic at once. "You think they'll care? We're talking Chula Vista. My sisters'd have their kids out of there in five minutes. And Mother would spray me with Lysol."

"Or Raid," said Emmett, thick as Florida honey.

Steven was detached as ever, sitting beside the one narrow window looking down on Highland, but he'd also developed a certain idle affection for the Thursday group. After five weeks he found himself perking up at the next chapter—Emmett's two-week fling with the dancer, Charlene's mother and grandmother who shared a room and didn't speak. He could see how the thin gray man was more peaked every week, the slight catarrh in his throat more pronounced. The group didn't really talk about how it would change if one of them got sick. It was part of the magic of meeting like this that they would keep the full-blown nightmare at bay if they just stayed in a circle.

No one knew very much about Steven yet. Like the others, he gave himself over to small talk before and after the meetings, always exchanging a word with Marina. But he rarely spoke in the meeting proper, confining himself to chiming in when the group cheered or groaned. By doing so he seemed to ventriloquize the feelings that otherwise escaped him. He didn't dare verbalize certain things, like his suspicion that Dell Espinoza was the Halloween saboteur. He shrank from knowing for certain, trying instead to keep his focus simple, like the rest of the group. Just to stay healthy, one step ahead of the creeping horror.

"I hate my friends who haven't been touched," said a stocky man on the bench below Steven. It was his second time here, and he'd cried last time. He didn't sound proud of what he just said. The room stirred with a murmur of guilty agreement. "The straight ones I can't even talk to anymore. They all say the same thing: 'You're not gonna get sick.' That just means they don't want to hear about it. And my roommate's negative, so he doesn't give a shit. He's got the rest of his life."

He stopped. It seemed as if he would cry again. The entire group poised to hug him. But he caught himself with a huge sigh that lifted the weight from his belly to his chest. He shook his head, ashamed of hating, and the group was silent a moment, ashamed too.

And Steven was thinking about the roommate: negative. Was anyone he knew negative? He couldn't imagine such a thing. For years, it seemed, ever since Spot appeared on Victor's ankle, he had assumed the worst scenario, that all gay men would die. Of course he meant the urban ones, and lately at least he'd come to see that the young ones would squeak through. But nobody he knew. They had connected one with another all too well. And though he heard now and then about somebody testing negative, he put no faith in it. The test was bullshit like everything else. Some time bombs ticked louder than others, and some were hidden very deep in the caves of a man, but still it was only a matter of time. In the black hole of his grief, Steven had taken some comfort in that, and he felt no guilt at all.

The thin gray man groaned with exasperation. "This is a big revelation to you, that straight people don't care? Where have you been? They just want us to shut up and cut their hair."

"Hey, chill out," snarled Marina. "It was us straight people knocked down 81." This was true. Just last week the quarantine proposition had gone down to defeat, fifty-three to forty-seven, surprising the pollsters and pundits.

"Gimme a break," scoffed the thin gray man. "You want to know who fucked Prop 81? The guy with the blood. He scared all the breeders. They decided to protect our useless civil rights so we won't go psycho on em."

"Easy, easy," said Tim, "we're getting on soapboxes again." He smiled around at his group, blaming no one. He was as drab as his turd-brown sleeveless sweater and the leatherette clipboard he held on his knee. Yet his very blandness served as a kind of anchor, backing them off from confrontation. "Remember, we're here to support each other. Let's try to say what we need and give it. Find the feeling."

This last was delivered in a Zen-like hush. There passed between Marina and the thin gray man a small nod of truce. It was like grammar school, thought Steven, learning how to behave for the teacher.

"Look, I'll be honest," said Andy. "I came here to get laid." The dumb laugh that erupted here was more like junior high, somewhere behind the boys' gym. "No, I'm serious. I thought this was going to be like a dating pool."

A bouffant queen with a murderous manicure, very Joan Crawford, stroked an eyebrow. "We call it a cesspool now, darling."

"I don't want to be with a guy who's not positive," continued Andy, ignoring the bitchy intrusion. "But he's gotta want to beat it as much as I do."

"Oh, you can beat it just as good yourself," drawled Miss Crawford, but no one laughed.

"Are you taking applications?" asked Mark, smiling across at Andy.

"Not from you guys. You're all just waiting to die."

"I resent that," blurted one of the new recruits, fierce in a Silverlake leather vest.

And they started the round again, just like they did every week, about whether it was worth it to get close to someone who might get sick. They would split down the middle as usual, between the romantics, who wanted to seize the day, galloping on white stallions toward the cliff, and the pragmatists, who wanted a little unentangled nooky but nothing more. Paramount was immunity, and whether love would boost your numbers or stress you out.

Steven tuned out of the discussion and watched the night traffic below on Highland, the straggling homeless shuffling up and down. The mere idea of courting someone was exhausting, like hauling cement uphill. Not to mention the rejection.

At least he was over Mark. Maybe not over the ache or the awkwardness, but the bristle of expectation had finally abated. He could tell, because he wasn't wiggy with jealousy watching Mark's casual flirt with the sandy-haired boy. Over four different lunches they'd talked it through about Sonny and the peeping Tom, managing some how to laugh about it, as if it were some kind of porn fantasy gone awry. They gave their predictable alibis. Mark ruefully hung his head, bemoaning his need for meaningless sex, passion without feeling, something he had been working on in therapy since Sonny Cevathas was eight years old. Steven pinned his own behavior on grief, the usual suspect. The loneliness and brokenness had left him with his nose against the window, watching life from the outside. He apologized for the laughable wrongheadedness of being hung up on Mark. Mark, they decided together, was just a symbol anyway.

But though they determined to put it behind them, a perceptible shadow had fallen. They still pretended to make plans every day to tool around like buddies, but half the time they canceled. Errands blew up out of nowhere, or one of them had the sniffles, or Steven was holding Margaret's hand in Ray Lee's room at Cedars. Worse, there was a palpable sadness when they did connect, as if their friendship had gone too far and they didn't know what to replace it with. Didn't know how to undo the nakedness.

There had been no repeat performance with Sonny. He was still in residence in the room beyond the garage, which may have been masochistic on Steven's part. He would have made a terrible landlord, a regular doormat. In any case, Sonny stayed rigorously out of his way for days afterward, all the while making himself indispensable with chores and little fix-it projects. Perhaps Steven let him stay to prove it didn't matter—plus a dogged sort of pride in keeping things intact, no matter how problematic.

Mark incidentally swore that he had barely gotten it up that night, despite Sonny's sultry demeanor and a mouth as foul as the Master Mario video. This was part of a larger picture Mark took pains to clarify, over cup after cup of decaf capuccino—that sex didn't mean anything to him anymore, he could take it or leave it. He didn't expect to solve that puzzle, not in the time he had left. Whenever he said it, he seemed to hope Steven would feel better, not take it somehow so personally. Fat chance.

Yet he looked across at Mark now, sitting between Marina and Uncle Fred, and felt the oddest dispassion. He didn't suppose he had loved Mark at all, nothing beyond the blur of infatuation, or just the idea of filling the empty hole in his heart. Meanwhile, the only notable change in his own dysfunction was a most ambiguous gift of heat. Now he jerked himself off at night, sometimes snapping a cockring on, sometimes a full trussing with the rawhide. Even in the fugue state of desirelessness that gripped him after Victor's death, he had managed to whip it up once or twice a month, but now it was every night. He'd even stocked in a few stroke books. But the fantasies were very careful—never Mark, certainly never Victor. In fact, he found himself roaming way back, to Boston fifteen years ago or his randy first summer in Europe, dicks of the ancient world. The deep past was the one safe place where a man could still let go.

"I ain't *never* had a date," declared Charlene with comic wistfulness, and Steven shook his self-absorption. "Girls I know," said Charlene, "they don't expect a man. They just wanna have chirren."

Charlene was the thirdest world among them by a long shot, however disenfranchised the militant gay ones felt. They never knew what to say to her, an ex-hooker with two kids no father would claim, four generations of women accordioned into an apartment off Pico. Yet Charlene never truly complained, so accustomed was she to bad shit, and seemed content with the sheer diversion of Thursday's men.

"Seem like you boys wanna fall in love awful bad," she drawled. "You better get movin', huh? I got me my chirren, where's your man? Time goin'. Stop *talkin'* about it."

A fitting enough end to a night of talking in circles. Tim announced there would be no meeting two weeks hence, on account of the dreaded holiday, and suggested they all come back next Thursday prepared to do some role-playing around the turkey issue. Instantly the mood was lighter as they fell to talking one on one. They'd all OD'd on angst and romantic longing, and now all they wanted to do was keep it simple and go have coffee with a Thursday comrade.

But not Steven, who grabbed his jacket and prepared to make a beeline for the door. He'd talked to Marina before the meeting, so there were no further courtesies required. He was over the threshold when Mark called out: "Hey, Steven, wait up, will you?"

Steven didn't turn around, but he stopped in the hall outside, staring at a safe-sex poster which showed a woman putting a condom on a banana. Just as well that they had five minutes together now—they wouldn't have to talk in the morning and pretend to want lunch, only to cancel by noon. Steven smiled and murmured good night to Uncle Fred, Charlene, the stocky man. When Andy stopped beside him and grinned, Steven had the queer-est impulse to look over his shoulder, assuming the grin was for somebody else.

"You run away so fast, I never get a chance to talk to you."

"About what?" asked Steven, genuinely baffled.

The boy laughed heartily, as if Steven was irrepressibly witty. "I'm Andy Lakin," he said, extending a hand that Steven didn't want to shake. He was old enough to be the kid's father. "You're Steven. Marina says you've been all over the world."

"Not unless they've got room service," Steven replied with instant caution. Since when did the others talk about his non-AIDS life? That wasn't the deal. "And not anymore."

"Well, I've never been anywhere. And I don't want to die without seeing Paris. Or the pyramids."

"Uh-huh." What did the kid want, brochures? Steven squirmed with displacement, and then saw with relief that Mark was coming out of the rap room. He turned and deliberately cut Andy off, perking his face toward Mark, but in the same motion trying not to look too eager. Nothing was simple. Mark, expressionless himself, didn't really notice the mood swings of Steven's face.

"They denied my disability," Mark declared flatly. "Lou screwed me."

Steven knew exactly what it meant. Unless Mark got a new job, his insurance would be gone in three months. Even assuming he wanted to work again, he was uninsurable, since the virus was catch-22—a preexisting condition. All Steven could think to say was "What are you going to do?" and he had the good sense to bite his tongue instead. Mark looked more beaten than ever, as if he hadn't been able quite to feel it till he could speak it to Steven.

"Cocksucker," Steven growled, finding the right pitch at last. Mark gave out with a short dry laugh more raw than tears, and Steven said, "Come on, we'll go have coffee." The rules of their disengagement were temporarily suspended.

But Mark flicked an eye to Steven's left and replied mildly, "I think you're busy," with the slightest ironic emphasis on the *you*, as if the shoe were on the other foot at last. Steven furrowed his brow in confusion, even as Mark softly punched his shoulder. "It's okay, we'll talk tomorrow," said Mark, gliding away and down the stairs.

Leaving Steven blinking in disbelief at Andy, who still hovered attendance. All the others had left by now. They were alone beside the picture of the starlet and the banana. "So you want to go to Paris," said Steven in his most neutral voice, one hand automatically reaching for the wallet where he no longer carried his Shaw Travel cards.

"Well, eventually," said Andy, brimming with mirth again. "Right now I'd like to go grab a burger with you."

"Uh..." Steven looked as if he needed to go to the bathroom, but also as if he meant to hold it till he got home.

"Look, do I have to draw you a map?"

Steven stared at him. He couldn't actually remember the last time a man had come on to him. He felt like a total asshole for being so thickheaded, though he could see that in Andy's eyes he was simply playing hard to get. He was amazed at the kid's cheek, and not a little moved by his willingness to be vulnerable.

"Listen, it's not you," Steven declared with a certain fervor, feeling as if he were turning down a date for the prom with the class geek. "I'm just not available. Here," he added, thumping his chest, where two weeks ago he would have thumped his gonads.

"For a *burger?* Look, I don't want to marry you. I just want to talk to a grown-up."

And still Steven blanched, because that was precisely the last thing he felt like. Andy tossed his head and made a bleating sound—half disgust, half despair—and turned to go down the stairs. It suddenly seemed pathetically absurd, to be so defended. All the ruinous pride that had kept him silent in the group came crashing down around him. He tramped down the stairs, past the dyke at the phone bank, groping his way through the knot of fallen angels hanging about the coffee machine.

He caught up with Andy on the curb outside, kicking his Reebok idly against a parking meter. They looked at each other warily. Steven shrugged and pointed across Highland to All-American Burger. They stuffed their hands in their pockets and crossed against the traffic, Steven suppressing a guilty need to look over his shoulder, in case somebody he knew should see them.

Andy Lakin hadn't been entirely honest, of course. He openly admitted now he was looking for something permanent, and always had his radar out for an older man with a sterling record. Steven's eight-year stint with Victor was thus like money in the bank. This was all shared with such unflinching candor that Steven wasn't sure if the kid was being ingenuous or disingenuous or both. Having grilled Marina two Thursdays running, Andy seemed to know all about him, requiring no further details. And so he filled the glaring fast-food time—the burgers speared with little American flags—relating his own rueful tale of near misses.

Steven relaxed and drank two mocha shakes, realizing there was no pressure to take the kid home to bed. He only wondered why he didn't want to—the eagerness was endearing enough, bright as the agate eyes and the dust of freckles below the tousle of hair. Ann Arbor, Michigan, twenty-six, played hockey in high school. Steven found himself wondering what Mark would have done, how he would have found a way to strip that eagerness bare. What he wouldn't think about was Victor being the same age when they met. As if the life of Steven Shaw—the usefulness of the past, the gathering of what little wisdom—stood utterly discounted, giving him no clue whatever.

"But you think we can beat it, don't you?" asked Andy, half a dare. "Everyone's not gonna die."

Steven shrugged. "Not right away, anyway. Some guys'll probably make it twenty years. So you might as well live like you have a future." He didn't think this at all, not a quarter of twenty years, but he wasn't going to be the one to challenge Andy's stubborn optimism. He was secretly pleased that Andy saw him as some kind of renegade in the group. His silence had somehow come across as disdain for the general carping of Thursday's men.

"So tell me about Victor," said Andy when his plate was empty, every last fry. Ingenuous surely, but dis- around the edges even so.

The question Steven had managed to duck or otherwise freeze in its tracks, never asked once since Victor died. Perhaps because he avoided anyone new. Yet for some reason it didn't threaten or annoy him now—something to do with the agate eyes and the curious Michigan trust, as if Andy really believed Steven Shaw possessed some special key to love.

So he talked, he who'd avoided a bereavement group and fired his shrink and stuffed the condolences in a shoebox. About locking eyes with Victor at a New Year's party in Venice, and ending up two hours later twenty miles up the coast at Zuma, wind-whipped and rolling in the sand as the eighties dawned. How they mightily resisted falling in love—four months, six months, still trying to stay apart two nights a week.

"The *last* thing Victor wanted to be was a couple," said Steven, his cheeks high-colored, in a whiskey voice, as if he were teasing Victor himself. "He couldn't stand them. He loved being single."

"So how did you get it to work?"

"My immense charm," retorted Steven. "Plus three weeks in Europe living like princes. He'd never been anywhere either."

He smiled across at Andy, making the bridge. The boy blushed easily, owing to his fair complexion, and insisted on paying the check, as if to prove he wasn't looking for any free ride. He was assiduous in fact, as they walked to Steven's car, about explaining that he understood completely. No wonder Steven wasn't ready for something new, after being twinned so deep. It would come in its own time, somebody totally different—certainly not another eager boy who'd never been anywhere. Andy was as unflinching in his pulling back as he had been coming on.

They stood with the door to the Volvo between them, Steven about to get inside, and Andy leaned over and kissed him chastely on the lips. "I'm just glad to know there's men out there who've made it happen," he said with appalling sincerity, a smile as wide as Lake Michigan. "Gives me hope."

Which left Steven exactly where he started, not wanting to get entangled, not wanting to be pursued. He drove away up Highland, and the wave that passed between them was a last wave—the ship pulling away from the dock. So why did Steven find himself flashing deliciously hot and cold? Though he'd just had a date that went nowhere, hardly worth a check-in call with Margaret, he felt as if he'd pulled off something quite extravagant, back in the tenth grade stealing a girl from Daryl Sawyer. A girl he didn't want, but let that go. More than anything it seemed to prove he was over Mark Inman once and for all.

He and Mark didn't talk that night or over the weekend, not in person, leaving a cluster of messages on each other's machine. Very nice messages, breezy and open-hearted, Mark full of tough assurance that he didn't give two shits about his disability. Perhaps one or two of the messages were left in the Hollywood way, at those vague dusky hours when no one was ever at home. And Sunday afternoon Ray Lee was released from Cedars. Steven had to be there literally to carry him up the stairs to his apartment. So he wasn't exactly avoiding Mark—just processing other things.

After only two weeks in, Ray Lee was as frail as a ten-year-old, sitting propped up in his little sofa bed and swearing he needed no help, he'd be back to work in a week. That was hard to imagine, since the stroke had left his hand too limp to hold a pencil and his mouth drooped to the left as if it were melting off his face. He could speak all right, if a little slowly, but the crackling hipness had disappeared. Ray Lee had always sounded as American as TV, and suddenly overnight there was a halting Korean accent hovering in his voice, as if he'd begun to emigrate home.

Margaret, of course, collapsed. She'd been on hospital watch for two weeks straight, and now she had to coordinate meals-on-wheels.

Steven took her out for dinner on Sunday night and let her cry. Her proud mane of hair was drawn back in a schoolmarm's bun. Victor used to tell her she was getting better-looking every day, ripe to be plucked by a zillionaire mogul. All of which seemed very remote tonight at Loretta's Shanghai Kitchen.

"This is the last one," said Margaret with bitter emphasis between bites of cashew chicken. "I'll go to the end. It's not going to be long, I can tell that already. But that's *it*. All the beautiful young men of West Hollywood will have to die without Margaret Kirkham's help. I go over to Richard's to spend the night, and all I do is cry. Real sexy."

Steven murmured agreement, whatever she said, and scarfed the tangerine beef. He didn't raise the obvious technical objection: present company excluded. Of course she'd be there for him, right down to the last handhold, bone-thin and purple with lesions, whatever final horror took him. But meanwhile she kept that corner of her mind uncluttered, believing it wouldn't happen, not to Steven. This was the standard het denial, which came up all the time at the Thursday meeting, infuriating everyone, but Steven was just as glad that Margaret had the breathing room of some small illusion. When it finally hit him full force, Steven already knew he would check out sooner than later, for Margaret's sake alone. He couldn't bear to think of her losing the dusty flower of her second youth on his account.

Meanwhile, he would shoulder some of the burden, which kept him running around for the next two days—renting a wheelchair, retrieving Ray's Siamese from the pet hotel, the small and mindless stuff so that Margaret would have some down time, which she spent watching forties noir thrillers on Ray's VCR. The two of them looked pretty noir themselves as Steven arrived with takeout from Pollo Loco—Margaret in robe and peignoir like Gloria Grahame in a lonely place, and Ray Lee curled with his head in her lap, inscrutable as Anna May Wong.

In any case, he didn't talk to Mark for real till Tuesday night. "Are you sure this isn't your machine?" Steven asked impishly when Mark picked up. The answer came back in a monotone: "No, it's me."

And that was about all Steven got out of him, not exactly a stone wall but nearly. Depressed, not hiding it, but nothing to say about it either. And Steven wasn't good enough at bullshit to tell him not to feel it. Despair was part of the cycle. So instead Steven told him about Ray Lee, and they both knew what he was really saying, that this was how the monster would come to them if it hit the nervous system first.

"It'll be in his brain next," declared Mark grimly. "Then he won't care if he's paralyzed."

"You know," ventured Steven, seeing they had dead-ended on the poor Korean, "if it's money you're worried about—"

"You don't get it, do you, Steven?" Mark's voice quickened with anger, as if he'd been waiting to have the chip knocked off. "You're too honest—you never swam with barracudas. Listen, I got *money* money. Stock options, last year's bonus—two hundred grand cash, plus my house. That's enough to die on, even if I last five years. But I don't want to die on *my* dime. I want that fuckin' disability so *they* have to pay." The tone here wasn't exactly loud or savage, it was cold, ice cold. Steven waited, working overtime like a saint not to take it personally. Mark shifted to withering irony. "You forget, darling, until two months ago I was a scumbag TV executive. You didn't know me. All I did all day was screw people with money. Stuffing it up their hole."

"So how about dinner tomorrow?"

"And now that they've screwed *me*, you know what I'd like to do? Pour blood all over their office, just like that terrorist out there. I'd like to see Lou Ciotta prancing around on his show, him so cute in his underwear, and he opens a beer and takes a swig and spits it out. 'Cause it's blood."

"I'll pick you up at eight, we'll go have Chinese." Big of Steven, whose heart still burned from the tangerine beef, but he couldn't answer rage for rage. He was only trying to give it room, like Margaret's exhaustion.

"Look, I'm better off by myself right now," said Mark, milder now and almost apologetic. "It's nothing to do with you. I get in these black moods—even before AIDS. I just have to sit with it." Steven nodded gravely, not wanting to say the wrong thing. He thought they'd pretty much wound it up when Mark threw a final curve. "So how was Andy Lakin?"

"Oh...nothing," Steven blurted, suddenly feeling cornered. "I mean, he's very earnest. I told him I wasn't available."

"Why not? He's got a great ass."

"Yeah, well, there's this small problem about my dick." Which was a lie now, of course. The instrument in question had been quivering like a tuning fork these days. Yet he seemed to want to hide it, as if the recovery of his carnal edge might somehow threaten Mark.

"Steven, you think too much."

They let it go at that. Still Steven would have pressed it again on Wednesday, maybe even done the unthinkable—driven over to Skyway Lane and dropped in with takeout. His life was a constant round of takeout now, and what was one more stop? But then, Wednesday turned out to be a nightmare start to finish, so he didn't have time to think. Ray Lee had an appointment with the eye doctor, and Margaret's car wouldn't start, so Steven had to pick them up and run them over to Cedars.

They sat all three in the front seat, Ray Lee regaling Steven with the plot of a stinko B, Ida Lupino and Robert Stack, convict on the lam holing up on a widow's farm. "Lotsa chickens, lotsa heartache," Ray Lee concluded, lilting the air with a delicate fine-boned hand—the hand that still worked. In the eye clinic waiting room he vamped about whether he might need glasses, promising himself a pair of tortoiseshells from L.A. Eyeworks. "Please, I rather be fashion victim than AIDS victim."

None of them said a word about the deeper issue—that if he was having neurological problems, overnight the horror might seep into the bright jet of his eyes. There were blind men all over West Hollywood now, some who saw shadows, some who saw Christmas lights, and four or five of them were sitting right there in the clinic, staring at nothing.

While Ray Lee was in with the doctor, Margaret told Steven he had to go by the office and pay the bills—by the fifteenth or the phone would be turned off. Steven felt a spurt of irrational rage, to think he had to take care of his own affairs, and as if it was all Margaret's fault. Which made him plummet with guilt, so that when Ray Lee came out of the eye exam with his sight intact, dancing in his wheelchair, Steven invited them both for Thanksgiving.

"*You*'re going to do Thanksgiving?" Margaret asked, incredulous.

"Well, sure, why not? We've always done it."

"Victor, you mean," she observed skeptically.

Touché. Last year Steven had spent the whole of Thursday under the covers, sobbing over the Macy's parade. But he'd been planning it ever since his last encounter with Dr. Buckey, even if he hadn't quite got his invitations out. Things being lately blurred with Mark, the moment never seemed right for making party plans. He'd been keeping his options open as to the guest list all along, with a vague idea of springing it on them the day before, so they wouldn't have time to dread it.

Ray Lee gave out with a shriek of delight, drowning Margaret's irony, and promised to make creamed onions and mince pie. "With a lattice crust," he enthused breathlessly, flashing his crooked smile at Steven, right side grinning, left side down, a Noh mask of the tragicomic.

An hour later, Shaw Travel was as still as Pharaoh's tomb. Inside the door where the letter slot dumped was a daunting pile of mail. Steven stepped over it as if it were a body and went around to Margaret's desk. He flipped the phone machine to playback, turned the volume up, then waded back into the mail. As the messages began to spill out, he pawed through the endless brochures and come-ons, trying to sort out the bills.

They'd been closed for only sixteen days, but it seemed like years. Call after call swept over him, people wanting holiday reservations, sometimes leaving three or four messages before they gave up. Old customers were especially persistent, leaving word for Margaret or Steven himself, cuddly with familiarity: "Fran and I want to go someplace special for Christmas. Some inn in the middle of no-where—big fireplace, no phones. You know what we like."

Steven found the phone bill, water and power, American Express. As he padded around to retrieve the checkbook from Margaret's desk, the calls grew increasingly desperate. A party of forty-eight teachers bound for a convention in Vegas gave up on the third try. Various gay professionals, used to princess treatment, sounded more and more wounded with every call. "I'm missing all the discounts," they whined, then pettishly rang off. The husband of Fran left a little mini-lecture, the text of which was I-scratch-your-ass-you-scratch-mine, and therefore Margaret shouldn't expect a discount anymore at Fran's killer boutique on Beverly Drive.

Frankly, by the time Steven had written the three checks, he wondered if they had any business left at all. He looked around at the silent office, no more eager to dive back in than ever. Ray Lee was out of there for good, and Margaret had made not a peep when they passed the two-week limit on the office closure. There was nobody left. But while the thought of closing down made Steven wince with emptiness, even that finality couldn't make him throw himself back in. He couldn't do this and tick at the same time. Could only keep himself from not waiting to die by staying adrift of time. And Shaw Travel was time-obsessed—every departure down to the minute, every checkout, every three-day cruise to nowhere.

Then, after a call from a frantic woman on Maui who'd missed her connecting flight, came a soft and tentative voice. "Hi, it's Heather. I don't know who's picking up messages, but I owe you all an apology. I feel just terrible. It's because I was scared, but that's no excuse. I want to see Ray, and I want to come back to work if you'll have me. You're the most fun people I ever met. Tell Ray I make a meatloaf that's to die."

Well now, wasn't that fortuitous? Shaw Travel would snatch victory from the jaws of defeat, all because Heather had faced her fear of death. Good for her! Steven felt positively lumpy with sentiment as he flipped the phone machine back to answer. He would make her Assistant Office Manager and send her on the next free gig from Princess Cruises. He'd call her tonight, and the agency would reopen again by morning.

He closed the door behind him with relief, still without a clue what the cash flow was these days, how close to the brink. What he was really thinking driving home was: if she made a dynamite meatloaf, she could probably pull together a passable sausage dressing for the turkey.

When he got to the house, he called Mark, not to push for tonight but to rope him in for the Norman Rockwell feast. Nobody home, and he didn't want to leave it on the machine, so he hung up. He stood in the dining-room doorway and studied his table. Nine: Ray Lee and Margaret and Richard and Mark and Sonny and Heather and him—

The doorbell. For some reason, as he moved to the foyer, he was certain it was Mark, as if he'd pulled him here by telepathic means. He threw open the door laughing. But no: a lean and pony-tailed Latina in jeans and a Mickey Mouse T-shirt. Immediately she looked away shyly from Steven's laugh. She was frightened, almost trembling, like a deer caught out of cover. Steven composed a meek and helpful smile, assumed she wanted to sell him something, or collect for some desperate cause. At last she sought his eyes again, miserable but trying not to plead.

"I'm sorry—I'm Linda Espinoza."

He didn't connect it right away, offering his own name in return, trying not to sound patronizing. She nodded as if she knew it already, presumably working from a canvasing list. She looked sad enough to be a Democrat. Then, because she could see he was still in the dark, she added with a certain stubborn dignity, "Dell's my brother."

Steven beamed. "Well, of course he is," he said eagerly, bustling her into the house. And she didn't get a word in edgeways for the next two minutes. He put a light on under the kettle, chattering all the while about Thanksgiving dinner. How he had meant to invite them all along, and there he'd been working out the seating when she rang.

To her he seemed slightly delirious, which maybe he was, with so many balls in the air. But something about him had seized on the holiday, something to do with pulling a family together around Ray Lee, who might not last till Christmas. Something to counter the awful gathering of blood clans everywhere, hiding their distances one from another, smothering them in gravy.

"Don't feel you have to cook or anything," Steven hastened to assure her, "but if there's something special you're good at and you have the time—"

He turned to hand her a mug of tea and saw the patience in her eyes. He held his breath to hear, and she spoke: "Dell's in trouble. He's the one trashed that church."

Of course, he'd known it all along. She was fighting back tears. He led her into the dining room and sat her down exactly where he planned to have her next week. Brokenly she told him about the police arriving with a subpoena. Dell had left a trail that was ridiculously easy to follow. Several of Mother Evangeline's parishioners had seen the pickup truck from which the ghoul emerged. Once it was ascertained that the blood was turkey, it was simple to track down the farmer in Riverside. Even a rookie could have followed the trail to the thirty-five-dollar deposit at Western Costume.

It all converged this morning at Dell's apartment, the banging of the police rousing Linda across the court. When they got no answer, they broke down Dell Espinoza's door. The mistake they made was coming at seven, when the gardener was always out by six. They found the tapes in the kitchen cabinet. They told Linda her brother was wanted for desecrating a church, for tampering with the mails, for attempted murder.

"He tried to *kill* somebody?"

"Because of the reservoir. They say he try to give people AIDS."

Finally she let out some of the tears, not squalls of them like Margaret did, but a few small sobs with her shoulders hunched. Steven laid a hand gently on her arm and murmured like a lullaby. He was juggling so many cases at the moment, he wasn't sure how much he had left to offer. Besides, his first instinct was fury at Dell for putting his sister through this, so if Steven did rush in to help, it would be for Linda's sake. And if Dell Espinoza thought he was going to ruin Thanksgiving, he was sorely mistaken.

"Where is he now?"

"He's at my friend Emilia's, but he can't stay. She's afraid her kids'll get hurt. He's waiting for me to call him."

"And tell him what? That he can stay here?"

He didn't say it so roughly, but her silence told him he was right. She took a deep breath. Steven looked forlornly past her into the living room, where the big leather sofa hadn't seen someone sleep over since they had nurses around the clock. He pictured what the terrified Emilia must be imagining: a shootout by the L.A. police,

Sheriff Noonan announcing to the Minicam crews that they'd bring him out dead or alive. Even if she survived, they'd send Emilia back to Mexico on a slow boat. Ruefully Steven conceded that his house would work much better for a shootout—no minors involved, nobody to deport.

"All right, but just for a few days," he said, and even as she clasped his hand in gratitude, he recalled saying something of the same sort to Sonny, and that was almost a month ago.

Only after Steven had agreed to give her brother sanctuary did Linda begin to pour out all her terror. How she had seen him withdraw deeper and deeper for months now, willfully almost—the opposite of putting the passion of his grief behind him, letting it fade to a dull ache the way it had with her. Dell Espinoza's passion only seemed to grow more violent and secret. In the month that followed the anniversary, she thought he was going to kill himself, and could even feel that the one thing holding him back was Linda herself—the last protective urge he felt as head of the family.

That was the word she kept using: passion. Rather formal and only half-translated, as if it meant something far more intricate in Spanish. Steven had never thought of grief quite that way before, like some kind of sexual hunger. Carnal and driven, obsessive, consuming. But he also understood what Linda meant, for the white-hot passion in Steven himself had dwindled at last to a quiet throb, like a broken bone that ached in the rain.

"He'll listen to you," said Linda. "You lost what he lost. Maybe you'll help him get rid of the anger, so it won't eat him up anymore."

Steven made all the right noises, promising to be a sounding board for her wayward brother, but in fact he didn't expect to make the slightest dent in the gardener's rage. He wasn't even sure he wanted to, startled instead to find himself feeling a surge of pride. He liked the idea of having his very own anarchist. Besides, he knew Dell well enough from fifty widowers' Saturdays to know he couldn't be budged. So all he would get from Steven was the leather sofa to crash on, seven nights max, assuming he behaved himself and made no crazy calls.

Linda phoned Emilia from the kitchen, speaking in rapid Spanish and making no mention of Dell by name. As they waited for the terrorist to be delivered, Linda explained that the pickup truck had been impounded. Though she didn't drive herself, she was trying to get it sprung so Dell's men could keep up with the gardens. Only now did Steven understand she had walked the half-mile uphill to his house, having taken the bus from Silverlake.°

He felt the oddest twinge of jealousy, having no brothers and sisters of his own. The brother he'd found in Victor, and a glimmer again in Mark—that vaguely apprehended shiver of incest whenever two gay men connected. But never anything like a sister. Margaret was too urban and neurotic, despite her fevered loyalty. There was nothing she wouldn't do for Steven, but this plodding walk uphill was something in the blood, stark and single-minded, a fire deeper than armies.

When they heard the car pull up outside, instantly she hurried into the dining room to gather her purse. She drew out an envelope and thrust it in Steven's hand, no nonsense: "There's eight hundred dollars here. I don't know what he's gonna need. Maybe a lawyer." Steven couldn't understand why she was making so much haste to leave. She hadn't even seen Dell since the police arrived. If anything, Steven wanted them to have some private time alone, but he shrank from intruding, even to offer it.

They went together to the door. Dell was in green fatigues and a tank top, dirt-streaked from the day's interrupted work, a truculent strip of blue bandanna tied about his head. A bandolier of bullets wouldn't have been out of place crisscrossing his chest, or an AK-47 tucked under his arm. And yet for all the sullen pride of his presentation, what Steven picked up immediately was the unmistakable fluster of shame. He seemed to blanch at the sight of his sister as he grunted hello to Steven, who understood now what she was trying to flee, his sense of having failed her.

She practically bolted by him, no embrace and no familiarity. Emilia waited below with the engine running, in a Band-Aid—colored Nova that was a symphony of misfiring. Linda ducked inside without a backward glance, and the Chevy stole guiltily away in the falling dusk.

Dell locked eyes with Steven and erupted in a hollow laugh, like a sneer given voice, and in the brittle sound of it was all the absurdity of the mess he was in. Steven couldn't think of anything smart to say. He motioned Dell to follow him into the living room, and as soon as Dell saw the sofa made up, he lumbered over and flung himself down, then stared up at the ceiling.

The room was nearly dark, but Steven turned no light on. He left to make another call to Mark, engaging the machine again. He puttered about in the kitchen for a while, cooking up three packages of Kraft Macaroni and Cheese. The living room stayed dark, and he assumed the terrorist had fallen asleep. As usual these days, he left the pot of food on the stove, knowing Sonny would pad in like a cat later on and finish the remains. Steven thought about leaving notes for both of them to alert them to each other's presence, but then he decided to let them do that dance themselves.

He retired to the bedroom end of the house and closed himself off. He slept fitfully, with long, jagged waking spells, where he'd turn on the light and scribble notes on the bedside table, beginning the Thanksgiving grocery list. The next morning when he came out groggy into the kitchen he'd forgotten Dell was there. Once more he tried Mark and got the machine, and he slammed the phone down, feeling betrayed and enraged that he had to make all the advances. Mark's black mood was no excuse. The old resentment resurfaced, that Mark hadn't really been through fire. He didn't have to watch Ray Lee's body shut down limb by limb.

And just then Sonny shuffled in the kitchen door in bicycle shorts and nothing else, his maddening Adonis body packed like a loaded gun, and Steven wanted to turn and fling the pot of coffee on him. "Hey, we got us a celebrity," Sonny drawled lazily, plopping the paper on the counter.

Steven glanced at the front page, bottom left: AIDS TERRORIST ELUDES CAPTURE. Without missing a beat, he crossed to the swing door and poked his head into the dining room. He could see the swirl of bedding on the sofa, but no Dell. He tried to grope back to the night before, to think if they'd set any ground rules. It should have been strictly specified: now that Dell was here in the safe house, he was grounded. Steven could feel the thin whine of hysteria building behind his eyes. Everything was on the brink of being out of control.

"He's in real deep shit," continued Sonny with a certain admiration, as he cut himself a quarter of a coffee cake. "I told him, you don't fuck around with Jesus."

Steven turned and glared at him, scarfing fifteen hundred calories and so lean you could bounce a quarter off his belly. "Where is he?"

Sonny shrugged toward the west end of the house. "My room."

"Oh really? You fucking him now too?" Sonny looked over, his cheeks bulging like a chipmunk's, but he still managed a grin. "No grass under *your* feet, is there?"

Sonny chortled with a kind of relief, as if he much preferred the bitch stuff out in the open. He swallowed his hunk of cake like a python consuming a rat. "He's borrowing some clothes, Steven," he declared dryly, playing the moment like a rope, seeing how far he could tease. "I told him to take a shower in my room so he wouldn't bother you. He's not my type at all. I'm not into ethnic. I like white boys." He reached across the counter for the coffeepot, stretching the ripples of his abdomen taut. "Or should I say white boys like me, 'cause I'm *their* ethnic fantasy."

Steven knew he was being goaded, that Sonny was just throwing back at him the tawdry clichés he harbored about him. "Nothing's changed, has it?" Steven hissed with contempt. "You're just going to keep getting your rocks off till someday you wake up dead."

Sonny leaned back with his elbows on the counter. A line of golden hair trailed from his sternum to his abdomen. "Hey, I'm not gonna die. I got a lot of plans for the year 2000. I've been waiting for that since—" He shrugged his shoulders helplessly. Impossible to measure the time in human years. "At least 2000 *B.C.* Except we don't really go by the Jesus calendar. We think in terms of dynasties."

"And all that bullshit makes your dick hard, does it?"

"Not exactly. That's just 'cause I'm young and horny. I could fuck in a nuclear war." He was teasing himself without any barriers here. They could take it wherever they liked, if Steven would only laugh. But he didn't: he needed to be snappish and gruff and put-upon. So Sonny made the concession. He leaned forward from the counter, drawing up his knees and clutching them with his powerful arms, as if to disengage his body, fold it up like a pocketknife. "I'm not as tortured as you are, Steven," he said with an odd tenderness. "I never was. Ellsworth and me, we were only in it to have a good time. I'm doing what I'm supposed to."

It was as if he had blanked out the agony of the vigil at Cedars-Sinai. Steven could see him still, curled in a ball in a plastic chair in the waiting room, sobbing that there was nothing left. The first week Sonny had been the worst of the three of them. And now he flashed a grin over Steven's shoulder, all of the bad behind him, the picture of California. "Hey, here's the masked man now."

Steven turned as if to a figure in a dream. The gardener's fatigues and bandanna were gone, replaced by a sky-blue muscle T-shirt and baggy French jeans. He'd shaved the black mustache, and the brush of his hair was slicked with gel into tailfins. He nodded to Sonny, acknowledging that they were now members of the same West Hollywood tribe, then turned to Steven, cocky in his new persona, but something in him looking for approval too.

"Well," said Dell softly, "here we are again, the three of us. All for one and one for all."

"Listen, we can get you in as a busboy at Monte Carlo," Sonny declared with eager confidence, as if the real power at the restaurant rested with the best-looking waiter. "Right off the street. No questions asked."

"You stay put," Steven growled at Dell, jabbing the air with a finger. "If you leave this house, you don't come back. Got it?" Dell nodded so imperceptibly there was scarcely any motion involved. Steven swung the withering finger to the Greek. "And you, you keep your mouth shut. No sleepover dates until further notice. This is *my* movie you guys are in, and nobody makes a move unless I say so."

His two guests hardly blinked, maintaining a submissive silence as they waited for further instruction.

"And put that out!" bawled Steven, swiveling back to Dell as the latter flashed a wooden match on his belt buckle and lit his Mexican cigarette. He poked the air again, indicating the courtyard outside the kitchen as the designated smoking area. He looked as if he would've happily cracked their heads together like a pair of coconuts. Then he swept out of there—the two younger men unprotesting, biting their tongues for the sake of a roof—in a lighthearted swoon, like a man who'd been gulping ozone.

It lasted about twenty minutes, until he walked into Ray Lee's apartment and found him sobbing because he couldn't remember half the people in the pictures on his dresser, and one of his ears was full of roaring, as though the sea had broken through. His body was turning against him now with little offbeat tortures. Steven was only there an hour, and he was destroyed for the rest of the day.

Yet the barking tone and the fume of sullen rage continued to sustain him, whenever the pressure got too intense. At Thrifty Drugs he shrilled at the pharmacist, who'd given the wrong milligram dose in Ray Lee's last prescription. The pharmacist blamed the doctor like pharmacists always did, but Steven pounded the counter anyway, making an awful stink, and felt terrific.

His next explosion came in the checkout line at Mayfair, where he'd stopped to pick up a few things for Ray Lee and also grabbed four cans of cranberry sauce and a package of cocktail napkins blazoned with strutting turkeys. Arms loaded, he stood in the 8-Items-or-Less line until he was challenged by a doddering pensioner behind him. "You got ten items," hissed the old man.

Icily Steven explained that his four cans of cranberry constituted a single item. Within five seconds they were screaming, and Steven knocked over the *TV Guide* rack, and the jar of pocket change for Jerry's Kids tumbled off the counter and smashed to the floor. The manager had to be called, who ruled in Steven's favor, but mostly to get the lunatic out of there.

He drove around leaning on his horn, roaring invective at piss-poor drivers on either side. So at least he kept blowing the top off the anger. But the queer thing was, none of it stopped being Mark's fault. There it was, ungainly and irrational: if Mark had only called him back, none of this would be happening. Steven had bent over backward not to fall in love with him, not to crowd him. The idyll of the last two months—the two buddies tooling around in a Jeep, a second chance to be boys at last—had vaporized somehow. All he could see when he thought of Mark was the self-obsession, enameled with those arrogant good looks.

Even Steven could tell he was mixing it up with the rest of his problems. Sonny's cold-blooded rutting, Dell's pointless anarchy, even Margaret's martyrdom and Ray Lee's last pathetic stabs at vanity—everything seemed a projection of what was wrong between Steven and Mark. More than anything, Steven was furious at the constant echo, thinking what Mark would think of things—the random humpy dude on the boulevard, the latest cure-of-the-week. But he also planned to get over it. He would see Mark tonight at the regular Thursday rap and take him out for supper after and not say a word about the irrational rage. They just needed to connect again. Finally Steven would let rip with his whines and complaints about all the others, and Mark would ring down curses on Lou Ciotta's house and issue, and that would be that. They could start over where they left off.

So it was in a peacemaking spirit, putting his tantrum to rest, that Steven bounded up the stairs to the meeting, fifteen minutes late on account of seeing Heather at the office, to let her squirm an apology and then to dump all the work on her. Steven sidled in meekly and sat by Marina, who squeezed his hand hello. The group was in the midst of a role-play, Uncle Fred and Charlene pretending to be Mom and Dad at Thanksgiving, laying on the rest of them a barrage of nosy questions.

The mood was animated and boisterous, a lot of camp and laughter—and Mark wasn't there. When Steven swiveled his head to check behind him on the upper bench, Andy Lakin winked at him. Steven gave him back a wan and distracted smile, feeling a surge of impatience at Mark for being late. The group was getting a little punch-drunk now, the thin gray man pretending to cough up sputum on his Aunt Louise's pumpkin tart. Emmett from Talahassee swore he would pass out condoms at the table when he made his antibody announcement, in case anyone in his family wanted to fuck him over any further.

"Hold it, hold it, one at a time!" bawled Tim like the referee, but without much hope of keeping the group in order. They needed the crazy release and a sense of holiday, safe among their own, before they ventured off one by one to the real families, agendas dense as sweet potato pie. Steven had already decided not to tell about the upcoming feast at his house, for fear they might question his motives.

"I have some announcements," said Tim, drawing his lumbering clipboard from under his feet, where everything was written down as grayly as a junior-high assembly. Something about vitamin therapy, something about a forgiveness seminar. Steven was trying to whisper a shorthand update on Ray Lee to Marina beside him, when he suddenly stopped dead at the sound of Mark's name.

"—called me last night," announced Tim blandly. "He said he couldn't be here for the meeting tonight, but he wanted to wish us all a nice holiday. Well, what he actually said was, 'Don't kill any members of your immediate family because it's very hard to keep your immune system up in jail.'" He read this part from the pad on his clipboard, smiling rather sheepishly as the group cracked up, whistling and applauding.

Steven could feel his face burning red with embarrassment, but he couldn't stop himself from speaking. "Where is he?" he asked in a voice that seemed to tremble with desperation.

"He went to Florida to see his dad," said Tim, unctuous with self-congratulation, as if he took personal credit for the reconciliation.

Steven was all alone with it, his chest constricting, a cold sweat creeping across his neck. To choose blood over Steven's ramshackle family of Thanksgiving orphans. Although it wasn't really fair to think that, since Steven hadn't quite got around to inviting Mark, who didn't even know Steven's dinner was happening—but Steven had had enough of being fair. He preferred to just stew in it, thank you, and cut his losses. He began to see how he might expend more passion getting rid of Mark Inman than he would in having him.

Marina nudged his ribs with her elbow. He looked at her blankly. "Your turn," she said. He stared around at the group, all of them watching him expectantly.

"I think he's somewhere else," observed Charlene, but gently, being a major drifter herself.

"We're making a wish list," reiterated Tim, his fabled patience intact. "We're going around the room saying what we hope to get out of the holiday."

"Like I decided to tell my chirren," Charlene said helpfully. "The oldes' anyway, she be nine."

"Emmett's gonna go by Century City and visit the AIDS ward," said Tim.

"Yeah, and give 'em all a massage with my magic fingers," Emmett drawled, who had a Florida mail-order license in chiropractic.

They all looked at Steven, more expectant still. He knew what he wanted, of course, but couldn't say it. To put Mark Inman behind him; to rid his house of squatters; to host a feast they would never forget. He really didn't have any other idea when he opened his mouth, but what came out was: "I just hope Ray Lee dies right after. This can't go on till Christmas."

And his eyes filled up with tears, so that Marina put her arm around him and rocked her head on his shoulder. The others were all so moved by his finally having spoken a feeling out loud that they didn't ask him to say any more. The meeting broke up with a final plea from Tim for openness and healing. "Don't come from anger, come from love," he said, increasingly oracular, his parting wave more than ever like a Papal blessing.

People would have come over to Steven. Marina herself wasn't finished smothering him. But as soon as they all began to gather their sweaters and bags, Steven turned around to Andy, totally un-rehearsed. "You want to come over to my place?" he asked. "I'll make some hot chocolate."

Andy looked confused. The hot chocolate was really a bit much. "Sure, but I thought—" And he let it hang there, waiting for clar-ification.

A wrinkled smile, utterly endearing, rippled across Steven's face. "Does it have to be so serious? Can't we just play?"

A pause the length of a held breath, in which they couldn't seem to read each other's eyes. Andy shrugged. "Why not?"

He preceded Steven out the door, and Steven nodded good night to the others as he followed, wishing them all a happy Thanksgiving. Not caring who saw the two of them leave together—wanting to be seen, in fact. Steven Shaw, who'd never been calculating enough, hopelessly straight, heart on his sleeve, never cold-bloodedly gone after anyone, fairly strutted down the stairs now behind the sandy-haired boy. Feeling nothing. As if it had all twisted around, and he who always fell plummeting into love had become like all his hood-lum gang. The thing he'd never quite got to work before and everyone else was trying to grow out of—a man who just wanted to get laid.

9

On the fourth tee of the Pitch 'n' Putt, a gaggle of blue-rinse ladies in pastel jumpsuits took a break from their golfing labors and waved in unison up at Rob Inman's third-floor balcony. Dapper Rob, sporting a cancerous tan and a matching sky-blue golf shirt and visored cap, stood up and returned the wave. "Morning, girls," he called, doffing the cap and grinning like Eisenhower. The ladies tittered with pleasure and went on with their game, none of them quite having given up on Rob, despite the obvious smolder between him and that bitch Roz Schwartz. Rob Inman never stopped flirting.

He sat down heavily on the slatted plastic chair, the balcony so narrow that his knees scraped the stucco unless he sat with them wide apart. Behind him the sliding door slid back with a screech, and his only son and heir stepped out with a cup of coffee and a danish. Mark sat down in the other chair, still muzzy with sleep. In his gym shorts and cut-off sweatshirt he looked a good bit younger than his thirty-eight years, but that may have been an optical illusion, given the fact that he looked so much like his dad. It was Rob who had the mottled skin, the belly sag, the crepey under-chin, the dwindling hair. This was the way it was supposed to be, but neither man seemed very comforted just now by the natural order of things.

They didn't speak right away, even to say good morning. Roz Schwartz, who'd poured the coffee and microwaved the danish, would have livened things up immeasurably, since she was a nonstop talker, but she had decided to leave father and son alone. They were pretty well talked out. The first two nights, Mark had let his father have the floor—railing in equal measure at his triglycerides, his doctor, and his pigshit diet. Alternately gushing with pride about the autumn beauty of Roz, then taking Mark aside to bewail the wound that never healed, the loss of his precious Kate.

He was a man given to bursts of drama in his old age, as if to compensate for forty years of pencil-pushing drabness. Growing up, Mark had thought of him as being almost pathologically even-tempered, a gelid smile for every occasion. Now he was a veritable tropical storm of highs and lows. At the dog track on Friday night, he'd been a Damon Runyon swell, back-slapping and leering one-liners. Then back at the condo two hours later, glazed with the fear of death, he'd wondered with thin-lipped eloquence where his life had gone.

There was no right time for Mark to speak, and no wish to make a drama of it. Saturday noon Rob took his son out for deli in downtown Lauderdale, sneaking a plate of knockwurst and beans while Roz got a manicure. Mark told him the gay part first. Rob stiffened and said he'd always suspected, then two minutes later began to sob that it was all his fault, not Kate's. Mark didn't have much patience for any of this, but gave it about five minutes, murmuring politically correct responses as he rolled the big gun out. Then he let him have it as matter-of-fact as he could, fancying it up with T-cell projections and the latest antivirals, surprising himself with his optimistic tone.

Rob stared at him stone-faced till Mark had run out of statistics. Then he said, "So how long you got?"

"Who knows? Two years. Maybe five, if they find a drug that works."

Grimly Rob went back to his knockwurst, asking no more questions. His silence was so profound for the rest of the day that Roz Schwartz took Mark aside. He told her the whole thing, partly because he refused to hide it anymore, partly because he liked her hummingbird intensity. She didn't blanch at the news, being a sophisticated lady who'd always had gay friends, far beyond the beauty parlor. She promised to talk to Rob.

But Saturday night's dinner had been a disaster. The three of them sat in front of the television, Rob spitting a running commentary, railing at every bad sitcom joke. As if Mark were to blame, as if all the insulting and mindless prime-time doodoo had been personally okayed by Rob Inman's son. It was hopelessly transparent, Rob displacing the anger he felt about Mark's double whammy. Anger that was patently self-centered: How could the father keep pissing and moaning about the indignity of his ailments, life on the edge of the cliff, when the son was already tumbling down the mountain? Mark had expected fear and lousy coping skills, but not this sense of having been cheated, as if he'd stolen his father's thunder.

And so he wasn't expecting a goddamn thing this morning, sitting beside the old man, staring out over the Pitch 'n' Putt to the palm-lined humid green of the Intercoastal. Mark was fine, because he realized more than ever that he wanted nothing at all. The one thing left to say was that he meant to go it alone when he got sick. Rob Inman didn't need to make an appearance, gritting his teeth like Job.

This was another way of saying Mark would not be flying in the other direction either. Rob would have to manage without the ancient bond of sons who helped their fathers die. They might get lucky, of course, and have years and years to go, both of them. But the bottom line of the visit was clearer with every hour. They weren't here to fix a thing, to make the relationship better. No, this was all about good-bye.

"Do you have someone?" asked Rob abruptly, watching his pant-suited foursome as they clumped to the fifth hole.

"You mean a lover?"

"Someone special," replied his father carefully, not quite comfortable yet with the idioms.

"No. I don't think I'm the bonding type." Amazed at his own casualness, as if there was no pain attached to it at all. It was just a quirk, like being left-handed.

"What do you do, just sleep around?"

"More or less. I don't sleep too good either."

He wondered if this part would have worked any better if they'd had it out ten years ago. Then it would have just been the gay stuff. Now it seemed ridiculous for a man this old to be telling his dad about his love life. Besides which, the whole territory was moot. It struck him with bitter irony that his father was getting it up more than he was.

"Well, actually there *is* somebody," Mark declared. "A friend, anyway. It's not like I'm alone."

"Do you love him?"

A strange prickle of shyness, like a dry sweat, crept across Mark's shoulders. He supposed he was blushing, a sensation entirely new to him and deeply unappealing. "I guess," he said. "But not like *you* mean." At this the father finally turned and looked at his son. Not judgmental, not even ironic, just curious to know how many meanings love could have. If he noticed the pink flush on Mark's face, he gave no sign, or chalked it up to the Florida sun. Mark shrugged and sighed. "The problem is, he's in love with me. So he gets hurt."

Rob was utterly absorbed now. He seemed to have gotten beyond whatever it was that still made him squeamish about gay. Or perhaps it simply astonished him that after four decades of avoiding his son, he finally had some advice to give.

"But that's exactly what happened with Roz and me," he said, more animated than he'd been since the knockwurst declaration. "She loved me first. I wasn't lookin' at all. It was never gonna happen to me again. But Roz, she just wouldn't let go. Thank God." He shivered with gooseflesh at his own good fortune, then reached out a hand and slapped his boy's bare knee. "So why don't you listen to him. What's his name?"

"Steven. It won't work, Dad. I'm not attracted to him."

Rob made an impatient waving motion, determined not to let the kid off the hook. "How old is he? He's your age?" Mark nodded curtly. "Good, good," said Rob, as if the numbers were very important here. "And he's got this virus too?"

"Uh-huh. He buried his lover last year."

"Well, then, *he* knows," retorted the father, his ruddy face beaming with satisfaction.

"Knows what?" Mark bit the question off, not quite sure what he was angry at.

"That's all there is, son. Someone to love. You ask anybody here."
And he gestured grandly out over the Pitch 'n' Putt, but also included
the mid-rise condos banked on every side, full of seniors in lonely
efficiencies. "They've either been married forty years, and they're
holding on to what little time they got left, or they're widowed and
only half alive. The lucky ones are like Roz and me, we get another
chance. We know it's not for long. Two years, three years—just like
you say. But it's all there is, so you'll take even a little. Everything
else is shit."

This final comment he delivered with both arms wide, like a prince
abdicating a kingdom. He never used to have this fierce dumb pride
back in Manhasset. He used to be as meek and laconic as he was
even-tempered, ceding to his hard-eyed wife the monologues and
sweeping judgments. Mark felt a knot in his gut, building like a
hairball of sourness as Rob extolled the glory of love. Resisting it
with every fiber of contempt he could summon up. He saw as if in
a diorama the string of Hallmark cards along the mantel, marking
every holiday and milestone. "To my beloved wife," "To the world's
greatest husband," all that mawkish packaged sentiment. No accident, perhaps, that Mark had turned into a man who flinched at the
very mention of the "L" word.

"I think it's great, Dad," he said, swallowing the bile. "She's a
classy lady."

"But that's what I'm *telling* you, boy. I didn't look twice at her.
Not my type." He uttered a short, coarse laugh at himself for having
been so blind. "If a woman didn't look like Kate, I didn't even see
her. Even then I couldn't get my pecker up."

Now it was Mark's turn to swivel and stare. His father had never
mentioned his penis before, had hardly ever appeared naked around
his son. He'd been sexless in fact, as far as Mark could ever tell, until
this very conversation, despite all the romantic gush around the
memory of his mother. And not very well-endowed. In the savage
world of his adolescence, Mark had experienced a surge of superiority
when he saw that his own heavy equipment would favor the genes
of the donkey uncles on his mother's side and not the pencil of his
father.

"But Roz, she took time," went on Rob Inman, unaware in the

spell of his own story that his son was fairly gaping at him. "We built up to it real slow. Sometimes you have to trust the other person."

Where had he come by this appalling casualness about sex? From watching Phil and Oprah? Fortunately he was so wrapped up in the sunniness of his own renewal that he seemed to have forgotten the relation of it all to Mark and Steven. And when the sliding door creaked behind them, bringing all the banality to a merciful end, Rob Inman turned with a beatific smile to greet his new beloved. Roz Schwartz, smart in a gray silk dress—the husband left her plenty, no polyester in *her* closet—glided between the two chairs, laid a manicured hand on Mark's shoulder, and leaned down and tenderly kissed his father's temple. They laughed as if at some private joke, at the sheer delight of being together.

Mark excused himself to go for a jog. He only had one more day to get through here, and then back to the house on Skyway Lane to brood about how his life had come to nothing. He trotted around the rim of the golf course, waving up at Rob and Roz on the balcony as he passed. What they couldn't see were the hundred other terraces, seniors sitting on every one, singles and in pairs, squinting into the morning sun.

Did they all understand they were just biding time? Everyone seemed to be old, wherever he ran. Coming off the ninth hole was a trio of stooped and shrunken men, but stepping spry. One wore a plaid tam and sported a George Burns cigar, and Mark caught his bloodshot eye as he jogged past. He could see the pang in the old man's face, his yearning to be young and swift. Mark wanted to laugh out loud and shout that he was dying too, but he kept on running.

The sweat felt good. His lungs were strong. He ran between two palm trees and onto the condo dock, his Reeboks drumming nicely on the wood. He watched two white-hulled yachts pass lazily in the canal. Everyone on both boats was white-haired and morbidly tan, but having the time of their lives as they laughed and chattered ship to ship. Mark stopped short at the end of the dock. Hands on his hips, he paced in a circle, warming down.

There were Chris-Crafts tethered all along the dock, retirees in loud Bermudas swabbing their decks and polishing brass. Nobody seemed to be dying. In fact, they appeared to be fairly bursting with energy. Mark had always found Lauderdale ghoulish, the anteroom of a funeral parlor, but now he felt a strange jealousy as he loped back up the dock. All these people had banded together here as a tribe, holding their own and finding one another, defying the shadow of death. Next to them his own body—still so fit and vivid, nothing wrong to look at him—felt alien and solitary, trapped in a shuttered house.

He pulled up the front of his shirt to wipe the sweat from his face. As he rubbed his neck, he happened to glance into the boat docked beside him. ULYSSES was painted in black on the blue hull, the woodwork dark and polished like glass. Just then the door to the cabin flew open, and a young god clambered out on deck. About twenty-four, in cutoff jeans and nothing else, blond and bronze and ridiculously good-looking. He carried a fishing pole in one hand, tackle box in the other. There was a frozen moment, eye to eye, in which they established the gay part. The god smiled and stared at Mark's belly where the sweatshirt was lifted up.

"Hot day," said the young man, putting the ball into play. Mark dropped the shirt, covering up. His eyes darted to either side, as if he'd forgotten his lines. He'd been at this brink a thousand times, remarking on the heat of the day in a dozen ports, from San Diego to the Pines. The god smiled effortlessly, not requiring a two-way hookup ship to shore. "I got some beer in there," he said, shrugging in the direction of the cabin. "If you want to kick back."

Still Mark stood awkward and silent. How many times had he visited Rob and walked this dock in a horny swoon of desire, too late to drive to the bars in Miami? He'd always been up for another encounter like this, the chance to plunder beauty. That was the point: you could never have enough. But now he could feel himself recoiling, and it shook him, because if he'd lost the pleasure of this, then what was left?

"It's my granddad's boat," said the young man, stroking the tip of the pole against his cheek. "Except he's in the hospital right now. Maybe you'd like to go out." He nodded out to the waterway, and in the toss of his head was every beckoning call to pleasure, every desert island.

Mark shook his head. "Sorry, I gotta get back to my dad," he said. He couldn't believe he was turning it down and still couldn't say why.

But the next moment helped. The god gave a lazy shrug, and something shifted in his eyes, so that Mark could almost see him thinking, *Who cares?* As if the day was still young, and he could do a lot better than a middle-aged man. And with all his indifferent perfection intact, he stretched to throw off the lines. There was no need to say good-bye or wave or pretend they would ever see each other again. No different, Mark thought bleakly as he loped away down the palm alley, than if they'd had the sex.

He let himself into the condo, thinking he'd tell them to get dressed up and he'd take them into Miami for lunch. He pulled off his sweatshirt and strode across to the balcony, something in him feeling proud to be bare-chested and sweaty, as if he wanted to prove to his dad that he was still a man in his prime. He stepped out, but the slatted chairs were empty. He turned to call their names into the apartment and just then heard them through the bedroom window, beyond the balcony wall.

Laughing. He wasn't sure how he knew they were making love as well—the laughter just as it was before, when he fled to go running—but he knew. And it made him blush red again. He'd never heard his father make love to his mother, or at least it was deep in the forgotten past. He didn't feel embarrassed exactly, or even ashamed, but like a fool. Suddenly Roz's laugh pitched to a trill, and there was gasping. Mark stepped in and closed the sliding door.

He went into the TV room, where the sleepover sofa was pulled out and neatly made. He flung himself down and stared at the ceiling, wiping his face again with the damp shirt. The raw funk of his own sweat filled his nostrils, but for once didn't make him feel sexy. So much about being a man was tied up with a kind of compulsive vanity, and here he was trapped in a place without mirrors.

He reached out for the phone and drew it close, resting it on his breastbone as he punched in his long-distance code. He thought he was going to dial his own number and retrieve the messages from his machine, but he made a mistake and dialed Steven's number instead. At least he preferred to think of it as a mistake.

Sonny answered the phone in L.A. "Steven Shaw's," he said breezily, chipper as a houseboy.

"Sonny, it's Mark."

"Hey, dude. You sound far away."

"I'm in Florida. Is Steven there?"

"No, he's over at Ray's. Hey, I used to commute to Florida. This bitch of a winter in Boston, I was freezin' my nuts off. Then I met this pilot, worked for Eastern, real big dick. And he'd bring me down every week on the Friday run. First-class, the whole bit—"

"Just tell him I called, okay? I'll be home tomorrow night."

"Yeah, sure. So like that went on for about three months, but then it was gettin' too hot in Miami. I don't dig humidity."

"Listen, I gotta go—"

"So you're comin' here for Thanksgiving."

"Uh, I don't know. No plans."

"Yeah, you got a place card and everything. Please, he's already set the fuckin' table." They laughed together, and Mark permitted himself the sudden small rush of pleasure, knowing he had a place to go for Thursday. "It's like musical beds since you were here. Like we have to eat breakfast in shifts."

Mark was stuck for a second, trying to process *since you were here*. He didn't like Sonny knowing he hadn't made an appearance at Steven's house since the night of the rawhide tryst. It almost seemed that Sonny took a certain satisfaction in the breach. Mark should have hung up right then, but he was a step behind. "Tell Steven if he needs anything, like wine or—"

"First we got us a fugitive," said Sonny, a bit too loud. He sounded drunk, but it was only 9 A.M. out there. "The fag Jesse James, holed up right here. Wearin' my underpants and everything."

"I don't know what you're talking about," retorted Mark, his voice even and cold, though in fact he was feeling pretty agitated. He heard the bedroom door open, and out of the corner of one eye saw his father saunter across to the kitchen, wearing an oversize green silk robe like a prizefighter's.

"But that's not the best. Listen—Stevie's got a *boyfriend.*"

"A what?"

"This kid. He's been here all weekend. Kinda cute—nice butt."

"Andy," said Mark quietly.

"Oh, you know him." Sonny sounded immediately deflated. Rob Inman appeared in the doorway to the TV room, sucking on a no-cal Popsicle.

"Just tell him I called, okay?" Mark barked abruptly, and depressed the button, ending the call.

He turned to his father with relief, anything to change the subject, and Rob said, "C'mon, get dressed. She wants to take you to see some garden. S'posed to be famous."

As Mark nodded, the green silk robe, unbelted, billowed open a crack. His father's penis was half again as big as Mark had ever seen it before. Not surprising, since it was just easing down after being at full throttle. Yet Rob didn't appear to be deliberately showing off, merely unconcerned and playing it real loose. The fingerbitten accountant was dead and buried. Rob Inman had become a sensualist, a South Florida Casanova, with nothing on the schedule but loveplay with Roz Schwartz. If it took him all day to come, all the better.

As Rob padded back to his bedroom, Mark didn't begrudge him a minute of it. It wasn't as simple as jealousy or envy, not like his own dick had suddenly become the stub of a pencil. No, it was sadder than that. He felt as if he'd never grow up and be a man like his father—a fatuous thought that had never once crossed his mind as a kid—and knew besides he would die alone. It didn't even matter that he was finally able to admit he loved Steven Shaw, because he'd lost him now. Driven him away.

There was nothing to do but put up the wall. He pulled off his running clothes and headed for the shower. Right then he was as old as the oldest man in Lauderdale—no options left, no second chance, nowhere to go but out to sea. At least he'd come out of the closet. He ought to be glad he could even admit to being in love. But all that mattered now was the wall. He looked the same, he looked fine. You would have had to have known him better than anyone he'd ever allowed. Too old and too young at the same time, sadder than he could even feel, but damned if anyone would see.

Especially Steven Shaw.

"Yeah, ride me, man," snarled Sonny Cevathas. "Do it!"

He straddled the soft belly, pinning Sean's wrists with his hands as he sank down on the stiff member, taking him all the way in. The fucking itself felt surprisingly good, considering how lifeless and unappealing was the dazed man lying under him. At least he had a big dick. The astonished look hadn't left Sean's face since Sonny climbed on top of him, so that Sonny couldn't be sure how close he was to coming.

But he kept up the pace of his pumping up and down, clenching his ass muscles and swaying his hips as he rode, expertly driving the guy crazy. Sonny was in total control—a little bored, a little impatient, but never breaking the flow of smut that spilled from his mouth.

"You gonna give me a load, Sean? Right up into my belly? Yeah, we got a lot of fucking to do. I'm gonna be your stud puppy, huh? Fuck me, man. Fuck my boy pussy."

The older man's mouth was pursed in an O, emitting short bursts of breath that grew more and more urgent. His eyes were wide with shocked delight. He'd held it in as long as he could, and now he grunted wildly, all the answer he could give to the torrent of Sonny's abandon. "Yeah!" Sonny shouted in triumph, bucking on the pole, shouting it over and over to punctuate every burst inside him.

Then Sonny let go of his wrists and sat up straight, showing off his warrior torso. The dick was still inside him, and Sean was still dazed. Sonny grinned, something between a purr and a growl. "Yeah," he repeated again, but softer, like a dirty little secret. His own dick swayed in front of him, about three-quarters hard, untouched. Sean didn't seem to notice that Sonny hadn't got off. Slowly the Greek lifted himself away, moaning nicely, as if to keep giving praise for a job well done. "You fill me up real good, Sean," he said with a small cry of regret as the head came out.

"You're beautiful," Sean Pfeiffer retorted, finding his voice at last. Which was true but a little beside the point: it was the animal heat that had really knocked him out. There were beauties on every corner, after all, but not with a mouth and moves like this.

And as if to prove it wasn't over even after it was over, Sonny shifted around, showing the butt that had riveted Sean's gaze for months at The Body Works. The Greek reached for the heavy meat and carefully slid off the condom. The reservoir end was thick with cum, white and foamy. Sonny cocked his head and glanced at Sean, still lying there in a dumb swoon. He held the rubber between his thumb and forefinger and swayed it like a pendulum, displaying the weight of the seed.

Then he lolled his head back and lifted the rubber to his mouth. Baring his teeth like a jackal, he started to chew on the bulbous tip, keeping one jaded eye on Sean, who looked appalled and thrilled at once. After a few moments the condom broke, and he sucked out the cum as if it were an overripe fruit. He made a smacking noise, then drew the back of his hand across his mouth, tossing the husk of the rubber away. "Now you came in me twice," he said, staring at Sean with a passion that appeared to have no limits.

"Very fucking hot," admitted Sean, always glad to see a new trick. "But are you sure you should do that?"

"You mean is it safe?" Sonny gave a languorous shrug, as if the question was beneath him. "The stomach juices kill all that. Besides, you're a total top man, aren't you?"

Sean nodded on the pillow, folding his white arms under his head. He seemed relieved at Sonny's unconcern, as well as highly pleased to be touted for his manhood. A total top and a total asshole. Though he bragged incessantly about business, Sonny still didn't understand remotely how cable franchise worked. The money he understood, however, and the post-mod house at the top of Trousdale, commanding a two-seventy view of the glittering prizes.

Sonny rose up off the Porthault sheets and swaggered across and into the bathroom, knowing Sean Pfeiffer's dazzled gaze was following him. Sonny caught himself in the river of mirrors that wrapped around three walls, and he stopped to pose, alert to every muscle, loving his deep reflection as he receded into infinity. He moved to the open shower, in a window alcove that hovered on top of Sean

Pfeiffer's mountain, the city far below shivering with light. Much higher up than Steven, or even Mark Inman just off Mulholland, whose property Sonny had checked out punctually the morning after their one-night stand, to see if the thing was worth pursuing. Not a chance. Sonny required an entire mountain.

He turned on the water full-force, as hot as it got, and the jets pummeled him. He swayed in the stream, almost dancing with himself. He felt terrific, though the crystal was beginning to wear a little thin around the edges. His butthole throbbed, but then, that was the price of admission, and in truth it hurt pretty good. Besides, Sonny knew how to compensate. In a day or two he'd check in with one of his fuck buddies and plow the shit out of him. Because life was a balance of power, something he'd known since the Second Cataract.

Not that he didn't have all the power here. Ever since he was sixteen years old, luring his Aunt Urania's husband onto the shoals of desire, he understood instinctively how a bottom stayed on top. Especially here, in the house of a vulgar man. He turned in the steam as Sean strutted into the shower. Sonny grinned lazily and reached for the soap. Vigorously he lathered Sean's tire-waisted body, inexhaustible as a geisha.

And Sean stood there dumbly, happy as a sheik in a harem. While Sonny soaped him down, he stroked the Greek with a meaty hand, lingering on the buttocks in a proprietary way. He had sunk two and a half mill in the Trousdale house, and three years later it was easily worth double. In truth, his whole life seemed to double every time he turned around, that was how rich he was. And yet this right here was the only reward that mattered: a man whose beauty took his breath away. It was what he deserved and what the world owed him. Though he couldn't leave Sonny alone, pawing him like a drunken suitor, he was also coolly appraising. For if he'd learned nothing else from having an ocean of money, he knew that the rich could own the beautiful.

It was close to 4 A.M. when they stepped out of the shower. As Sonny toweled himself dry in the hall of mirrors, Sean leaned over the sink and blew out his nostrils, thick with bloody gunk from the crystal. He hadn't done as much as Sonny, but he did it all the time, so his sinuses were shot. He didn't seem to care how gross was the sound of his nose-flushing. On the contrary, he appeared to take genuine delight in being gross and vulgar and rich.

The evening hadn't even started till one, when Sonny was through at the restaurant. The second date, the second night in a row. Last night they had tooted a little crank in Sean Pfeiffer's limo, pulling up at this travertine palazzo at the top of the city. Sonny had seen immediately how very high the stakes were, and on the spot decided to go for the gold.

In a voluminous white terry robe, Sean moved to Sonny, who was toweling dry his hair. He watched him for a moment, sated but still famished, as if all that counted was figuring out how to use him next. Then he frowned: "What's this?"

Sonny's head emerged from the towel. Sean put out a stubby finger and raked the swirl of hair in Sonny's armpit. There was a small crimson spot about an inch from the tricep, slightly raised, that looked sore. "Nothing," said Sonny, stiffening slightly at the offense. He didn't look at the spot himself. "It's a birthmark, why? You paranoid or something?"

He flicked his towel at Sean's ass, turning it into a playful moment, two guys horsing around in a locker room. The older man laughed and grabbed at Sonny, chasing him back into the bedroom, tumbling with him onto the bed. It was half a wrestle and half an embrace, but too late at night to take it either way. They were lying side by side, Sean puffing with exertion just from the little chase. Sonny dug a tickling finger between his ribs, put his face up close and said, "So you think I'm Typhoid Mary, is that it?"

Sean laughed, his belly shaking. Sonny was glad the fish-white body was wrapped in the terry robe, because he was sick of touching it. "Not exactly," Sean replied, lazily nuzzling Sonny's neck, "but you lived with a guy who died, didn't you?"

Sean couldn't see the startled look in Sonny's eyes, like something wild in a trap. But he didn't flinch; he had too much control of his body for that. Instinctively his hands parted the robe, and he began to play lightly with Sean's nipples. Sean groaned in protest, his tits having gone through a long delicious session at Sonny's hands before they got down to serious fucking. Tits were the only topwork Sean

Pfeiffer ever allowed, the only thing close to yielding. Now Sonny kept the pressure exquisitely light, the softest echo of a deeper throb, till Sean lay back on the pillow with his eyes half-closed.

Anyone else might have been glad to consider the subject dropped, but Sonny said quietly, his voice like a lullaby, "You mean Ellsworth? We were just roommates."

"I heard you were lovers," Sean murmured in reply. He hadn't got rich by losing the thread of conversations, no matter how nice his body felt.

"No way. I mean, like maybe we jerked off a couple times, but he never fucked me. I'm real picky." He gave the nipples a final twist, perfectly walking the tightrope of pleasure and pain, and Sean hissed in answer, reduced at last to a sort of white noise. "I need a man," declared Sonny, releasing the pressure points and closing the discussion all at once. Ellsworth, whatever else he was, had clearly not been what was needed.

Sean Pfeiffer gave a tremendous sigh of contentment. He began to breathe more rhythmically, surfeited at last and ready to sleep. Sonny leaned up next to his ear and whispered, "I want to wake up in the morning with you inside me." The ghost of a shit-eating grin suffused Sean's face, as if this last remark would ensure an X-rated dream or two. Then he was out cold, the strain of forty-six grubbing years visible now in the puffs and sags of his face.

Sonny pulled back and reached around to the bedside table. He'd hardly touched his flute of Dom before the session got going in earnest. Now he just wanted to savor his champagne. He'd put in a double shift tonight, Monte Carlo and here, back to back. And he had barely slept the night before, wired as he was from the crystal. He'd been running on pure adrenaline all day. He probably should've crashed and taken a major nap, but he'd gone to the gym instead and put in his regular two hours. It was almost as if he wanted to gauge his loss of power after a night of sex and drugs.

He passed the test just fine, benching as strong as ever. The only tangible effect was how spaced he was, jangled and slow on the uptake, which was why he neglected to pass on the message from Mark to Steven. And couldn't remember the name of Steven's new boyfriend, though he kept bumping into him all through the house.

He sat up and leaned close to the table, where a skim of white powder covered a small hand mirror. Enough for Sonny to scrape together a last line. He toyed with that for a moment, figuring it would give him the rest of the night to think. He even felt a perverse fascination with how it would be tomorrow, after *two* nights sleepless. How it would be, in other words, to push the limit here, play a little Russian roulette with the perfect tone of his body.

Strange, since he really wasn't into drugs. Not that he was so clean either, but he only took what his tricks would feed him—a joint here, a couple hits of amyl. For a while there in his early twenties everyone seemed to have coke, but that was passé now, at least among the hard-bodied types he played with these days. It really took finding a sleaze bucket like Sean Pfeiffer to get drugs thrown into the package. And frankly, Sonny was grateful for the carnal boost of the speed.

But the champagne was enough for now. He wandered naked into a living room the size of a barn, with half-acre splatter paintings on facing walls, in which obscure violent figures foamed up red and fought with beasts. Sonny didn't get the paintings at all, but then, neither did Sean Pfeiffer, who only required them to be expensive. Sonny crossed the room with a certain caution, knowing there was staff in the house, including the hulking limo driver who doubled as a bodyguard and looked as if he ate West Hollywood fags for breakfast.

Sonny hoped he wasn't tripping invisible wires, especially when he moved up three stone steps into Sean's office. A swirling Nouveau desk stood on tiptoes in the bay window. Sonny sat naked in the glove leather chair, brought the champagne glass to his lips, and tilted back to drain it. He liked the feel of the leather kissing his body and wondered what it would be like to lie naked in the back of the limo. He'd save that idea for Sean, who could ravish him as they purred through Beverly Hills.

Idly but methodically, he pulled out the drawers on either side— blue boxes of Tiffany stationery, business cards and letterhead for the cable company. Nothing so concrete as a balance sheet that would tell him in black and white what Sean was worth. He'd have to break into the office on Wilshire to root out that kind of detail, and even then he'd probably need an accountant. That didn't seem fair, given the fact that all his own assets were concentrated here, naked in this chair. Already Sean knew just what he was getting, after only two nights' feasting. If they were going to keep it on an equal footing, man to man, a financial statement seemed only fair.

Not that Sonny thought of himself as a gold digger, or not in the usual sense. Oh, he liked the feel of the palace around him, the privileges and accoutrements of empire. But he wanted no *things*. His own body was all he ever desired, the only object worth possessing. Sean Pfeiffer was power rather than gold, a prince on earth with a walled kingdom, and Sonny's perfect match, who wanted out of the world. Sonny had caught Sean at just that moment when all his domain was ashes in his mouth if he couldn't have love.

Sonny knew a terminal romantic when he saw one. Beneath the Neanderthal manner, the drivenness about money, Sean Pfeiffer's heart was shaped exactly like a valentine. Love to him was purely of the body, measured by beauty alone. Sonny would make him fall hard, like an eagle plummeting out of the sky. Tit for tat: his body for a kingdom.

He pulled open the bottom drawer on the right, full of prospectuses and promos. He wasn't looking for anything now, especially not any further clue to how Sean Pfeiffer ticked, since he knew all that already. He flipped through the second-class matter, bored by the very sight of print. Reading had never taught him a thing. Underneath was a black vinyl pouch, about six inches square. Sonny lifted it from the drawer and opened the flap.

It was full of pictures, but even so he wasn't burning curious. He didn't care what the past looked like, or who Sean kept for a keepsake. Only the deepest distant past had any resonance at all, beyond the reach of any record save what could be carved on a temple wall. But he couldn't not look either, the last blip of the crystal pushing him past his huge indifference to the world of the non-self.

The pictures fluttered out in the palm of his hand, a couple of dozen Polaroids. Men, but not their faces. Crotch shots—flashing their dicks and bound-up balls, bending over to show off their shaved holes, the red welts on their cheeks visible even in the crude half-light of the flash. The final submission being the picture. Sonny went through them one by one, unmoved, unshockable. He only felt a certain weariness to see how rapt Sean Pfeiffer was, how wed to all the ritual. There was nothing here that Sonny hadn't given himself to, one time or another, but it needed an awful lot of heat, and not the manufactured kind he was putting out for Sean.

He flipped one more, and the next was a woman. Finally, something that raised an eyebrow. Christ, he was bi. Sonny nearly laughed, to think there was anything in a man that could still surprise him. An entire series of women, mostly blondes, naked like the men and just as crudely objectified, but no S&M. They were posed modest and girlish, touching their breasts and smiling shyly, knees together. Not carnal at all—in fact, nothing that could be remotely construed as dirty.

Sonny felt an involuntary sneer of contempt, recalling with disdain the string of married men who'd hungered for his ass, all the way back to his bag-boy days in Fresno. They kept their whores and madonnas separate, even as far as separate sexes. After twelve years in the trenches, Sonny still wasn't especially gay, not in the sense of brotherhood, but he was a thousand lifetimes more evolved than those who were neither one thing nor the other.

And then he came to the last picture.

Another blonde, but he knew right off from the prickle of heat that rose up the back of his neck. Anyone else would have said they were all the same, the boys in thrall and the bashful women, but Sonny would have recognized her anywhere, even without the green shock that zigzagged like a lightning bolt across her bangs. Romy. Her cat's eyes were red in the Polaroid glare, but her smile was fixed on him alone, full of the pearls and agates with which she had cast his runes. His key to the XVIIth Dynasty, his window on the journey to his rightful place, commanding the land below the Second Cataract.

Whenever you come to an oasis, she said, *think of Romy.*

The joy of connection was so intense it almost choked him. He slipped all the pictures back in the pouch and closed the drawer, not even retaining the image of Romy, because he was free of things. He was all power as he rose from the desk and capered across the great hall. His life was his own again, completing the circle at last, his journey to the place he owned in every incarnation. He glided into the bedroom, drunk on the promise of sanctuary. Sean Pfeiffer lay on his back and snored greedily, as certain the world was his as Pharaoh, even in sleep. They would make a great team, he and Sonny, synchronized beyond the zodiac. The Greek would be transient no more.

He floated across to the bathroom to kill the lights and caught his myriad beauty in the mirrors one last time. He stretched his arms over his head, and his eyes went like a laser to the red spot under his arm. Of course it wasn't a birthmark. A month now and it hadn't gone away, and the lymph node under it swollen like a golf ball. The only way out, he'd known all along, was to find again the river and source of his ancient fate. The one thing that would freeze his beauty, aligning himself with a destiny deeper than all the dying men of West Hollywood, wed to a single incarnation.

He hit the lights and retreated once more to the royal bed, in a chamber protected by Nubian warriors and lions on golden chains. The only part of his body still here was the flesh with which he would capture and enchant the beast beside him. Otherwise he was a hundred generations, beyond decay and pestilence. From now on it was he who would call down plagues. And Death, he saw as he fell into a slumbering swoon, Death was only for slaves.

10

Dinner was called for four, and since the turkey was twenty-eight pounds, it had to go in the oven at eight in the morning. Heather delivered the dressing the night before, sausage and corn-bread, mounds of it, so all Steven had to do was get up and stuff it and stick it in. But then around midnight Wednesday, while he was stewing the peaches and cranberries and layering the sweet potato fool, Margaret called in a terrible state. Ray Lee had spiked to a hundred and four, talking deliriously in Korean, and she couldn't get hold of the doctor.

Steven dropped everything and went over. They bathed him with alcohol and washcloths dipped in ice water, bringing the fever down to 101 and bringing Ray back to English. The doctor called at two but didn't sound impressed. No need to bring him into the hospital, especially on a holiday, unless it stuck at 104, in which case go to the E.R.

So Steven didn't get home till almost three, and then had to finish the cranberry sauce and sweet potatoes. He dragged himself to bed at four—and nearly shrieked to discover the kid lying there fast asleep. They hadn't slept together since Sunday, and there was distinctly no standing invitation. But while Steven was at Ray's, Andy had come by, his trunk full of firewood, which Sonny helped him stack in the garage. He must've thought it would be a nice surprise for Steven, to find him curled up in his bed. But it only made Steven more sleepless, since it wasn't working at all. The upshot being that he overslept, and the turkey didn't go in till after ten.

Mark had finally called on Tuesday afternoon, biting his own bitter tongue that Steven hadn't called first, to welcome him home from Florida. For a minute they were excruciatingly formal, till they established that Sonny had never passed along the message that Mark had called. Then they got off a nice little riff of bitchiness at Sonny's expense, about his one-track piglet mind, and after the playfulness of that exchange Mark found himself promising a pair of pumpkin pies for Thursday. He didn't mention what Sonny had told him about Andy Lakin, nor did Steven bring it up. In some dim region of wishful thinking Steven still hoped to establish to Andy *before* the Thanksgiving dinner that their shipboard romance was over and let's be pals.

But the logistics of the coming feast grew madder with every hour, giving Steven time for nothing, and he ended up wishing Victor were there to make it all work. Not that he didn't have an army of help. Linda was there all day Wednesday cleaning the house, crawling in behind the stove and swabbing out cupboards that swarmed with weevils. Even Dell got off his ass, foregoing the afternoon talk shows to prune and clip the yard. And Sonny came home mid-afternoon having ripped off a centerpiece floral arrangement from Monte Carlo that was big enough for a concert hall. Also two trays of hot and cold hors d'oeuvres, which he didn't quite deliver to a catered affair in Hancock Park.

And even with all the blizzard of preparations reaching a sort of crescendo, Thursday morning didn't lack for a certain endearing camaraderie. One after another, Steven shooed Sonny and Dell and Andy from the kitchen, each of them snatching a bit of breakfast as he fled. Once he had the turkey cooking and had checked in with Margaret to make sure Ray had survived the night, Steven grabbed a mug of decaf and padded into the living room. The three were lined up on the sofa eating a box of doughnuts, watching the Macy's parade on tape delay.

"Maybe I'll go to New York," Dell announced as the camera panned the crowd in Herald Square. "Be easy to hide out there."

"But what would you do?" asked Sonny. "They don't have yards."

"I could bomb the U.N.," came the casual reply, and Steven whacked the back of his head.

He turned to see if Andy noticed, but the kid was dunking a doughnut and fixed on the parade. Dell was under strict house rules not to discuss with anyone on the premises his urban guerrilla status. As far as Andy or anyone else was concerned, he was a fellow widower down on his luck and bunking temporarily with Steven. Fortunately the police hadn't made any public announcement that Dell Espinoza was the AIDS saboteur. Presumably they were still watching his apartment, and Linda was very careful when she took the bus to Steven's house, in case she was being followed.

But already the case had been supplanted in the media by a serial killer of hookers and a crack bust involving a deputy mayor of Beverly Hills. The AIDS terrorism was yesterday's news, and Steven and Linda figured Dell could resurface again by Christmas, new name and new apartment, just another wetback, and start all over with a battered truck. That was what Linda hoped for anyway, and Dell hadn't contradicted the scenario of his resurrection.

Steven headed back to the kitchen to check the bird, something he would be doing compulsively every fifteen minutes for the next seven hours, and Andy called after him, "Can I help?"

Steven turned and faced the trio on the sofa. "Not right now. But you're all on call, so don't go far. *And* we have ladies coming, so I want some fancy clothes and the most piss-elegant manners you can muster."

"Shit, what time is it?" blurted Sonny in a minor panic. "I got a date."

"*What* date?" demanded Steven. "You can't go anywhere. You're booked."

But Sonny was already bolting, pulling off his T-shirt. "Don't worry, it's just a nooner. I'll be back by two," he said, slipping out through the dining-room doors and racing around the garage.

"What's a nooner?" asked Dell, culturally deprived.

195

"A fuck date," Andy informed him pleasantly. "Usually you have them during your lunch hour."

Sonny hadn't told anyone yet about Sean Pfeiffer. Indeed he was running up to Trousdale for a midday tryst, before Sean took off for Palm Springs and dinner with his family. Sonny preferred them all to think he was just going out for a meaningless fuck, not wanting to jinx the delicate negotiation of the permanent bond. Meanwhile, Steven stooped to the oven, annoyed at Sonny's casualness. You'd think that for one day he could leave his dick alone and just be part of the family. There was no getting around it: Steven wanted everything perfect. It was going to be that kind of holiday, brimming with expectations, the kind that left mothers weeping at the end as they dried the Waterford goblets one by one.

There were no juices to baste with yet, as the turkey had barely started cooking, but Steven crouched and peered into the oven window, counting the onions in the roasting pan as if the turkey might have eaten one. Suddenly he felt a hand ruffle his hair, and Andy leaned down and kissed the back of his neck. Steven stood up and faced him, the muscles quivering slightly in his jaw. Andy's eyebrows creased in an anxious frown.

"You didn't get much sleep," he said, stroking the stubble of beard on Steven's cheek. "Can you take a nap? I'll watch the turkey. How 'bout I give you a back rub?"

"No thanks." His voice was tight. Andy, constantly misreading, kneaded Steven's shoulders, as if he could be the cure instead of the cause of the tension.

"Sweet, sweet man," murmured the kid. On his upper lip was a milk mustache, which made Steven feel like a pedophile. Andy trailed out through the swing door.

Steven leaned his forehead against the refrigerator, between the two star magnets. He wasn't going to worry about what Dell might reveal, anarchy or otherwise. Steven would be crackers if he had to monitor all eight of them. Let them appall one another if they must. He turned with a sigh to survey his kitchen, the calm before the storm, all the counters clear. He realized—perverse as ever—he could hardly wait to see them mix it up. When the phone rang, he didn't tense at all. He was ready for anything. "Hello?"

"Steven Shaw? This is Angela. Ciotta. Lou's wife." She was halting and uncertain.

Steven's heart leaped at the total unexpectedness. "Well, of course. How *are* you? Happy Thanksgiving."

"Yeah. I don't know why I called, but like—I wanted to thank you."

"No, no, I should be thanking *you*. You had us up for that lovely tea, a month ago already. And I didn't even send a bread-and-butter note." My, but he was a veritable fruitcake of Sunday manners today.

"Hey, no problem. You were so nice. You remember that talk we had upstairs? In the closet?" Steven reached in the fridge and pulled out a double bunch of celery. As she talked, he cradled the phone with his shoulder, stripping and washing the celery stalk by stalk. "I been doin' a lotta coke, this whole last year. Kinda keepin' Lou company. And like, that day with you I started to realize, who am I foolin'? Ya know?"

She didn't expect an answer, though he murmured affirmatively. He started to cut the celery into three-inch lengths, finger-size. "So Lou and me, we been fightin' ever since. I tell him to stop, he tells me to go to hell. And with all that shit around, I can't stop takin' a taste. So I split." In the pause that followed, he heard her drag deeply on a cigarette and the clink of ice in a glass as she drank.

"You left him?"

"Yeah, night before last. I'm here at the Beverly Wilshire. But I'm checkin' in to Betty Ford tomorrow."

"Oh. Good for you," he said lamely.

"Like that was the first call I made. Second was Marvin Mitchelson. I'm gonna clean Angela up and clean Lou out." She laughed, but the joke was hollow. "Anyway, I just wanted you to know, it was you got the ball rolling. My moon's in Cancer, so this is a real healing time. But listen to me, so fulla myself. How *you* doin'? How's Mark?"

"Fine, fine. What're you doing for dinner?"

"Huh? Me, I'm just drinkin' Tab. My internist got me on Valium till I get to the clinic, just so I don't climb the walls."

"But it's Thanksgiving. Why don't you come here?"

She gave a little astonished laugh. Protesting right away: she didn't have any clothes, she was still in bed, her hair was a wreck. But he could tell she wanted to come. Flustered and insecure, she needed to be reassured, so he gave her the lay of the land, gently but insistently. The guest list, the menu, the geography of the house. No need to drive, she could take a cab. Her tiny phobic bursts of uncertainty began to abate. She did have a little black cocktail dress, and maybe it would be a distraction, but he had to promise to meet her at the door and tell her if she looked horrible. She'd leave the cab running.

Anything, anything. She promised to be there by six and then had to ring off, determined to drag her hairdresser out to the hotel, at least to give her a comb-out. By the time he hung up the phone, Steven had the celery fingers arranged on a serving plate, and he was spooning Kraft pink cheese and olives from a jar, slathering it on the celery. The Kraft was a bit low-class for the dinner he was serving, but was more or less a tradition here. Victor's mother in Montana always had a tray of stuffed celery on the table at Thanksgiving, and Victor had kept it up as a sort of kitsch homage to his frontier youth. But the irony was lost on Steven, who stuffed the celery now with grave attention. There were also jars of spiced crab apples and corn relish for condiments, exactly the brands that Victor used to buy. As if to veer even in small ways was to tempt chaos.

Through the kitchen window, as he worked, Steven could see the mangy dog dozing under the sycamore, lying on his back with his paws in the air. Except he wasn't looking especially mangy anymore. His coat shone sleek and thick from all the veal bones Sonny brought him. Steven had failed utterly to keep the beast in the jungle.

And as if to mock him further, Dell and Andy trotted out to the garden and started flinging a Frisbee, bringing the dog leaping to his feet and barking energetically. He sprang in the air as the disk floated back and forth between the two men. Where had they gotten a Frisbee? It seemed to Steven such a straight boy's prop, almost as suspicious as a football. But for all of that, he was smiling as he watched, doting again, as if there was something unimaginably safe about the day.

Heather and Linda arrived on top of each other, Heather apologizing profusely when she realized she'd driven right by as Linda trudged up the hill from Sunset, a crock of guava pudding under her arm. Linda hastened to reassure her, guilty to think she made anyone else feel guilty. The two women exchanged a smile, both overanxious not to offend, then converged on the kitchen. They shooed out Steven, who needed to shave and shower, then rearranged the masses of food with an inner logic that had escaped their host. Heather put up a pot of cider to mull, while Linda chopped greens for the salad. The bird had by now begun to spellbind the entire house with the smell of its roasting, bringing the boys in to pick at the cold hors d'oeuvres. The dog sat in a rapture of hope by the kitchen door, nose quivering.

Linda and Dell were still a bit tentative with each other, both tucking in like turtles when Heather teased them that they looked like twins. But once she had the salad fixed, Linda tugged her brother out to the backyard and drew a thick letter from her shoulder bag. Written by one of the sisters-in-law in Morelia, but dictated by Beatriz Espinoza. Linda sat on the whitewashed bench and read it aloud— the lazy narrative of days in the baking sun, punctuated by strings of Spanish names as her mother went through the roll call of everybody's children.

Dell listened quietly, gazing up the hill at the twisted chaparral above the house. November had been unseasonably dry, no rain since Halloween, and nothing was green. A dust shroud hugged the mountain. The turmoil in his heart rode so deep even Linda couldn't see it, and she was accustomed by now to his broods and glooms. He'd listened to dozens of letters from home, bored and vaguely embarrassed, annoyed to think that his mother imagined he cared about any of that. But today the flat details of life going nowhere, the slow-witted cast of characters, all of it left him agitated, listening like a man condemned. The final dispatch from a sunlit world beyond the prison wall.

For the first time in a hundred letters, he wished he could speak in answer, write back in the flowing hand that used to send letters to Linda herself. To thank his pious mother for the prayers with which she sealed each missive. To tell her that he loved and honored her every day and would one day rear a son who would know her name. All lies, of course, but just for the moment he wished he could tell them. As if he longed to be something else before he died—the gay son who had never left home, who stayed in the closet and took care of family, never moving out of the shadow of the mountain.

Linda read off the final flourishes, God and mother love mixed in passionate exhortation, but managed to keep her own voice carefully indifferent. As if she had learned too well not to be emotional in his presence, any emotion at all, or else he might shut down further. She folded the letter up matter-of-fact and tucked it back in her bag, filial duty done. She made no comment on any of its details and didn't dream of hazarding anything like a reminiscence. So it must have surprised her when he spoke, still looking up the hill and so softly melancholy she barely heard.

"Maybe you'll go back and visit," he said. "We could send you down for Christmas."

"Mm," she replied vaguely, realizing he hadn't included himself, and she would never go back alone. He moved toward the house, locked in his stubborn intensity where she could never follow. She reached into her bag again. "I brought you this."

He stopped. She held out the spiral notebook that he kept on the shelf under the bedroom phone. "I hid it the day the police came, so they wouldn't take it away."

He nodded rather formally as he took it from her. Of course they had never discussed it, though he'd never tried to hide it either. He flipped through the pages—first names only, measurements, turn-ons, the full repertoire of sex talk. Dell laughed. "They would have had a great time trackin' these guys down," he said. "Whole lotta men out there with cop fantasies."

On almost every page a phone number was scribbled beside the name. Though he laughed it off as a dirty joke, he could feel the rage like bile in his gut, that the L.A. pigs would muscle in on these lonely boys, accusing them of consorting with a terrorist. Suddenly he thought of Kevin, whom he hadn't talked to in almost a month. He wondered if Kevin missed him.

"It's none of their business," Linda declared, blindly loyal, her brother against the authorities. Her black mane framed her lean face, not a trace of makeup. She wore an off-white cotton dress with lace inserts at the shoulders, the dress she'd worn the day of her wedding.

"Alfonso brought me fourteen hundred dollars," she went on, dutifully changing the subject now that the notebook was returned. "He hasn't lost any customers, and he wants to know can he buy the truck."

Alfonso was the hardest worker among Dell's crew, a tree man who could scamper like a monkey. He was the obvious one to take over the business when Dell went underground. Alfonso was sweet on Linda and never failed to pay over her brother's cut. Dell shrugged. He trusted Linda's judgment in business, and only worried that Alfonso Nava might make a move to marry her, and Dell wouldn't be there to stop it. Alfonso might get rich, but he would always be a peasant.

A third time Linda reached into the bag, and this time brought out a camera. Dell frowned as soon as he saw it, cornered, looking as if he would turn and run. "I don't even have a picture of us," she protested. "If it comes out good, we can send one home, so they won't forget what we look like." She was talking rapidly, as if he hadn't even mentioned her traveling home for Christmas. What she didn't want him thinking was that she needed a picture before he got sick.

"Maybe later," he said.

"No, *now*. I don't have a flash."

She was bathed in the dusty sun that dappled through the sycamore, its palomino trunk rising behind her head. Dell reached for the camera. It was really a picture of her that was needed. But then the dining-room door slammed open, and Sonny Cevathas came lurching out, eyes wild as the Furies. He was heading for the room beyond the garage, and Linda called out to him, "Sonny, will you take our picture?"

He balked. All he wanted to do was get in his room and pound the walls. But something about her plaintiveness stopped him, as if he could hear her fear of where the time would take them if they lost the moment now. He turned. His face was flushed; he was breathing hard, snorting like an animal. Still he might have told them both to go to hell. Perhaps he understood they were all he had left, this marginal bogus family that had ended up at Steven's house.

His smile was more of a grimace, but he rolled his shoulders and tossed his hair and reached for the camera. Everyone's younger brother, he herded Dell over to the whitewashed bench. He made a squeezing gesture with his hands to make them sit close together. And when they still kept a shy space between them, Sonny went up and physically pushed them tight. He grabbed Dell's wrist and drew the brother's arm around Linda's shoulder. Then he scooted back ten feet and crouched. They looked hopelessly stiff and formal in the viewfinder.

"Hey, guys, could we lighten up a little please? Why don't you look at each other."

Suddenly face to face, they smiled as if a sort of reprieve were being granted, however brief, and they were brother and sister again. Sonny snapped once, twice for good measure. Then they faced him, tilting their heads together. Two more clicks. Steven would have loved it, a holiday reconciliation worthy of prime-time, boding well for a white Christmas.

The camera got all there was of it, though. When Sonny sprang to his feet and moved to return it to Dell, brother and sister had already pulled a hair apart. "Listen, I better go clean up," said Sonny, "or Stevie'll have my ass." He backed away, still oddly boyish and bobbing his head, riding the last of the nooner's speed, and trotted away to his own room. Dell and Linda hated to see him go, their only witness here to who they used to be. Pride was welling up again, a passion not to intrude, and the queer double shame that they weren't good enough for each other. Before the sun had left the dusty branches of the sycamore, their way would be paved again with eggshells.

"Me too," declared Dell wearily. "I gotta go put on a tie for Steven's gringo holiday." He laughed. "Like I'm going to a funeral." And gently handed the camera back to Linda, all the evidence in their favor.

As soon as Sonny walked into his room and slammed the door, he felt caged, but the cage was good. He'd been ready to pound the walls, but now he shrank from them instead. Not half an hour ago Sean Pfeiffer told him they were finished. Told him in the driveway, standing between the limo and the Mercedes. Right after they'd fucked for an hour, Sonny on his hands and knees taking it like a dog, then standing up spread-eagle against a glass door as he gazed west to the ocean. Another toot and they played Marines, Sean smacking his butt with a paddle as Sonny barked out the count: "...forty-nine, fifty, sir!" As if to see how much heat they could cram in an hour, so that Sean would go off to Palm Springs ravenous. Sonny had brought him the paddle.

And then they were in the driveway, not even time to shower, and Sean handed over an envelope. "I always think it's better," he said, "to stop these things before the heat goes. End on an up, you know what I mean? Always better to be a little sorry." Sonny was speechless, his body still on fire from the crystal. He stared at the envelope, as if to will it to be a love letter, with a key to the house taped inside. Sean slipped into the back of the limo and stuck his head out the window. "Don't take this wrong, but you really oughta go see a doctor, show him that sore."

Sonny let him glide away without even screaming, because above all else he didn't want to look stupid. He was supposed to have understood the deal from the very beginning. In the envelope were twenty new hundreds, so fresh they seemed unreal. At first he didn't feel betrayed or even insulted, only relieved that nobody knew. But by the time he got home, he could actually feel his body crawling with all that he hadn't washed off. He went in the house determined to beg off dinner, pleading sick, but couldn't find Steven. Then the encounter with Dell and Linda, so lost and afraid to touch, and he figured what the hell, at least it would be clean in there. No one at Steven's table was going to put their hands on him.

Now he pulled off his clothes as if he wanted to burn them. The sight of his body in the mirror above the sink made him wince. The red welts on his butt, the head of his dick raw, his swollen nipples, all like a sort of infection. The rest of his perfect body was numb and pale as death, next to the mocking soreness of his love zones. He felt as if he'd raped himself. He'd never done it for money. How far did he have to go to meet his fate halfway?

He began to blow the mucus from his nose, one nostril and then the other, expelling it into the sink, as bloody as Sean Pfeiffer. He was so sick of men, he could hardly breathe. He had a wild flash of understanding how sex criminals sometimes pleaded to have it cut off. Then he stepped into the shower, where the last thing he expected was to come out clean. And when the hot water hit the raw places, stinging like salt in a wound, still he couldn't make it hurt like the lesion in his armpit, which didn't hurt at all.

When Mark arrived at three with his store-bought pies, Steven was bearing the punch bowl full of steaming cider into the living room, where all the others were gathered. Mark crouched to the hearth to light the fire, and an overeager Andy knelt beside him and said, "I'll take care of that." Instantly Mark stiffened and backed off. Steven, grinding his teeth against a possible hernia as he set the punch bowl on the coffee table, wished he could call a time-out. It was only because Andy had brought the wood and laid the fire that he wanted the lighting honors. It was nothing more proprietary than that. Yet Steven could see Mark picking up on the fact that the kid had practically moved in.

Hastily Steven ladled the cider into cups, and Heather plunked a cinnamon stick into each one as she handed them round. Dell came trailing in, looking strangled in his tie, and they were six around the fire as Steven raised his cup, deciding not to wait for Sonny. "Long life, good health," he said, catching Mark's eye at last and smiling. The group repeated his hearty prayer and drank, cozy as all the last chapters of Dickens.

Then there was a funny moment when they didn't seem to know what to do, all dressed up in the middle of the day. Oh, they were maddeningly polite, right from the get-go. Andy told Mark how great he looked with his Florida tan. Mark lobbed a compliment about Heather's beaded sweater, which prompted from Steven an equal nicety on Linda's account. When they'd exhausted that tack, they took turns tossing out random remarks on the holiday, but kept it light, avoiding for politeness's sake the tortured Strindbergian dreads and scars that so possessed the Thursday group.

Heather recalled the snowy Thanksgivings in Wisconsin growing up, and her father actually slaughtering the bird on the family farm. "And it's really true, they run around with their heads cut off, bleeding all over the place." She laughed a bit shrill, the cider having gone right to her head. And didn't really notice the strained look that passed between Steven and Linda, or Dell casting his eyes to the fire. Turkey blood had a rather more immediate fix in some of their minds.

Merry and impromptu, Andy started in on the Pilgrims, recalling all the pious clichés of grade school, red man and white man together like brothers, sharing sharing sharing. He ladled another cup of cider and sat by Steven on the sofa, thigh to thigh. Now he launched into the story of John Alden, sent to propose to Priscilla for Myles Standish, pillar of rectitude but a dork when it came to women.

"As far as we can tell, ladies and gentlemen," Andy enthused, "we have here the only example of romantic love in America between 1620 and the films of Greta Garbo."

He laid a hand on Steven's knee. Steven shot a glance at Mark, who pretended not to see the knee maneuver, then pretended not to notice Steven's look. When Andy got to the punchline, he turned and put his face up close to Steven and delivered it with breathless histrionics: "Speak for yourself, John Alden." Clutching the front of Steven's shirt and affecting a swooning passion. They laughed around the fire, but barely. Linda and Dell didn't get the story at all, the cultural barriers being so queer, even if it hadn't been played for laughs.

Steven, rigid as stone, still felt as if the kid was all over him, though they'd resumed the simpler posture of hand on knee. An awful silence was starting to fall, as if they'd exhausted every lead, when they were saved by the creak of the dining-room door. Sonny walked in in a blue blazer and tie, hair spiffed back and squeaky clean, looking for all the world like an Ivy jock.

"I hope you realize, I only eat white meat," he announced with an impish smile.

At the sight of him Steven remembered the purloined hors d'oeuvres from Monte Carlo, and he leaped up from Andy's smothering proximity and ran to fetch them. He sailed around the kitchen, transferring the cold canapés to a silver tray, rustling up the turkey cocktail napkins, turning a drawer inside out for toothpicks. He couldn't recall exactly why he'd been so angry with Mark. He certainly didn't want him anymore, or anyone else for that matter. He only hoped the day would present an occasion when he could be unbearably civil, and prove to Mark there was no lingering romantic burnish.

The phone rang, and he grabbed it up on a millisecond's ring. It was Margaret: "Okay, we're ready, I got him in the car. He's a hundred and two, but he's talking English."

"Darling, can you wear the shawl? Angela's coming."

"Steven, I'm practically wearing overalls. Please don't expect a fashion statement. We'll be there in ten."

She rang off. Steven grabbed a mitt and pirouetted to the stove, grabbing the tray of dainties out just before they burned. He was on a roll. He whipped a white napkin onto a second silver tray and began arranging the little cheese cups and bacon-wrapped chestnuts. Then felt a sudden hand on his shoulder, and gasped and burned his finger and bellowed, "Shit!"

Of course it was Andy. "Steven, I'm sorry," he whimpered, "I didn't mean to scare you. I just wanted to help."

Steven reached to the sink and ran the sizzled finger under cold water. Then turned an eye on the kid that fairly glittered with domestic madness. "I'll tell you how you can help," he said softly. "Stop pawing me."

The milky face beneath the shock of sandy hair crumpled in bewilderment. "What do you mean?"

"This is not the time," Steven warned him, back to the cheese cups.

"You mean in there? I'm not supposed to touch you?"

"I think *maul* is the word you're looking for."

The face crumpled further, the eyes especially, tortured as only the very young can be by love's reversals. "I don't get you, Steven. You spend all your time pulling away. How did you ever last eight years?"

Not even skipping a beat with the canapés, making a second concentric circle, Steven drawled over his shoulder: "I would suggest that comparing yourself to Victor is very thin ice around here. *Very* thin ice."

"Why are you doing this? I'm supposed to be *ashamed* that we're sleeping together? Maybe you have a little more self-hatred about your sexuality than you realize. Did you ever think that?"

Steven picked up the two trays and faced him. "You take the hot and I'll take the cold."

"That's it? I don't get an answer?"

It had reached a kind of low-level hysterics for the sandy-haired boy. Not a pretty sight. Steven tried to be gentle, but his heart wasn't in it. "Honey, we've got to feed these people," he said, pleading from reason. "I'm sure you're right, I hate my dick, but please, I can't do psychology and dinner for ten at the same time. You'll survive. You're cute and sweet and sassy. But I'm not the one." He shrugged, not cruelly at all. There was more tenderness in him right now than he'd shown all week, and he understood the ache as Andy Lakin swallowed hard. But this was not the time. "Here, you better take the cold. They're simpler."

He handed Andy the cold tray, then whisked around him and through the swing door, no looking back. It didn't have to be done with such bad timing, except the young were so enamored of things blowing up in their faces.

Moving around the group by the fire, he was glad to see they had broken at last into smaller units. Sonny was regaling Dell and Linda with the crazy Greeks of Fresno, and Mark was being a trouper, answering Heather's starry questions about the magic of television. They all attacked the canapés with relish, two at a time as Steven passed.

"The bird's got about forty more minutes," he announced at large, his ace in the hole being Victor's passionate conviction that Americans overcooked fowl. "We'll eat by five, so don't overdo on the nibbles."

Andy, he could see, was standing rather gloomily off to the side, holding his tray dispiritedly and making no move to pass it around. He seemed to be trying to figure where he'd gone wrong. Steven let him be. But Heather, supersensitive by reason of a raft of self-help books, seemed to intuit Andy's blues and jumped up from the sofa. She squealed with pleasure as she popped hors d'oeuvres from his tray and asked him where he was from originally.

Steven seized the moment, leaned over Mark's shoulder, and said, "Can you give me a hand outside?"

"Sure." He stood up and followed Steven through the vestibule and out onto the front landing. Steven stopped and looked out over the city, and Mark stood beside him, hands in his pockets. The Catalina Eddy had rolled in over the setting sun, filling the basin below the mountains with chalk-white air, like very cold smoke. The low sun in the west was a disk in the fog. Steven shivered in only a shirt. Mark looked at him expectantly. "Uh, I thought you needed some help."

"Yup, in a minute. They should be right here. How's your dad?"

"Fine. He's found himself a fox." Mark chuckled and shook his head, digging his hands deeper in his pockets. Hooded as ever, his body language as tight as it used to be at the studio, ringed on every side by macho creeps. "He'll bury us all."

"I don't want to be buried anymore," said Steven, who in truth hadn't thought of it at all till now. "I want to be scattered." He accompanied this announcement with an outstretched hand and a slight flutter of the fingers, rather like a diva waving to the fans.

"But you have a plot and everything," retorted Mark. "Right beside Victor."

Steven made a soft little humming noise, as if he was trying to establish the pitch of what he would say next. He shivered again, but it didn't seem like the weather this time. "The first three months I visited every day. But he's not there." He was looking down at the roof of Mrs. Tulare's house, and Mark was looking sidelong at him. "I think I'll leave a couple of grand in my will. Then Margaret can take my ashes to Europe and have a little vacation too. Crete would be nice, say in the ruins of the palace at Phaistos." At last he turned and looked at Mark, rueful except it came out wistful. "Maybe I'll make it five grand, and you can go with her."

Mark snorted. "You think you're going to check out first? Excuse me—who's got four hundred T-cells? Not this pig."

"Two eighty-nine," said Steven automatically.

"Two forty," pounced Mark triumphantly. "So you'll be scattering me. I was thinking the woods behind my high-school gym, since that's where I first sucked dick, but the woods are probably gone by now. Your idea's better. Big Sur maybe, or Puerto Vallarta. Where would you like to go?"

"No fair. You have to pick. It's supposed to be a surprise, because I'll be prostrate."

Something about it cheered them both. Their shoulders grazed as they stood side by side, which managed to tip the scale from rue to irony. Casually Steven touched the back of Mark's hand, right at the fork of the veins. "Why don't we go there now," he said, "before one of us has to go in a box?" He seemed to mean this very moment, as if they had no other obligations here.

Mark nodded. "My place or your place?"

"Well, November's awfully windy on Crete. Puerto Vallarta might be terrific, and I can probably get us a shitload of discounts."

And then Margaret's fiery orange Celica rounded the knoll and drew up to the curb at the foot of the stairs. She got out on the driver's side looking drained and puffy, and no, she wasn't exactly wearing overalls, but the gray sack dress wasn't much of an improvement. She waved up at Steven and Mark as if she were surrendering, and Steven said, "We have to go help with the wheelchair."

Mark really didn't know anything about the case at all. Steven had told him about the stroke when Ray Lee first went in, but by now it had blurred with a dozen other horror stories currently making the rounds. They headed down the stairs to Margaret's car, the trip to Mexico dispersing into the chalk-white air. Mark and Margaret tossed off a cheery hello, as if they knew each other better than the one night back in September.

Steven opened the passenger's door and greeted Ray Lee, whose face was a skull with the skin stretched tight. "Well, I hope you're hungry, pardner," Steven said, " 'cause we got enough food up there to feed an Olympic team."

Beaming with excitement, the Korean lifted a covered dish from his lap and offered it to his host. His thin arms wobbled. Quickly Steven relieved him of the dish. "What's this?" he asked, lifting the lid a crack and sniffing. Then turned with a delirious grin to Mark. "The creamed onions!"

"Pie—lookit pie," retorted Ray impatiently, pointing over his shoulder. And there in the backseat, nested in a towel so it wouldn't be flung around, was the mince pie with the lattice crust. Steven hooted with pleasure, and Ray Lee wagged a bony finger. "Margaret help. She did crust."

But he looked just awful, pasty white and perspiring, shrunken in his visored cap and jacket, frail as an old, old man. This to Steven, who'd seen him every day for weeks. Mark was speechless, saucer-eyed, even as he shook Ray's wasted hand in greeting. Margaret had meanwhile flipped open the trunk and dragged the wheelchair out, expert as a stevedore. She wheeled it round to the passenger's side, and Mark and Steven stood back as she coaxed and gently tugged the Korean from the car.

He groaned once as he leaned against her, more in frustration than in pain, then collapsed in the chair, panting as if he'd just run up the mountain. Margaret stooped and placed his feet one by one in the footrests, grunting like an overworked nurse but every moment tender. She stood up, swiped a straggle of hair from her brow, and nodded at the two men. "Okay, guys, you take it from here."

She relieved Steven of the creamed onions and ducked in the back to retrieve her bag and the pie. Steven hadn't exactly worked out the logistics here. Sputtering at Mark, not quite making a sentence, he gestured at the chair and then the flight of steps, indicating they would carry him up. On either side they hunkered down and grabbed the seat bar just in front of the wheel and then the handle behind Ray's head.

"Wait," the Korean announced, and as they paused he reached in his jacket pocket and drew out the tortoise shades from L.A. Eyeworks. Carefully he put them on under the visored cap, then nodded for them to proceed.

Steven counted to three, and they heaved. It was surprisingly light. The chair was aluminum alloy, and Ray Lee weighed barely a hundred. The tricky thing was the climb upstairs, the space too narrow between the railing and the house to accommodate both men and the chair on one step. So they had to sort of straddle sideways, Steven one step up and Mark one step down, lugging and heaving, while Ray Lee sat serene as an emperor in a sedan chair, Margaret following a few steps behind bearing offerings like a priestess.

About halfway up Steven and Mark exchanged a red-faced look that was partly a goad, cheering each other on, and partly a ghastly

SOS, as if the disease had fallen on them like a meteor. Every step got a little harder, and Steven could see the cords standing out taut on Mark's neck. They grunted in unison, hunkered like Sumo wrestlers, and at last they reached the landing, Mark lifting his wheel over the last riser with a final burst of force that left him wheezing and panting worse than the patient himself.

"Thank you, gentamen," Ray Lee said, declining his head in a small imperial bow. Margaret handed him back his dish of onions and the pie, which he held proudly in his lap. Then she went around behind and made ready to push him in, waiting for Steven and Mark to catch their collective breath. They were both still reeling, but they pulled themselves together nicely, exchanging a nod of their own. Steven flung open the door and led the procession in.

They all knew somebody sick was coming, more or less, but no one was ready for this. The moment was so frozen, five heads turning as they came in the room, that Steven swore he could see the split between the men and the women. Dell and Sonny and Andy, who all had the virus, stared at the enfeebled figure in the movable chair with a kind of disbelieving horror, to see as if in a dark mirror the place where they were bound. Yet there was something else as well, a weird fascination, as if every case was uniquely appalling, and thus another lesson in how to die. Heather and Linda winced in pain, and a terrible grief sharpened their features. Then they both looked up at Margaret, to see if they had the strength to be where she was.

Steven started to introduce them all, but just then Heather sank to her knees beside the chair, laid her head against Ray's arm, and began to sob. Gently he stroked her hair and made a hushing sound. The rest stood dumb while he soothed her, refusing to let her wail that she had abandoned him. But he let her cry for a while, as if he understood that she was crying for all of them there.

Only when she was done, groping for a Kleenex in her bag, did Steven complete the rounds, so that each guest gravely shook Ray's hand. He loved the formality and the attention, then asked for a glass of champagne. Steven looked askance at Margaret, who shrugged as if to say what the hell, and Steven dug out a pony of Mumm's rusting in the back of the fridge.

Margaret came into the kitchen and declared the turkey cooked to a T—for it was she who had instructed Victor in the sin of over-roasting. "Americans like their turkey dry as sawdust," she announced to no one in particular, implying that those gathered here were devastatingly Continental. It was only three days ago she informed Steven that Richard would not be joining them for dinner. "He's made other plans," she said succinctly, indicating there would be no further discussion.

Now she insisted, before they carved it, that Steven bear the bird into the living room to present it to the group in its pristine state. Which he did, eliciting a round of cheers and applause. The moment served to galvanize them all, time for the under-chefs and galley slaves to get the feast set out in the banquet hall. Steven felt a knife of pain between his shoulder blades as he tottered with the turkey to the sideboard.

Mark was enlisted to carve, though he swore he hadn't a clue. Heather and Linda donned their aprons and began a frenzy of potato-mashing and gravy-making. Dell and Sonny fetched chairs from all over the house, and Andy filled glasses with water and wine and rather a droopy countenance. Such that Margaret murmured to Steven, both in the midst of bearing tureens, "Why is the boy so melancholy? Did you break his heart already?"

"Mm—cracked it a bit," he replied, trying not to sound too cavalier.

At last they had the myriad bounty lined up on the sideboard, brimming with delights. Ray Lee begged them to take a picture before it got spoiled, but Linda didn't have a flash. They swore a group oath to memorize it in all its cornucopian glory, and then they attacked. Lining up and serving one another with relish, swords beaten to ploughshares, peaceful as pilgrims and Indians. Steven stood back with folded arms and watched them load their plates, then remembered in a flash of panic that he hadn't put out the place cards.

The doorbell rang as Heather was taking a great dollop of cranberry sauce, so Steven had to leave them to their own devices to seat themselves. He opened the front door, and Angela gripped his arm wide-eyed. "Tell me the truth, do I look like shit?"

How could she even think so, drop-dead chic in the black silk dress with an alligator belt as wide as a cummerbund, a white angora cardigan around her shoulders. No, she looked fabulous, he told her three different ways, till the haunted look in her eyes began to soften. All right, she would stay. Steven was dispatched to run down to the curb to release the cab, in the process having to pay the fifteen-dollar fare.

When he came back up, she needed coaxing again before she entered the house, a thumbnail refresher course on who was there. He sleeked her ruffled feathers and bore her in on his arm, astonished to find his guests all seated without any bloodshed. The first thing he noticed was Margaret with the embroidered shawl about her shoulders, which she'd snatched from her bag when the doorbell rang. She winked when Steven smiled at her. The gray sack was magically transformed.

Steven had to admit, as he went round introducing Angela, that he couldn't have seated them better himself. Ray Lee was at the foot of the table, Margaret and Heather on either side. Next to Margaret was Mark, then Linda, then Dell, then a space for Steven at the head and Angela to his left. Next to Angela's place was Sonny, with Andy between him and Heather. No potential nuclear explosions.

Steven commanded them to begin, then steered Angela to the sideboard. He had to coax her through every dish, for she had a terror of getting fat, despite being cocaine-thin. Steven made sure she took a spoonful of everything, taking twice as much himself. By the time they sat down, the table was abuzz with conversations one on one, punctuated by waves of praise for the food. Margaret was heavily tête-à-tête with Mark, while Heather was practically spoon-feeding Ray.

Sonny turned from talking men with Andy to welcome Angela more warmly, his company manners as impeccable as his Ivy drag. Yet there was something else immediately, as if they caught in each other's countenance the trace of an old memory. "I bet you're a Gemini," Angela said, all her shyness vanished now.

"Yeah, as a matter of fact I am," Sonny replied with a grin, clearly impressed by her perspicacity.

She laid down the fork with which she had been pushing around her anorexic portions. She turned and looked deep in the Greek's eyes. A passionate flush had come into her face, vivid as the expectant look he returned. "You don't have very long, do you?" she asked in a dusky undertone. Slowly Sonny shook his head. Angela covered his hand with hers. "I knew it the minute I saw you. . . ."

Steven, who had been politely bobbing his head in their direction, waiting for an entrance, suddenly reached for an olive instead, avoiding by inches the New Age quicksand. Sucking out the pimento, he turned to his right, just in time to see Dell steal a glance at his watch. "Are we keeping you from something?" Steven asked in his crispest housemother tone.

"She's havin' a cable telethon at seven."

"She who?"

"Mother."

Steven swallowed his olive hard. He had been laboring under the assumption that Dell had put his obsession aside once he became a wanted man. The futility of it all was obvious to everyone. Mother Evangeline had gotten all the sympathetic press. The disks had been restored to their rightful place, and once again were spewing out weekly mailings to the faithful. Nobody ever even understood exactly what the terrorism was meant to protest. Linda smiled at Steven, thanking him effusively, as if she couldn't quite believe that the nightmare of the last weeks had resolved itself so peaceably. For her sake Steven pretended he hadn't heard the Mother Evangeline reference. Blocked it out, the way he blocked out Victor's first demented phrases, locked in his mind without any door.

He gazed around the table, satisfied that everyone was being taken care of. Ray Lee was nodding off in his chair but smiling beatifically. Then Steven looked to the right, where the dark was beginning to fall on the hillside. The sliding glass door was open about six inches. In the crack of the door lay the dog, head on his paws, nose in the room and the rest of him on the terrace. His eyes were open and staring cautiously at Steven, his nose still quivering moistly, raptured by the feast.

Steven pointed a finger at him, ready to cry "Out!" There were limits, after all, even if everyone else had decided to befriend the beast. But Steven found he didn't have the heart, not today. Deluding himself, of course, to think that any inch the dog had gained would ever be recaptured. Yet he had no choice. If he meant the house to be brimful of holiday cheer, everything perfect, an island in time, then he had to give a guinea to the chimneysweep.

He stood up at his place and reached for the bottle of Beaujolais Nouveau. The laughter was like music to him as he drained the last of the wine into Dell's glass and disappeared through the swing door into the kitchen. He stood for a moment dazed with satisfaction. Then he dropped the wine bottle into the wastebasket and looked around hopefully, as if it would come back to him in a second what he had come in here to get. He reached for the refrigerator door, but then pressed his head against it, between the two star magnets. "Oh Vic," he whispered in a strangled voice, and a rush of hot tears stung his eyes.

He was flooded for a moment by the pointlessness of it all. Stranger in his own house, wandering round the edges of this party like a ghost, no one to let him in. Even so, it wasn't a full-fledged cry. More like losing his breath, and a sharp stab of pain in the chambers of the heart. Victor was almost palpable to him, as if that guttural infectious laugh were spilling in from the dining room, beckoning Steven back. The old life, the lost one, was all that made any sense. It tantalized him like a mirage, clinking its glasses and chattering happily just beyond the door.

And then the door swung open behind him, and Steven turned from the fridge and quickly wiped his eyes, facing away from who-ever'd walked in. If it was Andy Lakin whining with need, Steven swore he would stuff him down the disposal. But it was Mark: "Hey, pal, you need some help?"

Steven stared at the butcher-block island, covered with pies and trifle and Linda's pudding. In two hours they would all be out of there, and then he could go to bed for a week. "No, I was just . . . taking a break."

Mark laughed as if he understood completely, that after pulling off such a production Steven might need a breather. He clapped a hand on Steven's shoulder. "Listen, it's going great. First Thanksgiving I ever had where I'm not the only fag. Except—is that guy gonna make it through dinner?"

"You mean Ray? Jesus, I hope so. He deserves a piece of his fucking pie."

They both grunted in disbelief at the awfulness of the poor Korean's situation. They couldn't have said how close he was to the end, but closer than either of them ever wanted to be. Like the other three ticking men at the table, both had made a sort of contrary vow when Ray Lee entered the portals of the feast: not to last so long. It was the timebomb at the edge of all their plates, like some ghastly party favor, the question of checking out before it got that bad.

"Margaret's dead on her feet," continued Mark, rubbing the spot between Steven's shoulders where the muscle was tight. "She's afraid to wish it was over and even more scared it'll just keep going." Steven nodded, stretching his neck as the muscle unknotted, happy as a dog being scratched. "She said uh . . . apparently you and the kid broke up."

It wasn't certain who pulled away first, maybe it was a draw, but Steven sidled out of the massage and turned to face him, brutally nonchalant. "I wouldn't put it quite that way. You have to have something to break up *from*. We were just—" But he couldn't think of the word, and he stood there in a kind of half-shrug, half-flail, wishing they'd all go away.

"I love you, you know."

"Uh-huh." Steven nodded dumbly. Still his palms were open, the shrug not quite finished.

"No, I'm serious, Steven. I really love you."

"Look, I don't think this is the time," Steven began miserably.

"Sure it is. An hour ago you were taken, and now you're not. I think my timing's perfect." Mark was somehow beckoning Steven out to play.

"But I don't want to be taken," protested Steven, as petulant and stubborn as a child. "I hate my dick—ask Andy."

There was a bare three feet between them, yet Mark seemed to take a great stride forward as he moved to grasp Steven by the shoulders. Even as he tilted his head and planted his open mouth on Steven's lips, Steven was thinking: *he doesn't kiss.*

For the moment Steven could scarcely process his own name. He stayed with it, tongue to tongue, as much as anything to give himself time to think. But he didn't think, he just kissed. And when the kitchen door swung open and Margaret froze on the threshold, pulling them apart at last, Steven wanted to say it was all a mistake. "What do we need?" he demanded—slightly panting, having just come up for air, but determined to focus things back on the matter at hand.

"It'll wait," she said with a gloat of irony, and ducked back into the dining room.

Steven gave Mark his fiercest look. "We're going back in there," he declared, not for nothing commander of this operation.

"Fine with me," said Mark, grinning as if he'd never stopped, all through the kiss.

"Why are you doing this?"

"Doing *what?* I'm finally acting normal. What's the problem? You've been in love with me for months."

"*Was,*" growled Steven, withering with contempt. "I'm totally over you."

"Bullshit."

Thus giving Steven the opening to exit in a defiant huff. He batted the swing door wide and strode back into his banquet hall, only to discover that everything had fallen apart in the interim. They'd all erupted out of their places. At the foot of the table Margaret and Heather hovered over Ray. For an instant Steven thought he'd died, but then saw the women were struggling to pull off the Korean's shirt, drenched with the lightning sweat that broke his fever. Otherwise the table was virtually empty. Only Linda Espinoza still sat at her place, eating her dinner with exquisite delicacy, smiling up at Steven as if she hoped he wouldn't notice that everyone else had run away.

"Steven," Margaret asked him briskly, "you think we can borrow a shirt?"

"Sure," he replied in a frazzle, darting away.

"And a towel," Margaret called after him.

As he cut through the living room, he saw Dell hunched on the sofa watching the tube. Mother Evangeline was offering a prayer on her holiday telethon, surrounded by a melting pot of fresh-scrubbed kids. Dell licked nervously at his upper lip. He seemed about to talk back to the screen. Steven hustled across the vestibule and through the study, where Angela sat at the desk speaking earnestly into the phone. Sonny was cross-legged on the floor in front of her, hanging on every word.

"He's a Gemini," Angela said, "and he's had an excellent regression back to Egypt."

Steven didn't wait to hear, but guessed she was talking with her channeler. He stopped and pulled a big white towel from the linen closet, then headed for the far door in the bedroom—Victor's closet. As he flipped through the clothes, he was only thinking Victor was closer to the Korean's size than he was. He took a cream-colored dress shirt off a hanger and a yellow cardigan sweater, the latter bought on an achingly clear November day in Pisa. As Steven shut the closet door, he could practically smell the fallen leaves of the chestnut trees along the Tuscan street.

Crossing the study again, he saw that Sonny had taken the phone, though he was still sitting on the floor Indian-style. "All the dominion below the Second Cataract," he was saying, while Angela zapped the base of his skull with acupressure. Neither one even looked at Steven.

Dell was still all alone in the living room, his eyes fixed on the TV screen. Mother Evangeline, in tight close-up, spoke with a low thrill, not a foot from Dell Espinoza's face: "To the homosexuals we say, thank God for AIDS, because it is bringing you home to Him."

"Why don't you turn that off?" said Steven, passing through. Dell turned and stared at him, uncomprehending, eyes on fire, as if he'd taken a dose of radiated light from the Sony. Steven didn't repeat his injunction but kept on walking, suddenly realizing that the crisis of Ray was simpler.

Mark had joined the women in the dining room as they ministered to the Korean, but he stood slightly apart by the sideboard. Hands behind his back and lifting slightly off his toes, looking out at the night with an abstract smile. Steven went right to Margaret. With one end of the towel, he wiped Ray's bony chest, every rib fearfully distinct, the strings of a human harp. Margaret vigorously rubbed Ray's head, his blue-black hair still full and sleek despite the waste of the rest of him. Ray moaned in a dreamy way, enjoying the massage.

Tenderly Heather slipped the shirt over his arm, and Steven crouched and pulled Ray forward so she could bring it around his back. The other arm was a bit of a struggle, but at last the shirt was on. Steven buttoned it up the front while Heather adjusted the sleeves. The memory of dressing Victor was very intense, but Steven didn't cry. For all his own tender ministrations here, he realized he had consciously chosen not to bring a shirt of his own. He didn't want to see any threads of his on a dying man.

"I think it's time we got you home," said Margaret, combing back Ray's hair.

"No," he retorted with startling force, the emperor again. "I have dessert."

The group around him burst out laughing, relieved to be restored so quick from hospital to holiday. Forget the seconds. Now they were galvanized by Ray Lee's spunk, and the women moved to clear the sideboard. Steven looked over and caught Mark's eye. Mark smiled at him serenely and spoke it again, quiet but firm: "Bullshit."

"Coffee," Steven barked in return, jerking a thumb toward the kitchen.

Mark followed him dutifully back through the swing door. Fast on his feet, Steven whipped open the freezer and pulled out a pound of decaf French. He turned and handed it off to Mark like a football, then barreled across to the island. From the cupboard underneath he yanked out the Krups grinder and the clunky aluminum coffee-maker, big enough for a church supper. These he set on the counter next to the stove, then crooked a finger to call Mark over. He crossed and set to work immediately.

Steven leaned very close to his ear: "And even if I still was— which would be staggeringly self-destructive of me, not to mention the stress which I don't need—it wouldn't get us anywhere. Because you don't want it."

"You act like I'm *accusing* you of something," Mark protested, and Steven slapped the counter to keep him focused on the coffee. Mark poured the beans into the grinder. "You stuck it out through all *my* bullshit. I was scared. I wanted to have it without giving anything back."

"And you're not scared anymore, is that it? Ha!" Steven was banging around in the china cabinet, lifting out dessert plates. Mark drew a breath to answer, and Steven hissed like a diamondback.

For the swing door had opened again, admitting the women in procession. Heather, Linda, Margaret, each bearing a plundered tureen or platter. Heather ventured to say there was enough food left for everyone to have a big doggie bag for take-home. Margaret measured out nine pills for Ray's 7 P.M. dose of last-ditch medicine. Linda poured the lemon sauce for the guava pudding into a small pan and put it on the stove to simmer.

Heather and Margaret disappeared back to the dining room, and Mark said, "Sure I'm scared." He was standing beside Linda as she stirred, measuring spoons of coffee into the pot, and Linda smiled at him blandly, just as she did when the women she worked for said things that didn't quite translate. Steven was silent, loading cups and saucers onto a tray. "We managed to go a couple of months," continued Mark, half to himself, "not calling it anything at all."

Steven's teeth gritted. "Please—don't romanticize our dysfunction." Linda made herself as small as a mouse now, turning the gas up high and stirring fast.

"I know, I was awful," Mark declared, steeling himself for his own hard judgment. "I just left you hanging there all the time. I didn't know what to do. All I knew was I didn't want you to go away."

"Do you want bowls or plates for the pudding?" Steven asked Linda, who could barely choke out an answer.

Then Heather and Margaret appeared with one last teetering load, declaring the dining room clear. Steven strode through the house, calling his wayward flock together. Once more they congregated by the sideboard. All the desserts were lined up in a row, anchored at one end by a bowl of fruit and at the other by a tray of Godiva mints.

Quite properly everyone insisted on a taste of all the homemade goods, so Steven and Margaret and Andy together fashioned samplers, a sliver of mince and a spoon of trifle and one of pudding, with Linda ladling the lemon sauce very carefully so as not to run into the rest. Mark declared with chivalrous good humor that he didn't expect any loyalty to his pumpkin pies from Gelson's. Heather poured the coffee. She was sitting beside Ray Lee, who had recovered his equilibrium dramatically since his sweat, so he was able to dispense the cream and sugar.

"One lump or two?" he said to each, not a trace of Korean in his voice, wielding the tongs with infinite precision.

They all took cream and sugar today, even the ones who took it black, for Ray's sake. Then they proceeded at Steven's command into the living room, laden with cups and plates. The television was silenced, and they clustered round the fire. Heather wheeled Ray in, brilliant in the yellow sweater, and the feasting began again, punctuated by murmurs of delight and lavish praise for the mince. Not that anyone meant to slight the excellent pudding of Linda's or Andy Lakin's terribly serious trifle, which had necessitated five separate cookbooks, as if he'd been doing a term paper. But the pie garnered most of the compliments, flung like handfuls of rose petals at the proud Korean. A mince pie better than Wisconsin, Heather swore, its lattice lighter than air. A blue-ribbon pie, dark with citron and raisins and laced with Courvoisier.

"Margaret helped," protested Ray Lee modestly, but beaming all the while.

They had nothing else to give him but this, and they made him promise to make another for Christmas. The flush of good fellowship rosied his cheeks. His eyes were bright and dancing. And they all ate their pie in little feral bites to make it last as long as they could, for Ray's sake.

Mark sat next to Angela on the sofa and was exquisitely charming, making it clear that his bitterness toward her husband didn't extend to her. That said, the two of them launched into an orgy of slurs against the person of Lou Ciotta. Across the way Heather negotiated an intricate discussion between Linda and Ray about household customs in Mexico and Korea, like a Berlitz class gone slightly haywire.

Sitting on the floor and eating off the coffee table, Andy told Sonny and Dell the tale of his coming out, blow by blow. He didn't seem to care that both his listeners were utterly preoccupied and lost in thought. Sonny cast blushing glances at Angela, smitten like a teenager. All the red and soreness of his flesh had vanished. He was pure spirit. Beside him Dell still seemed to be watching the blank screen of the Sony, as if he could see in the dusk there the shape of his next reprisal.

Margaret sidled up to Steven where he stood with an elbow on the mantel, as placid as a pipe-smoking duke, and said: "Well?"

"It's not what you think," he whispered.

"What do I think?"

"Happily ever after. That's what you *always* think." It was very hard in a whisper to get the proper disdain across.

"He's in love with you, don't deny it," she purred.

"He likes boys," retorted Steven, spitting the noun like venom, as if he was talking nine-year-olds. Then turned his back on the room and stared at the fire. "He's had about three hundred boyfriends. He doesn't know how to commit."

Margaret watched his flickering face for a moment. "So? Dying makes people grow up sometimes."

"Yeah, the big D. See how fucked it is? Who wants to even get started if everyone's just gonna die?"

Margaret plumped the shawl at her shoulders, running the fabric through her fingers, studying the fringe. "I'd take a year in love," she said.

Steven gave a vague toss of the head at the room behind. "Oh, really? Even if that was the second year?" he asked dryly, and she knew he meant Ray.

"Maybe I'd just be selfish and take the first year first. Then see about later later."

"Margaret, don't be so wise. Does Richard know he's dating Bette Davis?"

She winced, very slightly. "Richard hasn't a clue," she said. "About anything. He thinks I look for this shit." She nodded over his shoulder, as vaguely as he had, putting Ray in the third-person neuter. "Like I'm some kind of tragedy junkie. At least that one lives"— and she nodded over his other shoulder at Mark—"on the same *planet* you do. Even if he is no good at it, you are. That's what he's probably drawn to."

"Not my ravishing body?"

"Bodies are very overrated, dear. They last about fifteen minutes. *He* knows that."

"Look, why don't *you* go out with him, Margaret?"

They laughed at that like old conspirators, for Victor always used to sigh, whenever one of his buddies got summarily dumped by a bad man, "You should go out with Margaret." Steven pulled her close into a hug, tasting the shivering fringe of the shawl, grateful for the sisterly advice. Which he might toss out without a second thought, but that was to be expected. What had really happened here was Margaret's giving her blessing. It hadn't been required for Andy Lakin, who was by definition nothing from the moment Steven invited him home. Something much more ancient was needed for this, especially in the absence of everybody's family. The force of a dowager empress, with ties to the old kingdom of Steven and Victor. Someone to say it was time.

They unclenched from the hug to find Heather an inch away, smiling anxiously, rubbing her hands together as if she'd taken a chill. "He's had a little accident," she said.

Even as they turned to look, Steven was thinking that accidents used to mean crashing and screaming; now they were all silent. Ray looked at them sheepishly. "I peed," he said. Margaret bustled over, a nurse coming off her break. "I laughed too hard," Ray continued, his cheer not really dampened even now. There was nothing so grim as a puddle below the chair, perhaps because he was wearing a pair of billowing parachute pants. But Margaret tucked a hand under him, patting like a mother checking Pampers, and nodded crisply to Steven.

"I think we'll call it a day."

Immediately they all sprang into action. Linda and Heather hurried into the kitchen to make up a bag of leftovers. Andy went to get Margaret's purse, and Dell and Mark gathered dirty plates while Sonny stoked the fire. They needed to be busy so as to cover the uncomfortableness of the moment, a small pang of shame each had carried from his childhood—as if they'd all just wet their pants. No one could quite look anyone else in the eye.

Except Steven, who raised a bushy eyebrow to Margaret, asking what it meant. Her lips crinkled, and she shrugged, as if to say this was a new one. So they at least acknowledged the somber milestone, that at seven-twenty on Thursday night the twenty-sixth Ray Lee had slipped into a new phase. Steven recalled the exact moment when Victor first wet the bed, startled and embarrassed even in his swooning state. Linda had the same recall of Marcus, when she'd assured him it wasn't any different from a sweat. And kept it from Dell.

With Margaret pushing the chair, they crowded round in a group, wishing Ray well and squeezing his hand and praising the pie some more as they waved him out the front door. Heather set the bag of leftovers on his lap and bent and kissed him gently on the lips. Sonny and Dell, being the strongest, pushed forward to pick up the chair. But Steven and Mark had the same thought at the same moment, traded a look and got there first, assuring the younger men they knew the angles better.

Not that Steven didn't feel the knife in his back when he lifted up, but he could take it. For even more than the journey up, the journey down—step by shaky step, their faces bulging red—had the feel of a great ceremony. Ray Lee was more the emperor than ever, regal in the yellow sweater and waving grandly to the guests on the landing above. There was something wonderful too, the kind of thing that couldn't be taken away, about carrying a man when he was still alive. There were coffins enough to come. And the straining together, all their strength required, had a certain exalted symmetry for Mark and Steven both. Bearing him lightly, no false step.

They reached the curb and set him down and grinned at each other and panted. "Gentamen, you are the top drawer," said Ray Lee, reaching to clutch their hands. Margaret opened the door, and he stood up to totter in. Only now did Steven see the great wet stain on his backside, and he looked away for modesty's sake, as if the emperor mustn't be witnessed in disgrace. Margaret settled him into the passenger's seat, and as she closed the door, a last roar of good-bye came from the group at the top of the stairs. Ray Lee flung a bony hand out the car window.

Margaret went around to the driver's side. She winked at Steven as she slung herself in. "H.E.A.," she declared wryly by way of farewell. The Celica moved off, Ray Lee's hand waving above the roof, indomitable, and they whistled and shouted from up above.

Mark turned puzzled to Steven and repeated the code: "H.E.A.?"

"Happily ever after," Steven replied, no irony at all.

And then they moved to go upstairs shoulder to shoulder, a pair of stevedores who'd put in a brute day's work. The guests remained in a cluster on the landing, looking off down the mountain in various meditative poses, some of them simply glad to be alive, some wondering just how long. About halfway up the stairs Steven nudged Mark, and they turned face to face, inches apart. "Okay, so we love each other," he said, softly so no one would hear. "Now what?"

Mark shook his head with a mischievous smile. "You got me, pal. I was thinkin' maybe I wouldn't go home tonight."

Steven blanched. "At all?"

"Well, I could always leave at four A.M. in hysterics."

"Oh, good," said Steven, reassured, and they headed up to the top, herding the guests back in.

But the chain was broken. Now was the time when it might have been useful to have a straight man around, to help them segue into a football game. Otherwise they'd run out of reasons to keep this gang together. Linda and Heather went promptly to the kitchen, insisting over Steven's protests on doing the cleanup detail. Angela called a cab. She had to be up at the crack of dawn to be driven to the treatment center, and besides, her Valium was wearing off and she didn't have another one on her.

Sonny waited with her on the landing. She held his hand in both of hers, but they didn't really need to speak, so tuned were they to the same deep chord. On the strength of Egypt alone, she had managed to get him a private session with Salou for the following morning, though the master was booked through March. She had written down the address at Betty Ford so Sonny could write. But they made no further plans with each other because they both knew he was on the cusp of a great divide, just as she was. They had both been burning bridges now for days, and there was something wonderfully exhilarating about meeting a fellow traveler. In fact they made a beautiful couple, standing there in the moonlight, as sleek as a pair of second leads.

"I feel so free right now," she said, even though her teeth were faintly grinding from the coke withdrawal.

"Yeah. For the first time in years I feel like my journey's beginning again."

Andy Lakin had been acting restless ever since Ray Lee's accident, and had done about as much avoiding of Steven as he could handle. Being so unfailingly polite and helpful, he was the obvious candidate for breaking the women's lock on the cleanup crew. He did take a load of cups and saucers into the kitchen, but seeing Steven at the back door laughing, tossing scraps to the dog outside, suddenly he'd had it. Stiff with dignity, he walked over and touched Steven's shoulder. "I've got to be going," he said. "Could I talk to you for a second?"

Only fair. Steven followed him into the bedroom. Andy closed the door behind them, and Steven prepared for a dressing down. "There's really nothing to say," said Andy, cool and rather arch. "I don't think you're the type who's going to connect again. It's like climbing up a glass wall, trying to reach you."

"I'm sorry."

"I never should've come up here in the first place. I don't need men who run the other way."

"I'm sorry."

Andy opened Steven's closet and grabbed up a gym bag off the floor, his tidy overnight kit, underwear and jeans and a mini hair dryer. Then he ducked into the bathroom, unexpectedly touching as he rooted around in the medicine chest for his toothbrush, razor, allergy pills. Steven stood watching in the bathroom doorway, admiring his tough-mindedness and flashing pride and—wistfully—his perfect butt, ripe as a pair of melons. Steven wished he could say something very sage, so Andy would only remember the nice part.

"I deserve better," Andy declared, pushing him aside. He darted a glance around the room to make sure he'd gotten everything. So little mark did anyone leave behind, thought Steven. "On second thought, Steven, you might find somebody after all. Some guy who's given up just like you have. I wish I'd known you when you were my age."

Steven smiled. "Before the automobile."

But Andy was out the door. Making his rounds of all the remaining guests, saying good-bye with withering good manners. He even remembered to pick up his trifle bowl as he left the kitchen. And still Steven wanted to toss the kid a pearl of wisdom, hoping it would come to him at the last moment, right on the threshold with the city of diamonds below.

But then he opened the front door and followed Andy out, and Angela's cab was just pulling up. They ended up going down the stairs all four together, too many good-byes at once. At the curb Angela threw her arms around Steven's neck. "Thank you for saving my life today," she said, and Steven looked helplessly over her shoulder as Andy shook Sonny's hand. "And for letting me meet this extraordinary man," continued Angela, pulling back to look soulfully into Steven's eyes. Her Bronx accent seemed to evaporate on this high plain. "He is of the pharaoh's lineage. Your house will be blessed for a hundred generations."

"Take care, Steven," Andy called.

Steven, trapped in the priestess's arms, looked up to see him already walking away to his car across the street. "Yeah," he called after him lamely, and that was as wise as it got.

Angela turned to Sonny with a last Cleopatra smile. Wisdom poured out of her like musk. "Be free of things and be free with men," she said. "The path never stops." And then ducked into the back of the cab like a queen entering a golden coach. "Beverly Wilshire," she told the driver, and as they lurched away she called back over her shoulder like the scarf of Isadora: "I'll be home for Christmas!"

For a moment Steven and Sonny stood silent. Then Sonny said: "Unbelievable."

When they walked in the house, just four of them left around the fire, it was starting to feel like *Ten Little Indians*. And right away Heather announced she was driving Linda home. For they had become fast friends in the kitchen, or at least Heather had. Linda seemed much more tentative altogether, but it may have had more to do with her brother being present, as if she was betraying him in his isolation by laughing with somebody new. But Dell was the lightest of all, bantering with Heather that next time maybe she could give his sister a lift *up* the hill as well.

"And then teach her to drive," he teased, playfully tugging Linda's ponytail. "We gotta get her off the bus before she's an old lady."

Linda flushed with pleasure to see him cheerful at all. Her heart was easy as she gathered her bag and her camera, precious with the pictures of the two of them. Heather had promised to show her how the computer worked at Shaw Travel, one small lesson at a time. Already Linda imagined how it would be to have a job in an office and not be a maid. And by then the ruckus would all have blown over, and she and Dell could be together again. A two-bedroom apartment, so she could take better care of him. By next Thanksgiving maybe. She hadn't felt so ambitious since Marcus died.

Once again Steven did the honors, walking them to the door. "It breaks my heart to see him like that," said Heather, tugging Steven's arm. "I hope it didn't show in my face."

"No, you were wonderful," Steven reassured her. He had seen the stricken look on all of them, as if Death himself had walked into the room.

Linda was too demure to touch him, but clasped her hands together as fervently as Beatriz Espinoza at Mass. "Thank you, Steven," she said, wrenched with emotion. "You are so good to us."

It was the same intonation with which Beatriz called the parish priest a saint. Of course Linda meant a great deal more than dinner. In the fullness of her love for Dell, she thought of Steven as the man who'd saved him, simply by the influence of his sterling character and spotless life, like some kind of fag scoutmaster. Steven didn't like the responsibility one little bit, but he didn't want to seem ungrateful either, so he bore the canonization with a plucky smile. The two women going downstairs arm in arm were as improbable together as their hair—Heather's frizzed and frosted, piled on top of her head, and Linda's modest ponytail, clasped with the white barrette she had worn since grammar school in Morelia.

When Steven came back in, the musical chairs were down to three. They were all looking thoughtfully into the fire, Mark on the sofa and Sonny and Dell in the overstuffed chairs. Steven took a seat on the sofa but distinctly at the other end from Mark, a reflex shyness. Sonny was eating a bunch of grapes, spitting the seeds into the fire, but nobody's mom was around to tell him it was gross. He seemed completely at ease and untroubled, a tribute to the soul aerobics of

Angela Ciotta, since he had otherwise been stalking around in a nervous pitch for days.

Yet it was Sonny, mellow as Buddha, who broke the silence with a mordant laugh. "That was a dead man, wasn't it?"

Nobody contradicted him. The only thing that happened was that Mark laid his hand on Steven's. Not smothering like Andy Lakin, not proprietary in any way, but enough to make Steven blush crimson. Curiously, a not unpleasant feeling.

"You think he knows?" asked Dell.

"It's weird, isn't it?" offered Mark, glad somebody else noticed. "He's just floatin' away. Doesn't seem angry or anything."

"Antidepressants," said Steven succinctly, still two spots of pink on his cheekbones.

"Oh yeah? When do I start?" Dell put his feet on the coffee table, nudging the dish of Godiva.

"Not me," said Mark. "I don't want to get too fuzzy to pull the plug."

None of them wanted to talk about it for real. The only reason they mentioned it at all was by way of perfunctory good manners, like removing their hats in the street as a funeral lumbered by. The three widows had memories they couldn't bear. It wasn't just antidepressants. All of them had watched the disengagement of the brain, when the men with the tubes in their arms couldn't remember they were dying anymore. No more than they could remember being alive, or who the figure was sitting weeping softly by the bed. Steven, always so good about letting the memories of Victor flood in, could feel himself leaning like Atlas against the dike, a mountain of sorrow behind it.

"How old is he?" asked Dell.

"Twenty-nine, thirty." Steven shrugged.

"He looked fifty," Sonny declared, spitting the last of the seeds.

And then Sonny's eyes shifted from the fire to the two hands clasped on the sofa, chaste as a couple of pilgrims. He smiled slyly. He was the least romantic creature in all of West Hollywood, or at least possessed of a romance that had nothing whatsoever to do with love. The night he had gotten it on with Mark was full of the old disappointment that had dogged him ever since Fresno: one more man who wasn't quite as hot or dirty as he was. Almost, but not quite; never enough to get him over the top. And Steven to him was utterly sexless, but that was true of anybody married, though not including the wayward husbands who tore themselves to pieces at his feet.

He looked at the two men's faces, Steven then Mark. He could see quite clearly they were both in love. They were wholly undefended, and for the moment anyway there wasn't a trace of vanity in either of them. You couldn't have said, for instance, how old they were, though Sonny knew perfectly well they were both around forty. Not that they looked younger, just that it didn't matter.

Sonny reached over and swatted Dell's feet from the coffee table. "Where'd you learn your manners, boy? C'mon, or we'll miss the beginning."

"Of what?"

"The movie." And when Dell looked at him totally bewildered, Sonny's grin was as innocent as a bag boy at Ralph's. "Don't you know when it's time to take a night off? These dudes want to be alone."

Guiltily Steven slipped his hand out from under Mark's. "We don't want to be alone," he said, more than a little alarmed.

Dell was still lagging behind. It had taken him days to fully comprehend what Andy Lakin was doing there, assuming he was just another sudden tenant of the safe house. Besides, Dell was no friend of Sonny. They had kept a courteous distance ever since Dell moved in. But dead though his heart might be, it wasn't blind. He saw the heat in Steven's cheeks, the eyes that couldn't keep a secret. For all his sullen despair, he owed this man his freedom. Mark protested laughing that they didn't know *what* they wanted, but Dell was on his feet, beckoning Sonny.

"So get off your ass. I been waiting to ride in that sissy white car. Maybe after we'll cruise the boulevard, pick up a couple nineteen-year-olds."

"Dell, you can't go out," said Steven, rising as if to block him.

"It's okay, Steve, I don't have a bomb on me."

"Oh, that's real funny. Why don't you call 911 and tell 'em which movie you're going to?"

"Don't worry, I'll take care of him." Sonny darted across to the vestibule and pulled open the coat closet. He grabbed his leather bomber jacket and tossed Dell the orange parka.

Steven turned helplessly to Mark. "They're going to get in trouble."

"They're grown-ups," Mark retorted with a shrug.

Sonny walked over and shadow-boxed at Steven. "I only got one request, guys. Name the firstborn after him and me." Steven reached out to strangle him, and he danced away.

Dell was already out the door into the night. Steven caught Sonny's arm as the Greek headed over the threshold, and he looked back at his landlord with antic defiance. "It's not a joke," Steven hissed. "I promised his sister."

"Stevie, there's only a minute left—a second." He snapped his fingers in Steven's face, here and gone in the wink of an eye. "Me and the spick, we're the last two lonely guys. We got nothing to lose."

And he was gone, leaving Steven maddened in the doorway, a housemother who'd lost control of the curfew. He heard the Mercedes roar with power in the street below, and as it shot away down the hill, Steven slammed his door so hard the doorbell above his head shimmered like a muffled phone. He turned to find Mark at his shoulder, but hanging back with a quiet smile, giving Steven room to explode. Steven made a sound between a whimper and a growl. "They're both—" he began, but the mix defeated him. He sputtered. "It's like living in a juvenile detention center."

"But he's right. There's only a minute left."

"Oh yeah? How do *you* know? They may come up with a cure tomorrow, and then we'll have to endure each other for decades."

"Please—I'm practicing being a hopeless romantic." He grabbed Steven's skinny tie, pulling him close, then bent and began to bite softly at his neck.

Steven slipped his hands under Mark's sweater, riding up the bare flesh to his chest, where he took a firm pinch of both nipples. "I'm just trying to inject a little dose of reality around here."

"If it's your dick you're worried about, I promise not to touch it for the first six months."

Steven squeezed, and Mark gave a barely audible gasp. "Dick works fine. I just had the transmission overhauled."

Mark drew back and grinned. "Well, then."

"*That's* not the problem. How do we get out of it once we get into it?"

"You think too much." Playfully he began to push Steven back, out of the vestibule and into the study.

"No—for once in my life I'm not gonna leave a fucking thing unsaid."

"Do you have to say it all *now?*"

Still he shoved Steven's shoulder lightly, teasing him like a bully as they moved in a queer tango toward the bedroom. It took an immense act of will for Steven to stand his ground, catching Mark's wrist and gripping it tight as a pit bull. They staggered against the bookshelves, breaking the neat lineup of photo albums, where the past was bound up in a hundred shuttered rooms.

They were laughing now, giddy from so many feints, duelists sick of honor. They grappled into a breathless embrace, holding each other steady. And Steven made his final demand, swearing it like a blood oath: "You can't die, okay? Not for years and years. I won't go through it again."

Mark gave him back the steadiest look, his gray eyes clenched in a kind of amazement, about to go over a cliff. "It's a deal," he said in a husky whisper—his ancient bond, worth millions in the days of Bungalow 19.

"How many years?" goaded Steven, never satisfied.

"How many do you need?"

"Eight—no, ten." Shooting the moon.

"Deal."

There was nowhere else to go now. Freely like brothers in arms, they went to meet their fate, closing the last door. But the laughter continued, rippling under the door and through the feasted house. If this didn't work they were out of luck, and not a minute left for the next time. Somehow, waiting so long, it must have got easy. No one was ever supposed to laugh, yet there it was, like a knife through butter.

11

At the first session, the balding man swathed in Polo seemed as ordinary, as colorless as a white-bread shrink. Indeed, Sonny did most of the talking, beside a pool in the Palisades, the chairs placed so the man called Salou could take the sun on his cordovan face. If it hadn't been for Angela's enthusiasm, Sonny might never have stayed. And yet it surprised him to hear his own voice, spilling the long tale of the men in his life, details he'd never told anyone. He had to force himself to return to the Second Cataract.

Salou's eyes were mostly closed as he drank the November sun. At four o'clock he looked directly at Sonny, so piercingly that he stopped talking mid-sentence. "You're not gay," announced the channeler, not exactly dismissive but almost droll, as if someone had played a harmless trick on Sonny. "But you've stayed too long in one place. You've clipped your own wings."

In that moment Sonny lost all doubt of the other's gift. He felt a sudden pound of surf in his ears, and the hair at his nape shivered. An unbearable weight was lifted from him. It was as if he'd been waiting to hear it all his life, and always it was the opposite, one man after another wild to make him a pagan god. He understood there would be no further elaboration today, that the first session was meant to end with a sort of psychic diagnosis. Sonny was grateful for the breathing room, a chance to savor it overnight, pure as ozone. But he couldn't just walk away with his release. One thing had to be said, though his eyes flinched from the channeler's in shame as he spoke the words.

"But I have the gay disease."

"That will pass," declared Salou. "Once you leave the path. Your soul is too old to die young."

Sonny stared at the sun on the water. It flowed like a river in flood, uncontrollable, seething with life. He hardly remembered leaving the channeler's house and driving home. The evening had passed in a dream as he waited, awesomely calm, for the next day's session. Before he went to bed he cleaned his house. Tossed in a Hefty bag his porno tapes, his poppers, butt plug, leather straps. Even his jockstrap. All the evidence he could gather of his carnal ride across the world of the body. He regretted none of it, missed none of it, as he dumped it all in the trash can at the curb. Just an immeasurable sense of relief. For the first time since the summer of his twelfth birthday, he didn't come before he slept.

Immediately things began to go downhill, in a way that was horribly déjà vu. Ray Lee slept twenty-four hours straight after Margaret got him home, barely able to swoon up into consciousness so she could feed him his pills. His brave little plateful of turkey and fixings, topped with a sliver of mince, turned out to be the last solid food he ever took. He drenched his sheets with sweat every three or four hours, and a murmur of soft Korean scored his dreams, playing like incidental music as Margaret stared at the VCR, one forties weeper after another.

The doctor point-blank refused to let her bring him into the hospital: "What for? There's nothing we can fix." But Ray was just fading and fading, Margaret protested, and no one was even trying to figure out what it was. Did it really matter anymore? the doctor sighed wearily. After all, at least he was home. "Isn't that where *you* want to die, Miss Kirkham?"

On his end Steven practically bit his tongue through, so much did it not feel right to be gushing over Mark. Margaret didn't ask, not even when he brought over a turkey sandwich and helped her give Ray a sponge bath. Only on his way out did Steven manage to blurt the headline, that he and Mark had passed the night in each other's arms—news that was spoken in sober tones appropriate to the stench of death seeping around the seals of Ray's brief lock on life.

Margaret smiled politely, as if she only understood Korean these days. "Nice," she replied mildly, but Steven wasn't at all sure as he walked away that she didn't mean it ironically, as if to say, "*Now* you've done it."

They'd put in a wonderful sleepless night, replaying all the blind turns that had kept them apart so long. Each of them took full blame for the ridiculous delay, salaaming back and forth, but finally they agreed that Mark was the bigger jerk. And the love part went just fine, by the time they got around to it, hard as rocks. They groaned and roared when they got off, first one and then the other and then the other way around as the first streaks of morning combed the walls through the Levelor blinds. Mark whistled and applauded the first time Steven came, but that was because they were 1 and 0 from the previous round six weeks ago.

They had breakfast, lunch, and dinner together on Friday, all of it left over from the feast. While Steven was checking in at Ray's, Mark went over to Skyway Lane and picked up clothes for the weekend. For ten years boys had stayed over at Mark's because the places they lived in were like dorm rooms, not the right style for entertaining a CEO. On paper Skyway Lane was in every way superior to Sunset Plaza for falling in love: no widower tenants or memories of Victor. But already there was a tacit agreement that Steven had to be close to Ray's for the end run. And though he wouldn't admit it, Steven didn't dare leave his pair of delinquents entirely to their own devices. A house without a mother was not a home.

Mark liked the sudden feel of being transient, with no possessions but what he could pack in his gym bag. He had no sentimental attachment to Skyway Lane. He was also not-so-secretly pleased to be throwing a monkey wrench into the boardinghouse arrangements of Sonny and Dell. Mark didn't say it to Steven in so many words, but these two had to go.

Steven arrived home shaken from Ray's. "We're down to the short strokes," he told Mark, hugging him close in a way that was awfully melancholy for twenty-four hours in love.

They made up the last of the turkey sandwiches, stripping the carcass bare, then holed up in the bedroom. They ate in front of the television, gaping at each other now and again as if they still didn't quite believe it. They tried to recall the time when they couldn't stand each other, awful West Hollywood parties before the war. Steven did a dead-on impression of Mark at his most arrogant— "That's *senior* VP, and please have that boy delivered to my office for inspection."

"Oh, really?" Mark retorted with an arched brow. "I'm Steven Shaw and I've been everywhere. Pardon me while I drop some names."

"Actually, I'm a has-been actor," Steven purred maliciously. "The last time I played a kid I was older than my mom."

"Victor and I would never stay in a place without a concierge," said Mark, draining the last word of its full pomposity. "You must come over and see my pretentious collection of masks."

Steven flung a spiced crab apple at him, which he ducked, and it ricocheted off one of the masks in question, a lacquered red Balinese with its tongue out. They shrieked with laughter and wrestled each other to bed again, but it went no further than a sprawling kiss because they were dead from the night before. They definitely weren't twenty-eight anymore. They fell asleep in their clothes, Steven first, Mark gently stroking his hair, trying to pat down the cowlick, then going under himself. They woke around midnight, pitched off their clothes, and crawled under the covers in their Jockey shorts.

When the phone smashed him awake at seven, Steven felt the arm cradling around his belly and thought for a tilting moment it was Victor in the bed. He picked up the phone and knew it wasn't good news. When was the last good news in the morning? Margaret: "I think it's another stroke."

And as he listened to the appalling details—throwing up black all night and a nosebleed at dawn that sopped two facecloths, then rigid and twitching—Steven tucked himself deeper into the warmth of Mark's body against his back, the curl of the arm around him, all its muscles intact. Margaret was beyond drowning. She spoke as if she'd had a stroke herself. She didn't ask, but he said he'd be right over, anything to stop the litany of miseries.

Groggy but gallant, Mark staggered up and groped for his clothes. Steven protested, but only a little. They were still half-asleep as they tumbled outside to the Jeep, and Mark dug a hand in the pocket of his jeans and pulled out Steven's car keys. They'd put on each other's pants by mistake. For some reason it struck them as incredibly funny. They whinnied their way downhill, slapping each other's shoulder.

"*I*'m Steven Shaw," bellowed Mark.

Steven pulled the wallet from his back pocket, whipped it open, and flashed a rainbow of credit cards. "My life is platinum," he trumpeted. "Wednesday night is mine!"

Near delirious by now, they swung by Winchell's for a dozen glazed and coffee to go. Then they parked on Fountain by Arturo's Flowers, the dumpsters along the sidewalk rotten with heaps of dead Thanksgiving arrangements. Mark rescued a stem of yellow Thai orchids, and they tramped together to Ray's apartment, Mark's pants as baggy as Chaplin's, Steven poured into his like a hooker.

As they came up the steps to Ray's tiny porch, his white Siamese shrank back from them, unimpressed and vaguely offended. Steven rapped on the door, then leaned with a leering grin and kissed Mark wetly on the mouth. Mark made a hissing sound, commanding him to behave. They stood up straight and austere, wiping the grins like spittle as Margaret opened the door.

Her puffy eyes went straight to Mark, instantly suspicious. He was still a stranger to her. She stood back and let them in, pulling her flannel robe closer. Nobody said a word. She stared at the bag from Winchell's, which Steven guiltily passed to Mark, who in turn laid the sprig of orchids on a table, without any presentation.

From the bedroom Ray Lee was screaming a blue streak of invective, furious at somebody. Since Steven had expected him to be mute and paralyzed, he looked questioningly at Margaret, but all she could do was shrug. Steven moved toward the bedroom, and Mark hung back so that Margaret would understand he knew his place. The etiquette of a death watch was as elaborate as Kabuki.

Ray's naked body thrashed back and forth on the bed, the covers awry. His hands were balled into fists, and he thumped the mattress, pounding a beat like a Kodo drummer. He was clearly wrestling demons. The noise he made was singsong, all in Korean, roller-coastering up and down from shriek to the barest whisper.

"It started about ten minutes ago," said Margaret during a momentary lull.

He didn't seem to be in any pain. It was all rage. Startling because the Korean's demeanor had always been so placid. His rib cage was a pair of praying hands, every bone distinct. Steven couldn't help but see his dick, long and uncut, the foreskin tapering generously like an anteater's snout. Steven blushed at the violation of Ray's privacy, then flinched with self-flagellation to find himself wondering if uncut was the general rule for Asians. Surely not. They were so fastidious. *Shut up,* he screamed in his head.

Ray bucked and rolled on the bed, one arm slamming the bedside table, keeling over the lamp, which Steven snatched midair before it could hit the floor. "If it gets any worse," said Margaret, "I guess I should tie him down."

But the snarling and shrieking sank once more to a murmur. The convulsive fury abated, and Ray crossed his hands chastely over his collarbones, pure as a maid. "He looks so clean," said Steven, somewhat irrelevantly, but in his head he was still wrestling with the images of black puke and blood-soaked washcloths.

"Mm," she replied dreamily, asleep on her feet. "I wish I could just wrap him up right now in a white linen sheet and walk out of here."

Just then the snout end of Ray's dick gave a small shiver, and a stream of piss came out, fanning along his inner thigh, pooling by his balls. With a soft moo of resignation, Margaret reached for another white hand towel on the dresser. Even before he had finished dribbling, Margaret was swabbing it up.

"Honestly, I don't know where it all comes from," she said. "He hasn't had a drop to drink since yesterday afternoon." She spoke with a queer dispassion, as if it were nothing more than her own modest science project, like sprouting seeds on a windowsill. When she gently lifted Ray Lee's dick to wipe it, Steven was stabbed with a memory of Victor at Cedars-Sinai, the nurse about to plug the catheter in. He turned with a gasp and lurched to the doorway.

Mark sat quietly at the table in the living room, staring out the window at the preening cat. He had set the table with plates and mugs for three, the bag of doughnuts in the center. Sensing Steven's presence, he turned with a sad smile. Steven worked his mouth to speak, but nothing came out. He pointed at the table, where the little setup for breakfast suddenly seemed unbearably moving, for Mark could hardly boil water. Steven's eyes filled and blurred. Mark half-rose from his chair.

And then Margaret slipped by Steven briskly, holding the wet towel out in front of her, grimly matter-of-fact. For her sake the two men pulled back from too much feeling. She ducked into the kitchenette and tossed the towel in a bucket by the back door, where the washcloths floated in sudsy water pink with Ray Lee's blood. When she came back in, they sat all three at the table, Steven dry-eyed now, and passed the doughnuts. Mark transferred the coffee from the Styrofoam to the mugs. They each scarfed the first doughnut as if there was a famine on.

They waited for her to speak, halfway through the second glazed. "I don't even know who I'm supposed to call," she said, meaning about the body.

Mark and Steven exchanged a helpless shrug. All their deaths had been in the hospital. "The police, I guess," he said, not quite sure what the crime was.

Silence again, and they each finished a second glazed, then passed the bag and took a third. It was such a relief that they weren't assorted and nobody had to fight for jelly. They seemed content right now to focus all their energies on guilty pleasures, not making another move until the full dozen was polished off. The comfort of the sugar was like hiding under the covers.

So when the first feeble cry bleated from the next room—"Hey"— they didn't quite believe it. In some quite tangible way, Ray Lee was already gone, and this was the wake. Steven reached for the doughnut bag to pass out the fourth and last, and the cry sounded again, no louder but more insistent: "Hey!"

They all came out of the daze at once, rocking the table as they leapt up. They crowded through the doorway like a SWAT team, staring at the Korean in amazement, as if he'd just come back from the dead. Not very far back, but definitely struggling to raise up on one elbow, and with a certain determined grin on his ancient face. Margaret rushed to the bed, then knelt on the floor and cradled Ray's shoulder. "Careful," she said, but Ray succeeded in propping himself on the elbow, his grin widening as if he'd conquered Everest.

His milky eyes looked from one to the other. "What I miss?" he asked.

Margaret reached for a glass of water on the bedside table and held it to Ray Lee's lips. Dutifully he took a sip, but barely a hummingbird's worth. Then he made a face and pushed the glass away. And Steven was thinking: *Did* he have a stroke? And was he dying in fact, or was it the start of a hundred false alarms? He tried not to feel impatient.

Ray Lee murmured something to Margaret and pointed to a wicker chest of drawers. Grunting to her feet, Margaret padded over and opened the middle drawer, neatly piled with laundered shirts the Korean would never wear again. "Unnaneath, unnaneath," Ray prodded her. She slipped her hands beneath the shirts and pulled out a large envelope. From five feet away Steven could see the Shaw Travel return address printed in the corner. Across the front in a large hand, Ray had written, "Last Wishes."

Now he made an impatient gesture, a soundless snap of the fingers, indicating that Margaret should take out what was inside. She did so, drawing out two sheets of paper. Ray made a double jerking motion with his head, curt as a Samurai, calling Steven and Mark forward to look over Margaret's shoulders.

The first page was a receipt from Forest Lawn, neatly detailing with appropriate X's instructions for cremation and interment. Steven had filled out one just like it, wild with grief the morning after Victor died. Actually Margaret had filled it out because Steven couldn't hold a pen for shaking. By contrast this one seemed quite placid and undramatic, Ray Lee's elegant penmanship unhurried. Dated in August, before all his problems began, or at least before he couldn't hide them anymore. On the bottom line it said there was seven hundred and thirty dollars in an escrow account to cover expenses.

"Okay," said Margaret, mostly to break the silence.

Ray Lee nodded for her to go on. She turned to the second sheet,

240

lined yellow legal paper with a list numbered one to twenty-two. The first line said *white china dog and jade cuff links to Tony Yi*, with an address in San Diego following. Scanning down the list, Steven saw several addresses in Korea, the booty as minor as *yellow scarf* and *Walkman*.

Exhausted by his labors, Ray fell back against the pillow, panting. He had drawn the sheet up to just under his nipples, so the waste of his body wasn't so jarring as when he lay there naked. Margaret moved to his side again and said gently, "Will you have some more water?"

Ray frowned and shook his head as if the question were absurd. He squinted at Mark, not quite sure he remembered him. Then smiled because he did remember, and looked at Steven. "This your boyfriend?"

"I guess," said Steven, flushing. "I mean, we just got started."

" 'Bout time," declared Ray Lee.

The next moment he was asleep, breathing deeply, an odd, chilling pause at the end of every exhale. Steven leaned his shoulder against Mark's, indicating the visit was over. Margaret followed them out. They all stood for a moment staring at the table where their half-eaten final doughnuts looked completely unappealing, like wads of suet.

"I guess he came back 'cause he knew I had all these questions," Margaret said.

"Look, why don't we get a nurse," Steven declared. "This could go on for weeks."

"And who's going to pay, Steven? You?" She made a shooing motion at both of them, and they headed onto the porch, Steven vowing to check in later. There was a soft indulgent look on Margaret's face as she let them go. Her love for Steven—happy to see him happy—lifted its head briefly, as if Steven and Mark had made it onto the last train out of a war zone and she was blowing kisses from the platform.

It only sank them deeper as they guiltily stole away, almost ashamed to touch each other, almost afraid. Each knew just what the other was thinking, that all the world in front of them was a minefield, that every kiss might have to be paid in suffering three

241

times over, that one of them would be left behind. They piled into the Jeep like a couple of soldiers stripped of weapons, the dumpsters full of dead flowers mocking them like a mass grave.

Back home in the bedroom, Steven flung himself down and buried his head beneath the pillow. Mark straddled him, kneading his shoulders and neck, feeling the muscles unclench. Steven fell asleep almost as quick as Ray, once he gave into the notion of being taken care of. Only because it wasn't the real thing. Having spent the morning in the last room in the hospice, they needed the vanilla version, a man massaging his friend to sleep.

Even after Steven was softly snoring, Mark didn't move right away, taking comfort from the peaceful rhythm of his breathing. When he got up, he drew the sheet lightly over Steven, loving his own tenderness, daring it the way he used to dare things carnal. He unplugged the phone and closed the door quietly behind him. He was still flushed with protectiveness as he went in the kitchen, where Sonny Cevathas was sucking up a glass of milk and a peanut butter sandwich.

It seemed to Mark that Sonny was always eating, storing up food for the winter like a bear. Coolly he turned down Sonny's offer of half the sandwich, contenting himself with a glass of water. As he sipped it, he described in grisly detail the scene in Ray Lee's apartment. If he hoped to kill Sonny's appetite, he failed. Sonny went on from the sandwich to the last of the pumpkin pie, eating it with his fingers right out of the box.

"If he's lucky, he'll die today," Mark declared bleakly. Then, as Sonny smacked his fingers, not missing a crumb: "So tell me, what're your plans?" The slightest chill of emphasis on the possessive, as if he meant for Sonny to sketch the progress of his own demise.

Sonny smiled, mouth full of pie, taking no offense. "No plans," he said, "but I think I'm finished here."

Mark perked up. "You found a place?"

"Oh, no. I've stayed too long in L.A. as it is." He looked out the kitchen window, pondering a moment. He seemed to be gazing up the hill for dramatic effect. He really was an extraordinarily beautiful man, thought Mark, undamaged and somehow untouched, despite the hands that had mauled him. Would it be harder for him to shrivel and die, with so much beauty to lose? "And you know what's funny," Sonny said quietly. "The only one I'm really gonna miss is him."

Mark thought he meant Steven, but when Sonny's eyes stayed fixed on the hill, Mark finally turned to look. The dog lay dozing in the shade of the sycamore, fatter than anything wild in the mountains, its mottled coat sleek and free of snags. Mark winced at the florid sincerity, vapid as anything he himself had ever okayed for Wednesday night.

"Uh, why don't you take him with you?"

"No, he's a loner. Just like me." Dead-on serious, not a trace of irony, like a cowboy choking up over his horse. "Make sure Stevie takes care of him," he said, as earnest as a Cub Scout.

"He'll probably outlive us all," retorted Mark dryly. "Where exactly are you going?"

"Don't know yet. I've only had one session." He turned from the dog and gave Mark a glassy smile. "I should know better after today."

"I see," replied Mark, as polite as he could, and happily Sonny was already late. He darted out the kitchen door. The dog jumped up to trot after him as he headed around the garage. Mark didn't even feel any excess of contempt, so glad was he that the younger man was leaving Steven's house.

He moved to trash the pie box and wipe down the counter, something he'd never have done in his own house, because what else were maids for?

"He's pretty, that one, but he'll fuckin' believe anything." Mark turned as Dell stepped in from the dining room. "That's the kind they get to run the concentration camps. 'Cause God tells them to."

"Uh-huh," Mark replied, cynic to cynic. "And what do you believe?"

"Me, I'm a good Catholic. I believe in hell."

"And what are *your* plans?" Mark inquired, more brazen now, having struck paydirt already.

"Fuck, man, I'm out of here in a few days. Mexico." He seemed delighted Mark had asked, and went on with some excitement.

"Spend Christmas with the family. Take *mi madre* to midnight Mass. Get drunk with my sisters' fat husbands. Should be a blast." He rolled his shoulders and twitched his hips.

Mark laughed, though he wasn't sure exactly what was funny. "Linda's going with you?"

"No, I don't think so." Here he seemed reluctant, even disappointed.

"But you'll come back and start a new life," said Mark, pressing the point.

"I guess," replied the other vaguely, examining the palms of his hands, where the calluses of his previous life had practically disappeared. He barked his one-note laugh. "And if I don't, maybe I'll come back like Sonny. Be a prince next time."

They laughed together, though Mark was still an inch away from grasping the joke. He had a certain admiration for Dell's forays into urban mayhem, and wished he could do the same sort of damage to Lou Ciotta. But having acquired so much power himself, even if it all meant nothing now, he couldn't imagine being so far from power, learning an alien tongue in order to be a servant.

"You love Steven?" Dell asked suddenly.

"Yeah."

"For sure? You gonna stick with it?"

"Yup," said Mark. He was getting a little sick of having his vocation examined.

" 'Cause if you hurt him, I'll break you in little pieces," said Dell, his voice as even-tempered as could be, his smile pleasant. For an instant Mark could see the dead calm at the bottom of Dell Espinoza's rage. He was strangely serene in his fury, the eye of his own storm.

Mark groaned. "Are you for rent, by any chance? There's someone I'd love you to terrorize in Beverly Hills."

"Sorry. I don't want to fuck with my amateur status."

They parted as equals, a couple of tough guys. A deal had been struck between them, though its terms were mostly unstated. Mark left the kitchen with the curious satisfaction that if they ever needed a bit of serious revenge, the knees of their enemies whomped with a baseball bat, Dell Espinoza was their man. It was such a comfort to have your own terrorist.

He crawled in under the sheet and tucked himself up against Steven, who stirred himself from the green lagoon of his nap and murmured, "What? Did anything happen?"

Mark slipped a hand under his shirt and rubbed his belly. "I think your tenants just gave notice," he said, trying not to sound smug about it.

Steven spoke in a sort of dreamy afterthought: "But where will they go?"

Mark was too groggy to tell all the machinations. "To meet their fate, of course," he said, glib in spite of himself. But apparently it was a good enough answer for Steven, and so they slept without apology, as if their house was all in order.

And in the living room Dell watched "The Three Stooges," mostly because nothing else was on, certainly not for laughs. His pillow and blanket were stowed in the hall closet, along with his 976 notebook and a change of clothes. He had kept up with his laundry, sensitive about leaving no mess. Once Dell was up and dressed, the living room was the living room again, no evidence of squatters. The entire month of November he'd lived in Steven's house without any privacy at all. He accepted this without complaint, like a man in prison who had no choice. Besides, even with the TV on, he had developed a certain radar for knowing when someone was about to walk in.

Yet he seemed to listen now with an extra sense of tension and alertness. His head was tilted, and he barely breathed. He heard the Mercedes drive away, so he only had to watch his left flank, in case Mark or Steven had to run out for something. Moe was bopping Curly on the head with a trumpet, while Larry played the accordion and sang. Dell moved off the sofa and knelt by the hearth. He opened a cupboard door low in the wall where firewood was stored. It was smutty with cobwebs and crumbled bark and a couple of fragrant cedar logs lying side by side.

He shifted one of the logs to the side. Underneath was a package about eight inches square, wrapped in crumpled brown paper. He lifted it out and unfolded the wrapping, the Stooges brawling over his shoulder. Inside was a black revolver that glinted with an oily shine. He just stared at it for a minute, slightly amazed, as if he was still trying to convince himself it was real.

Maybe he would have believed it more if he'd gone in and bought it himself. But it came to him like this, handed over by Alfonso Nava, no questions asked. Dell had called him Friday morning: "You bring me a gun, you can have the truck." Alfonso grunted yes without any hesitation. He knew a steal when he saw one, also understood that the real trade here was a shift of power. He wanted Dell to owe him one, a debt that would be satisfied by the hand of his sister Linda. Alfonso Nava had come to L.A. from the killing grounds of Guatemala. He couldn't have cared less what Dell Espinoza wanted with a gun.

Did he know what he wanted? Not quite yet. He was still making this up as he went along, since the very first call to the water department. He astonished himself every step of the way. It was all he had anymore to prove he was still alive, the surge of unlikeliness, the opposite of reason. Carefully he covered the gun again with the brown paper. The taste of metal was on his tongue, thrilling as blood. He replaced it under the cedar log, closed the cupboard, then stood up and lumbered into the kitchen.

All month he'd been careful to keep his calls local, not wanting to abuse any privileges. But now he dialed Manhattan Beach, taking the small liberty because his tenure in the house was almost done. When the kid picked up the phone, Dell said, "It's me, Lorenzo."

"Hey! I thought you dumped me."

"Sorry, I've been tied up. How you doing?"

Kevin chuckled. "Well, my dick's gettin' hard. What else is new?"

Dell ignored the provocation. "You getting along with your father?"

"That asshole? Gimme a break. You want to fuck me?"

"Kevin, listen—we're not gonna be able to talk anymore. I have to go away." Kevin was silent, didn't ask where. He seemed to finally hear the gravity in Dell's voice. "It doesn't matter if he's an asshole. You want him to send you to college. After he pays the bills, then you can tell him you suck dick."

"You mean I'm never gonna meet you?"

Dell felt a stab he didn't want to feel. "Did you hear what I said?" he asked roughly. "You get yourself a life that *works*. You understand?"

"Okay, okay. But don't I even get a kiss good-bye?"

Silence for a moment. There was a great strain in Dell's face, as if he were craning to listen for any sound in the house. Faintly from the living room he could hear the Stooges brawling. His voice dropped to a husky whisper: "Take off your clothes. . . ."

The call came through at five-thirty, on the hairline crack between dusk and twilight. "He died at five-thirteen," said Margaret. "They like to know the time, don't they?"

Mark and Steven were down there in twenty minutes, just in time to see the stretcher come out with the body bag. Margaret stood on the porch with the Siamese in her arms, watching them stow the Korean into a panel truck, on the side of which it said beneath the logo IN TIME OF NEED. When Steven and Mark came up the steps to hug her, she said dully, "They don't exactly use a linen sheet."

Nobody cried. They took turns on the phone calling the names in his little address book, but there weren't very many. They decided against sending a spate of telegrams to Korea, figuring the modest legacies would arrive there soon enough. In any case there was no family. Ray Lee had always been quite specific about that: "Just me. All alone like Marilyn." And since they were all the immediate family he had, they decided to make it short and quick. They didn't need a wake, and they didn't need to sit shiva.

Besides, it was the twenty-eighth of the month, and the rent was paid only through Monday. So Mark went out to an all-night Thrifty and bought wrapping paper and packing tape and double-strength garbage bags. Margaret and Steven sat at the table sorting Ray Lee's leavings, wrapping them up, tucking notes inside, half condolence and half legalese. They were a two-man assembly line, loving the mindless business.

And while they worked, Mark went around with a garbage bag, disposing of everything else. He felt like the Grim Reaper in the flesh, brutally unsentimental as he threw away all that was not on Ray Lee's master list. In the kitchen were canned goods and cleaning supplies still perfectly good, easy to pack up a bagful, shameful to waste. Regrettably, Mark was not in a discriminating mood. Despite all the hungry children in the Third World, he tossed the Campbell's soup and the packets of oatmeal into the bag.

By eleven, when they decided to break, Mark had four bags full to bursting at the curb. Steven had prevailed upon him not to trash the Korean's clothes. These were piling up on the bed as Mark went through drawers and closets, to be donated to Gay Central. Ray's relentless quest for fashion rightness would thus be passed on to the street kids of Hollywood, glints of chic in the bad parade along Santa Monica Boulevard. Meanwhile, Steven and Margaret had finished about a third of the grab-bag packages to Ray Lee's heirs.

When they turned off the lights and went outside, the cat was purring, rubbing up against the porch railing. Margaret shot Steven a searching look, and he boomed, "No! I've already got a dog I don't want." Margaret frowned. "But I'm allergic," she said fretfully. Then they both had a brainstorm. "Heather!" they crowed in unison, and the Siamese problem was as good as settled. They all agreed to reconnoiter at noon on Sunday.

Steven finally cried in the shower, sobbing into the drumming spray, for Victor more than Ray. He could feel the membrane of toughness crack that had kept him detached all day and fussing with details. He stared into the cauldron of what would never heal, and he hated Ray Lee and AIDS and the whole world, in that order. He didn't turn the shower off till the noisy part was behind him, but Mark knew anyway. When Steven came out of the bathroom red and wrinkled, rubbing his scalp with a towel, Mark was lying on Victor's side of the bed, watching the end of "Saturday Night Live."

He pressed the mute and felt a flood of inexpressible feeling, catching the barest stoop of grief in Steven's shoulders. "Maybe you want to be alone," he said, but with some topspin on the last word, turning it into a question that allowed no room for yes.

Steven sat down beside him, steaming a bit, and laid the flat of his hand on Mark's shirt. It would have been very sexy, one naked and one still dressed, if it hadn't been for the dead part. "You shouldn't have to go through this one," declared Steven with a sigh. "You don't even know him."

"Yeah, well, I guess it goes with the territory. From now on I'm going to have my boyfriends fill out a questionnaire. 'How many friends do you expect to lose in the next twelve months?' If it's over three, I walk."

Steven didn't seem to be listening. "You know what's weird? Getting used to it." He laid his head on Mark's chest, his hair still damp. "I don't mean getting *over* it. But it's like nothing surprises me anymore. I expect it all to be horrible, and it is."

"AIDS or life?"

Steven shifted his head, propped his chin on Mark's breastbone and gave him a baleful look. "There's a difference?"

They slept fitfully, each trying to stick to his own side so as not to wake the other with tossing. In the morning they snuggled for an hour or so, achy and blurred and putting off the day, but there was no question of making love. Somehow it would've been the height of inappropriateness. "Like farting in church," as Victor used to say.

So they picked up the Sunday papers and dragged themselves to Pennyfeathers for pancakes and sausages, Steven asking the waitress for an extra helping of nitrites, Mark requesting a small bowl of cholesterol on the side. The first time they'd really laughed since Margaret's call the night before. The waitress, no friend of Dorothy's, walked away unruffled. She didn't even listen anymore to the camp requests of mad queens.

"Are we really not going to work anymore?" inquired Steven, tossing the business section aside.

"You still have a business," Mark countered accusingly.

"Now, there's an idea," said Steven, dumping three packets of Equal into his decaf. "You can come work for us. We happen to have an opening."

"Interesting. Of course you'd have to match my salary. I'm very, very important."

"Please—Shaw Travel is a major player. And the perks are royal. Free theme-park weekends, vinyl flight bags, star clientele. Including Barry Manilow's hairdresser."

"In that case, I could start tomorrow. But there's one thing you need to know." Mark took a small pause as the waitress laid the plates down. "I'm sort of dying."

"Well, you'll fit right in then," Steven purred reassuringly. "All our male staff is on respirators. That's our motto at Shaw Travel— 'Keep moving, even if it's just a twitch.'"

This last was delivered with a gelid smile to the waitress, who was refilling their cups, sealing her ears to all they said. She knew AIDS talk when she heard it. They were just two blocks from Cedars, in the middle of the Warsaw Ghetto. Now she asked in a singsong voice if they needed more butter. And they let her go because it wasn't her fault, and the whole elaborate riff suddenly died for want of an audience.

They ate their pancakes greedily, like a couple of kids after Mass. They passed each other the funnies and "Arts and Leisure" and avoided sports like the plague. As for death, they didn't think they were handling it very well at all.

They didn't know just how well till they saw Margaret. Ashen and ravaged, not a wink of sleep, foundering all night long in a sea of tears. By the time she met them at Ray's, she was cried out and barely ambulatory. She collapsed on the sofa and stared at the ceiling, hissing like the cat when Steven crouched to speak. She didn't want to be home, but she didn't have an ounce of sociability left either. She was bottomed out on AIDS.

They understood completely. All afternoon they worked around her, Steven at the table packing up the remainder of the legacies, Mark with Hefty in hand, trashing shelves of paperbacks and tearing posters off the walls. Nobody needed to talk, which was a relief. Every now and then Margaret would turn her face to the pillows and weep softly, but only for a moment. About two-thirty the phone rang, and they all three froze and gaped at it as if it were something returned from the dead. Steven picked it up on the fourth ring, steeling himself to break the news, suddenly sure the call would be from Seoul.

But it was the mortuary phoning, to let them know the ashes would be available for pickup Monday morning. Before he knew it, Steven had been put through to an Interment Counselor. He cupped the receiver and asked Margaret what she wanted, but all she did was wave her hand like a white flag of surrender. Steven listened as Mr. Corazon ran through several grisly options. Steven said they would forego a chapel service and simply gather at the columbarium to place the ashes in the wall. No, no priest would be in attendance. Mr. Corazon sucked his lips, clearly disapproving, then asked how many they would be.

"Uh, 'bout ten," said Steven vaguely, realizing only then that he meant to invite the entire Thanksgiving table. Somehow they would stand in for all the lost threads of Ray Lee's life. Tomorrow afternoon at four would be fine. Steven should tell the mourners to park along Eternal Way and go to the North Garden of Repose. Mr. Corazon himself would greet them there.

"He sounds like Liberace," Steven observed, scribbling a quick list of his holiday guests. He saw right off that his ballpark estimate was overly optimistic. With Ray Lee gone and Angela in treatment, and any call to Andy Lakin bound to be received like salt in a wound, they were down to seven already. Still the idea seemed right, to pull together the sudden family the plague had left them with. Linda's phone didn't answer, so he left a message on Heather's machine, laying out the details and asking her to be in charge of bringing Dell's sister. Then he dialed his own number, hoping both his tenants were home.

Sonny answered—silent after the first hello, as Steven announced the Korean's journey was over. Then he extended the invitation to join them at the tomb, but made it clear there were no excuses. Two months' free rent in the room beyond the garage demanded his appearance.

"Sure, no problem," he replied, disarming as ever. "I can't get outa here before Tuesday anyway."

"Where are you moving exactly?"

"Nowhere," retorted Sonny with an easy laugh. A trifle thick on the astral plane, and he seemed to make an effort to bring it back to earth. "I figure I'll head up to Vegas, then maybe Wyoming. Doesn't really matter. The thing is to get off the path."

"Right," said Steven, impeccably neutral. "So, four o'clock in the North Garden. You know where that is?"

" 'Course. Ellsworth's just around the corner."

He promised to give the message to Dell. As Sonny hung up, he grinned at Steven's discomfort. He'd always gathered strength from the leeriness of unbelievers. It only made the link more clear between him and the rest of his rare breed, their souls wide open like windows on time. He was still almost dizzy with truth as he floated out the door to the back terrace. His bare feet left beautiful vanishing prints on the cold slate paving stones. He fell to his knees like a praying man.

And the dog rolled over on his back, his tail batting lazily between the roots of the sycamore. Sonny Cevathas, prince of Thebes, gripped the beast around the neck and wrestled into its arms. They growled with love, sparring and playing it tough as they sprawled on the brink of wildness. "Yeah, you're just a big baby, aren't you?" declared Sonny, pushing his wrist between the dog's bare teeth as if daring it to draw blood. The animal's white fangs clenched lightly, not breaking the skin. They both knew just how far to go.

His second session with the channeler had been much more metaphysical. Salou wore a purple caftan and two gold cobra bracelets. Again they sat by the pool, but this time on a wrestling mat in the shade of a pergola. They drank a cup of yellow tea, and then Salou went into a trance, abrupt as a station change. The XVIIth Dynasty, where he'd served as Pharaoh's chief healer, was as palpable as his own backyard. He gabbled a while in a disconnected monologue, jeweled scarabs and scented oils and even a mummy's curse. Then he began to talk to Sonny direct, cousin of Pharaoh, as if they were on a terrace of the palace, slaves fanning them with bullrushes. Cross-legged, head bowed, Sonny went with the flow, never quite leaving his body but utterly free of it now. They chatted back and forth, ancient to ancient, building pyramids.

After twenty minutes down the Nile without a commercial break, Salou pitched over onto the mat, lying in the pool of his purple gown. His breathing stuttered and his tan went pale, but the Greek wasn't worried. Death was the furthest thing. Sonny looked up through the green roof of leaves that covered the pergola. For a moment he thought he saw a cobra twisting among the vines, and even that was no bad omen. The world was nothing but change, liquid as a chameleon. When he cast his eyes once more to the prostrate figure, Salou was smiling peacefully.

"Where should I go?" asked Sonny.

"Everywhere," replied the shaman. "Just keep moving." Sonny nodded gravely. "Put down no roots for three years, and then you'll be ready."

"For what?" asked Sonny, sorry the instant he spoke. The channeler laughed softly. How could he know till he got there? He might as well ask where his next life would birth him. Off the path, out of the cycle—the point was to break loose from all destination. He'd done it once before, the day he walked out of his father's house. A new life waited beyond the slam of every door.

He could feel the dog's heart beating, twice as fast as his own. He hated to leave the creature behind, but understood they had crossed paths for just that reason, so he would have something to miss. He had a sudden impulse to sneak the dog into his room, give it a taste of domestic bliss, one night in from the cold.

"Would you like that, pal?" he whispered into the animal's chewed ear. If he wasn't gay anymore, perhaps he could reinvent being a boy from the bottom up. "Someday we'll go hunting together," he said, grabbing at any cliché as long as there was a dog in it. "Rabbit and deer and pheasant..."

The beast jerked beside him, then scrambled to its feet, glowering toward the house. Sonny rolled over and saw Dell Espinoza standing just outside the dining room. He hadn't caught sight of the two grappling figures on the ground till he stepped from the house. Now he stood awkward and uncertain, as if he'd seen too much.

"Big surprise," Sonny drawled. "The guy in the wheelchair died."

"Oh." Dell held a small brown package in both hands, as if he meant to set it down with the greatest care.

"Stevie called special. He wants us there at the service." Dell made no protest as Sonny reeled off details. They would ride over together in the Mercedes. "Actually, it's kinda perfect. Be the last time the three of us get together."

"Okay," Dell replied diffidently, moving to go in the house.

"Hey," called Sonny, and Dell half-turned back, "you can have my room when I'm gone."

Finally Dell Espinoza cracked a smile. "No thanks," he said, almost an apology. "Don't need a room."

Sonny swallowed the burr of disappointment, forcing himself not to care that Dell hadn't asked him where he was bound. In this at least he harbored no illusions. There wasn't a man in L.A. who would truly mourn his leaving. What startled him here was the stab of longing, wishing he had a brother. He understood he wasn't ready. It might take years, perhaps till the end of his wandering, before another man could clasp his hand as a friend. And then, cleansed of the rot of passion, his blood clear as a mountain stream, he would come to love at last.

For now it was enough just to reclaim his innocence. Still the dog stood over him, ears perked, mute as a sphinx. Sonny came up on one elbow and nuzzled his face in the white star patch on the beast's chest. He could feel the throb of the swollen lymph node in his armpit, but it seemed no more than a battle scar now. "Yes, yes, yes," he whispered against the dog's breast.

It started to rain at six, hard, the first real storm of the winter. By the time Steven and Mark got in, it was coursing down the crooked lane, waves and sheets of water. They had left Ray Lee's apartment bare to the floorboards. Goodwill had picked up the furniture, not including the mattress, which lay in a soggy heap by the hydrant in front of the house, leaching its viral residues and night sweats into the gutter.

Margaret said she would drop the key off at the landlord's on her way home. Steven told her she could spend the night with them if she didn't want to be alone. "Unless you're going to Richard's," he added hastily.

"Richard?" She stared in disbelief. "You don't understand, he thought he was going to get AIDS from the *turkey*. Richard and I are deader than Ray."

So she went home by herself, happy to collapse in her own bathtub, and Steven and Mark slogged uphill in the Jeep, drenched to the skin as they ran to the house. They stripped down and lay side by side in bed, not quite touching, numbly watching the news and weather—no mention of AIDS at all, let alone the death of a nobody Korean. Steven ordered a pizza from Domino's, pepperoni and sausage, large so there would be some left over for the boys. They were both in a sullen rage by now, not at each other but at It. Still, they were smart enough to know the ice was very thin. The slightest wrong move by either of them and the other might start railing.

They tried to project it as best they could. When the President came on, simpering in the rose garden, they spewed a load of bile in his direction. The last item on the local news was a cutesy bit about Christmas shoppers. The malls were full to bursting on the weekend after Thanksgiving, despite the torrents of Alaska rain. Clip after clip showed kids on Santa's lap, four-year-olds flirting deliriously with the TV cameras.

"White folks," Mark said darkly.

"Mm—partying in the holocaust. But hey, if I was negative—if this hadn't fucked *my* life—I'd probably be out there too."

An especially unappealing group of Valley girls, laden down with shopping bags, mugged for the camera. "If Victor was still here, you mean."

"But he's not," retorted Steven briskly, because some fights had to be ended before they got started.

The rain took care of the night. The drum of its rhythm on the roof finally sent them burrowing under the covers and groping into each other's arms. In the room beyond the garage, the dog lay curled beside Sonny's bed, back legs twitching, running away in a dream. Sonny, who'd always slept naked, wore a pair of baby-blue sweats tonight, as cozy as a kid's pajamas. In the living room Dell slouched on the sofa in the dark, not bothering to drag the bedding out of the closet. He held his gun in both hands as if waiting for an intruder. Out the front window the city below looked to be underwater. Nobody would have known three widowers lived in the house. They had nothing in common anymore except the roof.

In the morning Steven went out to have his dark suit pressed, the one he hadn't worn since Victor. He ended up at Shaw Travel, Margaret too, completely unplanned. Heather didn't know what to do with them, since she was busy on three different phones, but they seemed content to putter around with coffee and didn't get in her way. After a while they began to poke at the stack of second-class mail piled up on Ray Lee's desk, mournfully sifting through it. Ray had been in charge of brochures and schedules, able to rattle off flights and sailings with astonishing recall. The Siamese, which Heather had brought to the office, rubbed against everyone's legs as they worked, making sure no one forgot.

Mark went home to Skyway Lane to pack yet another overnight bag. He didn't have any sense that he lived there anymore, didn't feel attached to any of his things. In fact he had the creepy feeling that the house was waiting to be cleaned out, just like Ray Lee's apartment.

He hurried into the bedroom and grabbed underwear and shirts, wanting to get out fast. He and Steven had never actually talked about living together, but it was getting to be a *de facto* situation all the same.

The whole matter of Steven aside, Mark still had the idea that he was in transit, a moving target. He liked that part. He wished he could put a FOR SALE sign by the front stoop on the way out. He swiveled his watch to the back of his wrist to remind himself to call a realtor. He tracked down his gray pinstripe in the hall closet and was out the door when the phone rang. Perversely he turned to answer it, as if to prove no one had died here.

"We heard you had an earthquake," said Rob Inman, who never said hello.

"Well, it must've been pretty small, because I didn't feel a thing."

"Where was it?" Rob demanded off the phone, then back to Mark: "Hillsborough."

"That's up by San Francisco, Dad."

"He's okay," Rob called out to Roz. "You got her worryin' worse than me."

"I'm fine, Dad."

"How's Steven?"

This caught him completely off guard. "He's fine too," Mark said lamely. "Actually—" He'd never told his father anything real before. He stepped out into thin air. "We sort of got together."

"Well, well, well. That wasn't so hard now, was it?"

It could have gone either way. The tone of the father, buddy/buddy and cocksure, was perilously close to the leering he used to do over Mark's "girls." Rob was incorrigible. "No, it wasn't," Mark admitted, laughing in spite of himself. When his father joined in, it happened to be the first time they'd ever found the same thing funny. For that alone they let it continue, till they seemed to be laughing at nothing at all, just for the hell of it, man to man.

By three the rain had dwindled to a drizzle. Dressed in her black Chanel suit, a veiled hat worthy of Ray's beloved Alexis, Margaret arrived with Steven early at the cemetery office, to sign the final paperwork and meet up with Mr. Corazon. This worthy man, terminally unctuous but otherwise bland as a serial killer, insisted on driving them up to the North Garden in his own black Cadillac. He'd clearly mixed Ray up with another client, because he kept referring to Margaret as "the sister."

For some reason that misnomer cheered both Margaret and Steven, somehow keeping Ray Lee secret to themselves, as they wound their way through the golf-green hills to the travertine walls of the columbarium. They parked on Eternal Way, and the agile counselor held an umbrella above Margaret's head as the three of them headed up the pebbled path to the north wall.

Most of it was partitioned off into units three foot square, meant for a coffin to be placed behind each marble slab, rather like a wall of airport lockers. But at one end, set off by a picket fence in front, was the area reserved for what Mr. Corazon insisted on calling "cremains." Here the wall was sectioned into units six by eight inches, more like post office boxes.

As they came through the gate in the fence, a cemetery worker stood waiting by an open slot at about waist level. Beside him on a wheelbarrow was the box of Ray Lee's ashes, about the size of a portable tape deck. As Margaret and Steven stared at it, Mr. Corazon gave a small gasp of delight, collapsing his umbrella and pointing to the sky. The Irish mist had cleared, and the pewter clouds in the west had cracked, letting through a gilded shaft of the setting sun. Mr. Corazon flushed with pride, as if Forest Lawn had produced on cue this proof of the smile of God.

Steven could see the Jeep approaching up the hill, parking next to the Cadillac. About a hundred yards behind came Heather's blue Toyota. Steven went bowlegged with relief at the sight of Mark, the first time either one had ever seen the other in a suit. Mark had a bunch of roses in the crook of his arm, wrapped in green tissue. As he strode up the path, he caught Steven's eye and tilted his head in a melancholy smile.

Reaching the little group behind the picket fence, he bussed Margaret chastely on the cheek, then gave Steven a soft punch to the shoulder. Margaret introduced him to Mr. Corazon, the two men nodding crisply, then gestured at the box of ashes. "And you know Ray Lee, don't you?" she asked amiably.

Steven let loose with an involuntary bray of laughter, and Mr. Corazon looked aghast. Heather and Linda were just coming up the rise, both in raincoats, Heather holding Linda's arm and clearly very weepy, a knot of Kleenex dabbing against her eyes. They stepped through the gate, and Heather reached out to Steven and Margaret, who dutifully moved to embrace her. This was more Mr. Corazon's speed, but he still wasn't over Margaret's blasphemy. When the crew from Shaw Travel pulled out of their three-man clinch, the counselor raised his brows nearly to his hairline, then caught Margaret's eye and tapped his watch with a fingernail.

It was four on the button. As if on command, the group of mourners moved hastily into a ragged half-circle, facing the chink in the wall where Ray would lie forever. "Wait," said Steven, for the gray 380 had just pulled into place behind the Toyota.

Sonny and Dell climbed out, looking respectable enough, but neither one in Sunday clothes. As they jogged uphill to the waiting group in the fenced garden, they looked like a couple of guys going out to throw a few passes. They were both too restless and impatient, coming through the fussy gate when they wanted to leap the fence. Murmuring apologies, they split off to either end of the arc of grief, Sonny standing next to Heather and Dell beside Mark. All of them looked expectantly toward the figure of Mr. Corazon.

But he was damned if they would put it all on him, this motley crowd. He smiled gelatinously at Margaret. "Were you planning on saying something?"

"Uh—not really." Hopefully Margaret looked left and right, in case somebody else was moved. But no, they all kept quiet. Margaret lifted a hand and primped her veil, then nodded to the counselor. "Why don't you just go ahead and put him in?"

Mr. Corazon was as shocked as if they'd sacrificed a chicken on the spot. But he was a pro, accustomed to eccentricity. He gestured sharply to his underling by the wheelbarrow, who bent in a sort of bow and hefted the box of ashes with two hands. As he turned to place it into its slot in the travertine wall, Sonny thought irrelevantly of Dell the day before, bringing the brown-paper package out of the house and then in again. Beside him, Mark thought about his mother, the urn of ashes displayed in the TV room, unburied till his father sold the house in Manhasset. Margaret thought nothing at all except that this was the very last thing she had to do, for the rest of her life.

There was a grating noise as the workman slipped the box in. Then he reached for the bronze plate that covered the front and sealed the tiny tomb. Drawing a screwdriver from his pocket, he began to fix the cover in place. Heather, still the only one with tears, was thinking how awful it was that a full-grown man could be rendered so small, but then this was her first. Linda beside her, holding her arm, thought with a shiver how cramped and claustrophobic was the slot in the wall. Fiercely she comforted herself that Marcus Flint was scattered on the mountain, so at least his soul could breathe. Steven wasn't thinking of Ray or even Victor. He held himself back, abstracted, almost bored, yet hungry to be out of here and back in the soup of life. He felt selfish and loved the feeling, greedy to have his time with Mark. He glared at Mr. Corazon with loathing, as if that manicured queen were Death's doorman himself.

The workman put in the last of the four screws on the bronze plate. The lettering on it was all in Korean, ordered months ago as part of the package. The characters probably spelled out Ray Lee's name, but none of the mourners knew for certain. Maybe it was a Shinto scrap of wisdom. There was a proper moment of silence as the workman stooped to the barrow and wheeled it away. For a brief few seconds everyone stopped thinking and stared blankly at the finality of one life shut away.

All but Dell Espinoza, whose eyes were fixed on his sister's hand where it cradled Heather's arm. He hadn't stopped looking at that since he took his place at the end of the line. This time he was sure. He might have been jumping the gun, of course, since he had no way of knowing what had been declared, let alone consummated. But there was no mistaking the intimacy of the touch, the way the two women folded toward each other. Linda's shyness couldn't hide it, nor Heather's little-girl grief. He felt it in his viscera, the last rope slipping loose, the final heave of ballast weighting him still to the ground.

Mr. Corazon raised his brows once more to Margaret, indicating that Forest Lawn's part was over. In response, Margaret raised the veil from her face and tucked it up over the hat brim. The seven mourners broke ranks, turning to greet one another with the ambiguous relief of survivors. Mark laid his roses at the base of the wall.

No after-party of any sort was planned, no provision having been made by Ray himself, who was otherwise so punctilious. This was it. No lingering. Margaret led the way out of the garden, allowing Mr. Corazon to take her arm, and was followed by the others in pairs: Steven and Mark, Heather and Linda, Sonny and Dell. A regular procession.

When they reached the line of cars along Eternal Way, Margaret turned to Mark. "I assume you're taking my boss home," she said, hitching a padded shoulder in Steven's direction. The counselor held the door of the Cadillac open for her.

"Wait, I'll go with you," Steven protested.

"Please—can't you see Mr. Corazon and I wish to be alone?"

The counselor managed a wincing smile, but he looked as if he'd rather have a root canal than drive down the hill with Margaret Kirkham. She waved good-bye to the little group as Mr. Corazon started the car. Steven knew it wasn't just the wish to put Ray behind her that made her bolt, but also an awkward desire to get out of Mark's and Steven's way, no more crowd of three. Steven saw it and felt helpless, watching her drive away, feeling as if he'd failed her. It didn't seem fair that she had to lose Richard in the bargain, even if he did hate fags.

Dell and Linda were comforting Heather, who was still the most sniffling of all of them. Mark was already waiting in the Jeep as Sonny touched Steven's arm. "I'm leaving real early in the morning. If I don't see you, thanks."

"But you'll be back," retorted Steven, putting off all finalities.

Sonny didn't counter him, letting him believe what he needed to. "You know what, Stevie? You're practically the only guy who ever left me alone." A different sort of passion flashed in his eyes, a vast sentimentality worthy of his father, who wept at Little League games. Sonny threw his arms about Steven's neck. "I'm gonna start over," he said, choking on the emotion. "Wish me luck."

It was so raw and naked, how could Steven be cynical? He found himself wrapping the boy in a bear hug, tears stinging his eyes. "Yeah, good luck," he whispered fervently, touching wood for all of them.

He had never held Sonny before, and for all the rippling muscles in his torso, he seemed unaccountably frail, but perhaps it was just the spillover effect of this week's death and funeral. Certainly Sonny appeared revitalized by the embrace, as if he'd brought off another feeling that didn't stink of desire. He sauntered away toward the Mercedes, no good-byes for anyone else. He waited for Dell to finish with the women as Steven climbed into the Jeep.

"Can we please go get out of these clothes," Steven pleaded. "I can't stand being a grown-up one more second."

"I think you're very sexy in a suit. Can we go see Victor?"

Steven felt a sudden knot in the pit of his stomach, as if he'd just been found out. "I don't think that's necessary," he said.

"I'd like to."

Steven nodded, unable to think of a reason not to. Mark laid a hand on his knee, very gentle, and he covered it with his own. Tears blurred his eyes again, and he realized with an odd shock that he and Mark hadn't touched at all throughout the burial scene. Was it for Margaret's sake, or Mr. Corazon's, that they'd held themselves back? How would anyone have even known they were lovers? Now, as if to redeem the betrayal, Steven raised Mark's hand to his lips, grazing tenderly over the fingers.

"I love you, Steven Shaw."

Steven nodded, nuzzling his face in Mark's palm, then pointed left along the rolling hills. Mark had to disengage his hand so he could shift gears. He swung the Jeep in a brisk U-turn, not touching the grass on either side, where the graves came right up to the pavement. Steven gave a vague wave in the direction of the little group remaining.

Only Heather waved back, always an eye on the boss, even through tears. Linda couldn't focus on anything but her brother. There was an air of animation about him as he shifted from foot to foot, as if he had just emerged from a long hibernation. Maybe it was being outdoors again, the quick winter green of the lawn on every side. It didn't seem to matter that it was a cemetery. Something had brought out the gardener in him, like an omen of early spring. As he talked with his hands, he might have been casting seeds in a meadow.

"So we walk out of the zoo," he was saying to Heather, "and the little one's very quiet." He glanced impishly at Linda, the butt of his story. "'What's wrong, *poquita?* You eat too much licorice?' She looks at me very serious. 'Lorenzo,' she says, 'I don't want to be a horse no more. I want to be a panda.'"

Heather laughed, charmed by the gardener—but softly, so as not to be rude to the dead. Linda smiled coquettishly, falling back into the role of baby sister. Dazed by his sudden good cheer, she had no idea it was she who'd done it. She saw what she wanted to see, that Dell was coming back to life. She'd prayed for nothing else since Halloween. What she wouldn't see, as he teased her with the past, was how hyper he was. She'd been afraid of his gloom so long that she grasped at anything.

"So that's what you are," said Heather playfully, making Linda blush. Then to Dell: "I thought she was a unicorn."

"Because she's magic," said Dell.

"Stop it, both of you," Linda protested, never good at being the center of a circle.

"Let me give you girls a piece of advice," said the older brother, wagging a finger. "Stay away from funerals. The dead, they have each other. Don't forget now."

Bowing his head in a mock courtly way, he spun around to the gray 380. Sonny started the big engine as Dell climbed in. He turned to look one last time at Linda. Both women were smiling, still basking in all that charm. So it must have seemed like a trick of the failing light that he looked so sad. It was as brief as a spasm of pain, and the next moment they were off, but in that half-second the losses of Dell Espinoza were total. Linda went tense with doubt as the Mercedes pulled away. Then Heather turned and grinned at her.

"He's wonderful," she said—she who always found something nice to say about everyone. "And he's got great taste in baby sisters."

Linda smiled at her new friend, and for once let the worry go. Happiness was so simple. She turned to it like a flower in the sun. Fifteen months of being afraid to laugh, afraid to feel, and now it all came back, as easy as riding a bike.

"C'mon, panda," Heather said softly, taking her hand. They moved toward the Toyota, walking in a garden where death was banished. Everything was going to be fine now, Linda was sure of it. Not only had she found a friend, but Dell had blessed it. Soon he would cease to be a fugitive, and she would be a secretary, and all of them would laugh together like a family.

Across the bowl of the hills, where the cemetery's eastern edge bordered a gully choked with chaparral, dusk was feathering down as Mark and Steven came up the rise. To take the marble edge off death, Forest Lawn had mandated that there would be no gravestones in the park, only bronze plaques set in the lawn, so you had to know where you were going. Victor was between a pair of umbrella pines high on the slope, in an area sparsely populated. The old who did most of the burying couldn't climb that far. The two men's feet were wet to the cuffs by the time they reached the site, and both of them were breathing hard. It looked out over the Valley, clear after the rain all the way to the San Bernardinos. They stood there like a pair of mountaineers, catching their wind, not looking down at the grave yet. Steven straddled the plaque, Mark a step below, waiting till he was ready.

"If you leave flowers, the deer come down and eat them. Sometimes I bring lettuce. Or strawberries." Steven's voice was thoughtful, very private, as if Mark weren't meant to fully understand the protocols of deer. He stooped to the plaque, the wet grass shaggy around it, and still Mark held back. Carefully Steven gathered off the bronze the sprigs of pine needles blown down in the storm. "Well," he asked dryly, "aren't you going to say hello?"

"Hi, Victor."

Mark crouched down beside him. The bronze hadn't tarnished at all yet. It would take the second winter to fur the edges. In block letters it said VICTOR LOUIS OATES, and below that the dates, and below that NO REGRETS.

"He wanted it just to say 'Queer,' but I told him I didn't want him desecrated."

"You think anyone bothers to look at the people they don't know?"

"Sure. Me, I've read this whole neighborhood looking for dead fags." And he waved his arm, taking in the grassy slope from the line of umbrella pines at the crest to the Jeep on the road below, perhaps a thousand graves. "That's when I used to come every day."

"And where are you?" asked Mark, emphasis on the pronoun.

It might have been a question heavy with metaphysics, but Steven understood it in purely concrete terms. "Right here," he said, reaching to pat the grass to the left of Victor. "All paid for, just like Ray."

A moment's pause, in which they both stopped to wonder where Mark was going to go. He didn't even have a will yet. Where Steven was always waffling between having his ashes scattered and getting planted here, Mark was pointedly silent on the subject. Perhaps it didn't really matter to him, or else it mattered too much.

"How many, would you say?"

"How many what?"

"Dead fags."

"Oh, maybe twenty in the last three years." Unconsciously as he spoke, Steven traced his fingertips across the letters of Victor's name, as if he were reading Braille. "That's just counting guys under forty, where it says 'Beloved Son' or 'Baby Brother,' that kind of thing. Maybe a quote from *Hamlet*—always a telltale sign."

It was five minutes to five, closing time. Lights were coming on all across the Valley, and the traffic on 101, heavy with commuters, rippled like neon in the middle distance. The cloudy sky was darkening, and here on the crest of the ridge they were solitary as shepherds, shivering slightly in their suits.

"It's never going to be over, is it?" asked Mark, not really expecting an answer.

"Someday. Not for us."

"Will anyone understand what it was like?" It was curiously easy, perched on the mountain of death, to speak about the future when all of them would be gone.

"Maybe the gay ones will."

"Yeah, but they'll have to see through all the lies. 'Cause history's just white folks covering their ass."

Mark's knees hurt from crouching, but the only concession he made to redistributing his weight was to rest a hand on Steven's shoulder. In a few minutes a pickup truck would rattle along the winding road among the hills, stopping at every parked car. A worker would get out of the truck and, using his hands for a megaphone, shout among the graves that the main gates were closing. Always a car or two overstayed, a fresh widow, a prostrate orphan. A single shouted reminder was usually enough. No one really wanted to spend the night.

"We might as well travel, huh?" said Mark. "Think of all your discounts."

"Great. Where do you want to go?"

"Everywhere."

"Okay, but forget India—too many bugs. And Russia, because they can test us at the border and send us to Siberia. Otherwise, we can chalk up some fabulous mileage—"

"Steven." Mark tightened his grip on Steven's shoulder, pointing into the twilight, sharp as an Indian scout. Barely twenty feet away a deer cropped the grass, or at least it looked that way till the animal raised its head, and they saw in its mouth a bunch of flowers. Coolly it watched the two men as it chewed, big ears faintly quivering but otherwise quite unstartled. Living above the cemetery, where everyone came unarmed, it had unlearned the fear of hunters. When it had eaten all the flowery part, letting the stems and leaves fall to the grass, it trotted a few steps down the hill, but even closer to Mark and Steven. Again it dipped to the ground and fetched a fresh bouquet.

Mark slipped his arm closer about Steven's neck, hugging him fast. Perhaps it was that—the nearness, the smell of Mark's hair—that made him cry. Since when had he even isolated the particular smell of Mark? Or perhaps it was something about the deer, its ridiculous trust that men were harmless, or maybe its loss of the wild. They were tears that made no noise, flowing easy because there was someone to hold. Mark gripped him like life itself, looking over his shoulder at the deer. They were all that was left, the three of them, and only a moment more and a shout from below would scatter them.

12

Dell Espinoza got up at dawn because he always did. Neither the restlessness nor the dizzy sense of anticipation were any different today, for he was a morning person. What was new was the thrill of stealing away. He dressed himself in the green fatigues, the blue work shirt, the red bandanna, the very uniform in which he had arrived at Steven's house. Neatly he folded the clothes he'd borrowed from Sonny, which had made him look like any other West Hollywoo clone, harmless and shallow.

He went in the kitchen and forced himself to eat a container of yogurt and a slice of bread to settle his stomach. Then he took the revolver from its hiding place under the firewood one last time, crumpled the brown paper in a ball, and tossed it into the fireplace. He tucked the loaded gun—loaded by Alfonso Nava, because Dell didn't really want to learn how—in the inside pocket of his denim jacket. When he left Steven's house it was eyes forward, no looking back, closing the door behind him without so much as a click.

The first streak of the morning sun shot across the chaparral, highlighting the luminous jade of the sage, aching with scent after yesterday's rain. Passing Mrs. Tulare's house, Dell snapped a sprig of wild anis from a bush. He made a tight fist and crushed it in his

266

hand, then brought it to his nose and drank it in. Its licorice smell was wonderfully intense, deeper than a flower and sweeter than an herb.

No cars were out on Sunset Plaza Drive this early, since nobody in the hills had to be at work till a civilized hour. Dell had the road to himself, striding down the steep grade unencumbered, only the gun reminding him, heavy against his heart, that he carried any baggage. But it didn't prevent him from appreciating everybody's lawn and flowering shrubs. He was like an inspector, giving grades to all the gardens as he went by.

Halfway down to the Strip, he stopped and squinted at a stand of palmetto, rotting because it hadn't been cleaned of dead fronds. He itched to have his equipment in hand, pruning shears to shape it. Instinctively he reached for the wallet in his pocket, but of course it wasn't there. If it had been, he would've drawn out a card—DELGADO LANDSCAPING—and slipped it in the mailbox at the curb. That's what he used to do: ride up and down the hills in the pickup, leaving a card wherever a yard looked badly tended, what they called cold-blanketing the neighborhood.

It was seven by the time he reached the Strip, but he had plenty of time. The bus stop for the 41 East was by a croissant boutique. Dell didn't have the exact schedule, having lived a notch above his immigrant brothers who had no wheels, but he knew from Linda the wait would not be more than twenty minutes. He sat there placidly and turned his mind to Marcus Flynn.

Arm in arm with Marcus at the Gay Pride Parade, hip to hip on the Catalina ferry feeding sea gulls, Marcus in cap and gown for the Cal State graduation. The thoughts of a man who was past his grief, who had processed all the agony of dying, burned through it, leaving only the memories of wholeness. He could see the scholarly hunch of Marcus's shoulders, silent at his desk. Then saw him arched with passion, riding Dell like a stallion, exploding after all those years in the closet. Nothing was lost and nothing broken. At last Dell had become a man who could live in two worlds, the inviolate past and now. The suffering wasn't part of it anymore.

The 41 bus came sailing down Sunset, lurching suddenly to the curb like a tanker running aground. The door hissed open, and Dell scooted up the steps, dollar ready in hand. The driver was a black woman wide in the hips. She didn't pay him any mind as she took the fare, even if the bandanna was a trifle inner-city for this neighborhood. She certainly didn't care that the dollar was his only cash. He swayed down the aisle of the empty bus as it roared back into traffic, taking a seat in the middle. The bus people were mostly traveling west in the early morning, maids and other workmen bound for the garden districts, Beverly Hills and beyond. From west to east, everyone had at least one car—until late afternoon, when the maids rode home.

At Fairfax they turned south, and in front of Thrifty Drugs a second passenger got on. A gaunt, exhausted Latina, sinking under the weight of a pair of plastic shopping bags. As she fumbled in her purse for the fare, Dell took in the heavy surgical stockings, the battered shoes, the shapeless cardigan. Stepping as wide as a sailor, the woman made her way down the aisle, hoisting her heavy bags to clear the seats. In her mid-fifties, though she looked tired enough this morning to die happily of old age.

As she struggled to sit herself down two rows in front of Dell, the gardener stood up to help her with her bags. She shot him a look of panic, for thieves were everywhere, but his friendly smile won her over. She let him hoist the shopping bags and set them down on the inner seat by the window. She thanked him in Spanish, bowing her head. She wore a black kerchief that reeked of her own widowhood, and a crucifix round her neck, Jesus and all. Dell took the seat across from her as she drew out a small-beaded rosary from her purse.

It wasn't that she looked like Beatriz Espinoza, not in the least, and yet she was the same, guileless and long-suffering. Hard to say if California was any sort of promised land for her. She rode the near-empty bus, glazed and turned in on herself, much as she would have ridden the rattletrap line in Morelia, children spilling out the windows and chickens on farmers' laps. Dell smiled at the vividness of the parallel, but it wasn't exactly a sentimental longing for his mother. Mostly he saw the woman on the bus as somebody Linda would not become, just as she would never become Beatriz Espinoza. It made him completely calm inside.

At Farmers' Market the bus began to fill—Samoans, Filipinos, old Jews from Fairfax—and it headed down Third to downtown like a melting pot on wheels. Riders sat on all sides of Dell and the gaunt woman. No one dared to interrupt the reverie of her prayer to push aside her bags and sit by the window. As they came toward Korea-town, Dell began rubbing his hands on the thighs of his pants, to make the sweat go away. A man in the aisle beside him jostled his shoulder, but Dell smiled and didn't lose his temper. Anger wasn't part of it at all anymore. Anger might have veered him from the path. This was passionless, indifferent, not quite real.

He reached to yank the cord, but somebody got there first, buzzing the driver to stop at the corner of Third and Emery Place. Dell Espinoza stood up with care, huddling his left shoulder like a slightly broken wing. He wouldn't have bothered the woman across the aisle, but she looked up abruptly from her rosary and said, "Nice boy."

He fixed her with a helpless look, a hair-trigger second of doubt. "Pray for me, *madre*," he said. Then the crowd in the aisle stood back for him to pass, and his face was composed again, a mask of inertia as he hurried down the steps and out of the bus. It roared away, enveloping him in a brown cloud of exhaust.

He could see the parking lot was practically full. As he strolled along the sidewalk toward the church, he noticed that the neon sign across the portico was still lit, even in the morning sun. At the foot of the wide stone steps was a signboard, felt behind glass with tack-on letters. The text of the day was I AM THE ROCK AND THE REDEEMER. Below Mother Evangeline's name were listed the Sunday services. Below that, in block yellow letters set off with borders, like a special on a menu, it read: "1st of the Month. Family Prayer and Breakfast. 7:30 A.M." Nobody lingered on the steps outside, the way the young men in Morelia did, halfway in and halfway out of Mass.

Dell opened the tall oak door, expecting a cool dank breeze, startled instead by the bright lights and stifling heat thrown off by the cable equipment. He stood in the back to get his bearings. The crowd was standing-room-only, as polyglot a mix as on Halloween. The flood of the TV lights streamed over their heads, bathing the altar and pulpit. An Asian man in a suit stood at the pulpit, wrapping his tentative English around a passage from St. Paul. Mother Evangeline, in proper white vestments, sat on a sort of Tudor throne, downstage right of the altar. Even now she was on—rapt with attention, willing the reader to stumble through and break the language barrier, turning her honey-blond head to gaze directly into the light.

Dell was standing in a group of men who'd given their seats to the women and children. There was no way he could advance down the center aisle and get closer. Any move he made out of the shadows at the back would fix him in the light, his every gesture naked. Restlessly he scanned the baseboards, hoping the cable fed to an outlet he could disarm. And he suddenly locked eyes with the pale young man in the glasses.

Mother Evangeline's aide was standing slightly apart from the overflow crowd, directly beneath the control booth. As before, he had a fan of memos in his hand. Instantly he looked away from Dell, then two seconds later looked again. *Kenneth,* Dell remembered now, letting his own eyes drift to the front, but always homing back to the man in the shadows.

Clearly Kenneth didn't recognize him—dressed as a ghoul last time, disconnected from his manhood—and just as clearly the aide was cruising him this morning. There weren't a lot of single men in the Church of Family Love, and no one dressed so raw and sexy. Kenneth looked as if he could taste the bandanna. Dell smiled lazily.

The reader finished. Mother Evangeline rose from her throne and approached the pulpit, buoyed by the waves of applause that erupted to greet her. The cheering and clapping didn't seem out of place in the church, perhaps because of the game-show lights. Dell reached a hand to his crotch and lightly cupped his balls, casting a sidelong look at Kenneth. The aide was beside himself, memos fluttering, a thin mustache of sweat beading on his upper lip.

"Children of joy," said Mother Evangeline, "let us sing the morning. The armies of righteousness grow. Today we are welcoming viewers from Durham, North Carolina, and Lawrence, Kansas. Let's open our hearts and greet them."

Again the roaring swelled in the old Congregational church, like a halftime cheer, the children especially shouting with pleasure. Dell stroked the length of his dick where it lolled down the leg of his pants, pressing the fabric against it so it stood out in lurid outline.

Kenneth was riveted. Meanwhile, Mother was telling the flock about her latest crusade, just completed, culminating in back-to-back appearances on Sally Jesse Raphael and Geraldo. Once more Kenneth caught Dell's eye and nodded toward the side aisle. At first the gardener didn't understand, not having started teasing with any goal in mind except to make Kenneth crazy. But the aide was making motions, indicating Dell should follow him.

"Losing one election makes no difference," Mother declared. "It only means we have to give more. Decent family people like us have had enough. Next time we'll win—because who's on our side?"

"God!" they shouted like a battle cry.

Kenneth nodded again up the side aisle, more impatient now. About halfway down were the heavy velvet drapes that separated the church proper from the offices and storerooms. The idea seemed to be that Kenneth would suck him off back there, perhaps in among the choir robes. Dell hesitated a moment more, but he had no other plans. He moved toward Kenneth, and the aide turned and strolled purposefully down the aisle.

"I want every one of you here to choose a sinner—a blasphemer, a Communist, a sodomite. And then I want you to bombard that sinner with prayers!"

Dell followed Kenneth a few paces behind, and no one in the congregation gave the two of them a second look, because they were all accustomed to Kenneth darting about. He reached the velvet curtains and waited for Dell Espinoza. The expression on the aide's face was completely self-possessed. He was as casual as if he were showing Dell the way to the water cooler. When the gardener reached him, he gestured for Dell to precede him through the drapes. Dell, more courtly still, nodded humbly and drew one of the drapes aside, indicating he would follow. Kenneth swept through to the vestibule, his heart bursting with the promise of a little joy. Then Dell let the curtain fall back into place.

And here he was at last, twenty feet from the pulpit. None of it was planned. He'd never once walked through it in his head. But he had no hesitation, walking quickly past the front pews and directly into the glare of light below the pulpit.

"Come, all you sinners, and win with us!" exulted Mother Evangeline. Again there were cheers. She saw the man in the bandanna moving toward her, but her view was hazy because of the lights. She was used to people seized with God, stumbling forward to be reborn. The congregation was still applauding as Dell Espinoza pulled the gun from his jacket.

The ones who saw it first, in the front pews, froze in horror, but none of them was ready to step out into television. Dell pointed the gun at Mother, who threw out her hands to stop it, praying for once in her life. He shot directly into her face, no hate anymore, no reason. The force of it flung her backward, falling against the altar. Dell could hear the voice of the crowd change from cheering to wailing in pain.

Mother's white robe was ghastly now, and she had no face at all, though her arms still flailed to protect it. Dell turned as the crowd surged forward, blinking into the holy light. Kenneth was lurching toward him from the left, and a hundred more from the congregation. Dell seemed perplexed, not having figured the next part out. It was really almost an afterthought that he put the gun in his mouth.

"I'm sorry, but patients aren't allowed to take incoming calls."

"Well, could I leave her a message then?" asked Sonny plaintively as he pulled on his lizard cowboy boots, the gift of a two-week trick last spring. Not everything had to be thrown away.

"We can't reveal the name of any patient," replied the switchboard primly.

"Please—just tell her that Sonny called, will you?"

"I can't confirm that the lady is here," declared the resolute woman at Betty Ford.

But there was something in her voice that left the door ajar, an appreciation perhaps of his burning sincerity. Sonny rushed in to fill the gap. "Say that I'm leaving on a long journey," he declared with breathless fervor. "And when I'm finished I'll be back. But if I'm not—if I don't—" He couldn't even say the words, for fear he would jinx his voyage. "Then tell her I'll meet her the next time around."

"All right," acknowledged the receptionist, gravely accepting the commission.

Sonny rang off, convinced the message would get to Angela. He went in the tiny bathroom and grabbed up his razor and toothbrush, but as much to check himself in the mirror a final time, the last sight he would ever have of the incarnation he was leaving. He stared with cold dispassion at the end of his youth, Narcissus cured. Nothing so decadent as beauty looked back at him. For once he didn't touch his hair or arch his brows, but turned on his heel and left cold turkey. His pair of nylon duffel bags were by the door, and he tucked his odds and ends in a side pocket and zipped it. One look around, as little sentiment as if he were exiting a Motel 6, and he stepped from the room beyond the garage into the morning of a new life.

The dog was waiting sentry in the driveway just outside. He'd made no move to return to his old haunt under the lantana. Since Sonny let him out an hour before, he'd pissed in the bushes and come right back. One night indoors and he was hooked. It had taken him months to domesticate to the point where he'd wheedle for shelter, but he had reached that shameless place. He looked up at Sonny with beseeching eyes.

"You don't want me to go, huh?" Sonny asked playfully, touched when the dog trotted after him down the driveway. He went around behind the Mercedes, propped one of the bags on the bumper, and opened the trunk. It was empty except for one thing—his black canvas gym bag, which sagged open, a jumble of bicycle shorts and tank tops, sweat socks, Speedos, workout gloves, a pair of Reeboks tied to the handle. The full raw uniform of his sunlit days as Apollo.

He reached and lifted it out, then walked over to the trash barrels at the foot of the drive. He lifted the lid and stuffed the bag in, not even bothering to root out the shampoo and moisturizer, both still perfectly good. Did it mean he planned never to exercise again, that his hero's journey would unfold without aerobic conditioning? He didn't really think that far. He only knew he had to dispose of the weight of that persona, so charged with being gay, like a soldier burning his combat fatigues.

The dog sat patient beside the car as Sonny went back and hefted the duffel bags, stowing them into the carpeted trunk. He slammed the lid and grinned at the animal. "Next time we meet, you probably won't even be a dog."

Steven's eyes fluttered open when he heard the sound of the slamming trunk. He glanced over to the bedside table—8:37. Mark was deep underwater, arms across his face. Gently Steven slipped out from under the sheet and comforter. He padded naked around the bed, grabbing up the boxer shorts Mark had shed the night before. He closed the bedroom door behind him going out, then rushed across to the front door, dancing into the shorts, fearful Sonny would peel away without a wave good-bye.

But he was putting down the convertible top, folding it like an accordion into the hollow behind the seat. "Are you trimming your sails, boy?" called Steven from the top of the steps. "Should we crack a bottle of Dom across your bows?"

Sonny looked up startled, flushing with unexpected pleasure. He didn't want to leave unheralded after all. "Beautiful day for it," he declared, hearty and butch as either of his straight brothers. "You take care of yourself now, Stevie. I'm not gonna be around to watch you."

He opened the door and slid into the driver's seat. When he flipped the ignition, filling the morning air with power, it seemed no further words would pass between them. None were needed. Sonny was already waving over his head and pulling away from the curb when Steven suddenly bolted down the stairs in his shorts.

"Wait!" he shouted, and Sonny braked, eyeing Steven guardedly, leery of too much good-bye. Steven pointed to the dog, who sat in the driveway still, idly licking his balls. "Please—take him off my hands. I don't need one more thing to take care of."

"I can't," protested the Greek, wishing now he had slipped away unnoticed. "He's got his own destiny."

"Excuse me, but that's a crock. He's totally in love with you, and it's all your fault." Nobody else could have gotten away with it. The dog blinked stupidly, but was clearly aware he was the subject under discussion. Sonny hesitated, engine roaring to go like a stallion. "Besides," said Steven, "I can't stand him. Especially now that he's so *doggy*."

The last thing Sonny had ever permitted, the very last thing— except for Ellsworth—was someone in love with him, but that of course was the old life when he was still gay. *What the hell*, he thought, and reached over and flung open the passenger's door. The dog stood up, loped over and jumped in, casual as could be, as if he'd never doubted the outcome at all.

Steven slammed the door behind him, and the Prince of Thebes was ready. This time they parted with truly minimal ceremony, nodding a bare half-inch, so as not to call attention to the boy-and-his-dog maneuver. As Steven watched the 380 disappear round the turn, he thought how he didn't have a clue what went on in Sonny's head, and he supposed the feeling was mutual. Had he been good for Sonny? The question had no meaning. He'd simply been a sanctuary for a while, because life had happened to deal them exactly the same card, like a pair of Jews at the opposite ends of Europe, a Dutch banker and a Polish tailor.

When he came back in the house, all he wanted to do was go back to bed, but the housemother instinct made him turn and glance into the living room, to see if Dell was up. The pristine tidiness of the place, as if no one had stayed there at all, didn't especially surprise him, for he was used to Dell rolling and stowing the bedclothes. Yet it was something about Dell's insistent unobtrusiveness that drew Steven into the room, even though he ached to sleep. Sonny, by contrast, had taken over the house, and the beast he carted away was only the most extreme proof of the claim he'd laid. Dell had barely left a dent in the sofa cushions. Hardly ate, even on Thanksgiving. The only evidence of his presence was the green of the hillside where he'd watered, the rosebushes clipped to the bone for the winter.

Steven stood in the middle of the room and looked around. He saw the cupboard door slightly ajar in the wall beside the hearth, and the crumpled brown paper in the fireplace too, but none of that meant anything. A sort of vacuum gripped the place. He couldn't have said why he leaned over the sofa and pulled the button on the Sony, since he wasn't a fan of morning TV, except that the room suddenly felt colder and more silent than even Ray Lee's apartment.

A street reporter was shouting over the noise of a crowd. Right at that moment—"LIVE" flashed on and off in the upper left corner of the screen—a team of paramedics was barreling through with a body on a gurney, all zipped up in a bag and very dead. Steven wondered idly why they bothered to hurry so if it was all over. There was always a murder on the morning news. "Two dead," Steven was able to make out, a man and a woman, murder/suicide. A lover's quarrel, probably, or a marriage on the rocks.

Except for the size of the crowd, a mix of races that seemed to be beating their breasts with grief. Then, as the camera swung wildly to show the chaos, Steven could see the stone facade of a church in the background. His stomach seized with a slight clench of dread. "The second body is just coming out," declared the reporter, and another team of useless paramedics emerged with a gurney, three on each side like pallbearers. Only here there were several police officials as well, hovering close as if the killer might at any moment leap out of the body bag.

Steven knew it all now. He didn't require any further information. Nevertheless, the station broke away momentarily from the live report, and a still of Mother Evangeline flashed on-screen, her in the meadow surrounded by children, the Sermon on the Mount. The coverage was already starting to accrue the nimbus of martyrdom, and the body was barely cold. Back to the studio: a bimbo anchorlady with a honey-blond do just like Mother's.

"Police have not yet identified the killer," she intoned, "but it's believed he may be a member of the radical gay underground. Mother Evangeline has long been known for her vocal attacks on the gay lifestyle."

Steven could see just where it was going. Within hours the telegenic priests and rabbis would be coming out of the walls to denounce and decry. Mainstream guys, not just the Jesus fringe and the Aryan nuts. With one fell stroke, it seemed, Dell Espinoza had set things back a generation, all the making nice and the coalition-building.

And Steven could feel himself keeping his distance, here even more than with Sonny, as if it were some kind of test to see how shockable he was. You wouldn't have known to look at him that he was at all acquainted with the parties to the crime. The blood didn't drain from his face. He didn't cry or wince in pain. And the screen before him was full of examples of how to do it—an entire congregation keening and moaning, stunned to the soul.

All he wanted to do was go back to bed.

The telephone rang in the study. As Steven leaned over to turn off the tube, a psychologist joined the bimbo, to try to probe the mind of the killer. Steven recognized the man as an expert on California murder, who had proven indispensable after the McDonald's massacre. *No thanks,* thought Steven, tuning out. He shuffled into the study and picked it up on the third ring. It was Linda.

"What's he done?" she cried in anguish. "How could he do this?"

"Honey, I'm sorry," Steven said brokenly, feeling the rush of protectiveness. "There was no way to know. He had a pain we couldn't touch." This sounded, even as he said it, as mindless as the TV expert.

"But he *killed* somebody. Why?"

Steven bit his tongue, because he realized the killing didn't bother him. That part at least seemed to have some social value. As to why, it was perfectly clear why. Mother Evangeline was a pig.

"I have to go down to the police," said Linda. "They can't have him. I want him next to Marcus."

"Sure, I'll be right over," said Steven, remembering how he'd said the same thing to Margaret three days before. He didn't want to, but he had to. This was called being a real prince.

"No, it's okay. Heather's going with me."

Fine, he told her, let the two of them go to Parker Center and claim the body, and they would all meet later at Linda's to figure out the obsequies. *Later* was all he could think of, his eyes drooping as if he was drugged, as Linda turned the phone over to Heather, who asked if she could close Shaw Travel for the day. Yes, yes. Anything.

He hung up the phone and swam back to the bedroom, a man whose privacy had been restored at last, in a most ambiguous fashion. Mark was still lying on his back, arms across his face. The coverlet had slipped to just below his navel. With his torso stretched by his upraised arms, he looked ten years younger. Steven kicked off the shorts, surprised to discover his dick swaying out to quarter mast, more awake than he was. He crawled into bed beside the man he was still too shy to call his lover, except "boyfriend" sounded even worse, as if they were both sporting toupees.

He snuggled up close, one arm cradling Mark's chest, and breathed in the smell that was no one else. Mark stirred and reached an arm about Steven's neck, holding him tight the way he did at the cemetery. Still half in a dream, he murmured: "What was all that?"

"Nothing," Steven whispered. "Just the tenants leaving."

Mark accepted the half-truth unquestioningly, not of a mind to wake all the way, and burrowed into a full embrace. He felt the swell of Steven between them and mumbled, "You horny?"

"Uh-uh—let's just sleep," replied his friend, swooning now in the warmth of the body that held him, letting go of all his fellow widowers. Even going under he could taste the simple wish that overrided all the rest: to stay in the middle of this with Mark as long as he could. Perfectly selfish, except it was deeper than that—the last dance, the last pocket of air. Nothing else was happening right now in Steven's house, a luxury beyond calculation. The sleepers had all they needed. Only to lie like this between the bombs, dreaming away and not alone, because time was very short.